"IT IS NOT OFTEN THAT I SEE
A LADY AT HER BATH AND
THEN ADJOURN TO MY ROOM ALL
ALONE. . . ."

"May I say, Lacie, that you made a most delectable picture last night." Dillon's slight smile, coupled with a prolonged perusal of her casual attire, only caused her temper to simmer even hotter.

"You may say no such thing!" Lacie stammered, truly mortified now. She tried to dart through the gate and get away from him, but his quick side step only brought them face to face.

"You know, if you would just be honest with me, we would get along so much better." His eyes lowered from her angry eyes to her shocked, rounded lips.

"I don't want to get along with you!" she snapped, even as a flush began to color her cheeks. "All I want is for you to leave this place."

"I'm not leaving here until I get what I want," Dillon said quietly.

"Why don't you just give up now and save yourself a lot of trouble!"

"Ah, but it's really no trouble." He took a thin wisp of her long dark hair and wound it about his finger while staring deeply into her eyes. "I think I shall enjoy every minute of it."

Also by Rexanne Becnel

MY GALLANT ENEMY

Thief
of My Heart

REXANNE
BECNEL

A DELL BOOK

Published by
Dell Publishing
a division of
Bantam Doubleday Dell Publishing Group, Inc.
666 Fifth Avenue
New York, New York 10103

ISBN: 0-440-20622-7

Printed in the United States of America

Published simultaneously in Canada

May 1991

10 9 8 7 6 5 4 3 2 1

OPM

For David . . .
. . . for everything

You took my breath away from me
My thoughts you stole uncaringly
By day you lead a merry chase
By night I long for your embrace
Too late to say how it did start
I yield to you, thief of my heart

—anonymous verse

Prologue

Denver, Colorado Territory, May 1872

The letter lay on the cluttered desktop. One solitary sheet, it was a thin laid linen with ragged edges, as fine a writing material as could be bought.

Dillon Lockwood had recognized it at once as his brother's stationery, although the unfamiliar hand had puzzled him. It was delicate where Frederick's was bold, and precise where Frederick's tended to sprawl. But the neatly penned message had answered his unspoken question with one startling, crushing sentence:

> *. . . and so, as Frederick's widow, I regret to inform you of your brother's untimely death.*

Now the letter lay where he had flung it, still creased where the folds of the past weeks were permanently imprinted. But if the ivory-colored paper had been forgotten, the terrible news it bore still weighed heavily on Dillon Lockwood's mind.

Frederick was dead.

At one time he'd hated his older half-brother. As a boy, Frederick had enjoyed a comfortable home, while Dillon and his mother had eked out a meager existence on the fringes of society. Frederick had received all the respect due a son of the esteemed Kimbell and Allen dynasties, while Dillon had always known just who he was: the bastard son of Miles Dillon Kimbell.

But that hatred—that jealousy—had faded long ago. It had taken years, but he'd come to accept that his birth had not been Frederick's fault. Frederick had just been the most convenient target for his pain all those terrible years in the town of Kimbell.

Dillon stood at the unadorned window of his office and stared blindly at the activity in the street below.

It was Frederick who had unwittingly been the force behind his own desire to succeed; Dillon knew that now. How determined he'd been to prove that he could amass the fortune, the property, and even the place in society that Frederick had been born to expect as his due. The Kimbells had made their fortune in lumber, the Allen family had made theirs in shipping. Lockwood Enterprises had made fortunes in both, not to mention in construction in the fast-growing city of Denver.

Dillon ran a callused hand through his thick black hair, then slid one finger along the treble-carved mahogany window frame. He'd built his entire fortune just to show Frederick. And yet paradoxically, Frederick had been proud of his bastard brother's business successes. Then when the family businesses had floundered during the War between the States and the elder Kimbell had died, Frederick had come to Dillon for help.

It had been an unlikely alliance—Frederick's long-time connections, Dillon's indefatigable drive, and the combined clout of their money. Yet it had worked.

At first they'd kept their business interests separate. But as they'd prospered, this arrangement had become a stumbling block, based as it had been primarily on Dillon's foolish pride. Now almost everything was bound up in co-ownership. Except for Lockwood Lumber and Frederick's little school.

Dillon's dark musings were interrupted by a knock at the door. When Neal Camden stuck his head in, Dillon waved him entrance, then moved to a marble-topped console table and poured them each a whiskey.

"Bad news?"

Dillon grimaced, then tossed the amber liquid down in one stinging gulp. "Frederick's dead."

"What! When did this happen?"

"Three weeks ago, according to this letter from his widow." He picked up the letter and stared at it once more.

Neal took a sip from his glass. "I'm sorry to hear that, Dillon. I didn't realize Frederick was married."

"He wasn't. At least, not till now."

Neal raised his blonde brows and his expression turned from interested friend to intrigued lawyer. "Let me see that letter."

After a quick perusal of the carefully written message, he looked up at Dillon.

"If she's his widow, then she's your business partner now."

"*If* she's his widow."

"You doubt it?"

"Damn right, I doubt it!" Dillon snapped. He grabbed the letter, glared down at it, then crumpled it in his fist.

"Mrs. Leatrice Eugenia Montgomery Kimbell is what she's calling herself, but I'll stake my life that she's nothing but a greedy little gold digger. She saw an opportunity when Frederick died and took advantage of it."

"That'll be hard to prove. How can you be sure she didn't marry him? She'd have to be a fool to attempt such a deception."

Dillon turned his head to stare at Neal. "Many a fool has gambled for far smaller stakes than Frederick's estate." He looked away. "My half-brother and I may have had our differences in the beginning, and God knows we didn't agree on everything. But as time went on, we began to understand each other. And respect each other. He never married . . . he never married because he didn't like women. At least, not in that way." He cleared his throat. "But he hated that part of himself. Hated it and fought it. I've always thought that was why he turned that big old house out in the middle of nowhere into a charm school for spoiled little rich girls. It was his way of avoiding everything."

His jaw tightened as he realized that he would truly miss his older brother. Had Frederick ever known how much he meant to him? A sudden mist clouded his eyes, but he sternly willed it away. His fingers drummed an agitated rhythm on the table.

"This woman has shown up calling herself his widow, but I'm not about to give up all that Frederick and I built on the basis of this one letter. No"—he stood up and tossed the offending bit of paper into the empty hearth—"she's an imposter, and all she wants is Frederick's hard-won fortune. But she's not going to steal even one thin dime from him—or from me."

I

Kimbell, Louisiana, May 1872

Lacie Montgomery managed a smile only with considerable effort.

"Yes, Mrs. Mooring, the school has suffered a great loss. I'm not sure how we shall go on without Frederick. We will simply have to manage the best we can."

"Oh, and I'm sure you will. I'm sure you will. Of course, there's your own personal loss to deal with as well." The woman cocked her head curiously so that her fuzzy sausage curls fell along her plump cheeks.

Lacie lowered her gaze to a selection of lace collars in the glass-topped display case. She'd known this would happen and had tried to prepare herself by anticipating the inquisitive looks and the prying questions. But how many times in one day must she run this gamut?

"I was heartbroken when Frederick died," she murmured. That, at least, was not a lie. He had been teacher, father, brother, and friend to her. The problem was, he had not been her husband.

No matter how often she told herself that this deception of hers was justified—indeed, it was an absolute necessity if Sparrow Hill School for Young Ladies were to survive—she still could not shake off her feelings of guilt.

"And the pair of you so newly wed," Mrs. Mooring persisted, her eyes bright with the inveterate gossip's curiosity.

Lacie lifted her head and smiled grimly at the store-keeper's portly wife. "Barely a week before he—" She pressed a plain linen handkerchief to her mouth. "If you don't mind, I'd rather not speak of it."

That was true as well, Lacie thought as she made her way out of Mooring's Dry Goods. She did not want to speak of Frederick's death at all, for with every word she seemed to be digging a deeper and deeper hole for herself.

Still, it had been four weeks since Frederick had died. Surely the worst of the gossip was over, she reasoned. If she could just remain in quiet mourning all summer, by the time the students returned in the fall, everything would be smoothed over. Her biggest trial would be to get through the coming graduation ceremony.

Lacie was resolute as she made her way down the two blocks that constituted the town of Kimbell's main thoroughfare. She kept her face carefully downcast and murmured only a word or two to those she passed. But her back was straight and her stride determined as she crossed the street to meet Leland at the wagon.

"I settled the bill with Mrs. Mooring. Is everything in the wagon?"

"Yes, ma'am. I got it all." Leland hefted himself onto the high wooden seat and took up the reins. It was only when Lacie stood patiently on the plank walk, looking

pointedly at him, that he started in realization. If anyone could be both embarrassed and put out, the old
black servant certainly was. He was muttering under
his breath as he shuffled around the team of horses to
Lacie's side.

"I never been no driver to the ladies."

"I know, Leland."

"Mr. Frederick, he never needed no hand up."

"I'm sure he didn't." Lacie made the high step, then
carefully smoothed her skirts and settled onto the seat.
She watched Leland make his way back around the
wagon once more, then waited until he too was seated.
"There are many things that will be different now that
Frederick is gone," she began. "But all of us must
cope."

Leland did not answer. He only kept his eyes on the
road as he guided the horses through town. But his very
silence weighed most heavily upon Lacie. She fought
down an urge to slump in defeat as she considered what
lay ahead. Only the stringent reminder that proper
ladies always sat unbowed with their heads up and their
backs straight kept her from caving in then and there.
It was one thing to maintain a facade before Mrs. Mooring and the rest of the townfolk. But Leland was a part
of Sparrow Hill School for Young Ladies. If he didn't
support her—if the others didn't either—then how
could she go on?

Despite her prim exterior and her neatly folded, cot-
ton-gloved hands, Lacie was on the brink of tears as
they neared the edge of town. So caught up was she in
her depressing thoughts that she hardly noticed Leland
stopping, except when the meager breeze they'd enjoyed stopped as well.

Lacie wiped the dampness from her brow. When she spoke, her voice was sharper than she'd intended.

"Do get along, Leland. We've no need to be stopping, especially before such an unsavory place."

Leland's eyes stared straight ahead and his lower lip jutted out petulantly.

"Mr. Frederick, he done always stopped at the Half Moon on the way home. He always brought me out a little glass of whiskey."

Lacie's mouth dropped open in surprise. She could not imagine Frederick Allen Kimbell ever setting foot in a tavern, let alone encouraging someone in his care to actually partake of spirits. Yet as the moment stretched out and Leland did not budge, she realized it was true.

"But surely you cannot think that—that *I* could go into—into . . ." Lacie crumpled her handkerchief in her hand and blinked back tears. The old man's head sank lower between his shoulders, and his chin began to quiver.

"But Mr. Frederick—" he choked and wiped his eyes with the back of one large fist. "He done always looked out for me. Who's gonna look out for poor ol' Leland now?"

It was the final blow for Lacie. Her simple square of linen was woefully inadequate for her tears as she tried to stanch the flow. It was small consolation that the wagon finally did lurch forward, for once the tears began, they would not be stayed. It was awful enough to have lost dear Frederick. She truly did not know how any of them would cope without his reassuring presence. But to have all his responsibilities on her shoulders—the school, the students and their families, the teaching staff, and now even Leland's terrible sorrow . . .

Lacie bit her lip hard in an effort to control her runaway emotions. She had taken on this task, she reminded herself sternly. She had weighed the alternatives and had decided quite on her own to take on the responsibility for the school. Crying would not change that.

The wet handkerchief was quite insufficient, but Lacie did her best to dry her face. Then she straightened up and laid her small hand on Leland's arm.

"I know it's hard," she murmured.

The old man clucked to the team. "It ain't never gonna be right again. Not ever."

Lacie dropped onto her plain dormitory bed with a sigh that mingled sorrow and defeat. She pulled the long wooden pin from her hat and removed her newly dyed black bonnet. Her gloves were next, then the stiffly boned muslin bodice of her mourning costume. It was only midafternoon, yet she wanted nothing so much as a cool, refreshing bath. She grimaced as she arose and poured a thin stream of tepid water into a blue porcelain bowl with pink lustre accents. Unfortunately, she knew that whether she bathed only her face and wrists or took a complete bath in one of the enameled hip tubs, she would still not be able to rid herself of the guilty feelings that plagued her.

Lacie was patting her face with a damp cloth when a quick knock came at her door, followed by the fair head of Ada Pierce peeking around the frame.

"Oh, Ada," she called to her fellow teacher. "Do come in."

"I was wondering how you fared in town." Ada pursed her lips and stared seriously at Lacie. "Was it dreadful?"

Lacie's shoulders slumped, and she sat on her bed, clasping the damp cloth between her fingers.

"It was positively awful. No one came outright and said anything, but I could tell they were all still wondering why they hadn't heard of the wedding before Frederick died."

"They can't say anything—you have the papers."

"Yes." Lacie bit her lower lip. "At least we have the marriage papers. But I would hate to have anyone examine them very closely."

Ada took the cloth from Lacie's hand, then began to loosen the thick coil of hair at her friend's nape. "You underestimate your skill, Lacie. Why, your rendition of Reverend Hainkel's signature would confuse that good man himself."

"I'm just as glad that he'll not be here to verify it one way or the other. I only hope he's happy in his new parish and never, ever returns to Kimbell." She relaxed her shoulders as Ada began patiently to plait her hair. "If he would just stay in St. Louis! And if everyone else would just hold their silence!"

"No one else has anything to tell," Ada put in. She shook her head emphatically. "I don't rightly know just how you came up with such a brave plan to save our school, Lacie. I know you feel bad in one way, but you can't lose sight of the good you're doing either. Just keep in mind that letter that Mr. Frederick was writing when he became ill. It was clear that his brother had suggested that he close the school. But the last thing Mr. Frederick did before he died was to start that letter

telling him that he would never sell off Sparrow Hill.
Even though he didn't get to send that letter, it's clear
what he wanted. Why, it would be awful if Mr. Frederick's brother got the school, for he surely wouldn't hesitate to close it down now. Then what would happen to
all our girls? There are so few decent schools left since
the war. Where would they go?"

Lacie clasped Ada's hand fondly. "They won't have
to go anywhere. We're going to stay here and the students are going to keep on coming back year after year,
just as Frederick would have wanted. And if Frederick's
brother—half-brother—should try to claim the school,
he'll find he hasn't a leg to stand upon. Frederick seldom spoke of his brother, but he did say that he was a
well-to-do businessman. Why would such a man—probably well settled in Denver with a wife and children—
why would such a man want a school that barely gets
by? Heaven knows, the value of property has plummet-
ted since the war."

"Maybe he doesn't realize that, being from Denver.
Besides, some folks are odd about their inheritances.
Even if they don't have any use for it, if it's theirs, they
want it."

"But I'm Frederick's widow. I have the papers to
prove it. Even if he should send someone to snoop
around, he'd find nothing." Lacie stood up and took
Ada's hands into hers. "All we have to do is go on as
before, teaching our girls just as we've always done,
taking care of the school buildings and the horses, and
making sure Sparrow Hill School is a credit to dear
Frederick's memory."

They were brave words, and they carried Lacie
through the remainder of the afternoon. Not until the

evening meal was finished and Ada was leading the younger group of girls in their evening prayers did Lacie have a chance to contemplate once more the circumstances that had brought her to do such a devious act as feign marriage to a dying man.

Forgive me, Father, she prayed most fervently. *Please forgive my lie. But there was no other way to save the school Frederick worked so hard to build.*

Frederick's last coherent words had seemed to force her to it. *"My school,"* he'd whispered in that breathy shadow of his normally ebullient voice. *"Help me preserve my school."*

After that, there had been a week of silence. Then one night he had simply let go of life. Dr. Cromwell had said it was his heart and had signed the death certificate. He'd only looked at her with his bushy eyebrows a little raised when she told him she and Frederick had been married two days before he'd been struck down. By then, she had already forged the papers and donned a mourning gown. If the doctor had questioned her slightly desperate revelation, he'd clearly not mentioned it to anyone in Kimbell. Nor had any of the staff, although she was certain they had their suspicions. But they also knew that their livelihoods hung in the balance. There was no going back anyway, not since she'd sent the letter to Frederick's brother in Denver.

Her hand had shaken terribly as she'd written that dreaded letter. It had been bad enough to have to inform a man of his brother's death, even if they were hardly of the same social standing. But to lie and steal from the man and his family in the process seemed the most heinous of acts.

Still and all, that man did not need the school, and

they did. If Sparrow Hill were to close, she and Ada would be teachers without a school. Leland would be deprived of his lifelong home, and Mrs. Gunter the cook, the two housemaids, the stableman, and the gardener would be without any jobs whatsoever. Added to that, Monsieur Fontenot, who taught French and ballroom dancing, would also be quite without an income.

Then there were all the school's young ladies. Where would they find another school in the South that was more than just a finishing school? Frederick's girls received a well-rounded education by the time they graduated. That would be more important now than ever, with all the changes the war had brought.

Lacie shook off her doubts and made a devout sign of the cross. God would understand, she told herself. He would see that behind her sinful acts, she only wanted to keep the school going, and He would understand. Lacie grimaced to herself, then focused back on the restless girls.

"All right, young ladies," she intoned in her most serious voice. "We've all been silly and giddy this evening, for the term ends tomorrow. But we are still ladies, and we must still make a proper showing for ourselves. Not only will your own families be here to participate in the graduation ceremonies, but everyone else's families will be here as well. They'll be watching every one of you." She smiled at their sincere young faces. "You're the ultimate proof of the quality of Sparrow Hill School. So remember to be on your best behavior tomorrow."

Lacie stood beside the tall parlor door as the thirty-odd girls trooped out single file. There was something special about each and every one of them, she thought. Then she was suddenly enveloped by two chubby arms.

"Nina, whatever has gotten into you?" she asked as she gently unpried the arms that were wrapped so tightly about her waist. "Here, now. Let me see you."

"I don't want to leave you," Nina's sad little voice cried, muffled as she pressed her face against Lacie. "I want to stay here."

"But your parents want you to be with them, dear." Lacie led the weeping girl to the settee, then gathered her in her arms. "They have missed you so. Haven't you missed them as well?"

The plump face, set in a pink-cheeked frown, nodded reluctantly. She wiped a tear away with the back of her balled-up fist. "But what if you go away like Mr. Frederick? What if everybody goes away? Then what shall I do?"

Lacie's heart went out to the young girl in her arms. Something about Nina had always drawn her. Perhaps it was that Nina, too, had lost her mother at the tender age of eight. Bundled off to Sparrow Hill School a year later, Nina had never had a chance to warm up to her stepmother. Instead, she had lavished all her childish love on Lacie, who had been unable to resist.

"I shall be here," Lacie promised as she stared into the damp blue eyes of the grieving child. "You shall spend the summer with the new baby and your parents, and when you come back in September, everything will be precisely as it is now." She gave Nina a fierce hug. "I shall be right here as always, waiting for all my girls to come back."

When Nina scampered up the wide mahogany staircase, Lacie roamed through the empty rooms. She straightened a pillow on a settee and stacked several magazines more neatly. She smoothed a rumpled antimacassar and turned down the lanterns in the two parlors.

It was so rare that the big school building was empty. Only after the girls went up to their rooms in the high-pitched attic in the evenings did the grand old house quiet down. Then the two parlors and the great dining room would stand silent and still. The classrooms always seemed to lie in wait for the next school day as she routinely made her final rounds for the night. She usually felt a warm, reassuring contentment as she made her way to her own room on the second floor.

But Lacie felt anything but content this night.

She was taking a huge chance. Despite her brave words to Ada, she dearly felt the strain of keeping Sparrow Hill School for Young Ladies going.

Lacie let her hand slide lovingly along the smooth worn rail of the beautiful staircase. It needed a good polishing, she thought automatically. She would see to it in the morning. It was up to her to take good care of this place now, for who else was there? Frederick would have approved—she was sure of that. Sparrow Hill had been his home, just as it was hers now.

Certainly Natchez was no longer her home. The city house had been sorely damaged by shelling by Union troops, and the old plantation house had been burned even before that. Then the land had been lost to taxes.

Lacie sighed at the memory of so much loss. She could hardly remember those places anymore. Even her father's face was beginning to fade from her memory. All she had left was her mother's locket with its

small likenesses of her parents in their youth. That—
and this school.

Her hand moved to grasp the old-fashioned locket,
and her sense of purpose strengthened. She had always
kept her locket safe. She would be just as careful about
protecting Sparrow Hill.

2

The excitement in the house was palpable.

Lacie's hand shook as she slid two tortoise shell combs into place, then tucked her long dark hair into a plain black crocheted snood. Today was the ultimate test, she told herself. As this day went, so would her future at Sparrow Hill go. For if she could convince the parents of "her" girls that she could continue the school even though Frederick was gone, everything else would be simple.

No matter what doubts some of Kimbell's citizens had about her avowed marriage to Frederick, any gossip that might be circulating would eventually die down. But if the parents of her students did not have enough faith in her to return their daughters to her, she might as well give up this foolish idea now.

Lacie stared hard at herself in the small square mirror. If only she looked a little older! She had pulled her thick hair back severely from her face and abandoned any girlish attempt at curling the heavy, straight mass. It was oddly fortunate that the past few weeks had been especially tiresome, for it showed in her pale face. She was almost gaunt, with violet shadows beneath her wide gray eyes, and no color at all in her cheeks.

Yes, Lacie decided, she certainly looked like a mourning widow, for although Frederick had not been her husband, she nonetheless mourned his loss greatly. It was only her relative youth that might trip her up, she decided. Frederick had been forty-six years old to her twenty-four. While the difference in their ages was not really so unusual for a man and wife, not many people would expect a woman of her years to manage a business such as Sparrow Hill School with any degree of success.

Lacie stared at herself for another long moment. Then on impulse, she rose and made her way to Frederick's office. As she let herself into the big cluttered room, she half-expected to see him there still, sitting back in the big leather upholstered chair, playing thoughtfully with his pipe and going over the students' files. The scent of his tobacco lingered yet in the high-ceilinged room.

But he was not there—only his empty chair and his abandoned desk. His pipes were lined up on their oak stand, cleaned and waiting for the hand that would never reach for them again.

Lacie's sorrow intensified as she rummaged through the top drawer of the desk for the pair of old reading glasses that Frederick had worn when he thought no one was about. Once she found them, she hurried back to her own small, austere room.

They helped, she decided as she stared at herself in the now slightly fuzzy mirror. She certainly looked more severe, like a dried-up old schoolmarm. That image was uncomfortably close to the truth, but she refused to think about it. Right now she was determined to play the role to the hilt. She would convince every parent there today that she was completely dedicated to the welfare of their children and their school.

It shouldn't be too hard, she decided as she closed her bedroom door behind her. After all, it was the truth.

Downstairs there was bedlam. The older girls knew their responsibilities lay in keeping the little ones well behaved and in seeing that everyone's bags were packed and put in order in the small parlor, to be taken as each girl left. But for all that, the older and younger girls alike were filled with uncontrollable excitement.

Lacie glanced briefly into the big parlor as she crossed the enormous hall. All appeared in readiness. The schoolroom chairs had been brought in and lined up neatly so that everyone could enjoy the graduation ceremony. Ada's little girls had picked flowers from the rose beds and from the annual garden along the back path, so the entire room looked and smelled fresh and inviting. The lectern was set up before the huge marble mantel. There she would give her parting words to the girls.

"Miss Lacie, Miss Lacie!" There seemed an endless litany of calls and requests as she tried to calm the high-spirited group.

She took command at once. "Betsy, please help Sarah with her hair. Her ribbon has come loose. Lydia, you mustn't start biting your fingernails again, dear. Someone please help Julia with her bag before it drags her to the floor."

They were all such good girls, Lacie thought with a sudden burst of love. The little ones that Ada taught were so young and innocent and open to new knowledge. The older ones who were her particular responsibility would be going on to new lives of their own. She could only hope that she had exerted some positive influence on them.

Then there was no more time for sad reminiscences. All too soon the parents began to arrive from near and far. Many had come into town on the early train from Shreveport or had arrived the night before and stayed at one of the hotels there. Now they milled about the grand old house, walking with their daughters in the far-flung gardens or sitting on the deep porch that circled the house, in one of the many rockers and wicker settees there.

Lemonade and punch were served on the front porch along with a pretty selection of finger sandwiches, biscuits, and sweet muffins. Mrs. Gunter had outdone herself in the kitchen.

Ada circulated among the gathering, putting everyone at their ease with her sweet smile and always pleasant manner. Mr. Fontenot was at his most charming, and the entire staff seemed at their best.

Lacie even began to relax a bit herself after accepting numerous condolences for her sudden loss. Everything seemed to be going all right. It only remained for her to get through delivering her remarks to the graduates, and of course she must address the situation caused by Frederick's death.

Finally, she signaled to Ada, and the small mealtime bell was sounded. Amid much giggling from the girls and jostling for the best position, everyone slowly made their way into the big parlor. Lacie took a deep breath, trying to calm her shaking nerves. Everything would be fine, she told herself. It would all turn out fine.

She was about to enter the house when something made her pause. A small shiver snaked up her spine, and she glanced back over her shoulder. The scene looked peaceful enough: the well-tended gardens and lawns of the school; the azalea-bordered drive stretching down to the two huge oaks at the edge of the road.

But when she saw a rider, her heart's pace unaccountably quickened. He looked respectable enough: his black jacket was open as he rode, and a dark flat-brimmed hat shaded his face. But she knew at once— either from instinct or from a sense of foreboding—that he was trouble. Perhaps it was the ease with which he sat his horse, a huge black steed of striking lines and obviously high spirits. Perhaps it was the determined set of his wide shoulders as he drew nearer to the school building. Man and beast, both dark as night in the midday sun, seemed an ominous threat.

Lacie blinked once, then again, and tried to focus through the blurring lenses of Frederick's glasses. Surely her imagination was running away with her, she told herself. She squinted to see him better, but all she could ascertain was that he was not someone she knew.

She told herself he was no one she need worry about —only perhaps a tardy relative come to the graduation festivities. But then he turned his mount from the drive and cantered up the low hill toward the Kimbell family cemetery.

Lacie's heart stopped in that moment. She watched in rising panic as he reined in his powerful steed, then dismounted and removed his hat.

She knew then, with a sinking sense of doom, that he was no graduation guest come late to the ceremony.

No, he had come on account of Frederick's death. And on account of her.

She jumped in alarm when Ada took her arm.

"There you are," her friend whispered. "We must get things going, for Judge Landry says he hasn't time to linger."

Lacie's hand went to her throat nervously. It took all her effort to tear her eyes away from the dark figure silhouetted on the hill.

"Oh, bother Judge Landry!" she finally muttered. "He's forever in a rush and therein lies all of Jessica's anxiety."

"But you can't afford to offend him. He has three more little girls at home."

Lacie grimaced. Depending upon who that man was and what he intended, Judge Landry's three little girls might be the least of her concerns. Still, she had to be practical. There were some things she would never like about running Sparrow Hill School—and coddling difficult parents was most certainly one of them.

She took a long breath. Then with one last uneasy pat at her hair and a quick adjustment to her tilted spectacles, she moved to the front of the gathering.

"Welcome, parents," she began, trying hard to keep her voice low and calm, as she had so often instructed her students to do. "As you are aware, we end this year with far more than the normal portion of regret. Frederick Allen Kimbell, the founder of Sparrow Hill School for Young Ladies and its guiding force for all of its eighteen years, died quite unexpectedly this spring. He was struck down in his prime—" Lacie faltered. She could not help but think of the remarks she'd heard Frederick

make on graduation days, going back beyond even her
own graduation ceremony eight years before.

"I know it is impossible to think about Sparrow Hill
without thinking about Frederick Kimbell. He was everything to us—teacher, friend, even father." She
twisted the handkerchief in her hands and looked at
Ada, who was now weeping silently. Tears stung her
own eyes and a lump seemed to block her throat. She
continued on only with much difficulty.

"We who are left behind are determined not to let
the school that he loved so well die. I hope you will
extend the confidence that you felt in Mr. Kimbell to
me and to the rest of the staff here."

She had meant to say more. She had meant to go on
about the fine education their girls would continue to
receive and about the preparations they would receive
in history, mathematics, and literature. But Lacie was
afraid she would burst into tears in front of the entire
company and thereby disgrace herself.

Then Ada came to her aid with the silver tray of
diplomas and a reassuring smile.

"And now, we would like to introduce our valedicto-
rian. We will follow by awarding diplomas to the six
girls who will be graduating today after many dedicated years at Sparrow Hill."

It was a relief to step back and let Judge Landry's
eldest daughter, Jessica, make the valedictory remarks.
They were well-considered words—Lacie had helped
the nervous girl organize her thoughts—but the speech
was nonetheless similar to the many others that had
preceded it through the years. Still, it was reassuring to
hear the youthful enthusiasm of the girl as she spoke of

the unity of mankind and the understanding to be had through education.

Lacie let her eyes wander over the assembly. The thirty-four students were all dressed in simple white cotton dresses, and they sat together in the front three rows of chairs. Beyond them, their mothers and fathers sat, dressed in their summertime best.

But in the back a solitary figure leaned casually against the tall doorframe. It was that unknown man from the cemetery. And he was staring straight at her.

Lacie involuntarily brought her handkerchief to her lips and lowered her eyes. It took all her willpower to swallow her momentary panic, and her heart pounded painfully as she tried to calm herself. He would not find her out, she told herself. No one would. She'd been too careful. Besides, hadn't she half-expected this anyway? Hadn't she anticipated that Frederick's brother might send someone around to look further into the death? And the marriage? Someone to ask questions? She took a slow, shaky breath and tried to calm herself. She was being foolish and she was overreacting, she told herself, because she was feeling guilty. He was probably no one of any consequence at all.

Cautiously she looked back at him. How she wished she could remove the bothersome spectacles, but she dared not do so. Instead, she had to peer carefully over the metal rim to examine this intimidating stranger.

Despite his poor manners in staring, he was at least dressed appropriately, she decided. His frock coat was of black broadcloth, cut in a long fashion. Beneath it he wore a pure white linen shirt with a wing collar and a plainly tied black silk cravat. He held his black slouch hat in one hand. Yet despite these trappings of civility,

Lacie was aware of a dangerous air about him. He might have been a huge timber wolf, relaxed and at ease at the moment. But heaven help them when he became hungry!

Then a corner of his mouth turned up in a faint but knowing grin, and she realized that he had caught her staring.

She looked away at once, incensed that some stranger could be so rude, and in her own home! Her foot was tapping in irritation at his smug attitude when Jessica slowly closed her speech. When the polite applause ended, Lacie purposefully cast the aggravating stranger out of her mind and stepped bravely back to the lectern.

"Now we will present the diplomas. Miss Pierce, if you would assist me?

"Jessica Landry . . . Evangeline St. Pierre . . . Catherine Simoneaux . . . Marta Simpson . . . Regan Galliano . . . Regina Marsden."

With each girl's tearful acceptance of her diploma Lacie became more and more emotional. As much as she had looked forward to this day and a reprieve from teaching during the long hot summer, she felt an overwhelming sense of loss. The girls were still more dear friends whom she would probably never see again. Just as Frederick was gone, so now would her girls soon be gone.

Finally the ceremony was over, and both girls and parents met in excited embraces. There were tearful good-byes between the girls and happy congratulations by the parents. Then slowly the room began to empty.

"It went well," Ada murmured as they bade good-bye to still another family.

"I suppose. But my head is aching nonetheless."

"You should be relaxed now. There's no longer any need to worry."

"Then why do I have this awful premonition—" Lacie looked around suddenly. "Did you notice a man here? Tall, wearing a dark coat?"

"Oh, there were so many people here. Whose father was he?"

Lacie shook her head, then removed her spectacles and hastened outside without answering. The afternoon shadows were beginning to stretch out and in the dusty yard a faint golden haze lingered.

Then she saw him, and her heart quickened in unreasonable fear. He was standing next to Judge Landry's carriage while the older man gesticulated broadly. She watched as they both looked over at the house. Then the stranger nodded, tipped his hat, and stepped back from the handsome landau.

Lacie felt a certain sense of doom as the carriage pulled away, for now the man's interest clearly had turned toward her. He was trouble, she thought once more. But no matter who he was or what he expected to find, she knew she could not avoid confronting him any longer.

No more carriages remained in the curved drive, and none of the staff lingered on the porch. Lacie was quite alone as the man walked toward her. His stride was slow and easy; he appeared unhurried and completely relaxed as his long legs carried him across the lawn. Once more she was reminded of a huge timber wolf, and she had to force herself to stand steady before his approach. She knew it was no social call.

His expression was unreadable as he reached the

steps to the porch, although he scrutinized her closely. He was a big man, taller than she'd realized, with shoulders so wide as to almost strain the seams of his well-tailored frock coat.

But it was not his size that most frightened Lacie. What unnerved her more than anything was the watchful gleam that lit his startling green eyes. For a moment longer, she clung to her hope that perhaps he had nothing to do with Frederick's brother—that perhaps he was just some friend of Frederick's who was considering sending his daughter to Sparrow Hill School for Young Ladies. But that hope quickly vanished. She knew without a doubt that this man was no one's father. It was even hard to imagine him being the affable Frederick's friend.

She was staring at him quite openly when he stopped two paces from her. With a start, she realized how ill mannered she must appear—and how foolish. With a stern mental jab at herself, she cleared her throat and lifted her chin as primly as she could.

"Can I help you with something, Mr.—?"

He did not respond to her thinly disguised question. Instead, his sharp gaze slid quite assessingly over her. The clear jade of his eyes seemed to miss nothing, and Lacie had to stifle her outrage at such a blatant appraisal.

Then he smiled an odd, knowing smile, and her anger changed swiftly to wariness.

"Are you Mrs. Kimbell?" One of his dark brows arched upward. "Mrs. Frederick Kimbell?"

She nodded ever so slightly, bracing herself for she knew not what.

At that he gave a small mock-bow, sweeping his hat

in the air as he did so. His eyes seemed more watchful than ever. "Then let me introduce myself. I'm Frederick's brother—half-brother—Dillon Lockwood."

Words failed Lacie at the shock of that revelation. She'd expected that he had something to do with Frederick. But his brother? She could hardly believe it. Somehow she had pictured his brother as an older man, graying and tending to heaviness, as Frederick had been.

But this man was neither graying nor heavy-set. Coal-black hair fell across his forehead, and dark brows slanted above deep-set eyes of luminous green. She tried hard to discern a resemblance to Frederick, some shadow of him, in his tanned lean face. But there was none, either in his angular jawline or in the sensuous curve of his lips.

In dismay, she lifted her eyes to his. "You don't look like Frederick," she blurted out.

"No." His teeth showed whitely in an even smile. "But then, he and I shared only one thing in common."

Lacie did not miss the caustic edge to his voice, and she knew at once what he implied. She'd lived near the town of Kimbell long enough to have heard most of the gossip and rumors about the town's leading family. Everyone knew that Frederick's father had had an eye for the ladies, and that one of his mistresses had borne him a son. But during his teens, when his mother died, the boy had left town. Since then, there had been little word of him. Only in that unfinished letter of Frederick's had Lacie found any reference to him and his business successes. And his address in Denver.

Now it seemed she was about to pay for her soft-hearted gesture in writing him about Frederick's death.

As if he saw the path of her thoughts, his expression turned sober and his eyes seemed to harden. "So you know about me. Did Frederick tell you the details of our relationship?"

Lacie colored in embarrassment to discuss such an indelicate subject. "I know—I know that you have the same father, and that you have a thriving business of your own in Colorado."

He studied her for a long moment. "Yes, thriving. Tell me, where are your spectacles?"

She was caught off guard by his abrupt change of subject. "I—I laid them down somewhere," she faltered. Then she drew herself up to her fullest height. He had flustered her, first with his untimely appearance, then with the revelation of his identity, and now with his unexpected observation. If he was trying to keep her off balance, he was doing a splendid job.

But he would not anymore, she vowed. Fighting down her rising irritation, she put on her primmest expression.

"May I offer you my personal condolences for the loss of your brother, Mr. Lockwood? I'm sure you miss him terribly, as do we all here at Sparrow Hill School."

He did not reply but only stared at her thoughtfully. Then he took a step closer, and his nearness caused her to draw back in sudden confusion.

"Why don't you just call me Dillon, since it appears we are related? Now, aren't you going to invite me inside?"

Lacie's stomach tightened at his casually familiar tone, and she stepped farther back from him. Was he baiting her? Was he up to something? He'd not come here for nothing. With an effort, she lifted her eyes to face his watchful gaze.

"Why did you come here?"

It was his turn to be slightly taken aback, but he was quick to recover.

"A direct woman. How convenient." He cocked a dark brow. "I came to pay my respects, of course."

"You never visited him while he lived. Why would you visit him now that he's dead?" she challenged.

His eyes clouded at that, and an expression that might have been regret passed swiftly over his face.

"Let's just say that Kimbell is not one of my favorite places." Then he straightened up. "Do you intend to keep me standing on the porch forever?"

Flustered anew, Lacie led him inside. Once in the wide hall, she wasn't sure what she was to do with him. Somehow she simply could not see this man sipping lemonade and eating biscuits in the parlor. It occurred to her that she had no idea what refreshments to offer a man under such circumstances, or how to maintain polite conversation.

To her dismay, he hardly gave her a chance.

"I'd like to see Frederick's office," he started with no introduction, "and his business files."

"What?" Lacie drew back. She was alarmed by his bluntness, for she had not been able to go through any of Frederick's papers yet herself. There had been too many other matters for her to handle, and she hadn't known precisely where to begin. But if she let this sharp-eyed man go through them now, he might be able to determine that she had never been anything more to Frederick than one of his students and then a teacher. Frederick had left no will with his attorney, and she knew that she was the only thing that stood between this school and Dillon Lockwood. Only her claim of marriage could prevent him from inheriting Sparrow Hill. Even though the marriage license appeared to be perfectly legal, she didn't want to see it tested in court.

"Is there any reason why I may *not* see his papers?" Once more he gave her that strange, searching look.

"N-no, of course not," Lacie stammered, her mind racing to find a reason to deny him that very freedom. "It's just that—perhaps you would like to have supper first?"

It was hard to say who was more startled by her invitation. One of his jet-black brows arched up in clear surprise. And if she'd worried about maintaining a few minutes of polite conversation with him, what in the world would she do with him for the course of an entire meal?

But the damage had been done. A slight grin lit his face, and once more his eyes turned a clear, vivid green. "How kind of you to invite me. Actually, I was hoping to stay awhile. Now that the school has emptied, there's obviously no shortage of space. Why don't you see to the meal? My horse is still unsettled from the train ride. I'll take care of him, then get my things."

After that presumptuous speech, he gave her a last look and an abbreviated bow. Then he turned on his heel and with three long strides was through the door and on his way.

Lacie was caught between anger and dismay as she peered at his broad retreating back. Never had it occurred to her that Frederick's brother would show up at Sparrow Hill School. She'd hoped that he would ultimately abandon any suspicions he might have about the marriage due to the difficulties of distance and time. After all, why would a wealthy Denver businessman waste his time and money on a struggling girls' school?

But it was clear that Dillon Lockwood was not like other wealthy businessmen. Neither distance nor time had discouraged him from coming. It was clear the school *did* matter to him, and that she had a terrible struggle ahead of her.

To her dismay, Dillon Lockwood was looking more and more like a very hungry wolf.

3

Things were going better than Dillon could have hoped. Just as he planned, he was going to be staying in the grand Allen-Kimbell mansion—the mansion that rightfully belonged to him.

He slowed his stride and looked back at the huge old house. He had never lived there, but the house had loomed over his childhood in Kimbell. It had not changed in the nineteen years he'd been gone, although back then it had been his father's home, not a school. The oaks were bigger, and the peach and pear trees that had been skinny little saplings now made up a mature, healthy stand. One of the four pines that had marked the walkway down to the lake was gone. Probably to a bad storm, he thought as he cast his experienced lumberman's eye on the remaining towering trees.

But these were incidentals. The house still appeared as it always had: huge and imposing. Ten fluted columns soared two stories on each side, and a wide, two-storied gallery encircled the entire building. Its whiteness gleamed even more brightly against the dark contrast

of the deep purple slate roof. Five elegantly detailed
dormers pierced the roof on each side, dormers he'd
wondered about as a boy.

His mother had always refused to speak of his father's
house, and of the wife and son and mother-in-law who'd
lived there as well. But others in town had not been so
discreet. As a boy he'd learned only too well that people
were always eager to tell him about the father who
never acknowledged him.

Miles Dillon Kimbell had been a quick-tempered
man, given to bouts of generosity as often as he was
prone to acts of vengeance. Rich in his own right, he'd
married Amelia Allen, the sole heiress to her family's
fortune, and thus had come to call Sparrow Hill his
home. But his mother-in-law had been a hard-edged
woman, swift to throw her son-in-law's indiscretions in
his face. Between her constant harping and his flagrant
disregard, his pretty wife had not had a chance. Amelia's sole comfort had been her son Frederick, and she'd
kept him as much to herself as she could. Dillon wondered even now if Amelia had ever known about her
husband's bastard son.

He dragged his eyes away from the house, wishing he
could blot out all the painful memories of those days.
With an effort, he focused on the stable that lay ahead.
Frederick had built it shortly after the war. The old
barn had been torched by drunken soldiers. Dillon had
argued against the expense of building such a huge
stable, for what did a school need with so many horses?
He thought Frederick's money would have been far
better spent investing in the railroad lines that were
springing up throughout the West. But Frederick had
been adamant about building the stable.

As Dillon stepped into the shadowy center aisle of the whitewashed structure, he clearly remembered the time he'd been in the old barn that had once stood there.

He'd been caught picking pecans in the orchard behind the house. His friends had fled in a panic, terrified of the repercussions if Mr. Kimbell caught them. But Dillon had stood his ground. A scrawny twelve-year-old, tall for his age but skinny and awkward, he'd shaken off his captors' grasp, then marched boldly toward the barn, where his father waited to punish the culprit. What had he expected of that long-ago confrontation? he wondered now as he led his rangy stallion into a vacant stall. Had he been so foolish as to think his father would finally acknowledge his bastard son?

It was impossible to remember now what his motives had been. But he would never forget the agony he had endured that terrible afternoon. Miles Kimbell had been drunk and angry already. When he'd seen his bastard child he'd become even more furious. He would teach him a lesson, the older man had ranted. He would teach him a lesson about trespassing where he didn't belong and about stealing from his betters. Then with a loop of coarse jute rope, he'd beaten Dillon until his shirt hung in bloody threads on his back.

Dillon's shoulders twitched even now at the memory. That was the day his childish dreams of his father had died. That was the day his animosity had turned into hatred of the Kimbells and the Allens and all they stood for. That was the day he'd vowed to get even.

But he never had gotten even, he admitted now as he removed the saddle and bridle from his horse. Frederick, the last of the Kimbell and Allen families, had never done anything to deserve his younger brother's revenge. Despite Frederick's one flaw—his one perverse weakness—he'd been a good man. If anything, he'd been too good, too trusting.

And too easy to take advantage of. At that, Dillon's thoughts returned to the woman who now claimed to be Frederick's widow.

She had certainly looked the part, he decided as he rubbed the stallion down. She'd been covered in tightly laced black bombazine from her chin to her toes. By contrast, her skin had appeared pale to the point of translucence. Her dark hair had been pulled back so tightly that her cheekbones had shown prominently. Only her eyes, dark and wide, had given life to her face.

Still, there had been something about her. For all that she had appeared the mousy schoolteacher, timid and prudish, he'd nonetheless noticed a spark of fire in her. Beneath that facade of deep mourning, he was certain she was a grasping little thief. If she'd married Frederick—*if*—she had surely done so to inherit the considerable estate he had left.

But he still doubted that Frederick had ever married. If he'd wanted a wife—even if just for appearance's sake—he'd not have waited until such a late date in his life. No, she was a complete imposter. She wanted to get her hands on Frederick's money and had made the entire story up. Frederick was not a man to marry. There was no doubt in Dillon's mind about that.

As he made his way out of the cavernous stable, an old black servant drove up in a wagon. The man nodded slightly, but then he peered more closely at Dillon and pulled the team up hard. With round staring eyes he gaped at Dillon, but still he did not say a word.

"Do I know you?" Dillon asked as the man continued to stare.

"N-no, suh. You surely don' know ol' Leland."

"Perhaps it's you who knows me, then."

Leland nodded slowly. "You's Mr. Frederick's—his daddy's other boy."

"Now, how would you know that?"

The old man shrugged, but his morose expression had begun to lift. "I don' know. You just got that Kimbell look."

Dillon rocked back on his heels, and his brow creased into a frown. "You're seeing things, old man."

"I don' mean you looks like Mr. Frederick," Leland hurried on, "or even your daddy, Mr. Miles. But ol' Mr. Miles, your granddaddy. You favor him right well." He smiled faintly, showing several long yellowed teeth as he nodded his head.

It was Dillon's turn to stare hard at the old servant. This was something he'd never heard before, and somehow it disturbed him. "You've been around here that long? I don't remember my grandfather."

"No, suh. You wouldn't. You was too young. He took ill about the same time you was born. He didn't go out fo' a long time before he died."

That was just as well, Dillon thought sourly, for he would have been sickened unto death by his son Miles's callousness. Then Dillon's eyes narrowed speculatively.

"If you've been around that long, you must know everything that goes on around this place."

"Yes, suh. Yes, suh, I surely do. Why, before he died, Mr. Frederick had ol' Leland to help him with everything." The old man's smile slowly faded. "I surely do miss Mr. Frederick. Ain't nothin' 'round here been the same since he gone."

"No, I don't suppose it would be." Then he gestured back into the stable. "Why don't you show me where things are around here?"

With a sickening feeling of doom, Lacie watched Dillon Lockwood approach the house. She had seen Leland go into the barn while this man was in there. What had they spoken of in the endless minutes that had dragged by?

She jerked the heavy brocade curtains closed with a frustrated gesture, then turned abruptly from the window. But she could not shut out the image of the man who was even now bearing down on her, nor her dreadful feeling of vulnerability.

Unlike Frederick, his half-brother had a dangerous quality about him. Shrewdness, persistence, and—no doubt—vindictiveness, made him an adversary of no little consequence. To make matters worse, he was probably able to turn on his masculine charm at will. Handsome men usually could, she thought, remembering the smile that had lit his face. Still, it had been a false smile, and if he was handsome, it was a handsomeness too ruthless to appeal to her. No matter what his successes in business had been, he was undoubtedly a ruffian at heart. She'd heard wild tales about Denver and the Colorado Territory. Surely only the roughest of characters could survive in such a crude and lawless place.

His booted footsteps on the wide gallery brought her out of her worried musings. With a stern mental shake she moved from the parlor toward the hall. She was prepared, she told herself. She was more than a match for him and she would best him at every turn. Her hardest task would be curbing her temper if he continued to bait her.

"Do come in, Mr. Lockwood. Do come in," she greeted him softly, gesturing toward the small parlor. She had abandoned her spectacles—Frederick's spectacles—in favor of a small fan which she now waved with a forced air of lethargy. "I do hope you'll forgive me my poor manners earlier. I confess you took me completely by surprise. Why, Frederick never indicated you might visit Kimbell."

"Indeed?" He strolled into the parlor and looked around the room slowly. Then he turned back to her and gave her a cynical smile. "He knew me well, then, for I have not come back to visit Kimbell."

Lacie lowered her eyes at once from his sharp gaze. She should obviously ask him why he had come, but she feared the answer to that question. As the moment stretched out into uncomfortable silence her irritation grew. Finally she closed the fan with a snap and steeled herself. He was playing a cat-and-mouse game with her. But his game would only work if she let it, and she had no intention of playing the mouse for him.

Assuming her most regal posture she moved gracefully across the room, then turned at the black marble mantel to face him.

"Mr. Lockwood, I believe it would be best if we were honest with one another," she began.

His brow arched at her words and although he said nothing, she knew she had his undivided attention.

"While you have not revealed your reason for coming, I cannot pretend to be unaware that until Frederick and I were wed, you were his legal heir."

There was no response save, perhaps, that his eyes became an even deeper shade of emerald. But he didn't speak a word and only watched her steadily.

Still, that alone was enough to unnerve her, for that deep-set gaze seemed to see right through her.

"Perhaps"—she floundered for a moment—"perhaps you expected to sell Frederick's school and use the proceeds to finance some other venture. I can understand your disappointment to find yourself usurped. I assure you, however, that it was Frederick's desire that his school be preserved. I intend to carry out his wish."

She took a slow, shaky breath after she had finished her little speech. What would his response be? she wondered nervously. By bringing up this awkward subject had she defused the problem or had she only deepened his suspicions?

He did not respond at once. Instead, he picked up a small porcelain figurine of a shepherdess and her flock and examined it.

"Once more that unswerving frankness," he intoned in a curiously mild voice as he replaced the figurine on the serpentine mahogany commode. "And yet I wonder why you would ascribe such suspicions to me. Have you reason to be on the defensive?"

"I'm not 'on the defensive,' as you put it," Lacie responded more heatedly than she'd intended. "It simply seems odd to me that you show up now, after Frederick's death, when you might have come to see him anytime previously if you'd wanted to."

"That is none of your concern," he cut in coldly.

"No? Well, your presence here now is my concern.

And I assume that, like a jackal, you've come to fight over the remains!"

It was a horrid thing to say, and she regretted it at once. But once said, it would not go away. To her dismay, his lean face lifted in a sardonic grin.

"My, my! The proper schoolmistress certainly has become hot-headed. And with no provocation at all, I might add. Could there be something—unknown to me, of course—that has you so unsettled?"

Lacie was saved from having to respond to that baiting question by the abrupt entrance of young Nina.

"Miss Lacie, Miss Lacie. Dinner is to be served—"

She stopped and stared when she saw the strange man. Then she appeared to recall the manners she'd been taught, and she curtsied with a great show of dignity.

"Excuse me, Miss Lacie. I didn't know you were entertaining a caller," she said very seriously.

If it had not been so awkward, it might have been funny. But Lacie did not see it that way. "He's not a caller," she replied crossly. Then she forced a smile to her lips. "Thank you for coming, Nina. We shall adjourn to the dining room directly."

Nina disappeared at once. As the quick patter of her footsteps faded, Lacie eyed her tormentor with renewed dismay. However would she survive this meal?

But if she dreaded the coming ordeal, he seemed almost to relish it, for he smiled broadly.

"May I escort you to the dining room—Lacie?" He laughed when she bristled. "Somehow I doubt you would want me to call you 'sister.' And 'Mrs. Kimbell' doesn't seem . . . appropriate. And as for *Miss* Lacie

—well, that's suitable for a child to call you. But I'm no child," he added in a low, resonant voice.

He was no child. She knew that logically. And yet it was not logic that caused her stomach to tighten at his words. When he crossed to her, she tried not to notice the way he moved so easily, as if he were in complete control of the situation. When he put his arm out to her, she tried hard to disregard the challenge in his mocking green eyes. And when she finally took up the challenge, she had to force herself to ignore the firm muscles and unexpected warmth beneath her hand.

They had settled nothing, so why then did she feel he'd already won? she fretted as he led her across the hall.

Because he was acting as if he had. He was acting the proprietor, and she was reacting like a guilty child. Well, no more! she vowed to herself.

Before they entered the dining room, she removed her hand swiftly from his arm, ignoring the warmth lingering on her fingertips. She turned to face him, a haughty expression painted on her face. But he was too tall and too near. She took a step back, feeling her composure slipping already.

"I trust you will not bring up anything pertaining to the school—or any personal matters involving Frederick—before the dinner company."

He pondered her words a moment, then nodded his head. "If you prefer that our discussion continue later, in private, I'll be happy to oblige you."

That was exactly what she wanted, and yet the way he had said "in private" sent an unexpected tremor through her. Still, there was no help for it. With a curt nod at him, she moved peremptorily to the head of the long polished table, then sent him her most patronizing look.

"Please be seated, Mr. Lockwood." She indicated a chair to the left of Nina's and gestured for Ada to sit to her own right.

But he was not to be outdone. To her absolute frustration he insisted on holding her chair until she was seated. Then he did the same for Ada, not allowing Lacie to introduce him but performing the honors himself. Last, he seated Nina, to the child's sheer delight. Her little face glowed, and her eyes followed him adoringly as he sat down next to her.

Lacie met Ada's worried gaze briefly. They'd not been able to plot their course of action, for it was hard to tell just what Frederick's brother was up to. Still, it helped to have Ada in her corner. Lacie took some courage from her friend's silent support.

"Nina, perhaps you'd like to say grace tonight."

The little girl smiled a gap-toothed grin, then frowned and began in a solemn voice: "Thank you, Lord, for our supper. And our dinner and our breakfast. Thank you for everything you give us every day." She darted a quick look at the tall man at her left. "And especially thank you for sending someone to help Miss Lacie, now that Mr. Frederick is gone to heaven."

It took all Lacie's effort to give Nina an approving smile. But when she saw Dillon Lockwood's amused grin, her smile became more of a grimace.

"Would you care for stewed tomatoes?" Ada murmured tactfully as she forcibly handed the blue-and-white-pottery bowl to Lacie.

Tomatoes, mustard greens, potatoes and onions, and slices of smoked ham, as well as pan bread, fresh butter, and milk, made up the fare. Yet Lacie had no appetite and put very little on her plate. Dillon Lockwood, by contrast, filled his plate generously and even took a glass of milk. Ada had suggested wine or at least a bottle of Frederick's homemade beer for their guest, but Lacie had decided against it. She did not want him to get too comfortable. Let him drink milk, or else water as they did.

"You ladies certainly set a fine table. Do the students eat this well the year round?"

"Oh, yes," Ada said with a nod.

"No—" Lacie interjected at the same moment.

At the two contradictory answers, Dillon's brow lifted wryly. He regarded the two embarrassed women curiously. "Yes? No? Perhaps you just have differing opinions on what constitutes a good meal?"

"What Ada means—what I mean is that although the girls always get healthy meals, there is seldom the—the surplus that there is tonight. Funds are limited, and we must stretch every dollar we have to keep the girls fed."

"Yes." Ada nodded so vigorously that her blond curls shook. "Yes, the meals are always nourishing, but to-night's supper is especially good."

After that there seemed no topic for conversation, and a silence began to build. Although Lacie squirmed uncomfortably at the awkward situation, she didn't know how to rectify it. Even light chatter seemed quite beyond her tonight.

Dillon Lockwood, on the other hand, did not appear

the least perturbed by the dreadful silence. In fact, he seemed to enjoy the chaos his presence at Sparrow Hill School was causing, and he was clearly enjoying the meal as well. When he caught Nina's shy gaze, he gave her a quick wink that brought a smile to her little face. It was she who finally broke the oppressive quiet.

"Are you going to be the new headmaster for our school?"

Dillon leaned back in his chair. "I don't believe that I'm the right sort of person for that position," he replied. His gaze moved momentarily to Lacie. "Besides, I have a number of other ventures that require my attention. Now I have a question for you. Why have all the other girls gone home and yet you are still here?"

"My daddy's late because he's waiting for another baby to be born. So he said I could stay with Miss Lacie for a little while."

"It would be no trouble for me to bring her home, Lacie," Ada spoke up. "I'll be going right through there."

"You're leaving also?" His dark brows arched slightly in what seemed to be only polite interest. Yet Lacie felt an ominous foreboding.

"Why—um . . . yes. My great-aunt is visiting my parents, so—so I'll be going to meet them all." Ada shot an apologetic look toward Lacie. "But I won't be gone long," she hastened to add.

"And you'll be taking Nina?"

"No." Lacie folded her hands to keep her fingers from trembling. "Nina is going to stay with me until her father comes." She tried to smile encouragingly at Nina, but she knew it was a poor effort. "She and I shall enjoy having the house all to ourselves, won't we, Nina?"

Nina's chubby face bobbed enthusiastically. Then she turned her sparkling eyes up to Dillon. "But we won't really be alone. Not now that you're here."

4

Lacie had left the table with a pounding headache, a headache exacerbated by the obvious good mood of their unwelcome guest. As the meal had progressed he had become more and more pleasant, enticing smiles from both Nina and Ada. Like a practiced charmer he had entertained them with stories of the West and tales of his travels.

But he would not charm her so easily, Lacie vowed.

She had felt a certain satisfaction when Nina began to yawn and rub her eyes. It had been the perfect excuse for her to leave his presence. While she'd taken care of Nina, Ada had prepared one of the vacant rooms for his use.

That had left him alone, and given no polite alternative, he had adjourned to the shadowy gallery to smoke his slender cigar with only the evening cicadas for company.

Lacie smiled inwardly. They had not resumed their earlier conversation, and she was pleased that she'd gotten the best of him on that score. Although nothing was settled, he must nonetheless realize now that she was not about to fold at the first sign of his bullying. He might think he could manipulate her into letting down her guard, but she was just as determined to thwart him.

Still, there had been a few moments when he had turned that disarmingly crooked smile on her . . .

Lacie firmly shook off such thoughts. Then with a final smoothing of the thin cotton sheet, she stepped back from the bed in which Nina lay. The girl had been afraid to sleep in her attic room now that the other girls were gone. But safely ensconced in Lacie's own bed, she had quickly fallen asleep. Lacie looked down at the small cherubic face and smiled. Such a sweet child. What a blessing it was to have her staying longer, especially since Ada was leaving tomorrow. Although Nina would be no real protection against Dillon Lockwood's oppressive presence, she still provided a buffer between them, some common ground that allowed them to pretend to at least a semblance of civility.

Unfortunately, Nina would not be there for very long. And who knew how long Dillon Lockwood intended to linger at Sparrow Hill?

But no matter how long he stayed, she would outlast him. Common courtesy demanded that she not throw him out. After all, despite his awkward relationship to Frederick, he was nevertheless his half-brother. No, she would just have to suffer his unwelcome presence and hope that his business dealings would eventually draw him back to the Colorado Territory. When he saw the marriage license, he would surely give up hope of inheriting the school. Then Sparrow Hill would truly be hers, and she would preserve it just as Frederick would have wanted.

Lacie pushed a damp tendril of dark hair from her brow, then rubbed her aching temples. What a terribly trying day it had been!

She had gotten through the graduation ceremony with all the parents only to be faced with Dillon Lockwood. Then had come their confrontation in the parlor, followed by that dreadful supper. She thought she had come through it all fairly well.

But only by lying continuously.

She was living a big lie and supporting it by more and more small lies. Her head pounded anew at the thought of what she was doing. Lying. Stealing. Forging legal papers. What other terrible deeds would she do in the future?

Lacie pressed her fingers against her eyes for a moment, trying to recoup her strength. Then she straightened up. What else *could* she do? she asked herself. What were her options? She was only doing what she must.

At that thought she determinedly buried any feelings of guilt and donned her nightgown and wrapper. She was tired and had a dreadful headache. A long soak in a cooling bath would go far in restoring her spirits.

The house was quiet as she slipped out of her room. The second-floor central hall, which functioned as a library when school was in session, now loomed empty and dim. Only a solitary lamp near the head of the stairs lit the wide, book-lined space.

It was clear that everyone was abed: Ada in her room, Mrs. Gunter in her room, the servants in their quarters near the stable, and Mr. Lockwood in Monsieur Fontenot's vacated room. Lacie could not help tiptoeing as she crept past the narrow hall that led to Monsieur

Fontenot's room. Above all, she did not wish to alert
Dillon Lockwood to her presence outside his chamber.

It had always been Frederick's habit to let the students and female teachers use the hall if they were up
after dark, while he and Monsieur used the outside
gallery. But she knew she could no longer count on such
privacy. She held her soft slippers in one hand and two
squares of toweling in the other as she silently made her
way down the broad curving stair.

Downstairs there were no lamps burning, but that
did not slow her progress. She could have walked the
entire school blindfolded, so familiar was she with the
placement of every table, chair, and desk. Only when
she had to cross the small stretch of gallery to the bathhouse did she hesitate.

Was that the aroma of tobacco? she wondered as her
nose caught a faint scent. Then a light breeze moved
the air, and she shook her head softly. It was nothing,
only the tensions of this horrible day playing tricks with
her mind. Still, she gave a sigh of relief when she finally
closed the wood-paneled door behind her.

There were two wall-bracketed oil lamps on either
side of the door in the bathing room, but once again
Lacie opted for darkness. The three high windows let in
the faintest glimmer of moonlight, and that was all she
needed. She entered the center of the three curtained
bathing alcoves, then turned the water spigot on. The
water, collected in the huge copper-lined cistern just
outside, was cool on her fingers, but she didn't mind. It
felt good to be chilled, and she didn't want to be bothered with heating water tonight. She just wanted to lie
back in the tub and let both mind and body go lax.

She hung her plain cotton wrapper and nightgown

on a brass hook on the wall, then wound her sable brown hair into a thick coil on her head. Once it was tied in place with a thin strip of pale blue ribbon, she stepped into the enameled tin tub.

After the heat of the day, the cool water was a shock, but she quickly became accustomed to the temperature and with a sigh of relief, she leaned back in the tub. Normally she was efficient in her bath, using a minimum of water and time to accomplish her cleansing routine. But tonight was different. Tonight she let the tub fill until all but her shoulders and head were immersed. Tonight she let the soap and the cleansing cloth lie where they were while she enjoyed the luxury of her solitary soak.

Lacie lost track of time as she lay there. She had feared that her worries would dog her thoughts and that she would not be able to relax. But she had not considered her complete exhaustion. She had actually begun to doze off when a firm step awoke her with a start.

Her heart jumped into her throat when she heard the outside door open, then heard heavy, booted footsteps inside the bathhouse.

Lacie was too startled to move. Her first thought was that Yankee soldiers were back. Only one time had the school suffered unwelcome visitors and that had been at the beginning of the Yankee occupation. But that notion disappeared at once, for she knew the Yankee presence in northern Louisiana was slowly waning. Then her eyes widened as an even worse realization struck her. Dillon Lockwood had come into the bathhouse. Any minute now, her humiliation would be complete!

She sat motionless, listening to the sound of his movements as he felt his way in the darkness. Then she heard the sound of a sulphur match striking, and a weak glow lit the unadorned rafters of the room. The glass globe of one lantern was removed and then replaced, and at once the room was bathed in golden light.

Through it all Lacie remained as still as a stone, staring in fright at the whitewashed wall before her. Never had she been in such an awful situation! Only a slight turn of his head would make him realize that someone occupied one of the tubs. If he were a gentleman, he would leave discreetly, and nothing would have to be spoken of it. Neither of them would ever be forced to embarrass the other by referring to this unfortunate incident.

But it was not to be. A soft "I'll be damned" brought the horror of her predicament out in the open, and she cringed where she sat.

"What in hell are you doing taking a bath in the dark?"

"Get out," Lacie muttered from between clenched teeth. She did not dare look at him, for that would simply be too mortifying. It was scandalous enough that her bare shoulders and back were exposed to him. To twist about in the narrow tub would display even more of her anatomy to his view.

For a moment he was silent, and she wildly hoped he would accede to her demand. But then she heard the thud of one heavy boot against the wood-plank floor, then the other, and her heart turned to lead. He was an uncivilized barbarian without a shred of decency! And she was trapped in here with him!

"Please get out!" she demanded anew although this

time her voice sounded shrill and unnatural. "Are you so crude that you would embarrass a lady like this?"

"Ah, you want me to treat you like a lady? And here I thought we were getting along so well, just like family is supposed to. But then, we're not really family at all, are we?"

With every fiber of her being she wished to deny having any familial relationship with this ruffian. Yet she clamped her lips tight against her angry retort. He would not goad her into saying anything rash, she vowed.

"Yes, we are. We are family. But even true brothers and sisters do not bathe together," Lacie managed to reply as she sank as low as she could in the chilly water. "Now do as I say and get out of here!"

This time when he spoke his voice was low and rumbling, a quiet taunt just beyond her ear. "You're not getting rid of me so easily. And do you know why? Because I don't believe one word of your story about marrying Frederick."

It was what she'd feared all along, but hearing him say the accusation out loud caused her to shrink in despair. Then he slid his finger insultingly down her back from her neck to somewhere beneath the water, and she jumped as if she'd been scalded.

"Leave me alone! Leave me alone!" she squeaked as she huddled against the far end of the tub.

"Such soft, pale skin," he murmured. Then his voice sharpened. "No one would ever guess that under that rigid, corseted facade you wear like armor there is such a woman. But then, that's probably just one more part of this farce of yours. I suggest you leave off this act of innocence for me, however. I don't buy it."

Outraged by his callousness, Lacie felt her fear give way to fury. She clasped her arms before her breasts and twisted herself around just enough to see him.

"You are positively the most ill-bred clod I've ever laid eyes on! This is hardly the place for you to air your absurd accusations!" She stared at him with flashing eyes and as much affronted dignity as she could muster. When he only met her angry gaze with his own glittering stare, she took a deep breath. "If this conversation absolutely cannot wait till morning, so be it." She clenched her teeth before continuing. "Just vacate this room, and I shall meet you in the parlor as soon as I finish."

She expected an answer from him, but Dillon Lockwood once again proved to be unpredictable. Before her horrified gaze he began calmly to unbutton and remove his shirt. And all the while the smirk on his face grew more and more taunting.

"I'm not leaving this room until I get to the bottom of this. You can tell me right now"—he slipped off his shirt and flung it onto a bench—"or you can wait until I'm stripped down and sitting in the tub next to yours. But one way or another, we're going to have our talk."

So saying, he began to unfasten the buttons of his black buckskin trousers. Lacie was so stunned that she could hardly do more than stare at him while he unashamedly removed his shirt. His pants, however, were another matter altogether. With a gasp she jerked her head around and concentrated earnestly on the rolled edge of the enameled tub. But the speckled blue finish before her could not dispel the disturbing vision that lingered in her mind's eye.

She'd never seen a man's bare chest. Never. Frederick had even censored the art books that his students used. Consequently, she wasn't certain just how men were formed. But somehow she knew without a doubt that this man was formed perfectly. Even with her eyes tightly closed she could not escape the image of his broad shoulders and well-muscled arms. His chest rippled with muscles, only slightly concealed by dark hair liberally sprinkled there. That hair narrowed along his belly into a dark ribbon that disappeared—

Lacie wiped that picture from her mind with brutal determination. She dared not look around for fear of seeing his state of complete undress. Instead, she looked desperately over at her gown and wrapper hung so carelessly upon the small hook on the wall. Did she dare reach for them? Could she do so without completely baring herself to his view?

The answer was a disheartening no, but then she considered her towel. It was nearer and would afford her some protection.

As if he had read her very thoughts, Dillon reached for the white cloth. But Lacie grabbed it too. As they pulled the cloth between them, she glared at him furiously.

But her glower only caused his grin to widen. It was absolutely the last straw for Lacie, and with reckless determination she tugged harder on the towel. "Let go of my towel, you horrible beast!"

With a mocking wink he fed it to her slowly. But with every inch of cloth that she gathered in her arms, he moved nearer and nearer, still holding tightly to the other end. As furious as she was, his presence just inches from her was nonetheless intimidating. With a frustrated oath she abandoned any further thoughts of escape. Both fear and fury fought for dominance, but she wisely kept her silence. As his eyes captured hers, glinting like emeralds, she knew she could do nothing but wait for whatever it was he planned to do.

"There, that's better," he remarked as he released the towel with a casual flick of his fingers. He squatted beside her tub, his face level with hers. His grin turned up slightly on one side as he watched her gather the now-soaked towel before her. "Now that you're feeling a little more docile, perhaps we can have that talk."

"*Docile* is not the word for what I'm feeling!" she snapped, frustrated by how easily he had put himself in charge of the situation.

"Too bad. You'd get a lot further if you were a little more agreeable."

Lacie straightened up with a start. "You have your nerve! I'm not the one who's behaving so abhorrently! If you want an agreeable, docile woman, I suggest you go back to wherever it is you've come from!"

There was a pause. His eyes fell briefly from her angry gray eyes to her pursed lips, then farther still to her barely concealed breasts, heaving now with the force of her anger. Then his eyes met hers again and this time a different expression showed in his vivid gaze. Even his smile changed as he gazed at her. But it was his words that caused her stomach to tighten in a new, more violent emotion.

"I've never found docile women to be of much interest."

Lacie's eyes widened at the disturbing tone of his voice. What did he mean? she wondered. But she feared she knew and she began to shiver uncontrollably.

"Is your bath too cold?" he asked almost solicitously, letting his fingers play carelessly on the water's surface. She knew his interest was insincere and that he had asked the question only to unnerve her more. But far from feeling chilled, she suddenly felt uncomfortably warm as a slow, heated flush crept up her chest and neck.

"I—I would like to get out of the tub now," she whispered in a small, strained voice. She turned her eyes determinedly toward her knees, which lay just beneath the water's reflective surface.

"Suit yourself."

When he stood up, she turned in surprise at his unexpected cooperativeness. She tried not to notice his scanty attire of only silkaline drawers, but it was hard to ignore such a blatantly virile specimen of the male gender. To her complete dismay, a blush quickly colored her cheeks.

But instead of stepping away to give her privacy, he only pushed back the plain curtain that separated her tub from the next one. Then he proceeded to doff his last garment and step into the empty tub.

Lacie's cheeks were scarlet with embarrassment as he turned on the water, then leaned back in the tub. Never in her entire life had she been confronted with so impossible a situation! Never had any man so completely shaken her self-confidence—not even that horrible Yankee colonel who'd threatened to set fire to Sparrow Hill School and had torched the old barn. No, Dillon Lockwood had more gall than ten Yankee colonels!

She struggled to contain her myriad warring emotions—outrage, resentment, and defeat among them—

from showing. Her only satisfaction would come in besting him at his own game. But no matter how she twisted and turned the matter around in her mind, she could see no escape that would not bare even more of herself to his view. Her dark brows lowered in a furious frown as she admitted he had her bested. But this was just one battle, she told herself sternly, not the whole war. His strong-armed bullying only strengthened her resolve to keep Sparrow Hill out of his greedy clutches.

With a mutinous set to her jaw and a sullen expression on her face, she turned her hostile gaze on him.

"Whatever you have to say, just say it and get it over with."

His expression did not change, save for perhaps a slight, smug twist to his lips. His thoughts were well-concealed beneath his seemingly bland expression. Lacie knew, nonetheless, that something seethed beneath the surface. He had not come this far to challenge her claim to Sparrow Hill without what he considered to be good reason.

"I have a lot to say, sweet sister." His eyes glinted in the lamp's golden glow. "And a lot of questions to ask."

He reached forward to turn off the spigot, then took up a sliver of soap and a wash rag. For what seemed an endless amount of time he worked up a lather on the cloth. Lacie had to restrain an impatient remark before he finally laid down the soap and returned his attention to her. His eyes were dark and unfathomable as he watched her.

"I find you too young and too pretty—in short, a highly unlikely sister-in-law," he said as he slowly soaped his arms.

"How could you possibly know what sort of wife

Frederick would pick?" she answered curtly, but her eyes fell away from his face.

"Some things a brother just knows. Even a bastard brother."

Lacie's ears should have burned at his use of that crude term. But she was somehow too distracted by the lazy movement of the soapy cloth on his well-muscled chest. As the silence began to stretch out, she realized she was staring. With a jerk she turned her head and once again stared straight at the wall.

"Your opinion of Frederick's choice for a wife is hardly relevant. I *am* his widow. That's all you need to know."

"What you are . . ." He paused and his gaze moved boldly over her exposed shoulders and arms. Lacie felt as if his eyes actually saw further, as if even the meager protection of the water offered no proof against his brazen stare.

"What you are is an unexpected complication," he murmured so quietly that she hardly heard his words.

"A—a what?"

Abruptly he straightened, and his smile, which had almost seemed warm, quickly became cold and ruthless. "What you are is a very clever little gold digger. Frederick was not a man who was likely to marry, but you saw a chance to make a quick bundle when he became ill. I doubt that you actually married him at all. But even if you did, I've no doubt the deed was done while he was not in complete possession of his senses. Tell me"—his eyes glittered menacingly—"which scenario is closer to the truth?"

Lacie's jaw slackened at his brutal assessment of the situation. How could he have hit so close to the truth?

Still, he had no way of really knowing anything and no way to prove it either. She shivered as she faced his icy stare, so sure and triumphant already. It was hard to feel confident when faced with such a daunting foe. She had to remind herself that although she was indeed guilty as accused, her motivations were nonetheless pure. Frederick had wanted Sparrow Hill to survive. His last words had been of his school. But if this arrogant man inherited it there would be no way to prevent him from closing it and selling everything off. That thought gave her courage, and she lifted her chin in a brave gesture.

"If there's anyone who might be termed a gold digger, it's most certainly you. Poor Frederick is hardly dead and you're already here to pick his bones, trying to glean whatever you can from what he left behind."

To this he only snorted. "I should not be surprised that you turn the attack on me since you have no defense of your own to fall back on. But I caution you, Lacie, I have no patience with liars or thieves. And you, despite the innocence you work so hard at projecting, you, I'm afraid, are both a liar and a thief."

"I am *not!*" she shouted, sending a wave of bath water sloshing at the rim of the tub. "You are so greedy for everything Frederick had that you project your own wicked thoughts onto good and honest folks! You would not even want this school if you knew how meager its earnings are. Even the value of the house and lands are much reduced since the war!"

She struggled with the wet clinging towel that now hugged her breasts. "But you don't care about that, do you? You'd sell everything for ten cents on the dollar just to squeeze any penny you could get out of it. You'd sell Sparrow Hill and destroy a southern tradition—"

"I don't give a damn about southern tradition!" he thundered. "I don't give a damn about this charm school, and I don't give a damn about this town or any of the people in it!"

"You don't care about anything at all but your own greedy motives," she hissed. "Some of us try to rise above such vulgar emotions, but you would destroy everything for the few dollars you would gain by closing Sparrow Hill."

"My motives are none of your concern, and it is not *my* relationship to Frederick that is in question. You're the one trying to steal my rightful inheritance. You might as well admit it now, while I'm still willing to forget your crime," he added with an arch to one raven-black brow.

"I'm guilty of no crime," she vowed between clenched teeth. "You have no right to accuse me—"

"No? Let's examine the information I've gathered so far." He held up the fingers of one large hand as he ticked off the list. "Your marriage to Frederick came as a complete surprise to Judge Landry and to the rest of the people of Kimbell. Second, Frederick never so much as mentioned your name to me in any of his correspondence. Third"—he paused and gave her a chilling smile—"you clearly do not need glasses. The ones you wore today were strictly for show. What are you hiding? Why would a young woman of your obvious attributes disguise herself beneath such prim clothing and unflattering hairdos?" He paused and his eyes swept from her disheveled hair and flushed cheeks to her barely concealed breasts. "I'd guess your appearance right now is a lot nearer the real woman you are."

Lacie gasped at his horrible implication, but he continued relentlessly. "Unfortunately for you, you've seriously misjudged your man this time. You see, I know that Frederick never relished—" He stopped suddenly and seemed to reconsider his words. "I'm no fool to be taken in by a con artist, no matter how pretty she is. You're obviously the only one to benefit from this so-called marriage. There was no good reason for Frederick to marry you."

"How would you know why he married me?" Lacie cried furiously. "Why is it so impossible to believe that he loved me? Or . . . or that I loved him? But then, you probably wouldn't have the foggiest notion about such things!" she finished spitefully.

"Probably not," he agreed, but his smile was hardly amiable. A shiver shook her and Lacie tried hard to calm herself as she cleared her throat nervously.

"I hardly think Sparrow Hill is such a prize that you would want it so badly," she said in a strained voice.

"No? Well, there's a lot about me that you don't know. And if Sparrow Hill weren't a prize," he said sarcastically, "you wouldn't want it either. Why not give up this foolish scheme? Give up your claim to Frederick's estate?" He watched her closely. "I can make it worth your while."

At those words, Lacie peered sharply at him. Was he trying to buy her off? Her eyes were a stormy gray as she returned his bold stare.

"There's nothing you have that could tempt me to abandon this school."

For long icy seconds their gazes remained locked in

hostile battle. Then he slowly stood up and stepped out of the tub. Lacie's eyes widened in shock at his naked, dripping body that now towered so intimidatingly before her. This was man at his most natural, man at his most powerful. All her anger fled as she stared helplessly at him. Mortification and awe, horror and fascination struck her speechless as he glowered at her.

"I'm offering you a way out—mark that well." He leaned forward then and placed one hand on either side of her tub. Although she shrank back, she could not get away from his penetrating stare.

"You may have coerced Frederick—or perhaps sweet-talked him. But no fast-talking little conniver is going to cheat me out of what is rightfully mine."

Their gazes seemed to remain locked endlessly. Then his head cocked slightly and his expression changed.

"There's no reason why you have to be a complete loser in this, Lacie. As I said, I'm sure we can come to some arrangement." His eyes moved slowly down to her lips, then further to the white towel, soaked and clinging so revealingly to her rounded breasts.

There was no mistaking the implication in his brazen stare, and Lacie was dumbfounded by the thought. How could any man be so despicable? How could he make so disgusting a proposal to her?

When his hand reached forward she flinched, but he only tilted her head back with one finger beneath her chin. "I suggest you think hard about my offer, because it's the best one you'll get. Otherwise"—he paused and his eyes roamed her pale, wide-eyed face—"otherwise, you will find yourself locked in bitter conflict with me.

"And Lacie"—he smiled wickedly and rubbed his

thumb intimately over her full lower lip—"I fight dirty."

Then he calmly pulled on his trousers, gathered up his shirt and boots, and with only an arrogant wink at her, quit the room.

5

❧❧

The night provided no solace; sleep eluded Lacie as she tossed on her bed, all the while trying desperately to think of a solution to her dreadful predicament.

She should never have undertaken such an improbable scheme, she told herself. She must have lost all reason. Yet she could hardly have abandoned the school either.

Dillon Lockwood would exact terrible revenge from her now. He couldn't prove a thing; it was all just supposition, she reminded herself, but he would never let it rest.

Still, what else could he do?

Indeed, what he might do was precisely what worried her when she woke up once more from a fitful dream of rabbits and wolves. Although the eastern sky was just beginning to lighten in the hour before dawn, Lacie could not bear another moment in bed. Careful not to awaken the still-slumbering Nina, she eased from the moss-stuffed mattress and quietly donned a plain white blouse and a simple navy working skirt over her chemise. She did not bother with either petticoats or shoes and only smoothed back her sleep-tangled hair with one careless gesture.

She had no goal in mind as she went out onto the gallery that circled the house. She only knew that she needed some relief from her worried, restless thoughts.

At the gallery rail Lacie stopped and leaned out a little over the edge. In the dim light of predawn the school grounds appeared almost eerie. The trees were large shadows in a fuzzy gray world. The barn loomed almost indistinguishable from the haze, as did the smaller outbuildings. As her eyes grew accustomed to the light she saw the low layer of ground fog that so often blanketed the land in the early morning hours. Sparrow Hill might have been a land of dreams, floating on a cloud, not real at all.

How she wished that were so—that Frederick were still alive and the school just as it had always been!

But then a rooster crowed from somewhere near the barn, and reality intruded once more. With a sigh Lacie moved quietly along the gallery to where the outside stair descended to the ground.

Up till now, life at Sparrow Hill *had* been somewhat dreamlike, she admitted as she made her way silently down the stairs. It had been secure and comfortable, a haven from the war and its terrible aftereffects. Frederick had created his own little oasis at Sparrow Hill, and she had felt safe and insulated from the unpleasantries of life. Certainly she'd not had to deal with the Dillon Lockwoods of the world.

At the thought of Frederick's half-brother, Lacie's hands knotted in fists. Hang him and his ill-mannered ways! Who was he to come here and try to trample on her and this school? As she walked down the gravel

path that led to the barn, she was hardly conscious of
the dew that clung to her skirt and bare feet. She kept
remembering his shocking audacity—and the way he
had looked when he'd undressed for his bath.

Her stomach tightened at the memory—in anger, she
told herself. Only anger. But angry or not, she could not
pretend that he hadn't affected her. He had sent her
from absolute fury to cowering fear; he seemed more
able to control her emotions than she was. To make
matters worse, she was sure he knew it. Certainly he
took great pleasure from it.

Determined to put such thoughts out of her mind,
Lacie let herself into the feed room. With ease that
came from long familiarity, she filled an old bucket with
dried corn, then went outside to the chicken yard.

Summoned by the rooster's earlier crowing, the hens
were already scratching about in the dirt. At Lacie's
entrance they began to cackle and cluck in earnest,
clustering about her in eager anticipation. One hen,
however, stayed back, hopping slowly on one leg. Its
other leg was bent back in a permanently crippled position.

Lacie flung the kernels about her quickly, and the
chickens attacked them zealously. Then, as each tried
to best its neighbor for the choicest seed, Lacie moved
nearer the crippled old hen.

"Here, chick, chick, chick," she called softly. "Come
on, now. I've got a special treat for you."

As if it knew this routine well, the hen cocked her
head, hopping once or twice along the fence line but
not straying far. When Lacie was close enough, she
crouched down and placed a nice rounded handful of
corn kernels in a little pile near a fencepost.

"Come on, now. Eat up before the others find you out." Then she moved back toward the other feeding birds, tossing the last remnants among them.

For an instant she once again felt the dreamlike quality of the slow-dawning day. How many years ago had she first come to Sparrow Hill as a frightened, motherless little girl? Caring for the chickens had been the first chore assigned her, and for some silly, sentimental reason she'd never given it up.

She took a deep breath and closed her eyes, remembering the shy ten-year-old she had once been. Sometimes she felt that she'd not changed or truly grown up at all. Certainly there were times she felt just as scared and unsure and ill at ease as she had then. But she had only to open her eyes to see that time had passed. She had changed.

When Lacie did open her eyes, however, reality seemed truly remorseless, for it was the shadowy image of Dillon Lockwood that she first saw. He was leaning against a fencepost, smoking a thin-rolled cigarette, and watching her with his predatory stare. She was so taken by surprise that the grain bucket slipped from her suddenly nerveless fingers and rolled noisily among the chickens. Their startled cackling quickly died down, but Lacie's racing heartbeat only increased its frenetic tempo.

"Good morning," he called softly. "Sleep well?"

Lacie bristled. Even in making a casual greeting he obviously found it impossible to be pleasant. How did he think she'd slept after that dreadful scene in the bathing room?

Gritting her teeth she bent down to retrieve the bucket. "I slept rather poorly, as you no doubt can guess. You, on the other hand, probably slept just fine, considering that creating havoc seems to be your greatest pleasure in life."

His slight smile, coupled with a prolonged perusal of her casual attire, only caused her temper to simmer even hotter.

"Would it please you to know that I, too, tossed and turned upon my bed—"

"Good!" she cut in emphatically. "Now, if you'll excuse me." She turned toward the gate.

"But don't you want to know why I could not sleep?"

"No!" But she stopped short when he put his hand on the gate and opened it for her.

He tossed down his cigarette then and looked steadily at her. "It was you," he said, ignoring her words completely. "Every time I closed my eyes, I had a vision of your smooth pale shoulders and your lovely, delicate neck."

At Lacie's gasp of surprise and her stunned expression, his grin widened. "It's not often that I see a lady at her bath and then adjourn to my room all alone. May I say, Lacie, you made a most delectable picture last night."

"You—you may say no such thing!" she stammered, truly mortified now. She tried to dart through the gate and get away from him, but his quick sidestep only brought them face to face.

"Ah, but it's true, Lacie. Even when I did manage to sleep, it was only to dream of you."

"Oh, you must be quite mad to say such things!"

"Is it mad to speak the truth? I think not. You know, if you would just be honest with me, we would get along so much better." His eyes lowered from her angry eyes to her shocked, rounded lips.

"I don't want to get along with you," she snapped, even as a flush began to color her cheeks. "All I want is for you to leave this place."

"I'm not leaving here until I get what I want," he said quietly as his expression grew more serious.

"You'll never prove I'm not Frederick's widow. Why don't you just give up now and save yourself a lot of trouble!"

"Ah, but it's really no trouble." So saying, he took a thin wisp of her long dark hair and wound it about his finger, all the while staring deeply into her eyes. "I think I shall enjoy every minute of it."

Lacie's stomach tightened at that, and her heart seemed almost to stop in her chest. What did he mean?

But even without being told, she knew exactly what he meant. It was no longer enough for him to simply get Sparrow Hill. No, now he wanted her as well. He wanted to humiliate and degrade her because she had dared to oppose him.

With trembling fingers she tugged the lock of hair free of his grasp. "Then I shall do everything within my power to make sure you do *not* enjoy it," she countered as bravely as she could.

At that he laughed. "Lacie, Lacie, you are at your most charming when you are up in arms against me! Anger suits you far better than that cold politeness you affect."

"Oh, you are impossible!"

"At least your anger is an honest emotion."

Unable to bear even one more word of his taunting, Lacie tried to slip past him. He anticipated her move, however, and quickly blocked her way. To her dismay, he now had her backed against the fence, trapped by his arms on either side of her. In the tense silence that followed, she was wholly conscious of his nearness; all her senses were aware of him as she'd never been aware of any man before. He smelled of soap and tobacco; he radiated a disturbing warmth. She could hear his steady breathing—she fancied she could hear his very heartbeat.

Distrusting her own reaction to him, she tried to look away. But with a finger beneath her chin, he kept her face turned up to him and kept his face within her vision.

"Now perhaps you'll show me another honest emotion," he murmured.

"No, don't!" she whispered, fearing what was to come. She tried to avoid his devastating touch, but his hand was firm at her cheek as he held her still for his kiss.

The first brush of his lips was so light, so fleeting, that it could hardly be termed a kiss. Yet its impact was profound. She wanted to flee. She wanted to stay. She wanted to melt into the ground and disappear. She wanted to fly above the clouds and soar forever.

Then his lips moved more firmly against hers, and every conscious thought fled her mind. His mouth was at once soft and firm, sure and tentative. Its warm pressure was sweet, yet wickedly dangerous.

She had been kissed before, by three different suitors, in fact—all respectable citizens of Kimbell. But those kisses had been no more, she now saw, than the mere press of flesh against flesh. But this . . .

When his lips began to tease the corner of her mouth,

she let out an involuntary moan. But when his tongue slid silkily along the crevice of her lips, she pulled back in alarm. All her nerves seemed to be clamoring. From heart to belly to knees, every part of her was hot and trembling and out of control.

"Stop . . . please, stop," she whispered in a faint, wavering voice.

"We've hardly even begun," he answered, his warm breath stirring her hair. Then his hands slipped around her, and she was pulled intimately against him. For a moment they stood that way, fitted together almost naturally, it seemed. She had only to drop the bucket and slide her arms up around his neck to be perfectly cleaved to him.

But there was nothing perfect about what they were doing, she realized. Nothing.

"No, no!" She twisted away from the disturbing feel of his body pressing against her, and as his grasp loosened, she backed away from him.

"You—you—" Lacie fumbled for words as she stared wide-eyed at him. No man had ever taken such liberties with her. Never. If one had, she would have slapped him soundly for it. Yet this man . . .

"Why the shocked look, Lacie? After all, you *have* been married, haven't you?" He gave her a mocking smile. "You can't be a stranger to a man's attention— although I'll be the first to admit Frederick and I were cut from different cloth." His eyes were warm and alive, their green depths lit from within as he stared at her with a half-smile curving one side of his mouth.

Lacie fought to catch her breath and somehow slow the frantic pounding of her heart. He had done it again: he had unnerved her completely and taken control of the situation. But how in heaven's name was she to defend herself against such unfair tactics?

"A different cloth entirely," she managed to get out, ignoring his other taunts. "Frederick never demanded —he asked. He never forced himself on me like—like some beast might. He was gentle with his kisses." It was all pure fabrication. She knew it as she said it. Yet she could think of no other way to put him off.

But he only laughed, as if he saw right through her. "Such a little liar. Did no one ever warn you that in the end your lies will trip you up? Yours already have."

At those infuriating words, Lacie turned abruptly from him and began quickly to march toward the house. She would not bandy words with this insufferable man a second longer. He had insulted her. He had kissed her—

"May I have that bucket? My horse needs grain."

In an instant she whirled around and heaved the bucket at him with all her might, wishing more than anything that it would hit him on the head. She didn't know whether to be chagrined because she had missed him entirely, or because she had succumbed to such unladylike behavior. But when he began to laugh she let out a frustrated oath. Then she turned and ran as fast as she could back to the house.

Dillon remained next to the fence, staring after Lacie until she had disappeared around a tall clump of pink and white oleander bushes. Then, with a thoughtful expression on his face, he picked up the much-abused bucket and made his way slowly into the barn.

Leatrice Eugenia Montgomery—Kimbell—was hardly what he had expected.

Granted, she'd looked exactly the part yesterday when he'd arrived during her little social. Prim. Grim. Laced up tighter than a drum with those ridiculous spectacles sliding off her nose. Her chilly reception would have been enough to freeze any man's blood.

Yet his own blood was hardly chilled right now. When she was Lacie, she was another creature altogether. Softer, volatile. It took very little to trigger that temper of hers, and it was his profound pleasure to set her off. Actually, to do so was a good idea, for when angry, people often revealed far more than they intended. Eventually he would provoke her into saying something that would unravel her deception once and for all.

But why had he kissed her? he asked himself.

Dillon scooped a goodly measure of grain into the bucket, then closed the feed-room door behind him. He entered his big stallion's stall and gave the horse a friendly rub between his ears. As the magnificent animal dug eagerly into the meal, Dillon leaned back against the plank walls of the stall, his mind still on Lacie.

He had kissed her because—because her lips had been too inviting to resist.

No, that wasn't it, he decided abruptly. He had only done it to infuriate her, just as he'd referred to how she'd looked at her bath in order to infuriate her. He'd wanted to keep her off balance and unsettled, and he'd succeeded.

For a moment, though, before she'd remembered to be angry and insulted, for that moment she'd responded to him.

Dillon grinned ruefully as he recalled the sweet feel

of her body going soft against his. Where would things have gone if she'd not gotten so up in arms? For all that she was not really his type, she had felt damned good in his arms. And her lips . . .

A slow heat suffused him as he recalled the feel and taste of her rose-pink lips. They had been warm and soft, giving the lie to the cold, hard facade she tried to assume.

He should have pressed his advantage a little further, he told himself.

Then he straightened up and frowned. He had obviously been far too long without a woman if he was mooning after one Lacie Montgomery. She was either a liar and a thief, or else a cold-hearted witch who'd taken complete advantage of the ailing Frederick. In either event, she was trying to cheat him out of what belonged to him. Added to that, her pose of affronted innocence seemed highly unlikely for someone involved in such nefarious scheming. Besides, she was far from the type of woman who appealed to him. She was too slender and too plain, hardly the blond, blue-eyed beauty that he generally preferred.

Then, unbidden, a vision of her as she'd appeared last night came to him. Her shoulders had been so pale, her neck so delicately curved. The swelling of her breasts had belied her slenderness. Her eyes had been so wide with the longest, blackest lashes. . . .

There was no denying that his restless night had been caused precisely for the reasons he'd given her. He'd wanted her in his bed then. And this morning he felt the same way.

Dillon shook his head in disgust and heaved himself away from the wall, then gave his horse a pat on the rump. He had a hard enough task before him to prove she was a fake. It would not help things at all to have her leading him about by the nose—or by anything else. He would just have to forget about last night—and this morning—and concentrate on the task at hand.

Unless, of course, he could turn the situation to his advantage.

A small smile quirked the corner of his mouth as he let himself out of the stall, then retraced his steps through the barn. Perhaps the best way for him to get to the truth would be to woo his "widowed sister-in-law." Perhaps a few kisses—or even more—would aid his cause better than anything else. Whether she became angry and flustered, or soft and obliging, he could not really lose. One way or another, she would make a slip and he would be there, ready and waiting.

By the time he passed the chicken yard, Dillon was whistling under his breath. Whether she was a black-garbed widowed schoolmarm or a wind-blown, barefoot country girl, Lacie had better watch out. He was on to her game, and he fully expected to enjoy every minute of besting her at it.

Lacie slammed the kitchen door then slumped back against it. She was trembling from head to foot, confused by emotions that were too strong and too foreign for her to deal with. She took a long, slow breath, trying to slow her thundering pulse, but it did little good. Nothing she did could make her forget what he had just done. Nothing.

With a small cry of despair she pressed her fists to her eyes. That was what she feared most—that she would never be able to forget the unspeakably exhilarating way he had made her feel. So warm, so weak—not herself at all.

The sound of approaching footsteps suddenly caused her to back away from the door. Her eyes were wide and she was braced for the worst when the wood-batten door creaked open. When she saw it was Mrs. Gunter, however, and not Dillon, she nearly collapsed in relief.

"Oh, thank heaven it's you!" she gasped as she sat down hard in a spindle-backed chair.

"Ach, and who else would be in the *Küche* at so early an hour?" the florid-faced woman asked genially. Then she gave Lacie a curious look. *"Und* why are you here, Lacie?"

Lacie looked down at her hands, which were knotted in her lap. Indeed, that was a very good question. Why had she run into the kitchen instead of back to the house?

Perhaps it was because she didn't want to alarm Ada or Nina by her disheveled appearance and then have to explain what had gotten her so unsettled.

But more likely, she admitted to herself, it was that she thought no one would yet be in the kitchens and that she could be alone for a while and able to think through these terrible feelings that still assaulted her.

With a disconsolate sigh she raised her eyes to Mrs. Gunter's grandmotherly face.

"I—I was up early. I couldn't sleep," she explained weakly.

"So you went out to feed those chickens of yours," Mrs. Gunter prompted with a fond smile. "You know, if it weren't for you, I would have cooked that crippled bird long ago. You've seen to it that she's by far the fattest of that lazy lot."

Lacie smiled. "She's far too old now. She'd be too tough to eat."

"*Ja,* that is very likely so. But Lacie, it is not the chickens that have you trembling. And your hair! No shoes either!" The cook gave her a mock frown and shook her head in feigned disapproval. "I've not seen you look so since *you* were one of the students here."

At her kindly scolding, all of Lacie's reserve broke down. "Oh, Mrs. Gunter, I don't know what to do!" she cried. She rose and nervously began to pace the floor.

That the normally composed Lacie appeared so agitated made Mrs. Gunter frown in earnest.

"Now, now, *Liebchen,* don't get yourself all in a state. There's nothing can be so bad that we can't find a solution. Why, look at how well you've handled everything since poor Mr. Frederick—I mean, since your husband —died."

Lacie looked up swiftly at Mrs. Gunter's odd inflection. "What do you mean?" she asked warily.

Mrs. Gunter smiled broadly. "I mean that you've proven yourself to be a very—what is the word?—*ach,* a very enterprising young lady." She cocked her head knowingly. "I think Mr. Frederick would have been very pleased."

Once more Lacie sat down, staring at Mrs. Gunter in agitation. Did she know? Did everyone know? Oh, how stupid she'd been! she thought when Mrs. Gunter nodded reassuringly. Why had she thought she could ever pull off such a deception?

"Have I been so obvious then? Is that why that man is plaguing me so?" she asked defeatedly.

"*Ach,* now I see the problem. It is Mr. Frederick's

brother. Such a handsome man. Doesn't he believe you are a grieving widow?"

Lacie shook her head forlornly. "Not one word of it. But then, why should he? I've been a fool. He's determined to prove me a liar and get back the school for himself. But I know he's going to close it, and I can't let him do that. I must find a way to save Sparrow Hill!"

Mrs. Gunter did not reply right away. Instead, she filled a pot from the water keg and placed it on the iron stove. Then she began to build a fire from the embers that were banked from the night before.

"He does not believe you," she mused aloud. Then she looked over at Lacie. "I never see you without your hair up and neatly bound." She chuckled as Lacie tried futilely to twist her disheveled locks into an orderly bun.

"Tell me, *Liebchen*, was this brother of Frederick's also about this morning? Did you see him?"

"Yes."

At that grudging admission Mrs. Gunter laughed out loud. "So. You do not like him, but perhaps—perhaps he likes you?"

Lacie straightened up and stared in surprise at the now-beaming older woman. "I would hardly say he likes me except . . ."

"*Ja?* Tell me the rest of it."

"He doesn't like *me*," Lacie protested as her cheeks turned a bright pink. She wanted to be sure Mrs. Gunter understood things correctly. "He just wants to . . ." she faltered, not sure herself precisely what he wanted of her. "He just wants to convince me to trust him. But as soon as I do, I know he'll use whatever he finds out to prove his claim to Sparrow Hill. So you see, he is really quite a cruel-hearted cad."

"Did he try to kiss you?"

At Lacie's look of horror mingled nonetheless with guilt, the stout cook chuckled. "So, he kissed you. Well, that may solve all of your woes." The woman sat down across the table from Lacie and placed both of her hands flat on the smooth worn surface. "I tell you, *Liebchen*, listen to an old woman's advice. Marry him and everything will be fine."

6

Marry him!

Lacie grimaced in disgust every time she thought of Mrs. Gunter's ridiculous solution. As if that would help anything!

As if she would even consider marrying such a bounder!

As if anything as honorable as marriage were what he had in mind!

With a yank she tugged her wooden hairbrush through the tangled length of her sable-brown hair. He was a complete oaf, with the manners of a barbarian. A heathen, with no sense of decency whatsoever. A cad completely lacking in moral values.

But oh my, he certainly knew how to kiss!

At that aberrant thought, she tugged so hard at a particularly difficult tangle that tears sprang to her eyes.

"Ouch! Oh, damn!" she muttered furiously. Then she cast a guilty eye around the room. Thank goodness Nina had gone downstairs and wasn't here to see such an unladylike display of temper.

But that, too, Lacie laid at Dillon Lockwood's door. Never had anyone made her angry enough to lose her temper and actually utter a profanity. Yet he'd done it twice now, and she'd met him only the previous day!

Sighing in frustration, she smoothed her hair back as best she could, then caught it up in one hand and twisted it around and around. Once it was tightly wrapped upon itself, she looped it about her hand three times. Then, using an old-fashioned wooden hairpin, she deftly caught the underneath hairs and pinned the entire bun neatly in place at her nape. She then donned a fresh muslin blouse and stepped into a slip and petticoat before pulling on a black skirt of plain goods, adorned only with a triple row of tucks near the hem. Last, she hooked a plain black collar of severe design around her neck. Then she eyed herself speculatively in her small mirror.

Just as a widow would dress at home, she thought approvingly. Neat and simple and most respectable. There was no need in this heat to wear a black bodice over her blouse. No jewelry was necessary either, for a widow wouldn't wear anything—

Except a wedding ring!

Lacie's mouth gaped open at the thought of how stupid she'd been. Surely Frederick would have given his wife a ring, yet she'd not sported any such symbol of marriage. What should she do? Although he'd apparently not noticed her mistake yet, Dillon was sure to notice eventually.

There was only one thing to do, she decided nervously. She must slip into Frederick's rooms, find his mother's jewelry, and pick an appropriate ring. It would only be a loan, of course. She had no intention of using Amelia Allen Kimbell's jewelry any longer than she had to. Once Dillon was gone the ring would go right back where she'd found it.

All was quiet as she stealthily crossed the vast second-floor hall. No one saw her enter Frederick's apartments, but that only made her feel more like a thief. Skulking about in her own home, indeed!

Yet that was just what she did. She quietly searched Frederick's desk and his armoire and found a small intricately inlaid rosewood box in the bottom drawer of his tall mahogany dresser. A myriad of keepsakes and family mementoes crowded the drawer, but only the octagon-shaped box interested her, and within that, only the rings.

Most of them were too big, she realized as she slipped on an elegant pearl creation, then a garnet-studded band, and finally a dainty filigree piece with a pale emerald set up on six slender tines.

None of them would do, she fretted as she dug frantically through the chains and bangles. She was becoming positively desperate before she discovered a plain gold band stuck in a crevice at the bottom. Orange blossoms twined simply between narrow edgings in a classical motif. Although it was loose on her ring finger, it fit her middle finger perfectly.

Enormously relieved, Lacie quickly restored the other pieces to the box, stuffed the box into the drawer, and slammed it closed. Then she held out her hand to admire the ring.

It felt odd on her finger, strange and out of place. But she firmly buried that idea. It might feel odd, but it looked just right, and that was all that mattered.

She looked around Frederick's room then, wonder-

ing if she should move her things into it. She and Ada
had discussed that subject at length after Frederick
died. It certainly might be perceived as odd that she
still stayed in her old teacher's quarters when such a
fine apartment as this was available to her. But she had
simply not been able to force herself to do it. It was
stupid, and now that Dillon Lockwood was here, it was
probably dangerous for her pose. It would only feed his
suspicions if he found out.

But then, what did that really matter? she told herself
bravely. He already believed she was a liar and a thief.
He'd said so outright! Where she slept would hardly
affect his opinion one way or the other. Still, perhaps it
might be best if she did take over Frederick's suite.
After all, it couldn't hurt. And it didn't have to be permanent.

She quietly let herself out of the room, then took a
slow steadying breath. She felt as if she'd already gone
through a long, harrowing day although the morning
had scarcely begun. Despite her decision to skip breakfast, she knew she could not long avoid another confrontation with that man. What he would try next was
difficult to predict; so far, he'd taken a different tack
each time they'd met. Still, she was learning more
about him—all of it, unfortunately, bad.

Squaring her shoulders, she turned and proceeded
toward the broad stairs.

It was then that she saw him.

He was sitting in a high-backed chair, a comfortable
piece upholstered in wine-colored velvet. It had been
Frederick's favorite for those evenings when he'd gathered the younger girls around him for readings or story-

telling. But Dillon in the chair was a far cry from the comforting presence of Frederick.

He was holding a book, a volume dealing with the spread of railroads, she noted obliquely. But she was sure it was for show. He was waiting for her, and to her dismay, there was no way for her to avoid him.

"Good morning," he said pleasantly when she only stood there staring at him.

Lacie nodded curtly. She couldn't even pretend to be civil as she sent him a stormy look. But that only seemed to please him, for one side of his mouth lifted in a slight smile. Then he stood up and replaced the book on the dark-stained wooden shelf and turned to face her.

"Now that you're finally properly dressed"—he paused just long enough to drive home his little barb—"perhaps we can get on with the business at hand."

"Which is?" Lacie asked coolly, lifting her brows in a show of vague disinterest.

"Why, to prove that you're a liar, of course."

"What!" All her hard-won aplomb came crashing down at his deliberate taunt. "You are positively the crudest person ever to set foot in these halls!" she hissed. Then she forcibly calmed herself. "I am no liar, as you will eventually be forced to admit."

His grin became more a smirk at her words, and he rubbed his chin almost ruefully.

"Yes, looking at you now, all prim and proper, laced up with your hair pulled back so tightly it must hurt, I can almost believe you are Frederick's widow.

"But Lacie," he said more softly. "You forget that I've also seen you with your hair down." He walked toward her in slow, stalking steps. "I've seen you soft. I've seen you fiery. Why, I bet in the short time I've been here, I've seen more of you"—one of his eyebrows quirked up—"and learned more about you—the real you—than Frederick ever did."

Lacie could have cried. This wasn't fair! she thought frantically, trying to find some defense against his unsettling words. Even though a part of her could admit that he spoke no more than the truth, it was a truth that should never be revealed in polite society. He fought dirty, just as he had warned.

"You may bet on anything you like," she snapped in what she hoped was her most cutting tone. "In the meantime, I'd appreciate it if you would confine your comments to more pertinent matters."

"More pertinent matters?" His grin became truly wicked. "Tell me, Lacie, what could possibly be more pertinent to a man than having a soft, delectable woman in his arms?"

"Oh! You are truly despicable!" With that she whirled away, fully intending to flee down the stairs. Anything to get away from him and the awkward truth of his words.

But Dillon easily blocked her escape. Against her will, he took one of her arms and firmly hooked it in his, in what would appear to be the most companionable of manners.

"Once I settle down with Frederick's papers you may scamper off to whatever task it is that calls to you now. Until then, however, you'll have to stick right by my side."

So saying, he forced her to accompany him back into Frederick's suite of rooms.

Lacie was appalled at his nerve and aghast at his gall.

Yet it was not that shock which struck her speechless. It was, rather, the firm pressure of his arm against hers, holding it so warmly to his side. Then his free hand covered hers, and she was completely undone.

It was all she could do to maintain her composure and keep pace with his slow, unhurried stride. Once they were in Frederick's office she did find the presence of mind to tug her arm free of his disturbing grasp. But she had to turn toward the desk before she could find the wherewithal to address him again.

"Mr. Lockwood," she began in her iciest tone. "I would prefer that you not presume to touch my person—"

"To touch your person?" he mimicked. "And all along I thought it was your arm I had. Of course, this morning it was your lips—"

Lacie whirled around to confront his laughing expression. He thought it all a huge joke, but she was far from amused.

"This is obviously a frivolous matter to you," she said with much heat. "You neither need nor truly want anything Frederick left behind. Yet you do not hesitate to trample on all of us, to threaten us and insult us and—and make fun of us."

"I want and need my rightful inheritance much more than you'll ever know. Don't delude yourself on that score. As for your other accusation"—his voice grew cooler—"it is only you I'm threatening, only you whom I'm 'insulting,' as you term it. So leave off your pose of innocence. We both know that this manufactured scheme of yours is the only reason I came back to this miserable place. The sooner I find the proof I seek, the sooner I'll be gone."

The sooner she'd be gone as well, Lacie thought with a sinking heart. When he turned away from her and sat down at the desk, she was uncertain what she should do.

"Since you're so anxious to leave, go ahead. There's no need for you to stay and help me," he quipped dryly, glancing at her.

But that was precisely what she must do, she realized at once. She must stay at his shoulder and watch everything he did. There was probably nothing in Frederick's office to disprove her claim, but could she really be sure? Could she be sure he wouldn't plant something that could make her look bad? He was nasty enough to do something like that.

Lacie's face was drawn into a disapproving scowl as she seated herself on an old-fashioned walnut footstool. Dillon glanced over at her as she angrily arranged her skirts, and even though her eyes quickly darted away, she could not miss the slight, satisfied grin that curved his lips. He had her, she thought, in an untenable situation. She could either leave—and risk who knew what —or she could stay and suffer his obnoxious presence.

Her only consolation was that it was better to keep an eye on her enemy than to let him roam freely behind her back. For her enemy he most certainly was, despite his handsome face and beguiling smile. And seductive kiss.

She sternly buried that thought. He was first and foremost her enemy, determined to deprive her of her very home. No matter what, she must never forget that.

"So you're staying," he mocked softly. "Well then, the first thing I want to see is your marriage certificate."

Lacie's heart skipped a beat, but she swiftly composed her face and stood up. She was too unsure of her voice to reply to him, but stalked stiffly to a walnut bureau cabinet, opened the top right door, and produced the document in question. Then she thrust it in front of him.

She watched anxiously as he scanned the hand-lettered paper, telling herself all the while that he couldn't know the signature was forged. He might suspect, but he couldn't know for sure.

When he handed it back to her, giving her a hard, searching look, she felt a little better. He looked aggravated, and she took what pleasure she could from his annoyed expression. But she had no opportunity to enjoy this small victory for long.

"Very nicely done, Lacie. It looks good, but we'll see."

Time seemed to drag interminably after that. Lacie fidgeted in her seat and drummed her fingers impatiently on her knees. For his part, Dillon seemed much engrossed by his task. Drawer by drawer, file by file, paper by paper he went through Frederick's desk. Occasionally he made a notation on a sheet of paper, but primarily he seemed to be taking it all in.

"What are these?"

His deep voice interrupted Lacie's wistful daydream of Frederick walking into the room and quite soundly telling his half-brother off.

"What?"

"What are these?" Dillon held up a packet of papers neatly tied together with ribbons in notebook fashion.

"I'm not—I'm not sure," Lacie answered. Hesitantly she rose and drew nearer. "Give them to me."

She took them from him. "It looks like old files. Yes,

these are account records on girls who've gone on to graduate."

While she had studied them he had risen from his seat as well, stretching slightly as he did. Then he crossed to her vacated footstool and pulled it next to his chair.

"Here, sit down." He met her anxious gaze and grinned. "If you insist on staying, you might as well be comfortable."

Lacie could hardly be comfortable sitting less than two feet from him. His nearness was something she was acutely conscious of. From his dark hair to his sun-browned skin, to the sprinkle of black hairs on the backs of his hands, she found him impossible to ignore. Still, as he steadily continued through the contents of the desk, asking her more and more questions as he went, she had to admit, albeit grudgingly, that it certainly made sense for her to sit adjacent to him.

As the morning wore on she almost forgot her anger at him, for his questions were logical and his observations astute. Not until her stomach let out a low, very unladylike growl and he looked up did she realize it was nearing the noon hour.

"Hungry?" His eyes caught hers and at so close a distance she could see every glint of color in their green depths: the gold flecks near the center, the teal-blue ring that edged them. "If you had eaten breakfast instead of sulking in your room trying to avoid me, you wouldn't be making such unbecoming sounds."

Lacie's lips pursed contentiously. "I hardly consider you an authority on proper behavior."

"Because I wasn't born a gentleman?" he retorted. Then he reached out and lightly caressed her lower lip with his thumb. "You're right, Lacie, I'm no gentleman, despite the trappings of civility I now possess. But then, you're not who you say you are, either. We make a rather appropriate pair, don't you think?"

Lacie's huffy "No!" was somewhat lost in her undignified haste to quit the room. He was the most hateful man alive! she fumed as she caught her skirts in one hand and hurried down the stairs. He was cruel and devious and—and why had he touched her lip that way?

She nearly collided with Ada in her pell-mell flight from Dillon.

"My goodness! What's wrong?" Ada cried as she pulled up suddenly at the dining-room door. "What is it, Lacie?"

"It's that—that—that despicable man! What else could it be?" Lacie panted as she cast a baleful glare back toward the stairs. "I'm afraid I'm going to have to move into Frederick's suite of rooms after all."

"Oh, dear! Did he find something? Something that gives you away?"

Lacie shook her head and tried to slow her frantic breathing. Then she looked at Ada and forced a meager smile. "No, he's found nothing, although it's not for want of trying. It's just that . . ." she trailed off, unable —and unwilling—to explain how easily he unnerved her. With just his slightest touch, she had come undone. He taunted, criticized, and insulted her, and yet with that one touch her anger dissolved into a different, even more fiery emotion. What in heaven's name was wrong with her?

"I think I know," Ada murmured. A mischievous twinkle sparkled in her wide blue eyes. "None of us expected Mr. Frederick's brother to be so young and handsome."

In renewed dismay Lacie stared at Ada. Had he been testing his charms on her as well? That unsettling thought brought a frown to her normally serene brow.

"I suggest you show less concern for his handsome face and more concern for your own well-being," she said rather tartly. But when she saw Ada's surprised look, she was immediately chagrined. She reached a placating hand to her friend. "I'm sorry, dear. I don't know why I'm behaving so horribly."

"You shouldn't fret so, Lacie. You've been worrying too much, carrying the burden of us all. It's no wonder you're a little on edge." Ada smiled encouragingly and squeezed her friend's hand. "You know, I think he's actually more reasonable than he seemed at first. Why, he was absolutely charming at breakfast. And he's quite captivated our Nina. He even offered to drive me into town after lunch."

Lacie felt a shiver of apprehension. "I thought Leland was going to do that."

"Oh, you know how Leland hates dealing with anyone but"—she paused and smiled painfully—"anyone but Mr. Frederick."

Lacie didn't reply as they headed to the gallery. She was too worried about what Dillon Lockwood was up to. What information did he hope to gain from Ada? What devious trick did he have up his sleeve?

As was their wont on hot days, the midday meal was served on the shady gallery, cooled by a light breeze. Mrs. Gunter had laid out a simple meal of thick-sliced bread and stewed ham with collard greens on a square table draped in lace-edged linen. Four chairs had been pulled up to the intimate little table, and for a moment Lacie hesitated. She had no doubt that Dillon would soon join them. But what was the best seating arrangement? While she absolutely did not wish to sit next to him—she'd been doing that for too long already today —neither did she wish to suffer the direct penetrating power of his deep green eyes from across the small table.

For a moment she considered skipping lunch altogether, but another rumble from her stomach squelched that idea. She was famished and more than ready for a good meal. It was her misfortune that this delicious-looking repast would be ruined by that man's unavoidable presence.

"Well, everyone's here this time." Dillon's voice, low and mellow, caused Lacie to jump in alarm. She was even more unsettled by the tiny smile that flitted across Ada's face as she stared at her.

"Yes." Lacie cleared her throat. "Everyone's here, so perhaps we should sit down."

Dillon seated Lacie first, then politely pulled out chairs for the smiling Nina and Ada. When he sat down directly across from her, Lacie determinedly avoided his gaze and instead bowed her head most devoutly.

"Dear Lord, we thank you for this meal. We thank you for all the generous blessings we've received from you and pray we may long continue the work you have given us. We especially pray that you will keep all our girls safe until they can return in September. To start a new school year," she added quite pointedly.

She could not resist a quick, smug glance at him as she made a sign of the cross. But her little triumph at imploring God's help in opposing him was short-lived.

Although his expression revealed no hint of emotions, his eyes were clearly laughing at her.

She looked away at once, but the damage had been done. Nothing she could say or do—not even divine interference—was going to dissuade him. What was worse, he considered her and her efforts nothing more than mild amusement!

At that moment, if she'd had the power to, she would have had him struck down. By a bolt of lightning. By God's hand. By any means available. As it was, though, she could only sit there, pick up her silver fork with the fancy A and K entwined monogram, and begin to eat her greens.

Despite her own silence, the table conversation did not lag. At Dillon's subtle prodding, both Ada and Nina chattered about their homes. To Nina's delight, Dillon had passed through her hometown of Marshall, Texas, on several occasions and even knew the street where she lived. Ada was clearly just as captivated by his familiarity with Plano.

"The train from Denver paused there only briefly, but even so, I could see that Plano has grown considerably since I was last there."

That was when Lacie felt his gaze on her, and against her will she raised her eyes to him.

"Where are you from, Lacie? Certainly not from around here."

"Kimbell is my home," she answered coolly. "I've lived here most of my life."

"But you weren't born here," he persisted.

Lacie paused. Although she hesitated to tell him anything about herself, she knew she was only being antagonistic. Telling him about her early childhood could hardly help him determine the truth about her marriage to Frederick.

"I'm from Mississippi, a plantation near Natchez. My father sent me here just before the War for Independence. My mother died the year before, and my old nanny was too ill to continue with me." That should be enough to satisfy anyone, she thought.

But apparently it did not satisfy Dillon Lockwood.

"You were sent here to school, then. Why did you stay?"

Lacie was sorely tempted to say, "Because Frederick could not bear for me to leave." But she feared Ada might inadvertently laugh and thereby ruin the effect. With great effort she stilled the nervous clenching of her fingers, then looked straight at him. "After the war the townhouse in Natchez was no longer there. The plantation had been burned. Taxes took the land. I had lost my father." She paused, caught between anger at this impertinent stranger and sorrow at all she'd lost. "There was nothing left to go home to."

For a moment she thought she saw compassion in his gaze. For an instant his dark green eyes almost seemed to glow with warmth instead of with the wicked fire she had seen in them up to now.

But the instant was too brief for her to be sure, and it was too far-fetched to be true. He harbored no compassion in his shriveled, unfeeling heart, least of all for her.

It was Nina who filled the uncomfortable silence. "You can come live with me, Miss Lacie."

Lacie smiled fondly at her young charge and reached over to stroke the girl's silky brown hair. "I can think of nothing I'd like better, dear heart. Who would take care of things here, though, if I were to leave?"

"But I'm gonna miss you. Please, come home with me."

"Now, Nina," Lacie began as tears welled up in the child's sad eyes. "There's no need for those tears. I promise you, everything will be just the same when you return after the summer." She couldn't resist shooting a baleful glare at Dillon. Couldn't he see how his selfishness was going to hurt everyone, not just her?

"I'll tell you what, dear heart. If you'll wipe those tears away and try to be brave, I'll let you ride into town with Miss Ada today."

"Into town?" The girl sniffed twice and blinked her damp eyes at Lacie.

"Yes, and I'm sure I have an extra penny for a peppermint or two." Then she glanced over at Dillon and assumed her most casual tone. "I'm sure you won't mind if Nina and I tag along while you drive Ada to the railroad station in Kimbell."

If he was disappointed that she'd foiled his attempt to interrogate Ada, he didn't show it. But Lacie couldn't resist a small secret grin of triumph. He thought he was so smart—most men did. But she was a well-educated woman, and well-motivated too. He might have a few tricks up his sleeve, but so did she.

7

The pungent scent of smoke and ashes lingered in the air even after the train disappeared from view. As Lacie stood on the recently built wooden platform, she felt unaccountably alone.

All around her people milled, voices boomed, and activity abounded. An elderly woman was being escorted off by a crowd of youngsters, clearly her grandchildren come to meet her; three gentlemen stood in a knot, cigar smoke circling their heads in the still afternoon. Another well-dressed man shouted instructions to four laborers as they cautiously led away two fine-looking mares that were jittery from their noisy train journey.

Everyone else had someone to greet them, or some purpose for being there and doing things. But she was entirely alone, Lacie thought morosely. She had no one, other than her students. Being a teacher was all she had. But even that was threatened now, for her life at Sparrow Hill hung on the strength of her terrible lie.

She released a long, slow sigh. How she wished Ada had stayed! She knew that if she'd only asked her to,

Ada would have stayed, but that would have been unfair, Lacie acknowledged. Ada deserved to have some time with her family. There was no reason for Dillon Lockwood to ruin that, too.

The high-pitched laughter of a child brought her depressing thoughts to an end. When Lacie turned, she saw Nina and Dillon heading her way.

What an incongruous pair, she thought as she watched their approach. Nina's bloomer-clad legs took three steps for every one of Dillon's ground-eating strides. She was pink and white and ruffled, as opposed to his dark and simply garbed silhouette. Her bonnet strings were flying as she scurried up the steps and ran giggling over to Lacie.

"Miss Lacie! Miss Lacie! He says if I ride my pony astride, I'll get bow legs. Is that true? Is it?"

Lacie smiled down at Nina's eager young face. "I suppose you might."

"But my daddy rides astride. And so does he." The little girl looked back at Dillon. "He doesn't have bow legs, does he, Miss Lacie?"

Lacie could not help glancing at Dillon as he stood there, tall and straight, his legs a little apart, his hat shading his face. Unbidden, a picture of that same body, but unclothed as if for a bath, came into her mind. His legs were not bowed at all, she recalled. They were long and well shaped, the muscles not disguised a bit by the even sprinkling of dark hairs.

Lacie's eyes jerked up to his face abruptly. She would not remember such things or think such thoughts, she told herself sternly. Yet gazing into his serious green eyes was hardly a remedy for that, she realized in dismay. Still, she was unable to look away.

"Are you ready to go?"

Lacie heard his quiet words, but she was slow to respond. "I suppose there's no reason to linger," she finally admitted, casting a last wistful glance down the now-empty train track. How she wished she had family to go home to! Then Nina slipped a warm hand into hers, and Lacie turned away from the tracks.

"To answer your questions, Nina. I don't know why some men develop bow legs and others don't. But I do know that proper young ladies use a sidesaddle and never sit astride."

"But that's so hard," the little girl complained as they stepped down from the platform and crossed to where the school's carriage waited in the shade of a low spreading oak.

"Yes, it is harder," Lacie agreed. Then she smiled conspiratorially at Nina. "I doubt either your father or Dill—or Mr. Lockwood—could ride sidesaddle nearly as well as you!"

That brought a delighted giggle from the child. "I bet you're right, Miss Lacie. I bet I *can* do it better than them. But I'm still not as good as you."

"Such a sassy little tyke," Dillon teased. Then he grabbed Nina, raised her up high, and deposited her before the driver's seat of the brett. As Nina's giggles began to subside, he turned to Lacie.

"Shall you ride alone in the back? Or will you grace us with your company up front?" His eyes were dark and unreadable, shaded by the brim of his hat, and Lacie wondered what secret thoughts moved through his mind. He was a strange man, unfailingly polite to Ada, patient and kind to Nina, and, on occasion, quite the gentleman with her. But then other times . . .

"Oh, up front. Up front!" Nina insisted eagerly. "And don't forget, you said you would show me how to drive a pair," she reminded Dillon.

The ride into town had been uneventful. The stay had been brief and unremarkable. As long as Nina was there, what harm could it do to ride up front with Dillon? With a small agreeable smile she nodded her assent. But as she turned to place her foot on the high step, he stopped her. Then with a low murmured "Allow me," he placed his hands around her waist and lifted her effortlessly up to the driver's bench.

For an instant their eyes locked as she braced her hands against his wide shoulders. Then she found her feet and immediately leaned away from him. But it was a moment before he released his hold on her, and in that split second her pulse began to race.

Flustered, she sat down on the oilcloth bench seat at once. Even after he untethered the pair and climbed easily aboard the other side, she felt an undeniable breathlessness.

Lacie was silent as Dillon expertly guided the team through town. Once they had passed the Half Moon and he began to show Nina how to handle a team, there was no real reason for Lacie to speak. Nina was too full of questions and Dillon too willing to answer each one for Lacie's reserve to be noticed. As he showed the girl how to thread the reins through her fingers and keep just the correct amount of tension on them, Lacie's mind wandered in the most disturbing direction.

Why must she react so perversely toward this man? Him above all others? Richard Beasley's courtship had left her unmoved; Walter Reynolds's single kiss, pressed so politely against her forehead, had only annoyed her;

and Angus Hawsley's avid attentions had not affected her whatsoever. They had all been respectable sorts—well, perhaps Angus had been a trifle questionable on that score, but at least he'd been sincere.

But this man? His reputation was hardly sterling. And despite his wealth, his motives were completely selfish. She knew that without an ounce of doubt. Yet he was the one—he alone—who turned her knees to jelly and her mind to mush. She who had always prided herself on her logical thinking and unemotional reactions was time and time again undone by his slightest touch.

She was so engrossed in her own agonizing thoughts that she did not at first respond to Nina's call.

"Look! Look, Miss Lacie! I'm doing it all by myself!"

Lacie forced a smile to her troubled face. "So you are. So you are, my dear. My, how quickly you've caught on."

"That's 'cause I've got a good teacher."

"So you do," Lacie murmured as she glanced cautiously at Dillon. He was leaning back against the seat, one arm stretched out behind Nina, his hand resting near her own shoulder.

"Perhaps I have more in common with Frederick than we thought," he said slowly, his gaze trained steadily on her.

Lacie averted her eyes at once. Although she did not know precisely what he implied, she knew there was some further meaning hidden in his softly spoken words. Everything he said, everything he did, seemed calculated to taunt and test her. But she was no faint-hearted miss to buckle under the double-edged sword of his masculine appeal and his barbed words. He might consider her prey to his predatory stalking, but she would not be an easy victim. She lifted her chin and continued to stare straight ahead.

"Frederick was a very particular horseman. The two of you do seem to share that trait."

"That's odd, wouldn't you say? Our father's concern for his animals extended only as long as they won on the track."

She glanced sidelong at him from beneath her thick lashes, unable to mistake the hard edge that had crept into his voice. "Frederick was never cruel to the horses he kept."

"No, he wouldn't be."

"I wouldn't ever hurt a horse," Nina threw in as she concentrated on holding the reins just so.

They continued in silence for a little while, following the hard-packed road that led past fields of ripening tomatoes, strawberries, and beans, and through dense stands of pine trees. There was something soothing about the rhythmic rocking of the well-sprung carriage. That, taken with the pleasant warmth of the afternoon sun, conspired to make Lacie relax against the tufted back of the seat. Then she felt a hand on her shoulder, and she stiffened in alarm.

Her angry glare, however, was met only by Dillon's crooked smile.

"I think our driver has fallen asleep," he murmured quietly.

"Oh." Lacie looked down at the dozing Nina, who was leaning comfortably against Dillon's side. She felt quite foolish for her hasty reaction to Dillon's touch.

"Take these reins," he instructed. Then before she could question him, he scooped Nina up and deposited her gently on the wide seat immediately behind theirs.

Then he settled himself back on the driver's seat and stretched out his long legs, watching her as she drove.

"You've a good hand for driving," he commented. It was the first nice thing he'd said about her, and it unexpectedly pleased her. "You're apparently a good horsewoman as well, if Nina is any judge. And I have to assume you're a more than adequate teacher if Frederick kept you on staff. So tell me." He paused, and Lacie once more felt the light movement of his fingers upon the starched lace that circled the neckline of her modestly cut blouse. "Are you good at everything you do?"

Lacie leaned forward at once. Whether from his unexpected touch or his suggestive words, she could not say, but her heart's pace most assuredly trebled.

"A lady strives to excel at everything she does," she blurted out, but she knew he wasn't really looking for an answer.

"Everything?" His voice held a distinctly amused tone. "That may explain how you've covered up your trail so well. I do have to give you credit, Lacie. I made some subtle inquiries while you and Ada waited for the train, and there certainly appears to be no real reason to doubt your tale of a marriage to Frederick."

"It's no tale!" she snapped.

"If it *is* true," he continued as if he hadn't heard her at all, "that may also explain Frederick's unexpected death so soon after your marriage."

Lacie shot him an uncertain glance. "What is that supposed to mean?" Then she became alarmed. "Are you accusing me of somehow doing something—of having anything to do with Frederick's death?"

"No, no, nothing quite so terrible as that. I only wondered . . ." His eyes moved down slowly to take in her entire body. Then they returned to her face gleaming with some new and unknown emotion. "Well, if you *were* married to Frederick and if ladies *do* strive to excel at everything, it's reasonable to assume that despite your prudish demeanor, it was your passionate lovemaking that caused his heart to give out."

Lacie could not muster the words to respond to such an outrageous idea. She was too astounded. But as he continued to stare at her, waiting for her reply, she felt a violent blush stain her cheeks. How could he have said such a dreadful thing? Did he dare to jest about her wifely relationship with his own deceased brother?

But he was hardly smiling, and Lacie became even more confused by his serious demeanor. With a flick of the reins she forced her attention back to the horses. Then she felt his finger once more, toying this time with a wisp of her hair that had come loose at the nape of her neck. In an instant all her confused and distracted emotions jelled into the security of righteous anger, and she turned a furious face toward him.

"You may assume whatever you wish, Mr. Lockwood. I refuse to be drawn into your greedy little game. And I consider it the height of callousness to speculate so crudely on Frederick's death!"

"Actually, it was Doc Cromwell who suggested that possibility. Of course, if you're sure that can't be the reason . . ." He trailed off with a shrug.

From anger to caution, Lacie's expression suddenly altered, and she bit her lower lip in concern. Was it possible? she wondered. Could the private doings between a man and his wife actually cause his heart to fail? She'd never heard of such a thing. But if Doc Cromwell had brought it up . . .

If. That was the catch. With one last searching look at him, Lacie turned her attention once more to her driving. He could be lying, or he could be telling the truth. She was not sure which. No doubt he did one as easily as the other.

Taking a breath, she finally replied. "If that was the doctor's speculation, he did not mention it to me. But then," she added caustically, "he's far too polite to make such a crude observation to a grieving widow."

So saying, she sent him a smug look.

But her remark, intended to cut him down, only brought a grin to his ruthlessly handsome face. "If you think me crude and lacking in manners, Lacie, say so. You don't need to beat around the bush with me. I told you, I like direct women, not docile ones." Then he gave her a knowing wink, pulled his hat down over his eyes, and settled down for a nap.

Lacie was irate. She could not win with him! she fumed. She just could not! If she said she was not docile, then she was direct. But she did not want to profess to be the sort of woman he preferred. Likewise, although she was willing to claim Frederick as her husband, it was another thing entirely to take the blame for his death due to—due to—

Oh, he was truly the most devious, hateful man who had ever lived!

8

Lacie was getting quite an education. She thought she had known everything about Sparrow Hill School and about Frederick. And certainly everything she *needed* to know about Dillon Lockwood.

But as the days went by, she realized she had known little more than nothing.

As Dillon went through the myriad files and the confusing account books for the school, she kept an eye on him to protect herself and the school. But at his elbow she was finding out all sorts of—often unpleasant—information.

How in heaven's name had Frederick kept the school going? she wondered in amazement as she studied the column of entries for the previous semester's accounts. Tuition barely covered the salaries of the staff and the household expenses. Everything else—the school books and supplies, the heavy taxes on the property, and the exorbitant cost of maintaining the stable of riding horses—seemed to be financed by Frederick's own personal funds. But at such a rate, with no outside income, even a fortune would eventually be depleted. How long would the school have been able to maintain itself at that rate?

Lacie rubbed her forehead in dismay.

"Not a pretty picture, is it?" Dillon closed the account book with a thud, then sprawled back in his chair. His jade-green gaze was sharp upon her as he laced his fingers casually across his stomach.

Lacie only gave him a quelling stare. He'd been goading her whenever he could, snorting in disbelief at certain expenses, complaining when the records were unclear. He had even sworn when he saw how much Frederick had paid for two show mares.

"Show mares!" he had thundered. "What in God's name do a bunch of prissy little girls need with a pair of damned show mares!"

Lacie had to admit, although only to herself, that it had indeed been an unimaginably huge sum of money. What had Frederick been thinking of? Yet she was hardly prepared to side with Dillon against Frederick. That would be unthinkable.

Still, she fully intended to make some drastic changes in the way the school was run once Dillon Lockwood was out of the way.

"If you find the finances of the school so dreadful, why do you want it so badly? Why don't you just give up this absurd witch-hunt of yours? I married Frederick. You saw the papers yourself."

His jet-black brows lowered in a frown at her words, but then a cynical smile curved one side of his lips. "Let's just say I have a perverse interest in witches."

Lacie stood up in a huff. She was unwilling to bandy words with him any further, for it seemed she invariably lost when she did. Despite her every effort to confound and frustrate him, she inevitably came off the poorer in their exchanges. With a slow steady look or a few choice words, he would always unnerve her.

"I believe I've had quite enough of this," she snapped as she moved away from the huge cluttered desk.

"But we've only just begun," he drawled. Then with one smooth motion, he leaned forward and caught her by the wrist.

"Oh! Let me go!" Lacie cried as she was whirled about to face him.

"Where are you going?"

"That's none of your affair!"

"Aren't you afraid I'll find something to prove you're a fake?" His brows arched in query, but his amusement was nonetheless apparent.

"You won't find anything, so you might as well quit wasting your time," she retorted, trying all the while to tug free of his warm grasp. But Dillon was clearly unready to release her. Instead, he stood up and drew her a little nearer.

"If there's nothing to be found, why have you been my little shadow these past three days?"

Lacie was not about to answer that question, for the answer was very uncomfortable for her. There was something about him that drew her. Like a moth fluttering nearer and nearer the flame, like a struggling swimmer unable to resist the tide, she could not stay away from him.

It was increasingly apparent that he would find nothing in Frederick's papers to condemn her. Yet still she insisted on being there whenever he sat down at Frederick's desk. Now, however, the situation was getting out of hand. Her proximity to him was clearly far more dangerous to her than whatever scribblings of Frederick's he might find.

"Let me go," she whispered again in a voice more tremulous than she intended.

For a moment longer he kept his fingers wrapped firmly around her wrist. Then he let her go and she stepped back a pace. Distance, however, did nothing to dispel the disturbing heat that lingered where they had touched—like a brand almost—but imparting no pain.

"I think we both need a break from this drudgery." He smiled, then took a step forward. "Come riding with me, Lacie. A good hard gallop will do us both a world of good."

Her answer was slow in coming. It was not that she did not intend to go, for riding was precisely what she needed to clear her mind. But his smile . . .

To have a man—this man—smile just so with no hint of mockery nor gracious attempt at politeness; to have him ask her to join him just because he wished to have her company; that was, she suddenly perceived, exactly what she wanted of him. It was a dreadful realization, one she wanted to deny with every fiber of her being. But it was nonetheless true.

Even as she nodded a silent assent to his request, she knew his invitation could not be without an ulterior motive. He wanted something from her, and if he could not get it legally or by force, he intended to get it by guile. Yet despite that knowledge, she agreed to go and, even worse, was willing to pretend, at least for a little while, that it was really no more than the sincere invitation she wanted it to be.

Dillon was obviously surprised by her agreeable response. But he wasted no time and smoothly tucked her arm in his. "I must have caught you in a docile mood," he murmured near her ear.

At once she pulled her hand free. It was disturbing enough to feel his warm arm beneath her hand, but to have his breath move her hair and hear his low voice vibrating so seductively was too much.

"I'm only being polite, not docile. Oh, you've forgotten your coat," she added archly.

"I won't need it." He ran an assessing eye over her and grinned. "You might want to dress a little more comfortably yourself, Lacie. It's hot already, and I'm not planning a short sedate ride around the grounds." One of his brows arched in that familiar, infuriating manner. "Are you sure you're up to it?"

"Quite," she snapped. Then she hurried off to her room, more determined than ever to show him.

Lacie wasted no time in preparing for their ride. Off came the extra petticoat and her heavy starched slip. Off came the stiff mourning collar. She donned riding boots and found her gloves, then pulled down her wide-brimmed straw hat. When her careful coiffure did not accommodate the crownless hat, she swiftly unwound her hair, then plaited it and tied the end with a short length of black grosgrain ribbon. She spared only a quick glance in the small looking glass, then left her room, frowning at what she'd seen. She looked positively childlike, she thought, more like a student than a widowed schoolteacher. But there was naught to be done about it. She practically flew down the stairs, and by the time she reached the stables, she was almost out of breath. Yet even still, she knew that the color in her cheeks and her breathless state were not caused solely by her haste.

It was Dillon Lockwood and the thought of this ride with him that had her in such a state.

One part of her said that it was just a ride. It might not be sedate, and they might gallop or even race. But it would still be just a ride.

Yet another part of her said otherwise. It would be dangerous. It would be exhilarating. It would be unforgettable.

Sternly, she tried to banish those last thoughts. But some new, obstinate part of her would not let go of those possibilities. When she entered the wide stable opening and saw him bending down to pull his steed's girth up tight, she knew her cause was lost. He was so tall and handsome, so wickedly virile in his snug buckskin trousers and thin lawn shirt.

Then he looked up at her and slowly smiled.

It was that smile, she thought obliquely as his gaze slid approvingly over her. That smile was the problem. If he would only quit smiling at her, she would be all right.

For an endless moment their gazes remained locked across the short space of the stable aisle. Then Leland shuffled up leading her mount, and the spell was broken.

"This here mare's full of spunk today, Miz Lacie. I done told Mr. Lockwood she weren't a fittin' mare for a lady. But he said you could manage."

At the old man's look of doubt, Lacie's resolve strengthened.

"She'll do just fine, Leland. I'm rather in the mood for a vigorous ride anyway."

"Thanks, Leland. I'll assist Miss Lacie in mounting."

"Yes, suh. Yes, suh. You all have a good ride and ol'

Leland'll be right here waitin' for the horses when you git back."

Lacie stared at Leland as he moseyed away. When had his morose mood lifted? When had he become so talkative and so obliging? Then her gaze shifted to Dillon and the answer was obvious. A man was back in charge at Sparrow Hill. At least that was how it appeared to the aging stableman. There was a man in charge, and everything was going to be all right again.

She wanted to feel angry, but all she felt was depressed. How could she expect Leland to have faith in her when she herself was so uncertain that she could keep the school going? It was even worse now that she'd seen how serious their financial problems were.

"Ready to mount?"

Dillon's voice next to her caught her quite by surprise.

"I—I can manage," she replied as she started for the mounting block. But Dillon was there before her, once again offering her his hand in assistance.

"I said I can manage," Lacie repeated crossly, deliberately sidestepping him.

But her poor temper seemed only to amuse him. "I've no doubt you can rise to any occasion, Lacie. It's only common courtesy for a man to offer a lady a hand up. Don't you teach your young ladies that? Tell me, do you react to all men so snippishly, or is it just me?" he finished with a slow, lazy grin.

Lacie was at a loss to reply. It *was* just him. She knew that without a doubt. Every time he touched her, she felt hot and nervous and her stomach tightened in the most disturbing manner. But that was something he must never know.

"You and I are on quite opposite sides of the fence, Mr. Lockwood. I see no reason to pretend otherwise."

With that she stepped up into the stirrup, then swung her right knee forward to catch around the high horn of the lady's saddle.

"I see," he replied with that same maddening smile that made her worry that he really *did* see. Then she felt his hand on her booted foot, adjusting it within the stirrup, and her heart began to pound. As irrational as it was, the gesture struck her as embarrassingly intimate. It was no more than Frederick had done for her a hundred times, but with Dillon it was a different thing entirely.

Appalled by the perverse path of her thoughts, she pulled suddenly on the reins. At once the eager mare danced away from Dillon and the mounting block. Without a word Lacie wheeled her around, and with one firm kick, she sent the mare catapulting from the stables.

She was barely settled on the saddle. Her skirt was still bunched around the horn and in the horse's swift flight both skirt and slip flew back, revealing the entire length of her calf and the edge of her plain cotton pantalets. But she was too rattled by her reactions to Dillon to care. As if her flight could help her escape all the terrible pressures and fears that beset her, she leaned forward and urged the mare on.

Down the dusty trail to the drive they flew, then on at a thunderous pace toward the road. The mare's mane stung her face while her own heavy plait flipped behind her like a flag in the wind. She almost felt as one with her exuberant mount and when they reached the road, she did not hesitate one whit. Across the road they sailed, then with one breathless leap they were over the weathered cross-tied fence and galloping across a meadow toward the bayou.

She had wanted to ride to banish her cares—and to be with Dillon. But now Lacie was determined to cast him completely out of her mind.

Yet he was not a man easily put off. Before she was even halfway to the green band of trees that marked the bottomlands along Brush Bayou, Lacie heard the sound of his pursuit. One wild glance behind her revealed how close he was. Yet that only made her more reckless.

"Go! Go!" she shouted to the mare, bending forward as low as she could in the saddle. But it was useless. Within a moment he was upon her, and with a grim look on his face he leaned over and caught her reins.

"Let go!" Lacie shouted as her mare turned slightly toward the larger horse. But Dillon ignored her completely, and when the horses were running shoulder to shoulder he determinedly slowed them both.

"Are you a complete fool?" he demanded when they came to a stiff-legged halt.

"I am a perfectly competent rider!" Lacie snapped back. "The only fool is you for grabbing at me so!"

"Dammit, woman! That was an idiotic move and you know it! I should never have allowed a crazy woman to ride such a high-spirited animal!"

"Allowed? *Allowed!*" Infuriated by his high-handed attitude, Lacie tried to pull the reins free of his hold. But he would not release them, and in a fit of temper she rounded on him.

"Let go of my horse this minute, Mr. Lockwood. In case you've forgotten your place here, this is my school, my home, and my horse. No matter what accusation your nasty mind has concocted, the fact remains that you're in no position to *allow* me anything!"

For a moment he only stared at her, his eyes glinting as hard as emeralds as he took in her flushed and disheveled appearance. Then he shifted slightly in his saddle, and his lips turned up sardonically.

"What a quick temper you have, Lacie. Perhaps if you looked at the situation from my point of view, you'd be more understanding. If you *are* Frederick's widow, it's my responsibility to look out for you. And if you *aren't* his widow"—the grin widened a fraction—"then it's my responsibility to look out for *my* horse."

Lacie was so incensed by his smug words that she did not pause to think. "You—you are the most arrogant bastard I have ever laid eyes on!" But when his face grew taut and his eyes turned cold, she knew her choice of words had been unwise.

"An arrogant *bastard?*" He leaned forward and caught her arm so that their faces were only inches apart. "An astute observation, my dear. I've often been termed arrogant, and I've never denied being a bastard." He smiled, but his eyes remained icy as he ran an insultingly thorough gaze over her. "Now, why don't you be as honest as I am, and admit exactly what you are."

Lacie trembled as she stared into his harsh face. She was a fool, she told herself. A fool to think she could deceive him and an even bigger fool to see anything worthwhile in his cruel and greedy nature. He was a hard, ruthless man, and nothing she said, no insult or cutting remark, would bother him in the least. She tried to free her arm from his steadfast grip, but it was to no avail. Then he pulled her closer and her heart nearly stopped.

Their horses were side by side, and now her leg pressed snugly against his. He reached his other hand over and fingered a fold of her exposed slip. Then she felt his hand rest intimately on her exposed knee.

"Let me go!" she demanded in a voice that shook with both anger and fear.

"Why should I?" he murmured, close enough now that she felt his warm breath. "What could you possibly do about it? There's no one nearby. No one to hear you or help you." He paused, and a wicked gleam lit his deep-green eyes. "Actually, I thought you brought me here so we could be alone."

That final remark was too much. With a sharp oath Lacie wrenched her arm free and, with one thrust of her booted foot, drove the horses slightly apart. When she saw he still held her reins, however, she quickly slid from her mount without a thought for the danger. Then she lit out running just as fast as she could, her plait loosening with every frightened stride.

A part of her knew it was useless. She could neither make it back to the house nor to the safety of the thickly wooded forest before he would be upon her. Yet Lacie refused to stop. Even when he called out to her in a loud chuckling voice, she would not slow her headlong flight. When she heard the thunder of his horse's approach, she darted in a different direction. But like an experienced rider cutting a calf off from its mother, he deftly turned her, and then in one swift movement, he lifted her clear of the ground.

With a startled gasp she found herself seated firmly before him, held securely with one of his powerful arms around her as he turned the horse away from the bayou. For a moment Lacie could not speak. The hard gallop, followed by her futile attempt to outrun him, then this abrupt capture left her breathless. Only when she saw her mare now calmly grazing as they steadily rode away was she able to find words.

"What do you think you're doing? Where are you taking me?" she cried as she struggled against his firm grasp.

"Sit still," he grunted as he jerked her even more tightly against him.

His arm was around her waist, holding her in the most intimate manner against his chest and thighs. She was slightly off balance, with his face just to the side of hers. But when he looked down at her, she turned stiffly away.

"What do you think you're doing?" Lacie muttered once more, holding herself as rigidly as she could, given their intimate proximity.

"I'm taking a ride, just as I'd planned," he answered curtly. "Take off your hat."

"What?" Lacie reached up to hold the plain straw brim.

"It's poking me in the neck. Take it off." When she only held tighter to it, however, his voice lowered threateningly. "Take it off, Lacie. For if you don't, I surely will."

"Insufferable high-handed bully," Lacie muttered as she hastened to untie the ribbon bow at her chin and remove the hat. Toadying to him was the last thing she wished to do, yet she was hardly going to give him a chance to remove it for her. Oh, he would enjoy that, wouldn't he! He seemed to derive his pleasure mainly

from humiliating and tormenting her. However was
she going to get rid of him?

The ride seemed interminable. True to his word, he
set his well-bred mount to a steady ground-eating
canter that quickly took them beyond view of the
school. Despite her precarious perch, Lacie did not fear
falling. She recognized him as a true horseman, and she
knew he was not about to let her slip despite the horse's
rocking pace. No, it was rather his close hold on her that
had her worried. That, and where he was taking her.

They were heading down a half-overgrown trail, one
that she'd been told as a child had been a path for the
Caddo Indians for centuries and centuries before. Of
course then her childish imagination had been both
fascinated and terrified by the thought of some tall
black-haired savage lying in wait for unsuspecting
schoolgirls. Now, however, as a schoolteacher she had
to fear a far different sort of savage. As they moved out
of the bright sunlight and into the shade of the forest,
she spoke up once more.

"You've made your point, Mr. Lockwood. You're
stronger than I. You ride faster. Is there anything else
you wish me to concede?" she added archly.

"Ah, there are a great many things I wish you to
concede, Lacie," he murmured, amusement clear in his
voice.

"If you mean the school, you might as well forget it,"
she snapped.

"Well." He paused, and his arm tightened ever so
slightly around her. "Perhaps we can find something
else."

She knew at once what he implied, or at least she had
a general idea. But more outrageous than what he said

was the strange knot that formed in her belly at his words. She had to forcibly squelch the uncomfortable warmth stealing over her and stiffen away from him.

"I'll concede you nothing," she muttered. She tried futilely to tug his arm away from her waist, and when that failed, she finally turned directly to face him.

"Look, this is accomplishing nothing. If you wanted to embarrass me, you've succeeded. Now, why don't you let me down?"

For a long moment his direct gaze held with hers. Warm, fiery emerald clashed with dark, smoky gray. Then he smiled.

"It's not my goal to embarrass you, Lacie. Besides, if there's no one here to see you, why be embarrassed?"

"You're here," she retorted, but her irritation was giving way to a more confusing emotion.

"Now, how have I been embarrassing you? Making you angry, yes—I can see that you might be feeling a little angry right now. But embarrassed? It makes me wonder what else you feel toward me that you could be embarrassed."

His casual tone only made things worse, but Lacie refused to examine any feelings she might have toward him. Most certainly she would never reveal them to him.

"I find it irritating—and embarrassing—to be man-handled as you have *repeatedly* done," she snapped.

"I see." But he made no attempt to comply with her request to be released. Instead, he turned the horse down another path, then crossed a small sandy creek. All the while Lacie was forced to sit there, fuming at his arrogant attitude.

Above them the branches of oaks and sweetgum interspersed with an occasional pine to create a living green canopy. Squirrels chattered and played, darting around the trunks and leaping from branch to branch, tree to tree. Birds flitted about, unconcerned with the passage of the horse and riders below. The calls of blue-jays and sparrows, mockingbirds and even the tell-tale sound of woodpeckers in the distance—the forest was alive with movement and sound in the warm May after-noon.

But Lacie could take no pleasure in the beauty that surrounded her. She was too uncomfortably aware of the man on whose lap she unwillingly sat. When the horse began to ascend a hill, she leaned forward, trying to avoid any closer contact with the broad muscular chest behind her. Dillon leaned forward as well.

"We're almost there," he said quietly, his lips too near her ear.

"Where?" she asked in spite of herself.

"It doesn't have a name," he replied in a voice that was a little more grim. "It's just a shack."

This must be where he grew up, Lacie realized when they approached a ramshackle cabin in a now-over-grown clearing. The roof had long ago caved in, and one corner of the narrow porch had collapsed where a falling tree had glanced off it. In the yard wild black-berry and elderberry had taken over what had proba-bly once been an ambitiously planted rose garden.

Dillon stopped the horse before a vine-covered wall, and for a moment they both sat in silence. Lacie had not known about this out-of-the-way cabin, so near to Spar-row Hill, yet nonetheless a world away. In her mind's eye she could see a dark-haired little boy there, draw-ing water from the well, playing with sticks and rocks and maybe even a puppy, while his mother tended to the roses that now grew in such untempered abandon. He had probably been happy here. But he had never had a father.

Maybe that was why he wanted Sparrow Hill. Not because it had been Frederick's, but because it had been his father's. He could never have back the childhood, but he could have the home he must have pined for back then. When he shifted in the saddle, then sighed, she could not deny the pang of sympathy that ran through her.

"How long has it been?" she murmured softly.

As if her words roused him from painful memories, Dillon stiffened. "Not long enough," he muttered. Then he abruptly wheeled his tall stallion about and urged him forward. Although their pace was no swifter as they left than it had been coming in, Lacie was aware that he was more than anxious to be gone from the clearing. They did not speak on the ride out, but their silence was fraught with entirely different emotions than previously. Dillon was no less in command of the situation, but it was not quite the same. There were chinks in his seemingly invulnerable facade, weak spots in his tough hide. Yet Lacie found she could not fully savor that knowledge, for instead of satisfying her, it only softened her opinion of him.

You're a fool, she told herself angrily.

But he's hurting, she rationalized.

So what? He deserves to hurt. He wouldn't hesitate to hurt us, to destroy everything that's good about Sparrow Hill.

But logic did not hold when Lacie thought about the little boy he must have been so long ago. She knew what it was to lose a parent, to feel abandoned and lost in a world peopled only with adults who suffered too much over their own loss to ever recognize the child's. She did not pause to consider her words.

"When did your mother die?"

She could not see his face, but she felt a slight tensing of his arm.

"A long time ago," he answered curtly. "And yours?"

Lacie sighed in frustration at his caustic reply. Why had she thought they could ever have a normal, thoughtful conversation? Then she felt his face lower, and he rubbed his cheek against her loosened hair.

"We're both orphans, aren't we? Two lonely souls in a cruel, grasping world. Perhaps we should join forces, Lacie."

His husky words, low and rumbling in her ear, caused Lacie's stomach to tighten and her heart's pace unaccountably to quicken. Then his lips found the soft, sensitive skin along her neck, and she could not prevent a gasp of surprise as all her senses jumped in alarm. She felt his fingers splay open to caress her waist. His well-muscled thighs shifted slightly beneath her so that she settled even more intimately against him. Even the slide of her own dark hair, caught between his cheek and hers, seemed suddenly sensuous, something she'd never quite felt before. Then his lips slid farther down her neck, warm and wet as they tasted her skin, and her head fell back against his shoulder.

It was a moment of wonderful madness, snatched from reality, almost like a dream. Yet it was no dream, and when his hand moved up to cup her breast, Lacie jumped in sudden alarm.

"No. No!" she cried, fighting her own lethargic response to him as much as his heated touch.

"No?" He pulled the horse to a stop just at the edge of the woods. "Why not, Lacie? For all that starched primness you display, I know there's fire just below the surface."

"You—you don't know any such thing. Nothing at all!" Lacie stammered as she tried to gather her wits.

But he only chuckled. "I know you'll come out the poorer for fighting me. Why not accept my offer? I'll give you more money than this place is even worth. And you'll give me . . . what I want."

"You can't buy me off!" she shouted, struggling to free herself of his grasp.

"Everyone can be bought off," he answered darkly. "It's just a matter of agreeing on a price."

"Well, I can't be," she muttered furiously, seeking to squirm down from her perch on his lap.

"Oh, yes you can," he stated grimly as he tightened his hold until she could hardly breathe. "I knew you were a liar—and a thief—when you said you were Frederick's widow. And thieves always have a price. It's part of their nature."

"How many times must I tell you that I *am* his widow!"

"You can say it until you're blue in the face, Lacie." He turned her abruptly so that their faces were but inches apart. "But I know that Frederick didn't care for women. That's why he didn't marry."

"He surrounded himself with women. And girls," Lacie countered. "He loved this school and everyone associated with it. For you to imply otherwise only proves you did not know him at all."

He laughed at her then, a dark, troubled laugh. "Let me explain it better, my sweet innocent. My brother—" He paused, and his eyes flickered away from hers. Then, as if steeling himself for what was to come, he looked back at her with a bitter twist to his lips.

"Frederick fancied young men. It was something he abhorred in himself, yet he could not deny the fact."

When Lacie only stared at him for a moment, perplexed by his strange words, his face grew grim.

"His lovers were not women, Lacie, they were men. He would never have desired to touch you as I just did." He took a harsh breath, then squinted toward the horizon. "I have no doubt he liked you, but no better than I might like any one of my male employees. And as for the school, it was his protection. It kept him away from temptation and allowed him at least to live with himself."

Lacie was too stunned to reply to his terrible revelation. She could scarcely believe her ears. A man might desire other *men* as lovers? It was too ludicrous to be true. And Frederick . . . A shiver of fear shook her as she tried to understand.

She did not struggle when he urged his horse forward, nor did she protest his snug hold as they crossed the field and approached the house. But all the while her mind whirled in complete bewilderment.

It was not true, she told herself. It could not be true. Frederick was too good a man to be involved in such . . . she shuddered.

Still, she sensed a disturbing grain of truth in Dillon's words that she could not entirely ignore. Frederick *had* used the school as a buffer against the world—she had always sensed that. But she had thought it was only because he was a quiet man, not like his neighbors who cared more for hunting and fishing and shooting. He had just been different.

But what if it went deeper? What if what Dillon had said was true?

Not until Dillon pulled his horse to a halt before the wide porch steps was the silence between them broken.

"Perhaps now you're ready to strike our bargain," he said, sliding one long strand of wind-blown hair from her shoulder.

But Lacie only shrugged off his touch. Then she gripped the saddle horn and slid down from her perch on his lap.

"You may make what accusations you like about Frederick, but no one will believe you," she vowed as she backed away from him, then nervously mounted the steps.

Dillon leaned over a little, the leather of his saddle creaking in the quiet afternoon. "You already know it's true."

As much as she wanted to deny it, Lacie could not. What he'd said made too much sense. Dear, dear Frederick! No wonder he'd never married. She looked up into Dillon's unsmiling face and her mind thrashed about on this new, uncertain ground. Would he expose Frederick's secret in order to discredit her claim? Would he be so cruel as to do that?

Then she remembered what he'd said before: he would fight dirty. He had said he would, and now she believed it was true.

For a moment longer she stared up at him, so handsome, so cruel. But she did not know how to counter his subtle threat, and to her complete chagrin, she could only gather her skirts, turn, and stalk away.

It took all her strength not to run.

9

Nina was close to tears. So was Lacie.

The little girl's father had sent word that instead of coming himself, he would have a trusted servant come for Nina. She had to be at the station in Kimbell by ten thirty to catch the train to Marshall, Texas. But the child did not want to leave any more than Lacie wished her to go.

Still, Lacie could not keep Nina against her father's wishes. She knew Nina was no protection against Dillon, only a slight mediating buffer. But she dreaded the child's absence nonetheless.

To appease Nina's fear of leaving, Dillon had promised to drive her to town. He needed his horse shod, he said, so it would be no trouble at all. Lacie could not bear the idea of accompanying Dillon anywhere, but she was not able to resist Nina's tearful plea that she, too, see her off. So it was that the first dawn's light found the three of them headed toward town, Nina sitting in the middle demanding attention from them both, and the tall black stallion trailing behind the Sparrow Hill carriage.

Lacie was not prepared for all the activity they encountered when they finally arrived in Kimbell. Banners were strung across the main road. Flags fluttered from every balcony and porch, and the streets were crowded with wagons, horses, and people.

"What's happening?" Nina asked in wide-eyed wonder.

"It must be the Founder's Day celebration. It hasn't been celebrated since before the war, but I'd heard it might be held this year since the Yankees have finally ceased occupying this area." Lacie looked around in surprise. "I'd forgotten all about it."

"Oh, can I stay? Can I stay?" the little girl begged, looking first to Lacie, then turning pleading eyes on Dillon.

"I'm afraid your train won't wait, little one," he answered. Then he looked over at Lacie. "But we have time to buy you a few treats to make your trip more fun. Let me drop off my horse at the livery first."

By the time Nina boarded the train with the stout woman who had been sent to fetch her, the child was smiling with delight. She'd already eaten two lengths of taffy and had four huge suckers, a small bag of mints, and an endless loop of licorice wrapped in butcher paper. In addition, equal lengths of red, white, and blue ribbons were tied in her hair, and a whirligig on a stick spun wildly every time she waved it.

" 'Bye!" she called from the open window of the railroad day coach. She waved the stiff paper toy back and forth. " 'Bye, Miss Lacie! 'Bye, Mr. Lockwood!"

"Good-bye, Nina. Have a good time!" Lacie called as the train began its noisy departure. She waved her linen handkerchief until Nina's face was but a blurry speck in the distance. Then her smile faded.

Now she was in for it, she thought nervously. Now there would be no avoiding Dillon Lockwood. She looked at him from beneath the shelter of her thick lashes. On the surface he appeared calm and relaxed, not at all the predator she knew him to be. Perhaps it was the well-cut black trousers and the finely tailored white shirt that he wore with the neck open in the hot May weather. With his hat off and his brow clear, he was an astoundingly handsome man, the sort whose attention any woman would love to have.

Yet when he straightened from where he leaned against a post, put his dark slouch hat back on, and turned his emerald gaze on her, Lacie knew it was all illusion. This same man might decide to destroy Frederick's reputation in order to get what he wanted, she reminded herself. He was a wolf in sheep's clothing, and she had better be careful.

She stiffened when he crossed to her, then tried to pull away when he took her arm.

"What are you doing?" she hissed, but not so loudly that anyone else might hear.

"Going to the Founder's Day activities, of course. I think we both could use a little fun. Don't you?"

"I can't imagine it ever being fun to spend time with you," she muttered as she tried once again to yank her arm free.

But his grasp was firm, and he would not let her loose.

"You're making a spectacle," he warned in a stage whisper. "People are beginning to stare."

At once she stilled her struggles and glanced cautiously around. To her chagrin, a grizzled old man was staring curiously at them, but he quickly looked away. No one else, however, seemed to take much notice of them.

"Let me go," she demanded as quietly as she could.

"No." His hand moved over hers, and his thumb stroked lightly along her knuckles. "Why don't you just calm down and try to enjoy yourself? This is my first real chance to reacquaint myself with the good people of Kimbell. You can provide the introductions. After all, you are my sister-in-law." He grinned that infuriatingly smug grin of his, and Lacie turned her head away in frustration.

"You hardly believe that, so why continue to goad me with it?"

"Because you're so beautiful when you're angry."

Lacie tried to ignore the immediate response that his low, husky words aroused in her. He was lying, she told herself, and making fun of her in the process. Yet even that knowledge could not prevent warmth from flooding through her. Would that his words were sincere! the traitorous thought crept up on her. Would that he were a true gentleman and could be trusted! She might even reconsider Mrs. Gunter's ridiculous suggestion that she marry him if she thought he could be trusted, for that would solve all her problems. And his.

But he *couldn't* be trusted, she reminded herself harshly. He'd warned her that he fought dirty, and she knew from personal experience that it was true. What he hadn't been able to achieve by bullying, he was now trying to gain by flattery and seduction.

But it wouldn't work—at least not as long as she kept her wits about her and didn't succumb to his smooth words.

She kept her eyes straight ahead as they strolled down the street. Only occasionally did she nod to someone she knew. She was aware of the curious looks they were receiving, first from the barber and two of his cronies, then from Mrs. Mooring and her son. When they passed a group of young ladies, however, she realized there was another sort of curiosity growing.

"Hello, Miss Lacie," a shy Jessica Landry called to her.

"Hello, Jessica," Lacie replied, nodding to the several other young women clustered with her. Two of them were former Sparrow Hill students, while the other three were unknown to her.

But they were all looking straight at Dillon without a glance for her.

"Good morning, ladies." Dillon tipped his hat to them. Then when Lacie looked over at him, he slowly smiled. "It certainly is a lovely day for a fair."

At the girls' quick and animated replies, Lacie felt a sudden hollowness. She quickly shook it off, for good manners demanded that she make the introductions, at least to the girls she knew. After she had completed the introductions, she was obviously no longer needed. Clearly they all knew that Dillon Lockwood was Frederick Kimbell's brother, though no one alluded to the disparities in their social standing. It was readily apparent that in their eyes his dark good looks completely outweighed any deficiencies in his upbringing.

As Lacie watched a particularly buxom young blonde dressed in a pale blue muslin confection that was the exact shade of her eyes, she could not deny that the dark emotions seething within her were uncomfortably close to jealousy. Why she felt that way, she couldn't fathom. The girl seemed to be a hussy, she told herself, and she really shouldn't care.

In irritation she pulled her arm from Dillon's grasp, and this time he did not stop her. For several more minutes she managed to stand there. Then, after a few brief words to Jessica, she murmured a quick excuse to the group, turned, and left.

She tried not to hurry as she made her way along the crowded street, but Lacie wanted nothing more than to run away from the place. Everyone around her was smiling and laughing and enjoying themselves in the company of people they cared about. She was the only one who was alone, the only one who didn't belong.

Unexpected tears stung her eyes, yet she refused to give in to them. In a flurry of wilting black bombazine, she stepped down from the plank walk and hurried across the dusty street toward the carriage still parked alongside the train station. She would drive herself home, she vowed. There was no reason why she should not. After all, Dillon's horse was here being reshod. He would not be stranded. And even if he were, why should she care? Besides, now that he had all those silly young girls flocking around him, he would hardly notice her absence.

When she reached the brett, she was quite distraught. As she was fumbling with the long reins, blinking back angry tears, she was abruptly caught by the arms, then spun around.

"Where in hell do you think you're going?"

Lacie stared up at Dillon's angry face, but her blurry gaze would not hold against the hard jade of his.

"I'm going home," she said stiffly, turning her face away.

"Why?" When she didn't respond, his grip tightened, and his voice grew harsher. "Why?"

"Because I want to!" Lacie burst out. "Because I don't want to stand around and watch you flirting with those—those—"

She immediately wished she could take back her words, for an amused glimmer lit his dark eyes. "My, my! If I didn't know how cold-hearted and calculating you are, I'd almost believe you're jealous, Lacie." His lips curved in a mocking smile as he considered her. "But then again, you *have* always responded so warmly to my kisses. Perhaps you *are* jealous."

Had it not been for the tears that trembled so perilously on her lashes, she would have corrected his conceited notion once and for all. It wasn't jealousy at all! It was just—just *everything.* But she could hardly explain that to him, and she would not risk crying before him. She was only able to choke back her tears and mutter under her breath, "I want to go home."

For a long moment he didn't respond. Then his brow arched slightly, and a speculative gleam lit his deep-set eyes. "Of all the good citizens of Kimbell, you should feel right at home here today. After all, you *are* the heir to the Kimbell family's good name and holdings. Why do you feel such a desperate need to flee?" He chuckled when she averted her eyes.

"If you're going to play the part of Frederick's widow, Lacie, you're going to have to do better. I know you're a liar, but one thing I've never suspected you of was cowardice."

He released her arms then and stepped back. He reached for a thin cheroot and lit it neatly with one stroke of a match against the carriage wheel.

Lacie was caught between tears and an angry retort, between defeat and outrage. Damn him! she thought as she stared at his darkly handsome face and his taunting grin. Yet for all that she wished to escape this place, she recognized the truth of his words. She had proclaimed herself to be Mrs. Frederick Kimbell. Now she must play the part, no matter how painful. With grim determination she set herself to the task.

"I'm no coward, no matter what you may think. I'm sure you are the only one here who would begrudge a recent widow her grief. No one else would find my departure amiss."

"But it's not your grief that you're running from. Why not be honest, at least with me? After all, I already know the truth."

"What you *know* is only what you *wish* to be the truth!" she retorted as her anger restored her courage.

He gave her an odd look, his expression almost curious. For an instant she felt as if he were seeing all the way inside her. When he spoke, his voice was quieter.

"I know those young ladies made you feel less than they were. You're a mere schoolteacher, whereas they have socially elite positions in town society as marriageable southern belles." He paused. "Even though they haven't yet recognized that their elite society has ended, surely you can see that life in the South will never be as it was before. There's no need for you to feel beneath them."

Emotions seemed to catch in her throat as he spoke, and Lacie looked quickly away from his serious face. He had started off by taunting her and calling her names. Why had he now become so perversely compassionate? She took a shaky breath and then brushed at a bit of nettle that clung to her skirt. I can't trust him, she told herself. I can't trust his sympathetic tone and reassuring words, for that is precisely what he wants.

And yet . . .

And yet she wanted to. He knew what it was to be an outsider, never quite belonging. Perhaps for once he was being sincere. Perhaps this one time he was showing his true self.

"I don't feel beneath them," she insisted. But her words sounded weak even to her ears.

Their eyes met for a long trembling moment. Then he frowned, tossed down his cheroot, and ground it with his heel. "I suggest you work a little harder at playing your part, then. That way, when I finally find you out, you can at least play to the sympathy of the townsfolk here. They'll think I'm the horrible bastard brother who robbed the poor widow of all she had." He gave her a mirthless grin, then reached for her arm. "Shall we go? Our audience awaits."

Walking the streets of Kimbell with Dillon Lockwood was a confusing experience, especially after such an emotional confrontation. It was difficult enough to feel the warmth of his arm beneath her hand and to brush shoulders with him as they made their way through the crowded street. Lacie could not ignore the terrible attraction she felt for him. It only made things worse to know how selfish and single-minded he was. Yet her heart refused to heed those warnings and instead clung to those rare instances when he showed his better nature.

He was wonderful with Nina and always knew how to cheer her up. And when she had tried to run away from the fair, he had somehow understood how like an outsider she had felt.

She looked up at him cautiously, not sure what she expected to see. He could be thoughtful and kind, but then—then he had turned right around and warned her that he nonetheless intended to wrest Sparrow Hill away from her. She stared at his hard-chiseled profile, trying to understand the man he was—at once cruel and good-hearted, generous and vindictive.

"Is something wrong?" His amused words cut into her troubled thoughts.

"What? No, nothing's wrong." Lacie looked away, chagrined to be caught staring at him. His hand covered hers warmly, and her heart began to race unaccountably. Once again she had a wild urge to flee, yet she knew it would be quite impossible to outrun the overpowering feelings he created in her. She cast her eyes frantically about, desperate for a distraction from the intense emotions building within her.

"Oh, look," she gasped in relief. "There's to be a race!"

"A race?" he murmured, keeping his eyes on her flushed features. "How interesting."

"You—you should enter," she stammered.

"Why?"

Lacie took a deep breath and tried to compose herself. "Because you like to win at everything." She finally dared to meet his avid gaze. "And I would really enjoy seeing you lose."

That brought a grin to his face, and his expression grew speculative. "What makes you think I'd lose?"

"I'm an optimist," she quipped. But she had to stifle a small smile herself.

"We'll see." Then he purposefully steered her over to a flag-festooned table where a number of men milled about.

"We got us another rider?" Mr. Mooring of the dry-goods store shoved a pen at Dillon. "C'mon, sign up. It's only fifty cents to ride."

"Fifty cents? And what's the prize?"

"Why, your lady's honor, of course." The balding shopkeeper gave Lacie a wink. "Her bonnet goes up with the rest. The winning rider picks up the bonnet he wants when he rides across the finish line. And then he gets a nice lunch basket to share with his lady."

"Don't forget the kiss," another fellow threw in. "The winner gets to claim a kiss from he owner of the bonnet."

"I'm in," Dillon said at once. He dug into his pocket for the coins, then casually turned to Lacie and began to loosen her small black bonnet.

"Oh! Stop it! What do you think you're doing?"

"You heard the man," Dillon replied amid the good-natured laughter of the other men. "You'll have to put your bonnet up."

"I'll do no such thing!" she gasped in alarm as she tried to slap his hands away.

"Now, now, Miss Lacie," Mr. Mooring interrupted. "The race is gonna start real soon. There's no time for hemmin' and hawin'. Just give the man your bonnet and wish him the best."

Lacie could not have been more humiliated. Her cheeks were burning by the time Dillon untied the ribbon beneath her chin and removed her plain dyed bonnet. She could do nothing about it as he handed it to Mr. Mooring. If only she had not mentioned the race!

"Do you wish me the best?" he murmured for her ears only.

"I hope you get thrown and break your neck," she muttered, turning away in irritation. She heard his amused chuckle but she refused to watch as he left to get his horse from the livery. She did hope he lost, she told herself. She wanted him to lose and be bucked off, to be completely humiliated. And she wanted to be standing at the finish line when it happened.

But as Lacie squeezed up to the front of the crowd gathering for the race, her anger turned to dismay. A slew of hats and bonnets dangled down from a hastily built overhead frame. Blue-dyed feather hats, pink-be-ribboned straw bonnets, a forest-green confection with a curving rooster tail, and a cunning lace and velvet one done up in an elegant dove gray. There were even several flat straw boaters with wide brims and colorful streamers dangling down.

They twisted and turned in the summer breeze, swinging from thin strings as the riders assembled for the race.

But there was only one black one.

Against all those other colorful bonnets, her own mourning cap seemed pitifully out of place. Not only was it small and plain, it seemed in poor taste amid the gay hats of the other girls and women. She was a recent widow. Such frivolity as this was terribly inappropriate for her, she realized.

For a moment she considered running out and snatching it down, even though everyone would probably laugh. But then, she would never be able to reach it up there so high. Perhaps she could have Mr. Mooring remove it for her, she thought in desperation.

But a drum sounded, and it was too late. As a hush descended upon the gathered crowd, Lacie's heart sank to her feet.

"All right, folks, we're about ready to start the race. Now, riders, keep to the route. No shortcuts. Down Main Street, around the courthouse, and out Kimbell Road to the big oak tree. Around the tree and back by the same route. And don't forget—you can't win unless you remember to grab a hat.

"Mothers, keep your young'uns in hand and out of the way. And may the best horse and rider win!"

There were at least thirty riders, Lacie saw, mounted on everything from plow horses to high-spirited Thoroughbreds. She quickly spotted Dillon, now coatless with his sleeves rolled up. His black slouch hat was pulled low over his eyes, giving him a dark, rakish look.

I hope he loses, Lacie thought vindictively. I really do.

Yet a nervous knot in her stomach belied that emotion. When the shot sounded that sent all the horses lunging forward, her heart leaped as well.

"Go, go, go!" a hundred voices seemed to yell in unison as the riders flew by in a thunder of hoofbeats and a cloud of dust.

"Oh, he's right near the front," a soft feminine voice cooed from somewhere behind her.

"Oh, yes. I see him," another answered. "I do so hope he wins!"

Lacie had no reason to think they were referring to Dillon, yet she could not help but turn around to see who had spoken. When she met the blue-eyed smile of the buxom young blonde from before, she knew.

"Yes, I do hope he wins," the girl cooed once more to

her friend, as she stared straight at Lacie. "And that he picks my bonnet."

"Oh, you goose! You'd have to kiss him in front of everyone! Why, your mama would swoon if you kissed someone like him. You know, without even a family name."

"I don't care," the girl replied, tossing her thick blond curls arrogantly. "She'll get over it."

Lacie turned abruptly. That girl *was* a hussy, she thought furiously. She wouldn't hesitate to kiss Dillon Lockwood right on the lips in front of the whole town. She'd probably press herself up against him and not care at all what everyone thought. It would serve the blonde right if he won and didn't pick her prissy little bonnet at all.

But what if he did pick it?

At that dreadful thought Lacie's shoulders slumped. He had made her put her own plain cap up there, so she had assumed he would pick it if he won. But what if it was all just another way for him to humiliate her—this time in front of the whole town?

She pressed her lips tightly together and clutched her small gathered reticule. Oh, please, don't let him win, she prayed. Please, please, let him lose.

Yet it appeared that God was not listening, for as the riders rounded the oak tree, a young man perched on the edge of the saloon roof shouted down the standings.

"A big black horse is neck and neck with Stan Harris! And Cliff Carney is close behind them both!"

Then Lacie could see the lead riders thunder toward the courthouse. Around the back, then straight toward the finish line they came. The entire crowd was on its feet, jumping and screaming as the three horses flew toward the line of hats fluttering in the wind. The riders were hunched low, urging their laboring mounts on, but Lacie could not miss Dillon.

No, no, no! her mind cried.

And yet as he galloped in the lead under the hats, yanking one down in passing, she could not help but rejoice, for it was her modest little cap—none other— that he raised triumphantly in his hand! Although the other riders thundered in behind him, grabbing at the other bonnets as they came, Lacie was aware only of Dillon's jubilant expression as his eyes found and locked firmly with hers.

At once she was circled by jovial townsfolk who drew her forward to where the victor awaited. Even Jessica, who along with her friends had hoped that Dillon would hold her own bonnet aloft, joined in the crush of people. It was all Lacie could do to maintain her footing in the crowd.

Only when she had been helped up onto the back of a buckboard wagon in the winner's circle did the people quiet down.

"All right! All right! Come on right here, Miss Lacie. Don't be shy." Mr. Mooring smiled widely at her. She tried to smile back, but it was a weak effort. Then he grinned over at Dillon, who still sat his horse.

"Well, we got us a winner, and if he will just get over here, he can collect his prize."

His prize. At those words Lacie cringed. Never had she felt more conspicuous. Never had she wanted more to disappear. But there was no place to go and no way to avoid the coming humiliation. As Dillon edged his horse up to the wagon, dismounted, and handed the reins to an eager boy, she painted a painful smile on her face and refused to look at him at all.

"Okay, now. Quiet down. Quiet down!" Mr. Mooring waved his hands for silence, then wiped his perspiring brow with a large handkerchief. "This year's winner of the annual Founders' Day Race is Dillon Lockwood, only lately returned to Kimbell."

A slight buzz began to run through the crowd at that announcement. Anyone who hadn't known that the winner was Miles Kimbell's bastard son did now.

"And the bonnet he snatched belongs to Miz Lacie— or should I say, Mrs. Frederick Kimbell."

The hum of whispers grew louder, and Lacie could have died. Why had he done this? Why? As angry as she was at him, however, she was equally angry at the people who were staring so curiously at them now. All they wanted was a spectacle, some entertainment, and they didn't care who was made uncomfortable by it. Determined not to give them any satisfaction, she grimly raised her chin and turned to face Dillon.

"Your bonnet," he murmured with a slight smile.

"Thank you," she replied stiffly as she took the black felt bonnet from him.

"Here's the lunch basket, Miz Kimbell. Why don't you give him his prize? Then he can have his kiss, and we can all go enjoy a good lunch."

A good-natured applause followed Mr. Mooring's words, but Lacie paid no mind to the crowd. Dillon was staring straight at her, his sharp green gaze as clear as emerald but as undecipherable as ever. She took a deep breath as she grasped the handle of the well-stocked basket, but inside she was shaking.

"Congratulations," she muttered as she thrust it toward him.

"Thank you, Lacie." His hand wrapped about hers, and the basket was suspended between them. Then he bent forward to claim his kiss.

Lacie froze as his face approached hers. Her heart beat painfully in her chest, as much in fear and embarrassment as in anticipation. She knew she was mad to feel so, yet she could not deny that she did. His lips would be firm, yet tender upon hers, clever and cajoling, making her warm and weak all over.

Slowly his mouth descended to hers, and without conscious thought she closed her eyes, shutting out everything but the strange and overpowering sensations that raced through her. Then she felt his breath on her skin, followed by a feather-light kiss on her cheek. At once the crowd came alive with sound: claps of approval from the matrons, giggles from the younger ladies and the children, as well as more than a few groans of disappointment from the men in the crowd.

Lacie too felt a guilty wave of disappointment as she tried to back away from him. But his hand still circled hers on the basket handle, and she was forced to endure his scrutiny. Her cheeks were scarlet, her eyes glistened with emotion, and her breath came quick and shallow. Everyone else thought she was simply shy and somewhat embarrassed by her sudden and unfamiliar visibility before the townfolk. Yet she knew it was more than that. It was his touch and his kiss—and an unacceptable wish for more—that had her so chagrined.

What was worse, however, was that she feared he knew it.

To her enormous relief, Mr. Mooring, Judge Landry,

the mayor, and the second- and third-place riders quickly surrounded them, heartily slapping Dillon on the back and offering him their congratulations. At least she was no longer on such public display, nor need she fear a cynical comment from him in this crowd. But she was still unable to pull away from his firm grasp. He kept his hand securely around hers and even maneuvered her nearer his side.

It seemed hours that she stood upon that wagon bed, although she knew logically it was only a few minutes. By the time the crowd began to disperse to their own lunches and the men had all clambered down from the wagon, she was uncomfortably warm, and a bead of perspiration trickled down between her breasts. Still, her face was set in a determinedly pleasant expression as she bade the other men good-bye.

Then only she and Dillon were left.

"Allow me," he said as he finally released her hand, took the heavy basket from her, and set it down. In one easy jump, he was down from the wagon. But as he held his hand up to help her down, Lacie hesitated.

"I'm quite capable of getting down without your help."

"No doubt you are," he answered agreeably. "I've learned very well that your appearance quite belies the woman you really are."

When she bristled at his clear innuendo, he only laughed. "Come on, Lacie. Be a gracious lady. Take my hand, and let me help you down. Your obstinance is only drawing more attention."

To her vast dismay, it appeared he was correct, for not only were Jessica and her friends covertly watching them, so were Mrs. Mooring and several of the other town matrons. Still, it was hard for her to show good grace as she stepped nearer his great grinning countenance.

"You are vile," she hissed as she grudgingly took his hand.

"You're just saying that," he murmured with an amused twist to his lips. Then he took her by the waist and easily swung her down to the dusty street.

"Thank you," she muttered as she stepped stiffly out of his grasp.

"You're welcome." He smiled down at her. "Now, where shall we eat this delicious-looking lunch I've won for us?"

"I'm not hungry." She smiled smugly, then turned to slip past him.

"Then we'll just stroll around together until you work up a better appetite," he replied as he casually took her arm in his.

"No!" Lacie cried, pulling her arm abruptly from his. When several faces turned curiously toward her, she quickly averted her eyes. "I don't want to stroll around with you," she muttered more quietly. "I don't want to eat lunch with you or—or even to be here at all."

Dillon stared steadily at her, his gaze calm and far too perceptive. "All right, Lacie. If you want to leave, we can do that too."

That was no solution to her dilemma, she thought distractedly as he waited for her response. She was trying her best to avoid being alone with him, yet no matter which way she turned, he seemed always to be lying in wait.

If only his interest in her were sincere.

But that errant thought she swiftly squelched. She

knew far too well why he was interested in her. Yet still she was hard pressed to feign indifference to him.

"Perhaps we should leave," she finally answered, without looking at him.

"As you wish." There was a note of wry amusement in his voice that she could not miss.

As they made their way through town, his great stallion behind them, she was uncomfortably aware of the many curious looks the townsfolk sent their way. She hated to speculate on which bit of gossip intrigued them more: her suspicious marriage to Frederick Kimbell; the return of Miles Kimbell's bastard son; or the very odd pair the two of them made. Whichever it was, she wanted nothing more than to be away from it.

When they reached the carriage, she took advantage of his preoccupation with the horses to scramble up to the seat. She knew he noticed and that he found her defensiveness immensely amusing. But what else was she to do?

"I can drive the carriage myself. You can ride your horse," she stated briskly.

"I'm afraid he's worn out from the race. I wouldn't think of riding him now. No"—he grinned, then climbed easily up to the driver's perch beside her—"I think I'll ride here with you."

Unnerved by his sudden nearness, Lacie quickly set the picnic basket between them. Then she smoothed her skirts and took a calming breath, although it did her little good.

They did not speak as he skillfully guided the team through the crowded street. The strains of merry harmonica music drifted to them and merged with the sounds of gay voices to create a pleasant, relaxed back-

ground. Yet Lacie could not relax, nor could she enjoy
the town of Kimbell, even today at its most congenial.
The man sitting so near her had insured that. Every
move he took seemed designed to aggravate her. In
fact, everything that had happened today seemed part
of a conspiracy against her.

The only good thing she could find was that the sun
had gone behind the clouds, and the wind had picked
up. At least the ride home would not be made worse by
the midday heat.

"How about digging into that basket for some
lunch?"

Lacie glanced warily at Dillon, but he was watching
the team. Something in her wanted to say no to him, to
every request he made, no matter how small or how
reasonable. But that would accomplish nothing. With
her lips pursed in annoyance, she lifted the lid of the
large oak-split basket and poked around inside.

"There's fried chicken, cornbread." She lifted out
two bundles and investigated further. "Pickles, tomatoes, shortbread. And two bottles of sarsparilla."

"I'll take some of everything." This time he looked at
her with a familiar half-smile. "If you would be so kind
as to make me a plate."

"I wouldn't want you to starve." Her agreeable words
were colored by the faint sarcasm in her voice. Still, the
two of them managed to make a decent meal of it as
they headed south along the road that followed Brush
Bayou. Lacie even dared to hope that the entire trip
might pass without any discomfiture on her part. But
then he leaned back in the seat and turned his vivid
gaze on her.

"Tell me, did you enjoy the race?"

She met his eyes briefly, then willed herself to look away. "I would have preferred that Mr. Harris had won. Or young Cliff," she stated as she stared determinedly at the broad withers of the off-side horse.

"And here I thought you were rooting for me." He laughed. "Didn't you enjoy this nice lunch I won for us? Or perhaps it was the kiss you were unhappy with?"

At that Lacie abruptly turned to stare at him. Why was he bringing up that uncomfortable subject?

"Come to think of it," he continued, his eyes glowing with a warmer light, "that wasn't the kiss I really deserved for riding such an inspired race."

"You deserved?" she gasped. "You received *much more* of a reward than you deserved."

"All right. I'll go along with you on that. I don't deserve a real kiss for my ride." Then she felt his knuckle slide along the side of her neck, and she began to tremble. "It's you who deserves a kiss—for giving me a reason to win."

Lacie could not tear her eyes away from his dark compelling gaze. Logic deemed this a perfect time to dismiss him, to cut him down, and make him look the fool. Yet it was beyond her ability to do so. With his lightest touch and potent gaze he seemed to command her will, for all she could think of was how much she had wanted his kiss as she'd stood on that wagon bed.

And how much more she wanted it now!

With a low groan of dismay for her weakness, she turned her face away. "Don't do this," she ordered, trying to summon up anger to replace the confusion that always swept over her when he touched her. "Don't do this!" But Dillon was not so easily shaken off.

"Come on, Lacie." His finger slid once more along

the sensitive skin of her neck, then farther along the
curve of her jaw. "I could have taken a real kiss from
you in front of the whole town."

"So why didn't you?" she blurted out, not clear in her
own mind whether she was relieved or annoyed that he
had not.

"I didn't want to make things more difficult for you
than they already are."

"Since when do you care about me?" she accused
softly, trying to shrug off his disturbing touch.

He did not answer at once but instead picked up the
basket between them and set it behind their seat. Then
he put his arm around her shoulders and drew her quite
firmly next to him.

"What are you doing?" she gasped as a hot knot
coiled deep in her belly. She struggled weakly to break
his grasp, but he only tightened his hold.

"Give me my kiss, Lacie," he murmured huskily in
her ear. "I earned it. And anyway, you want me to have
it."

She wanted to deny it. With every fiber of her being,
she wanted to deny it. But she could not.

She was shivering in his warm embrace, trembling in
both fear and longing. She felt his hand at the back of
her head, and the loosening of her hair beneath his
clever fingers. She felt the heat of his strong body
pressed now so warmly against her. She even heard the
rumble of thunder and the dull flash of lightning beyond the low hanging clouds. But none of that mattered. What dominated all else was the way he was
looking at her.

Those eyes might have been swallowing her whole,
so fiercely did they devour her. Yet Lacie could not

truly fear such complete surrender to him. All she knew
was that his kiss would be divine and that she wanted it.

When his face lowered to hers, she stared at him as if
mesmerized. Emotions smoldered in his eyes—desire,
most certainly, and triumph as well. But she could not
begin to fathom the rest. Then his lips met hers, and her
eyes closed in willing surrender.

Could a kiss be at once sweet and wicked? Could lips
be tender and passionate? Could she both long for and
fear this intimate embrace? Lacie shut out those confusing thoughts as she drowned in the fierce emotions that
captured her. Her head fell back against his arm as their
lips clung together. Then Dillon shifted a little, and
they were suddenly fitted together in the most intimate
of embraces. Her arm reached up to circle his neck; her
mouth parted beneath the seductive teasing of his
tongue against her lips. She was caught up in a glorious
passion that she nonetheless feared terribly.

He was not to be trusted, she tried to tell herself.

Yet it was futile, for she was already lost.

When his hand moved sensuously down her side, she
arched helplessly toward it. When his kiss deepened,
becoming more urgent and more demanding, she only
opened more fully to his wicked onslaught. Lightning
flashed and thunder rumbled, but they only seemed
part of the violent storm that shook her now.

She was not aware when the horses stopped nor how
she came to be lying back upon the meager driver's
seat. She only knew that the weight of Dillon's body
pressing upon hers felt incredibly right. His hips
pressed against her belly. One of his legs rested intimately between hers.

"So sweet," he murmured to her. "So sweet, and yet so filled with fire."

Hadn't she secretly longed for just such passionate words from him? Hadn't she thought about it as she lay in her bed at night?

No, she told herself. No, she never had. Nor had she ever truly wanted this wild, out-of-control feeling that overwhelmed her now. Frantically, she tried to clear her head and gather her wits.

"Dillon . . ."

He raised his head and gazed down into her eyes, glazed still with passion. For once his own expression was unguarded and easy to read, and Lacie had to turn her face away from the clear desire she saw there. His desire was no less than her own, and a part of her leaped in eager response to that knowledge. But desire was not love—and he still could not be trusted.

"Don't turn away from me," he murmured huskily. He cupped her face with one warm palm and forced her to meet his gaze. "It's so good between us, Lacie. Don't turn away now."

"But it's—it's *not* good," she managed to say despite the sudden catch in her throat.

"It could be. Just don't fight it. Don't fight me."

"But I—I must. I must fight you."

He shook his head softly at her words. "Ah, you stubborn little fool." Then he lowered his face and took her mouth in a kiss of searing intensity. As if he were determined to wipe away every opposition in her mind, he pressed his sensuous advantage.

Lacie could not long resist his fierce ardor. When his kiss moved down to her neck, then to the soft hollow of her throat, she ran her fingers through his raven-black hair. When his hand found her breast, she gasped in exquisite pleasure. Then she felt his other hand sliding along the tender flesh behind her knee and upward toward her thigh. She jumped in alarm.

"Oh, Dillon. No—you mustn't . . ."

"Hush, sweetheart. Hush." He quickly moved to kiss her lips, but she shook her head in rising panic. She pushed at his shoulder, but it was to no avail. He only caught her hand in his, then brought it to his lips.

"Don't stop me now, Lacie. This is what we've both been waiting for."

"No, no," Lacie moaned as she pulled her hand free. Another bolt of lightning lit the sky, and thunder boomed in its wake.

"Dammit, Lacie! I know you want this as badly as I do. Don't start up this farce of yours again. Not now."

"It's no farce. It's no act!" she gasped, struggling in earnest to push him away.

Dillon stared at her for a long moment. Then the warmth in his eyes faded, replaced by another harder emotion. "If this is no act—" he began. Then he stopped and after a moment slowly pushed himself away from her. "You can tell me all day long—and all night long, for that matter—that you don't want this. But we both know you're a liar."

He smiled bitterly as she scrambled from him, trying to cover her bared legs with one hand while she struggled with her loosened neckline with the other. "Didn't anyone ever tell you that honesty is the best policy?"

In her shame and mortification Lacie struck back blindly. "You're not honest! So don't you preach to me!"

"Ah, but I *am* honest," he said, grabbing her wrist and forcing her to face him. "I told you from the beginning that I wanted my rightful inheritance. And I'm telling you now that I want you too. In my bed. Naked and writhing beneath me," he added harshly. For a long tense moment, his eyes bored into hers. Then he let go of her wrist and leaned back in the seat.

Lacie was shaking with anger. But that could not entirely disguise the confusion and the incredible longing that still had her in its grip. To make things even worse, tears of humiliation sprang to her eyes. She turned away at once, trying to hold them back, but she could not prevent a wayward tear from slipping free and sliding down her cheek. Furiously she wiped it away with the back of her fist, but not before he saw it.

"Lacie . . ."

She heard his voice, softer now. Huskier. But she was too afraid to look at him. Then without any warning the clouds opened up, and they were deluged with rain.

She heard his muttered oath as the horses jerked forward. But he quickly applied the brake and brought them under control.

"Get in the back," he ordered, then held her arm as she struggled to clamber over the seat. Once she was within the sheltered portion of the brett, she fell back on the upholstered seat. For a brief moment their eyes met in a look that encompassed all the terrible and difficult emotions that loomed between them. Then he turned away from her, pushed his hat low over his eyes, and hunched forward in the driving rain. The horses leaped forward at his command, and the carriage was soon careening toward home.

In the gloomy recesses of the carriage, Lacie tried ineffectually to untangle the damp length of her long thick hair and to smooth the rain-splattered bombazine of her skirt. But her eyes did not stray from the unyielding posture of Dillon's broad back.

Nor did she try to wipe away even one of the hot tears that streamed down her pale, stricken face.

10

Mrs. Gunter dusted the marble-top table with a generous handful of flour, then plopped the twice-risen bread dough onto it. With a deftness come of many years experience, she flipped the dough several times before she commenced to knead the fragrant, elastic mass.

Lacie followed Mrs. Gunter's motions intently, staring as the cook neatly divided the dough into four equal portions, expertly shaped them, and placed each one into a bread pan.

If only she could divide her confused feelings for Dillon so easily, Lacie brooded as she watched the cook. On the one hand, she knew she had no real right to Sparrow Hill. It was Dillon's, and she was both a liar and a thief to try to take it. But on the other hand, he didn't really want the school at all, only the money he thought he could get for selling it. Worse, he might go so far as to ruin Frederick's memory by revealing his dead brother's shameful secret. Although he hadn't threatened to do so outright, how could she be sure that he wouldn't go that far?

Yet despite all her worries, she could not prevent

herself from mooning over him endlessly. What on earth possessed her? With furrowed brow and pursed lips, she followed Mrs. Gunter's movements intently until the other woman stopped abruptly and placed her flour-stained fists on her hips.

"What is going on here, *Fräulein?* I never see you watch me so close. You wish to learn to bake *Brötchen?*"

Lacie jerked her eyes up to the cook's face, unable to prevent the guilty blush that crept into her cheeks.

"Perhaps—perhaps I should. My cooking ability is sadly lacking."

But Mrs. Gunter only frowned and shook her head, clearly unconvinced. "You want to cook, I teach you to cook. You want to talk"—her florid face softened—"then I will listen."

Lacie stared at Mrs. Gunter for a long, indecisive moment. She probably did need to talk, for she was sorely confused after that scene with Dillon the previous day. But she was not in a mood to hear the older woman's fancifully romantic advice regarding Dillon Lockwood. Marriage was the last thing on his mind—and on hers too.

With an effort she drew a calming breath.

"I don't know what to do about that man." She quickly raised her hand to forestall the eager reply she sensed the cook was preparing. "Don't talk to me of marriage to such a man. Even if I were willing—which I'm not—he is hardly casting about with such honorable intentions. No"—she shook her head adamantly—"your idea might work in one of your sweet German fairy tales, but not here. Not with him and me."

Although Mrs. Gunter said nothing, only raising her gray brows curiously, Lacie knew she'd not completely convinced her. Nervously she reached across the baker's table and picked up a small remnant of uncooked dough. "He says I'm a liar," she said in explanation. "And since I'm a liar—and a thief in his eyes—I don't warrant any polite consideration." Her blush deepened to discuss such a private matter, but she pushed on. "That's why marriage is out of the question."

"Hm." Mrs. Gunter stared at Lacie. Then she picked up a blue and white linen cloth and draped it over the four loaves of bread. "You say you think he won't consider marriage—"

"He won't!"

"Sh, sh, sh. Let me talk. Now." She wiped the flour off her hands then sat down on a ladder-backed chair. "How do you feel about marriage to him?"

"That's too ridiculous to even answer!"

"*Ach*, just humor an old woman, *Liebchen*. Would you find Mr. Lockwood an acceptable husband?"

Lacie did not want to answer that question, for she knew her emotions were too muddled where Dillon Lockwood was concerned. Yet Mrs. Gunter clearly awaited an answer, and Lacie knew she needed to unburden herself.

"On the surface," she began in a resigned tone, "on the surface he is agreeable. Certainly he seems to attract women to him," she added tartly.

"Oh? And what women could that be? Besides you, of course," the cook said with a knowing smile.

"All those girls in town," Lacie blurted out. Then as Mrs. Gunter's smile deepened, she added more defensively. "And you! You're obviously quite taken with him yourself. Why else do you constantly bring up that absurd idea of marriage to him?"

"Humph. Because you haven't got any better idea. Besides, I think you are the one most taken with him. *Ja*"—she nodded her head sagely—"you like him. If you did not, you would send him away."

"He won't go!"

He *wouldn't* go, Lacie told herself later. He wouldn't go, and there was no way she could make him.

Yet she hadn't tried very hard to make him go, she had to admit. She hadn't exactly ordered him away. She had hoped that after he examined all Frederick's papers and files, he would graciously concede the school to her and go back to Denver without too much trouble. But it was clear he had no intention of leaving anytime soon. She hadn't helped her cause at all, either, with her own foolish actions. She'd gone riding with him. She'd gone to the Founder's Day festivities with him. She'd even let him kiss her. Not just once, but twice.

And worst of all, she'd kissed him back.

A small moan escaped her lips at the thought of how wantonly she had responded to his beguiling kiss. Even the memory of it heated something deep in her belly, and in impatience she jumped up from the armless rocker she'd been sitting in.

She'd been acting like a silly schoolgirl, she thought as she paced the small parlor, not like a mature woman with numerous responsibilities. She should not be worrying about his kisses. His terrible accusations about Frederick were of much more importance. Could he prove she had never been legally married to Frederick? More important, would he go so far as to ruin his half-brother's good name in such a despicable manner?

In agitation she bit at a fingernail. Then she deter-

minedly balled her hand into a fist. She would have to
force the issue and see. She would have to tell him to
leave. He had no further reason to stay. Besides, it
wasn't proper for him to be staying in the big house
with her. Yes, she would tell him to go.

Lacie steeled herself to her task, unwilling to deal
with a thought that lurked just beyond her decision.

If he left, she would never see him again.

Good. That's exactly what she wanted.

Then again, he might not go, despite what she did.

Yes, he would. He had no reason to stay. Why, he
might already realize that despite his threats, this was a
useless endeavor on his part. After all, she did have the
marriage license. And as for what he'd said about Frederick, that was only talk. He couldn't prove anything.
Yes, she thought with a small sigh of relief, even now he
could be planning to leave.

Lacie halted before the heavy wine-colored drapes
and stared through the lace sheers out past the deep
porch. He could be planning to leave. Although it was
what she wanted, a wave of unwarranted panic coursed
through her. In a moment she was out of the parlor,
hurrying down the hall, then quickly across the porch.

Fool, fool, fool! she berated herself as she tried to slow
her frantic pace toward the huge barn. Why must I seek
him out this way?

Yet she could not make herself turn back. When she
finally entered the barn, she was quite out of breath and
completely flustered.

"How do, Miz Lacie." Leland bobbed his head obligingly as he led two horses down the stable aisle. "If you
want a horse saddled, I can get to it in just a minute."

Lacie looked around the barn, then sighed wearily.

"Thank you, Leland. I don't think I'm quite up for a ride today." Then when he led the horses up to the carriage, her brow creased in concern.

"What are you doing? Where are you going with the carriage?"

"Mr. Lockwood, he's sendin' me to pick up his friend at the station in Kimbell."

"A friend of his?" Lacie said in surprise. "A friend of his is arriving at the station? Who is it? And why is he coming here?"

Leland looked over at her and shrugged, but he didn't stop what he was doing. He backed first one horse and then the other into the traces, then methodically buckled the harness in place. "Mr. Lockwood, he didn't tell me nothin'. Only to git the carriage ready and be in Kimbell for the two-oh-five train."

"Mr. Lockwood told you that, did he?" Lacie placed her fists on her hips and stared hard at Leland. When the old man only ducked his head and doggedly kept on working, however, her irritation turned to anger.

"Well, you can just unharness those horses. If he wants to send *my* horses and *my* carriage and *my* stableman on an errand, he had just better ask me first!"

At her outburst, Leland straightened up, staring at her in confusion. Then his eyes moved beyond her, and Lacie turned at once.

"Is there a problem?" Dillon walked toward them in long easy strides. He neither hurried nor hesitated. He neither smiled nor frowned. He was as contained as always, showing no emotion save that damnably cool composure.

Lacie, however, found it almost impossible to appear unaffected by his sudden nearness.

"Why do you have Leland going into Kimbell?" she asked him angrily.

"To pick up Neal Camden."

The name meant nothing to Lacie, yet she felt a moment of sudden panic. What was he up to now? Still, she could not back down. "I presume you're bringing this person here?"

"Certainly." He stopped before her. He was too close for comfort, but she refused to be intimidated.

"You are taking far too many liberties around here, Mr. Lockwood."

"Dillon," he corrected with a faint, knowing smile.

"Mr. Lockwood," she retorted firmly, "I would like to remind you that this is *my* home. Mine. I would appreciate it if you would consult with me before issuing any orders to Leland or any of the others under my employ."

At that he cocked one of his brows and smiled at her. "I don't really think you want to open that debate in front of Leland, do you, Lacie?" At her angry scowl and her guilty glance at the old servant who openly gaped at them both, he laughed softly. Without warning he took her arm and firmly turned her around. "Finish up, Leland. Mr. Camden is in a big hurry to get here." Then without even asking her leave, he pulled her along with him.

"Let go of me!" Lacie muttered furiously. "Who do you think you are?"

"Never lose your temper in front of the servants," he responded, not slowing his pace a bit. "You should know better."

"Don't lecture to me!" she hissed. "You have no right to order Leland around. Or—or even to be here!"

"Oh?" He stopped then and turned to face her. "We both know that's not true."

With an angry shrug she pulled from his grasp, but she was still held captive by the piercing quality of his eyes. She *did* know it wasn't true, and so did he. But she could never admit it.

"You don't belong here," she insisted. "Why don't you just leave? You hate this place."

"You couldn't be more wrong, Lacie." He smiled, then reached out to graze her chin with one finger. "I like . . ." His gaze slowly moved from her wide gray stare down to her lips, then boldly took in every aspect of her feminine form. She might not have been well-covered in starched white cotton and stiff black sateen, so avidly did he seem to drink in her image. "I like it here very much."

Lacie was not prepared for her intense reaction to his light touch and softly spoken words. No reply came to her mind, no swift words of retort rose to her lips. Yet in every other way, her body leaped in violent response to him. Her heart thundered in her chest; color stained her cheeks with a becoming flush. Even her breath quickened as they stared at each other. But most alarming of all was the disturbing tightness curling up in her belly. She should not respond to him like this, and yet there was no preventing the terrible longings he inspired in her.

In self-preservation she took a step back from him, then another. "You hate it here," she whispered hoarsely, her eyes still locked with his. "You're only staying to cause trouble." She took a shaky breath. "Why don't you leave?"

The air between them crackled with emotion as the silence stretched taut. His face was serious as he spoke.

"I'll leave, but in due time. And not just yet." He paused. "Not yet."

In polite conversation his simple words would have been almost unworthy of note. Yet spoken in this situation, they could have been either warning or promise, a threat of trouble to come or a triumphant prediction. Lacie did not want to speculate as she stared at his lean masculine features. Unnerved by his steady perusal of her, she struggled for words.

"Who—who is this person, this man coming to see you?"

"Neal is a business associate of mine. He's a very perceptive attorney. My right-hand man, you might say." His face softened in a faint smile. "I'm sure you'll like him."

"I doubt it," Lacie muttered. She looked away from his discerning gaze to where Leland had finished harnessing the carriage team. "And how long does he plan to stay?"

"As long as it takes."

He was trying to scare her, Lacie thought as she peered warily at him. His ominous-sounding words were just that, only words. Yet a decided quiver snaked up her back. He was up to something, but what?

Lacie was suddenly sorry she had ever sought him out, and she wondered at her deplorable behavior in doing so. Her brow creased in an unwilling frown. "If you wish to linger in this area, there is a hotel in Kimbell that will accommodate both you and your friend."

"There's plenty of room here."

"But I don't want you here!" she insisted.

"Oh, yes, you do."

Those soft sure words were her final undoing. With a small cry of frustration, Lacie turned away from his arrogant taunt and hurried back toward the house.

But distance did little to diminish either the impact of his words or the dreadful truth of his remark. She was ten times a fool, she thought as she scurried up the back steps, then flew around the corner of the porch. She should be fighting fire with fire, yet time and again she was disarmed by his beguiling smile and seductive words.

She paused on the front porch and stared wildly around. What was she to do? she wondered desperately. What was she to do? In despair she took one step down, then another. Finally she sat down on the steps— most unladylike, she thought obliquely—and clasped her hands fervently together.

Prayer seemed her only remaining alternative.

II

Lacie vowed to avoid Dillon from then on. What he was doing and where he was were of no concern to her, she decided. But late in the afternoon, when she heard the brett returning from Kimbell, she could no longer remain in hiding. Still, she had no intention of being even polite to this man Dillon was bringing here. He was obviously coming to aid Dillon in his quest to discount her claim to Sparrow Hill—and perhaps even to destroy Frederick's good name. That made him her enemy, and she saw no reason to be hospitable to such a person. She stayed in the shadows of the second-floor gallery as the carriage pulled up to the front of the house. Although she was curious and wanted to see the man, that was as far as it would go.

The man who descended from the brett to be greeted warmly by Dillon was well dressed in a suit of gray broadcloth with a black-satin-striped silk waistcoat. He held his hat in his hand and Lacie could see his fair hair and pleasant features. He certainly didn't look cruel or heartless, she thought grudgingly. Then he turned to help someone else down and she tensed in dread. Had even more of Dillon's confederates come to badger her?

To her complete surprise, however, the slender figure who next alighted was that of her dear friend, Ada. Lacie rushed to the gallery rail to stare down at the small group, perplexed by this unexpected turn of events.

Then Dillon looked up to meet her confused stare. He must have known where she was all along, she realized, and that she would be watching. Although it galled her that he had read her so easily, Lacie nonetheless could not dwell on that. What Ada was doing in the company of this Neal Camden, a slick attorney brought in to wrest Sparrow Hill away from her, was a question she could not answer. Still, she had no intentions of leaving sweet Ada to the merciless manipulations of those two.

When Lacie got downstairs and emerged from the house, the two new arrivals were being escorted by Dillon into the cool shade of the porch. Mrs. Gunter appeared as if on cue with lemonade and biscuits, and the traveling bags were whisked inside. All in all, Lacie thought, a most charming domestic scene on the surface.

But something was afoot, and she was not about to allow anything damaging to happen.

"Hello, dear," Lacie said, giving Ada an affectionate hug even as she shot Dillon a furious look.

"How good it is to be home!" Ada answered sincerely. "I couldn't stay away another day. I was so worried about you . . ." She trailed off and sent an embarrassed glance toward the two men. "I mean—well—"

"Never mind," Lacie replied warmly. "It's good to

know you were thinking of all of us back here." Then she hooked her arm in Ada's. "Let's go upstairs, shall we? I'm sure there's lots we have to catch up on."

Ada started to follow but then she hesitated. "But Lacie, you haven't met Mr. Camden."

Lacie stopped in midstride, caught between anger and guilt. More than anything she wanted to ignore this man, yet something in her could not be quite so rude. Still, her expression was hardly welcoming as she turned to face him.

"Hello, Mr. Camden."

"Nice to meet you, Mrs. Kimbell." He nodded, giving her an amiable smile.

For a moment she hesitated, forcing a weak smile and chagrined by her ungracious behavior. But then she glanced at Dillon and her smile grew tight and bitter.

"If you'll excuse me?" Then she firmly pulled her friend inside the house with her. Lacie knew she had shocked Ada. She had shocked herself as well, for never in her entire life had she been so deliberately rude to anyone.

She was justified, she told herself. Her back was to the wall. The wolves were quite literally at the door. Yet she could not completely escape her guilty feelings of remorse.

"Lacie?" Ada's voice was soft as they went up the stairs together. Yet Lacie could hear the question in it. And the gentle chiding.

"I know, I know. I was rude to him. But you just cannot imagine how bad a predicament we're in!" She turned to her friend earnestly. "That man—that man is here to challenge the marriage papers. I'm sure of it. He's a lawyer, and he's here at Dillon's request." She paused to catch her breath. "I just couldn't greet him as if he were a welcome guest. I don't want him here at all."

Ada's brow creased in concern. "I'm sure Neal—ah, Mr. Camden won't force his presence on you if you wish him to stay elsewhere."

"He'll do Dillon's bidding."

"Dillon?"

It was Lacie's turn to be embarrassed, but she quickly rallied. "It doesn't matter what he's called. He's a devil by any name."

It wasn't until they entered her room that Ada replied. "Neal speaks very highly of Mr. Lockwood. Of Dillon."

Lacie looked at her friend, then sighed and sat disconsolately upon the bed. "They're no doubt two of a kind. Why wouldn't he speak highly of him? Besides, he works for him. Dillon pays him to do as he says."

"Yes, that's true," Ada murmured as she removed her dusty traveling bonnet. "But Dillon really has been good to Neal."

Lacie looked up at the thoughtful tone in Ada's voice. "You seem to know an awful lot about this man."

Ada quickly looked down at the bonnet in her hands. "We—ah, well, he was on the train when I boarded in Plano. But I didn't realize who he was coming to see until we were almost to Shreveport," she added sincerely. "By then it was too late to begin ignoring him. Besides, I thought I might learn something useful."

Lacie's shoulders slumped dejectedly. "Did you?"

"Well, I did find out that Dillon is quite well respected in Denver. He's a self-made man with all sorts of businesses."

"Yet he's still greedy enough to want our school."

"Yes, well, it appears he does," Ada said more slowly. "But he has his benevolent side too. Neal told me he is very generous to Denver's orphanages. And he put Neal through school to be a lawyer. Surely, he can't be all bad. There must be some way to reason with him."

"He's completely unreasonable! There's only one agreement he's willing to make—"

Lacie stopped abruptly. She did not wish to recall the one compromise Dillon had offered her.

"An agreement? Oh, tell me! What is it?"

"It wasn't anything," Lacie demurred. But she could feel her cheeks heating in a blush, and she knew Ada was bound to become even more curious. "He's not a very nice man," she finally said. "He made the most insulting offer."

"Insulting?" Ada stared at Lacie, struggling to understand. "I suppose he still doesn't believe you ever married Frederick."

"It's far worse than that," Lacie blurted out, frustrated by the terrible predicament she was in. "He is such a cad, such an ill-bred, low-life—" She stopped to catch her breath, then began to pace the small room. "He offered me money if I would drop my claim to Sparrow Hill. Then he—then he said we could have a special arrangement." She cast an embarrassed eye at Ada. "He made a completely improper suggestion regarding him—and me."

Ada's shocked face and absolute speechlessness only caused Lacie's face to go even more scarlet. She turned to the window, staring blindly at the sheer linen hangings as she struggled with the confusing emotions that Dillon Lockwood always caused inside her. Despite her

justified anger at his insulting proposal, and her humiliation at admitting it to Ada, there was still a part of her
that yearned for him.

But that was only her silly, foolish nature, she
thought. As long as the strong logical side of her pre-
vailed she could ignore those other unwanted feelings.
She took a deep breath.

"So you can see, Ada, he is not a man who may be
reasoned with." With a small forced smile pasted on her
lips she turned back to face her friend.

Ada, however, no longer had a stupefied expression
on her face. Instead, she was smiling at Lacie with the
most hopeful of expressions.

"He is taken with you. He must be!"

"He is only trying to intimidate me!"

"He finds you attractive or else he wouldn't have—"

"He finds ownership of Sparrow Hill attractive! If he
can seduce me"—her face went scarlet again—"then
he thinks he can somehow wrest the school from me."

Ada shook her head. "He's not married. Neal told me
that much. The two of you together would be a very
handsome couple. You would make him a very nice
wife. Oh yes."

"Not you too! Don't you see? It's not marriage he's
proposing. All he wants is a—a—"

"A paramour?" Ada pronounced carefully. "Yes, well,
that may be what he's saying now."

Lacie threw her hands up in dismay. "Is everyone
here so besotted with him that they cannot see the
truth?"

But it was clear Ada had made up her mind. With a
sigh of defeat Lacie stared at her friend's smiling face.
"I think I shall take a walk," she said shortly. "If I stay in

this house one more minute, I fear I shall go just as mad as the rest of you!"

They *were* all mad, Lacie vowed as she stalked down the white gravel path that led through the rose garden. Completely crazy. Ada with her foolish romantic notions. Mrs. Gunter with her outrageous suggestion. And Dillon—Dillon with his insulting proposition to which he was smug enough to think she would agree.

But she herself was clearly the craziest one of all, she admitted as she hurried along. Despite all she knew of the man, she could still not stifle the wild urgings that the mere thought of him aroused in her. It was quite insane, yet it was nonetheless true.

Beyond the rose garden the path became narrower. Wild blackberries grew untamed, catching at her skirts as she passed. Black-eyed Susans nodded as she went by. But Lacie was too beset by her dark thoughts to notice. Not until she reached a weathered, somewhat ramshackle gazebo near the edge of the duck pond did she pause to look around her.

The woods were still. The late afternoon heat hung heavy and damp over the earth, seeming almost to press down upon her solitary gloom. A storm was coming, she noted obliquely. Towering thunderheads were approaching from the west. With any luck, a good long rain would cool things down.

As it had yesterday.

Lacie let out a forlorn sigh at the thought of the rainstorm yesterday. Certainly it had saved her from complete humiliation at Dillon Lockwood's hands. But cool things down? Hardly. His touch and his kiss had aroused her to frightening heights. Even now she shivered at the memory. Would every rainstorm forever remind her of those wonderful, terrifying few minutes?

Lacie slowly made her way toward the old gazebo. She cleared off the leaves and dust from one of the painted benches, then wearily sat down and leaned her head back against the fancifully turned column. As was always the case these days, her mind was filled with thoughts of Dillon: Dillon that first day at the graduation; Dillon in the bathing room that night; the time he'd kissed her in the chicken yard; their ride together . . .

Angrily, she tried to cast those disturbing thoughts away. She stared up into the rafters of the gazebo, trying to note the repairs needed, and the painting. But thoughts of him still beset her.

He'd raced and won—and chosen her bonnet.

Then he had claimed his winner's kiss.

She was oblivious to the breeze picking up, and to the gray clouds that moved relentlessly across the sky. She was oblivious to all but her dark and troubling thoughts of Dillon. She wanted him in the way . . .

Abruptly she bit her lip, wishing she could deny the truth of her feelings. But she simply could not. She wanted him the way a wife wants her husband. It was as plain as that. Even though he was pursuing her only because he thought it would help him take Sparrow Hill from her, she still wanted him.

Lacie covered her face with her hands, wondering abjectly how she had ever come to this. All she had wanted was to preserve the school. She hadn't wanted to cheat anyone out of anything. Yet here she was: a liar, a thief. And even worse, she was actually contemplat-

ing the most unseemly and wanton behavior possible
for an unmarried woman!

As if to punctuate her truly wicked thoughts, a huge
bolt of lightning split the gloomy sky, followed almost
immediately by a sharp crackle of thunder. Lacie
jumped in alarm and warily peered beyond the shelter
of the gazebo. A brisk wind ruffled the surface of the
pond. The branches of the trees swayed in erratic gusts.
A splatter of heavy raindrops swept across the surface
of the water, then fell like quick, angry drumbeats on
the cypress-shake roof above her head.

Now she was in for it, she thought in dismay. She
could either stay put and be trapped for who knew how
long. Or else she could risk a good soaking and make a
run for it.

For a moment longer she debated her choices. Then
a blinding flash of lightning decided for her. The hairs
on her neck were standing on edge either from the
nearness of the lightning or from fear. She didn't know
which, but she didn't pause to find out. Holding her
skirts high, she sprinted up the winding trail, praying
with every step that no bolt would strike her when she
ran through the trees.

Lacie was huffing from her run by the time the school
came into view. The wind whipped around furiously,
sending leaves and small branches flying. The rain was
sporadic, swirling about and stinging her face and arms.
Still, she was almost congratulating herself on reaching
the shelter of the school building safely when she froze
in alarm.

For a split second she stared in wide-eyed horror,
willing it not to be so. It was only a lantern swaying
crazily that was casting the eerie glow from the open

stable door, she told herself. But even as she watched, the orange glow grew brighter, and she could not deny the terrible truth.

"Fire!" The ever-dreaded word burst from her lips as she charged toward the stable. "Fire!" she screamed as she ran, unmindful of the violent wind that tore at her hair and skirts. The barn was on fire and all the horses inside would be burned to death if someone didn't get them out!

She paused when she reached the opening to the stable. The frightened snorts and whinnies of the horses, combined with the ominous roaring of the fast-growing fire, was an awful sound to hear. Smoke already filled the interior, and to the rear of the barn she could see flames leaping.

Lacie could not have been more terrified. The thought of entering the burning building was too horrifying to contemplate. Yet the hoarse squeals of the trapped horses forced her on. But when she crouched low and started to enter the smoky barn, she was abruptly halted as a strong arm jerked her back into the fresh air.

"Get back, you little fool!" Dillon's harsh voice ordered her.

Why was he here? she thought wildly. This was not his problem. Yet a part of her felt enormously reassured by his commanding presence. "Dillon! I have to get them out!" she cried. "They'll die. They'll all die!"

"Leland has already brought some of them out. Neal and I will get the rest. Now, you stay back from the fire!"

Lacie's eyes stung from the smoke. Tears blurred her vision as Dillon dragged her away from the heat of the burning barn. Then she felt Ada's small hand clutching hers, and she turned a desperate face to her friend. With the back of her fist, she wiped her tears away.

"Dear God in heaven! How can this be happening?"

"It was the lightning. We heard this terrible sound, and then Leland screamed for help!" Ada clenched Lacie's hand tightly. "If it would just rain a little harder—"

But instead of stopping the fire, the storm made it worse. In a matter of seconds the violent winds whipped the flames to a frenzy, sending them leaping into the barn's upper lofts and igniting everything in its path. Any thoughts of putting it out were banished as the heat intensified.

Smoke obscured the opening of the barn, but the sound of the terrified animals was unmistakable. Then one horse bolted from the stable in a wild-eyed gallop. Then another, and another, followed by Dillon crouched low on the back of his big stallion.

As soon as he was out of the stable, he slid down from his horse and looked around.

"Where's Neal?" he yelled above the roar of the flames.

"He didn't come out!" Ada cried in agitation. "He's still in there!"

At once Dillon started back toward the inferno. Then with a loud crash, a new fountain of sparks and flames leaped into the sky.

"No! No!" Lacie screamed. She grabbed Dillon's arm in desperation, trying to stop him from going any farther. "Dillon! You can't go back in there. You can't!"

But he shrugged off her hold at once. "Neal's in there!" he thundered. Then he ran into the smoke.

In absolute terror Lacie strained to see him, hardly aware that Ada and Mrs. Gunter had come up beside her. Together the three women stood there, holding on to one another for strength.

Then Lacie saw a movement, and she tore away from the others.

"Dillon! Dillon!" She was sobbing as he staggered out of the barn. He almost fell when she reached him, he was coughing so hard. But he had Neal over his shoulder. With her help, he managed to get him to a grassy spot away from the barn and then lay him down.

"He's hurt . . . don't know how bad." He coughed again and wiped at his burning eyes and soot-covered face. "Help him, Lacie . . . help him—"

In an instant the three women took over. Ada went for water and clean cloths. Mrs. Gunter hurried off for her box of medicinal supplies, while Lacie checked the unconscious Neal for injuries.

"He's breathing," she noted as she gently probed with careful fingers. "There's a deep gash here, just above his hairline."

"I found him just beyond a fallen beam." Dillon took a wet cloth from Ada and swiped at his face. Then he took a deep, grateful drink of water.

"How is he?" Ada asked anxiously.

"I don't think he's burned, but this cut isn't too good." She slid her hand down his left arm, eliciting a sudden groan from the man. "I think his arm may be broken too."

Suddenly the heavens seemed to open. Like Noah's flood, it fell in huge drops—in buckets, it seemed. And yet for all its blessed relief, the first sizzle of the rain striking the fire sounded like the hissing of devils at the gates of hell. Then the billowing black clouds of smoke became lighter, spreading out under the onslaught of the rain, and everyone was forced to retreat once more from the choking, blinding mess. As they were hauling Neal back from the barn, he roused. His eyes opened and he stared about him in dazed confusion.

"Here, let me see to him," Mrs. Gunter ordered as she knelt beside him. *"Ach,* but he'll be needing the doctor. That's for certain."

The rest seemed almost a dream to Lacie. Dillon found Leland and had him bring the still-harnessed carriage around. Then the two men lifted Neal inside, despite his weak protests. Leland took the driver's seat as Ada and Mrs. Gunter got in to tend Neal. In a matter of minutes the brett was heading down the drive, Leland hunched over as he tried to keep the skittish team of horses under control.

And throughout it all the rain came down in a hard, merciless torrent.

12

❧

Lacie stared through the rain at the still-smoking barn.

"Get inside now, Lacie. Go on." Dillon took her arm and led her toward the shelter of the porch. She took a few steps along with him, for she was still stunned by all that had happened. But then she shook off her numbness and stopped.

"What about the horses?" she shouted through the dull sound of the pouring rain. "We can't leave them running loose in this storm. They might have been hurt."

For a moment Dillon only stared at her without answering. In the dreary afternoon light his features looked somehow different. The gray film of smoke and soot that covered him heightened the strong planes of his face. Yet even as she stared up at him, the rain was washing him clean in one rivulet after another. His eyes were a midnight shade of jade. With a careless motion, he pushed his dark dripping hair from his brow.

Then he reached for her.

It was only to push a long clinging strand of hair back

from her cheek. But it seemed the tenderest of gestures.

"The horses will find shelter from the storm. We can round them up in the morning."

"But what if one of them is hurt? What if in their panic they fall or run away?"

"I don't think any of them were hurt, Lacie. They're probably in the next field under some tree." He took her arm and steered her once again toward the house. "There's no need to argue out here in the rain."

But Lacie shook her head stubbornly. "They're Frederick's horses. His pride and joy. I know you don't care about that, but I do. I have to take care of them."

At once she regretted her words. She wished she could take them back, but once said they would not go away. How could she be so ungrateful when he had just risked his life to save those same horses?

Dillon's face closed against her; his jaw tensed and she felt him stiffen.

"I didn't mean that. I—I'm sorry, Dillon. Truly I am." She reached one hand towards him, then hesitated and pulled it back. "I'll never be able to thank you enough for what you did to save Frederick's horses."

He looked down at her. "Yes, Frederick's horses," he repeated. Then he gave her a reserved, distant smile. "Well, perhaps we should finish the job."

They made a strange partnership, Lacie thought as they set off in the rain. Dillon was completely drenched. His shirt clung to him like a gray-streaked second skin. With his hair slicked back by the rain and every portion of him lovingly outlined by his soaked clothing, he appeared to be a gallant warrior of old, silent and intent as he pursued his task.

She, by contrast, was bedraggled and floundering, weighted down by her heavily trailing skirts and tripped up by the mud. Her hair was a bothersome mess, sticking to her cheeks and neck and streaming over her shoulders and down her back. Yet still she struggled to match his pace.

Only when Dillon grabbed her hand and pulled her along, however, was she able to keep up with him. Despite the chill that enveloped her, his hand was comfortingly warm and reassuringly strong. It almost felt as if they were somehow connected in a higher, purer way. Lacie wiped ineffectually at the rain on her face and peered up at Dillon. They were connected through Frederick, she realized. But whereas previously that connection had made them adversaries, for now, at least, they appeared to be working toward the same end.

For a moment she relived the horror of the fire and her absolute terror when Dillon had plunged into the fiery barn. Why had he done it? she wondered. To get his own horse? But she knew with an unshakable certainty that he would have done it even if his stallion had not been among the hapless horses in the barn. He would have risked his life for anyone or any animal that might have been trapped within that terrible inferno.

In a gradually dawning wonder she stared at him, confused anew by this unexpected facet of his personality. What manner of man was he?

But she had no time to ponder that question. Up ahead, the blurred shapes of two horses showed through the unremitting rain. With a quick motion Dillon bade her stay still while he moved off the road toward the two.

The larger horse spotted him at once and flattened his ears in warning. But with a long, low whistle Dillon calmed the animal. Then with a nicker of greeting, the big stallion ambled over to his master.

Lacie could not mistake the true affection between Dillon and his great stallion. Hadn't she read somewhere that animals and children were the best judges of character? If that were so, judging by his relationship with both Nina and this huge horse of his, Dillon had a very good character indeed. Even Ada and Leland had been won over by him, not to mention Mrs. Gunter.

Only she seemed unable to get along with him.

But that was not her fault, she told herself. If he weren't so greedy, they might get along very well.

Yet she knew with a feeling of distinct discomfort that if she had not lied about being Frederick's widow, she and Dillon would have had no cause to battle one another so fiercely.

She pushed back a dripping strand of hair and watched him swing up easily to mount the horse. Then with his hands and knees he guided the animal over to her.

"Come up before me," he said, reaching a hand down to her.

She knew she shouldn't. It would be a terrible mistake to sit so close to him. Yet Lacie could not refuse. She was tired and wet and cold, she told herself. Walking in a drenched skirt through muddy fields was just too hard.

Still, when Dillon hoisted her up, then settled her before him, her shiver was not caused by any chill.

"Swing your leg over. You'll be more secure riding astride."

She did as he said without reply, then pressed her lips together when he leaned close and put his arms around her.

"We can round them up and herd them into the field beyond the barn. They should be able to find shelter in the stand of sweet gum."

Lacie only nodded. It was hard enough to ride the rain-slick stallion bareback. It was even more difficult to be settled between Dillon's thighs, his legs pressing against hers, his chest warm against her back and his arms circling her.

With the ease of a born horseman Dillon guided the stallion across the field, looking for the other stray animals. It seemed to take forever, yet only a few minutes passed before they found the remainder of the panicked horses. Besides the one that had stayed with the stallion, there were the two work horses, her favorite mare, and four other riding mounts.

The animals seemed more than willing to stay together, almost as if they knew that someone was here to take care of them. In short order Dillon had them all in the fenced-off field. Only then did he slide down from his horse and reach up to help her dismount.

"There. Are you happy? All of Frederick's horses are safe. Now, can we get out of this damned rain?"

Lacie stared at him. Despite the easing of the storm's fury, the rain still came down in a steady rhythm, clinging to her lashes and dripping from the end of her nose and chin.

"I don't know how to thank you," she said with heartfelt sincerity. "I couldn't have managed."

"There are any number of ways you can thank me, Lacie," he answered quietly. Then at her shocked expression, he grinned faintly. With one finger he caught a drip as it clung to her chin and let it slide down his finger. "I saw no reason to let such fine animals die."

Lacie frowned, disturbed by his first suggestive comment and aggravated by his casual nonchalance as well.

"What if they had been old broken-down plow horses? Are you saying you wouldn't have tried to save them then?"

For a moment he only stared at her. Then he looked over at the smoking, gaping remnants of the barn and shrugged. "Who knows? Besides, that's unimportant. What is important is that we both get into warm, dry clothes."

So saying, he took her arm and steered her toward the house. Once they were on the porch, Lacie pushed her hair back from her forehead and cheeks, then wrung the long length out. She lifted her skirts, trying to shake the water away, but it was futile. Already a huge puddle was gathering at her feet, yet she was still drenched to the bone. It was Dillon who took charge of the situation.

"Go on in the bath house and take that dress off."

"I have to get something else to wear," Lacie argued, moving toward the front door of the house.

"What? And ruin the Tabriz in the hall, or the Bijar runner on the stairs? Why, old Mrs. Allen would turn over in her grave." He grinned cheekily at her and took her arm. "Go on to the bath house, Lacie. I'll find something suitable for you to wear."

"If you think I'm going to let you go through my things—"

"I promise you, I won't be shocked." Then he headed off to the stairs.

"Don't you dare!" she cried in dismay as she headed after him. But her soaked skirts tangled in her legs, and she had to grab the door frame to prevent herself from tripping and falling. She watched in sinking despair as he disappeared up the stairs.

Lacie could not have been more outdone. Who did he think he was, ordering her around! Taking over as if this were his home!

But it *was* his home. She knew it, and he knew it. Lacie shivered as she stared into the gloomy hall, still unlit with either candles or lamps. It *was* his home, but as far as the rest of the world knew, it was legally hers. Besides, that wasn't the question. Whether the house was his or hers, he had no right to enter her room and sift through her clothes. Did he think she had left some incriminating bit of evidence against her claim lying around?

Angrily, she started into the hall, lifting her sodden skirts high before her. But although she tried to inch around the magnificent old Tabriz silk rug, her ruined skirts left a soaking trail. She was at the bottom of the stairs peering doubtfully at the beautiful red wool runner that lined it when Dillon appeared up above.

"I found a lavender dress. And of course, all the necessary undergarments." He raised a hand filled with delicate white cotton garments as he descended the stairs, looking for all the world like some hero bearing the spoils of war. "Here." He offered them to her. "Did I forget anything?"

Lacie was too horrified—and too furious—to respond. Her face was scarlet with humiliation as she grabbed her personal items. But when she turned to flee, the clean pair of pantalets was stretched between their hands, dangling horrible in plain view. In mortification she yanked at them, only to hear a telling rip as the fragile fabric gave.

"Slow down, sweetheart," he murmured softly as he caught the ruined garment in his large hand. "Why don't you just let me help you—"

"No!" Lacie cried, pulling abruptly away from him. "Don't you dare touch my pantalets!"

At her scandalized expression, Dillon began to laugh. "I only meant to carry your clothes for you. But instead —instead I think I'll just carry you."

So saying, and without any warning, he abruptly picked her up.

"Oh!" she gasped. "Put me down at once! Let me go, I say!"

"In good time," he answered in a low, mocking tone. Then he moved across the hall and out the door, carrying her as if she were no heavier than a kitten—and leaving a trail of his wet boot prints and a swish of dripping skirts.

Lacie was lying as still as stone in his arms by the time he stopped before the bath house. It had suddenly occurred to her that everyone else was gone—Ada and Mrs. Gunter and Leland. Even that other man, that Neal Camden. She and Dillon were alone in the house and that knowledge caused her heart to race in the most unseemly manner. She was terrified, she told herself, terrified to think what such a scoundrel as he might do under the circumstances. But there was a part of her that trembled with anticipation. Even now, wet and bedraggled as they both were, his body was warm against hers. His arms were strong, and he smelled faintly of smoke and rain and horses.

In frustration she bit down on her lower lip, determined to kill such terrible traitorous thoughts. Yet when Dillon set her on her feet before the bathhouse door, the loss of his warm touch left her chilled and feeling vaguely empty. In the deep shadows of the porch they stared at one another. Tall and dark, he loomed just before her saying nothing, only watching her with that familiar hooded gaze.

"I—ahh . . . I'll be quite brief so that you . . ." She faltered as unwelcome memories of their other encounter in the bath house besieged her. He had been so threatening that night, so powerful and domineering. She cleared her throat. "I'll be quite brief so that you can also clean yourself up."

Still staring up at him, Lacie reached back with one hand and groped for the doorknob. Then Dillon reached around her and grasped the knob just when she found it. For an eternity he gazed down at her, his hand warm around hers, his body mere inches from her own. Then with an excruciating slowness he bent down to kiss her.

It was the most exquisite of tortures. There was an aching sweetness about the way their lips clung, something tentative and yet very, very right. But beneath that tender touch of his lips to hers, there was a groundswell of other emotions. Tenderness would quickly give way to unreasonable desire. And Lacie knew that what Dillon wanted—what she too wanted in some awful, primitive way—could never, ever be right.

"Please, don't," she murmured, turning her face away.

"Don't what?" he answered, his breath a warm

whisper in her ear. "Don't think about how good you feel in my arms? Don't dream about your sweet kisses?"

"No, no!" Lacie cried in true distress as an incredible warmth welled up from her belly. She tried to twist away from him, but Dillon pulled her hand from the doorknob. Then, with his arm about her waist, he steadily drew her to him. By the time she was pressed intimately against him, she was trembling like a leaf in the wind.

"Lacie, Lacie," he murmured as his hand gently swept her wet hair back from her cheek. "How you have tormented me." Then his lips met hers once more, and her protests died unsaid. It was like being touched by fire. Burned. Consumed. Beneath the seductive move of Dillon's mouth on hers, Lacie could do little more than gasp for breath. His tongue traced the edge of her mouth and she seemed to melt inside. Then it slid between her parted lips and a new inferno flared.

Lacie could not fight the onslaught of feelings that overwhelmed her. Every portion of her body seemed to respond to Dillon's passionate kiss. Where his chest pressed hard against her, she became softer and more malleable. When his tongue licked and probed, teasing her own to meet him partway, she could not hold back.

Then when their tongues did meet, the lightning seemed nothing compared with the flame that leaped between them. He was fire to her ice. Steel to her velvet. Lacie's free hand went up to circle his neck as she opened fully to his kiss. The clothes he'd brought down to her were lost somewhere, fallen and forgotten. Nothing else mattered but this intense longing that gripped her. Dillon had inspired it. Now only he seemed able to slake it.

"My sweet Lacie. My sweet, sweet girl. God, How I have wanted you!"

Lacie heard his words, and she thrilled to what he said. Yet still she tried to ignore the reality they brought with them. He wanted her. He wanted her! And she wanted him. Wasn't that good enough?

Yet she knew it was not enough.

"This is wrong," she whispered against his seeking lips even as she felt herself succumbing to the passion he had aroused in her.

"Nothing this good can be wrong," he answered as he moved his kisses down to her neck in the most sensuous manner. Lacie was faint with desire, aching for more of this madness as the buttons of her blouse gave way to his persistence. She could not rightfully say how they came undone. She only knew that somehow, in the midst of this haze of exquisite passion, he had unfastened them. Now her shoulders and chest were exposed as was the unadorned front of her white muslin chemise. Then he kissed the creamy flesh at the upper swell of her breast.

"Such beautiful, soft skin." He smiled at her with eyes smoky and alive with warmth. "I've wanted to touch you like this since that night I interrupted your bath. Did you know that, Lacie? Have you known all along how much I've wanted you?"

Then without warning he lifted her up, wet clinging skirts and all, and started for the front door.

"What are you doing? Where are we going?" she asked in confusion. Her senses were still spinning, and she could do little more than cling to his neck as he shouldered the screen door open, then crossed the hall to the stairs.

"I'm taking you upstairs—where I should have taken you long ago."

As he mounted the stairs, two at a time, Lacie stared at him in a dawning comprehension. Although she longed for him with an intensity that was truly frightening, she nevertheless knew that in the morning she would regret such a surrender.

"Wait, Dillon. Oh, please wait. We mustn't do this. It's not right—"

"Ah, but it is right. I can't think of anything more right than you and me together. I want it, and so do you."

Up the wide stairs he went, giving her no more than a glimpse behind them of the red carpet, marked now with a dark wet trail. Then they were at the entrance to her suite of rooms—Frederick's suite—and panic set in.

"No. No!" She squirmed within his possessive embrace to no avail. Her hand caught on the carved doorframe as he deftly kicked the paneled door open. "We shouldn't do this, Dillon. We shouldn't!"

"We should, and we will." he vowed hoarsely. Then he looked down at her pale face and seemed to recognize her panic.

"Lacie," he murmured. He lightly put her on her feet but kept her still within his arms. "It's the right time for us, sweetheart. There's no going back."

She shook her head stubbornly. It was not right, she told herself. It could not be more wrong.

Yet the touch of his hands . . . the feel of his strong body pressed against hers . . . There was a rightness there that she recognized innately. Something drew her to him powerfully. Despite all the reasons that such feelings between them were impossible—and that such an act was unthinkable!—she nonetheless desired it with a fierceness she could scarcely comprehend. When he maneuvered them into the room, she did not protest. When he closed the door behind them, she voiced none of her fears. She only pulled away from his embrace and moved hesitantly into the room.

The high-ceilinged sitting room was dim, for the meager afternoon light was further restricted by the deeply covered gallery. The sound of the steady drizzle seemed to muffle everything else, and Lacie felt as if they had somehow stepped into a place quite apart from the rest of the world. Then she felt Dillon's hands on her shoulders and his warm breath against her cold skin as he came up behind her.

He did not speak but his hands were more than eloquent as he deftly untied her skirt and then, when it fell in a sodden heap on the floor, circled her waist with his arms and drew her back against him.

"You shouldn't be here," she murmured even as a thrill of desire surged up from her belly.

"You want me here," he countered.

"But we're not married."

"No." He turned her around to face him, then smoothly drew her blouse off her shoulders and down her arms.

No. He didn't deny that they weren't married. Nor did he suggest that they could be, Lacie thought hollowly. But then, she'd known all along that marriage would never be a part of his plans. Still, the pain of his rejection struck cruelly at her vulnerable heart.

One last time she tried to pull away, averting her eyes to hide her feelings from him. But Dillon would have none of it. He only gripped her more firmly, then tilted her face up to his.

"It's too late for objections, Lacie. You knew it would come to this. You knew when you lied to me about Frederick. You knew when you refused my offer that first night." His eyes were dark as he stared at her and she was unable to tear her gaze away. But it was not anger that drove him, and even as she stared up at him, his eyes grew warmer and his voice became lower. "You've known it every time we've touched."

Then she had no further chance to protest. Like a man unable to hold back even one more moment, Dillon took her lips in a violent kiss. It was harsh and forceful. It was passionate and thrilling. It was at once both demanding and beguiling, and it touched the most primitive part of her.

In helpless abandon she melted against him, somehow triumphant in spite of his domination. Perhaps even because of it. As Dillon's mouth moved sensuously against hers, as his tongue seduced hers and lured her into complete acceptance of him, Lacie gloried in every portion of her feminine being. His kiss—indeed, his embrace—was one of pure possession. She was his now, in every way imaginable. She could not protest because he would not allow it. And yet her very submission seemed to empower her with a new strength, a power she'd never suspected she might have.

Recklessly she clung to Dillon, drawing him to her, accepting his kiss and returning it with impetuous passion. This could not be her, one remnant thought whispered. Yet it was her. For once it was truly her, she realized. Not Miss Lacie, the teacher. Or even just Lacie, the good little girl. And it certainly was not Lacie

Kimbell, the woman who had been living such a terrible lie these last weeks. It was another her, buried, yet nonetheless real. She could not help but rejoice in the knowledge.

Dillon's movements were brusque and swift, yet he was not rough with her. In one motion he drew her to the wide méridienne lounge. Then he eased her down upon its velvet surface, his lips still linked passionately to hers.

Lacie was unmindful of her wet hair tangled beneath her. Nor was she even aware of her scanty attire as Dillon's weight pressed her back into the rich burgundy velvet. She only knew that she wanted him in some primal way, and that no one before—or after—could ever affect her so.

Her arms were wrapped tightly about his neck and shoulders. His thigh rested between her legs and a new warmth was building deep inside her. She wanted to get closer even as she feared she never, ever could get close enough. When Dillon pulled away, then propped himself on one arm above her, she moaned softly in dismay.

"My God. My God, Lacie," he murmured hoarsely as his eyes roamed her flushed features. For once her eyes did not fall away from his direct gaze and for an endless moment they stared at each other. Then his hand smoothed down her cheek to her neck, and then slowly, slowly down her chest to cup her breast.

In an instant every part of her tightened in anticipation. It was as if by his merest touch he commanded all her emotions, and her breath came quicker and quicker.

His hand was warm and gentle around her sensitive

breast as he stared into her eyes. Then his thumb moved lightly across her aching nipple, and she closed her eyes against the exquisite pleasure.

"Dillon . . ." Her cry came weak and helpless as his thumb continued its sensuous torture.

"Finally I see you stripped of all pretense," he whispered huskily. "Finally you're being honest with me."

Then he pulled his hand away and Lacie groaned with the loss. But it was not his intent to leave her for long. With an economy of movement he stripped off his ruined shirt, removed his boots, then peeled down his trousers.

A quiver of desire shook Lacie as he removed his last garment, and she closed her eyes once more to hide the emotions she knew he could see. She wanted him. She was no longer able to deny it.

Then she felt him over her and her eyes flew open. "This must come off," he whispered as he began to untie the laces of her chemise. Like a new form of torture he opened her chemise bit by bit, his fingertips grazing her oversensitive skin in a deliciously random caress, until he had bared her breasts to his view.

Lacie could scarcely breathe, she was so overcome with tumultuous feelings. Her longing for him was raised to a fever pitch, yet she could not help but squirm in extreme humiliation that he could see her so.

But he was only beginning. His own breath was coming faster as his hand moved to rest on her smooth stomach. "Now these," he murmured as he unfastened the tapes that held her pantalets on. Instinctively Lacie tried to tighten her thighs together. But Dillon's knee prevented her, and to her complete mortification he pulled her pantalets apart and slid each side off her legs.

Then there was no hiding from him. Fear fought with desire for dominance. Like a leaf tossed in violent winds, Lacie's emotions twisted and turned as Dillon's eyes swept her pale, trembling body. Yet it was hardly the body she was familiar with, for never had such feelings been evoked in her. Her nipples stood out, dark rose and rigid, aching for his touch. In her belly a fire burned, curling and knotting inside her until she was sure she must burst.

When he placed his hand firmly over her lower belly, she softly cried out with ecstasy.

"Ah, my beautiful, beautiful girl," he murmured in a low triumphant voice.

Then he lay down upon her and caught her mouth in a kiss of desperate fervor. In wild abandon Lacie rose up to meet him. Breast to breast, belly to belly. Their lips clung together in mindless passion. She opened completely to his devouring kiss, holding nothing back from him. When his lips moved down to her breasts her head tossed back and forth on the méridienne's curved headrest. In wicked nibbling kisses and exquisite, swirling tugs he teased her nipples to aching erectness, bringing her arching off the plush velvet upholstery. She was gasping for breath and crying, lost entirely to the world he created for them.

Then she felt his hand move down past her belly to the burning center of her desire. When he slid his finger between her thighs, she tensed in sudden fear. Yet with his first touch upon her most private woman's place, she lost the will to resist. In slow sweet strokes he raised her higher and higher. When she cried out in mindless ecstasy he kissed her lips. Only when she was weak and helpless and slick with sweat did he nudge her legs apart a little wider.

Then he was over her, his eyes direct upon hers, glowing with emerald fire despite the shadows in the room.

"It's now, Lacie. It's right."

She felt the thick heated length of him pressed boldly against her body. Then he slowly raised his hips. For a moment she felt him, huge and erect, probing the entrance to her feminine being. Then with a slow steady pressure, he came into her.

Her eyes widened in surprise, as did his own. Then with a muffled oath he pressed farther until he was completely buried within her.

Lacie's quick cry of pain was smothered by his kiss. The tears that sprang to her eyes were wiped away by his thumbs. She tried to swallow a sob and pushed at his shoulders, but he would not budge. He only remained large and intrusive within her, a shocking interruption to the glorious arousal she had been feeling.

"I've been a fool."

Lacie heard Dillon's low muttered words, but they did not register for she was much too distraught. Her eyes were tightly closed, and her head turned sharply to the side as she vainly sought to hide from him. The pain of his entry was as nothing compared to the pain of this complete humiliation. She had been lulled into complacency—indeed, swept away by his seductive manner. She'd known all along she would regret trusting him in any way, but she'd never expected this.

Lacie fought to hide the tears gathering and stinging behind her eyelids. But as he always did, Dillon seemed to know her very thoughts.

"Don't pull back from me now, Lacie. I didn't know . . . ah, damn. I should have suspected you were a virgin." Then she felt his lips against her neck, moving slowly in heated kisses.

"Leave me alone!" she cried brokenly.

"Never."

"Haven't you done enough?"

"I haven't even begun, sweetheart."

At that decisive pronouncement her eyes flew open in alarm. But before she could formulate a reply, his mouth caught hers in a surprising kiss. Her stomach tightened again at the warm pervasive feel of his lips moving upon hers. It was a wicked pleasure, yet it had a new bittersweet quality, and Lacie could not resist it. As he once again raised her to forbidden heights of enjoyment, the pain and humiliation of his entry began to recede.

His tongue stole into her mouth, then pulled away, then entered again, only bolder and more beguiling. Then once more, and again. In a teasing, seductive rhythm he drew her higher and higher until she was soaring with excitement.

It was only then that he began to move within her. At first she was hardly aware of it, so caught up was she in his devouring kiss. But then she felt him, rubbing hard and hot inside her, sending new tremors through her that met and overpowered all the others.

Lacie could hardly contain herself. Surely he was a devil to bewitch her so. Her entire body—her entire being—was aching only for him. Like a fire she raced out of control, arching now with him, wrapping her arms desperately about him, and even her legs.

Wild and reckless, she succumbed to him, taking everything he gave in complete ecstasy. Harder and faster he moved, thrusting deep within her until it seemed they were no longer separate but were joined in body and will.

Then it began, and she cried out in helpless surrender. Like a live thing, no longer a part of her at all, the very center of her being tensed, then exploded violently. Wave after wave, one hot pulsing rush after another swept through her until she was faint and weak, slick with sweat and gasping for breath.

At once Dillon's pace increased to a furious tempo, raising them both off the now-damp velvet méridienne. On and on he pressed, until he suddenly tensed and with a huge burst of energy found his own release.

Lacie clung to him still, her hands sliding upon his damp shoulders as he slowed his pace. He too was gasping for breath. His entire body trembled from his massive effort. Then he slowly rolled a little to the side, drawing her with him. Her hair was caught beneath his head as he turned to look at her and his legs remained entwined with hers.

Lacie was too stunned by what had just happened between them to raise her customary reserve. Her eyes were hazy with lingering desire as she stared at him in amazement.

For his part, Dillon seemed well content. His eyes were warm as she'd never seen them. His face was relaxed and a contented smile faintly curved his lips.

"Lacie, Lacie," he murmured softly as he reached to smooth one dark strand of hair from her rose-flushed cheek. His touch was so tender, his smile so natural and unguarded, that Lacie closed her eyes against it. It was all too right, too perfect. Something—even if only her ever-present doubts—something was certain to spoil this moment. After all, she was nothing more to him than an obstacle he must surmount, a challenge to be overcome.

And now he had overcome.

With her eyes tightly closed and her face turned away from him, she sought futilely to shut out what must surely come. Even as her body hummed with the sweet lingering aftereffects of their lovemaking, her mind braced itself against the coming rejection.

Yet when his lips moved lightly upon her brow and he stretched languorously against her, fitting her comfortingly to him, she was caught off guard. His warmth was her warmth. Their sweat was mingled as she slid slightly against him and his musky male scent seemed to surround her.

Did *her* scent surround *him?* she wondered for a weak and wishful moment.

Then his arm slid beneath her. As if she weighed less than nothing, he pulled her onto his lap and swung himself into a sitting position.

"What—what are you doing?" she asked in a voice too soft and shaky to be her own.

"As much as I have enjoyed the méridienne," he answered, "I believe we'll both find the bed more comfortable." Then he grinned at her round-eyed expression.

She had no time to object before he dragged back the maroon paisley bedcover and placed her squarely in the center of the wide half-tester mahogany bed. He paused then and let his eyes slide slowly over her pale and naked body. A wave of painful self-consciousness washed over her, and Lacie hastily reached for the protection of the bedcover. But Dillon quickly stopped her with one knee upon the rumpled cover.

"Don't hide yourself." His hands caught hers and brought them down to her side. "You've been hiding yourself from me all along. But now you can see how much better things are when we're honest."

Their eyes held for a long trembling moment, and although the silence seemed almost tangible, filling in the spaces around them, there was nonetheless a clear and vivid communication between them. It was unspoken, and yet it increased her heart's pace and made her breath come quicker. When she could bear the exquisite suspense no longer, Lacie broke the quiet in the room.

"Will we . . . are we to be—to be 'honest' with each other once more?"

A distinct grin lit Dillon's darkly handsome face then, and he moved onto the bed, letting his magnificent naked body slide over her.

"Oh, yes. We most certainly will."

13

Lacie was warm. Even in her sleep-drugged state she was aware that her skin was already damp in the early morning humidity. Reluctant to awaken, she stretched beneath the linen sheets, feeling positively catlike as she arched in drowsy contentment. But in spite of her groggy state, she was intensely aware of every place the sheets slid against her skin. Like a smooth fluid caress the soft fabric both soothed and aroused her bare, sensitive flesh.

At once her eyes flew open.

She was naked beneath the sheets. Neither nightgown nor chemise and drawers covered her!

Then she remembered, and with a low moan of dismay every minute detail of what she'd done came rushing back.

Dillon . . . and her.

She rolled over and buried her head beneath the sheet as she recalled every intimacy they'd shared. He'd held her. He'd kissed her in ways she could hardly believe real now. And he'd come to her in all his masculine glory. As a man comes to his woman. As a husband comes to his wife.

Oh, what could she have been thinking? How could she have given in to him?

But how could she have resisted? she wondered. How could she have stilled the wondrous panic that only he raised in her? Even now the thought of lying so with him caused her nipples to tighten in anticipation, and an unbidden wave of heat to rise from her belly.

If only it had meant as much to him as it had meant to her! she thought wistfully. If only it had meant more than a casual conquest. Or another business triumph. She sighed and pushed a tangled strand of hair back from her cheek. Then she heard a noise from the adjoining room, and she froze.

The door opened with a faint creak, followed by the light sound of bare feet on the wooden floor. Like a mouse numbed by the cat's approach, Lacie lay still as stone before Dillon's steady approach. But when the mattress sagged beneath his weight, she cringed and pulled the sheet tight beneath her chin.

"What are you doing?" Her voice was shaky as she shrank back to the far side of the bed.

"So you're up." Dillon sat on the side of the bed and stared at her with a well-pleased smile on his face. He was not dressed, naked save for the meager protection of a towel he'd wrapped about his hips. Yet he was clearly not the least bit discomfited by appearing thus. She, by contrast, was humiliated beyond description. Her cheeks were scarlet and she was suddenly breathless. In vain she tried to look away from him, not wanting to see the wide expanse of his chest or note the smooth tan that colored his skin. Seeing him so made her recall just how he'd felt pressed naked against her. Watching a smile curve his mouth brought back memories of his lips on hers. And the look in his sea-green eyes . . .

It was that look that finally forced her gaze away, for it was possessive and knowing, and it confirmed everything that she wanted to blot out.

"Lacie."

At that softly spoken word a shiver of unwelcome longing snaked up her spine, but she sternly—desperately—willed it away. She had been weak and foolish last night, giving him that part of her she should have reserved for a husband. But this morning she would gain control of herself. When she spoke her voice was low and under tight control.

"I think you'd better leave."

"I think I'd rather stay."

Her eyes grew larger as she stared at him. "Why?"

"Why?" His smile turned cheeky then. "Why? Because I like you naked better than dressed. Because I plan to continue where we left off."

Lacie's face paled in horror. It was bad enough what had happened last night. But it was morning now and—and—

"You—you can't mean that!"

"Like hell I can't."

At that calm, unaffected response all of Lacie's hard-won aplomb disappeared.

"Get out. Get out! I knew you weren't a gentleman! You're nothing but a cold-hearted—a cold-hearted . . ."

"Bastard?" Dillon supplied the word with only a slightly raised brow. "I see you're back to playing the affronted schoolmarm. But Lacie"—he leaned across the bed and tugged on the sheet she gripped so tightly —"don't you think it's a little late? You know I much prefer you honest."

"A lot you know of honesty! Haven't you just gleefully robbed me of my honesty?" Then she burst into heart-rending tears.

After only a brief hesitation Dillon pulled her into his arms. He was strong and warm as he held her, absorbing the sobs that shook her body. His comfort was the last thing she wanted—he was the very cause of all her woes—yet it was hard to fight the lulling warmth he offered her. In a moment of weakness she yielded to the luxury of being held by him. Despite everything she knew of him, she was reassured by the sweet comfort she found in his embrace.

"Don't cry, Lacie. Come on, now. I swear to God, I didn't realize you were a—that you had never lain with a man before."

But that only made her cry harder.

"Listen to me, sweetheart. It's not the end of the world."

"But it is!" she sobbed. "I'm ruined forever."

She heard his sigh of frustration as she buried her face against his bare chest. Then he firmly took hold of her shoulders and gave her a little shake.

"You're not ruined at all. Besides, no one expects a widow to be a virgin."

His words sobered her at once, and she raised her tear-filled eyes to meet his gaze. Was that what this was all about? she wondered in a new, dawning horror. If she were truly Frederick's widow, she would not have been an untried maiden. Was last night only a way for him to prove once and for all that she was a liar?

A cold wave of dread washed over her as she stared up into his enigmatic eyes. Could any man be so cruel? Could he? She wanted to believe it was impossible, and yet—

"So you've found me out," she whispered very quietly.

His jaw tightened ever so slightly, and he took a long, slow breath. "I found out." His eyes seemed to become opaque. "Now am I going to get an explanation?"

A knife seemed to pierce to the very center of her heart. She could hardly breathe for the crushing pressure in her chest. Still, she knew that unless she could explain her maidenly state after having been married, she could lose the school entirely.

"Frederick . . ." She faltered, then raised her eyes resolutely to him. "Your brother was ill."

When Dillon only stared at her, she hesitated again. For once she was certain she could read his every emotion. He knew she was lying and it only made him angry. But there was no other way for her. She took a breath.

"He was ill, and besides, you've already said he didn't . . . he didn't care for women. Not like other men do." Her cheeks burned with color. "I don't see why my virginity should be so surprising."

"Don't make it any worse than it is," he said in a cold, unemotional voice.

She had tried to steel herself against his doubting stare. But she was not impervious to the pain as his glare turned to disgust, then something akin to disappointment.

No, not disappointment, she told herself. For he'd wanted to prove his claim from the beginning. Now he had.

When she pulled away from him he did not stop her. As she fumbled with the rumpled sheet, trying to wrap herself in it, he only watched her. Lacie could hardly think, her emotions were so destroyed by this new and bitter understanding. He was truly a man without a heart, bent only on his own gratification. And he'd received twofold from her performance last night. She was trembling with hurt and humiliation when she finally struggled to her feet.

"I'd like you to leave now," she managed to say.

"Why?"

At that cruel taunt she glared at him. "Get out!"

"There's no reason we can't establish a new relationship between us, Lacie. I think it's obvious that both of us will enjoy it."

In horror Lacie stared at him. "I will not be a—a—a whore for you!"

"Dammit! Would you stop being so melodramatic? A mistress is a far cry from a whore."

"They're the same thing. They just have different names," she insisted as she backed away from him.

Dillon rose to his feet as well, clearly angered by her furious rejection. "Where in the hell is all this moral rectitude coming from? You're the same little liar—and thief—that has been trying to steal my property from me. Now you're balking at an honest offer to keep you well clothed, well housed, and well fed, all in exchange for a little honest affection!"

"I—I am not a whore," she maintained, but in a decidedly weaker tone. He had her dead to rights, she realized. He had no reason to think any better of her. But that did not ease the anguish that enveloped her.

"Listen, Lacie," he said more calmly as he followed her step by step across the room. "I know you're not—" He exhaled noisily. "I know you have your morals. And believe it or not, I have mine too."

"Does that include ruining this school? Robbing all of us of our livelihoods just because you want this house? Why don't you just admit that you don't really want this school? It's just a financial drain and even the property isn't that valuable. You only want it because it was Frederick's—and your father's!"

Her words stopped him cold, as if she'd finally struck a nerve. For an endless moment he simply stared at her, his eyes narrowed to slits beneath his lowered brows. Then he spoke and his voice was icy with anger.

"My reasons for wanting this place are none of your concern. Nor are they in question here. It's your motives that are under scrutiny. I think it's clear that you are the one motivated by greed. You saw a good thing, and when Frederick died, you decided to claim it."

"Yes, I claimed it. But not for greed. I'm a teacher! Frederick loved this school and so do I. Even though it's losing money, I want to preserve it."

"Even now you're still lying! Dammit, woman! I would respect you a hell of a lot more if you'd just be honest! You may want this school, but that's just the tip of the iceberg. When you claimed to have married Frederick, it wasn't to get this house, this land, or even this stupid charm school. Hell! If I'd believed it was only that, I would have given it to you gladly! No"—he shook his head all the while keeping his angry, glittering stare on her—"you wanted it all and there was no way I was going to let you have it. I offered you a way out. A compromise. But you refused." His eyes ran boldly over her, and one of his brows lifted arrogantly—insultingly. "I recommend you give it further consideration."

Lacie was so outraged by his effrontery and by his vulgar appraisal that she was momentarily speechless. Her mind struggled to find the right words, the most cutting and cruel response possible. But before she could respond he took a long, slow breath.

"You're on shaky ground, Lacie. So think twice before you find yourself with nothing and with noplace to go." Then he turned away from her, and without any concern for his completely inappropriate attire, quit the room.

In the still, oppressive aftermath, Lacie trembled in absolute fury. With no outlet for her consuming anger she could only stand where she was, shaking uncontrollably as she held the linen sheet up to her neck.

He was the most horrible man in the entire world! A villain with no limits to his cruelty! He'd used her in the most unfeeling manner. He'd taken her virginity and broken her heart, and all because he wanted Sparrow Hill. Now that he'd proven her a liar he was going to take over the school, and all of her efforts would be for naught.

Like a wooden puppet, numbed by shock, she moved slowly to the méridienne to sit down. But then she jerked back from the velvet-covered piece. Too vividly, everything they'd done on that wide upholstered burgundy seat played back in her mind. The way he'd held her. The way he'd kissed her and touched her. Unbidden, a tingle warmed her body, and she abruptly turned away from the solid chaise longue.

He'd planned it all, every whisper, every touch, just to get his way. And she'd been foolish enough to give in.

Tears stung the backs of her eyelids as she thought of how easily he'd duped her. With his easy smile and smooth lines, he had lured her in, much as a fisherman might pull in an exhausted fish. Oh, he was too evil to believe. Why, she'd even been idiotic enough to think he might be relenting just because he'd not said anything to anyone in Kimbell about Frederick's unnatural leanings. She should have known better.

If he hadn't said anything about Frederick it was because he was afraid no one would believe him. Now, however, he had something new and better to reveal. After all, gossip about the living was always more appealing than gossip about the dead.

Lacie sat down on the bed and drew her feet up beside her. What would he say? What would he tell his lawyer to do?

A tear slid down one cheek but she angrily brushed it aside. Whatever he said she would deny, she decided. Then her bowed back straightened a little. How could he prove she was an untried virgin? It would only be his word against hers. In fact—she stood up and nervously began to pace—in fact, he had no more proof about her than he'd had about Frederick. It was all just so many threats. As long as she stood her ground, he was no better off than he'd been before.

Except that he'd taken something from her that she could never have back again.

Lacie wrapped her arms about herself, shivering a little despite the warm morning. She'd been a fool. She'd gambled and lost. But not entirely. If she could just be strong she might still win Sparrow Hill. He expected her to fold, to cave in. But she would deny everything. She tried not to think about how adept she'd become at lying. It just couldn't be helped.

But what if he still ruined her reputation? What if no one would send their daughters to Sparrow Hill after he slandered her?

Lacie sighed. She might still lose the school, but not without a fight.

Determined to fight him, she moved to the walnut highboy she had taken over and found a clean chemise and a pair of plain linen drawers. As she dropped the sheet, however, she saw bloodstains on it, and she stiffened. Yes, the evidence was there, but she'd quickly cleanse it away. Then she'd fight him more fiercely than ever. He thought Sparrow Hill was a foolish venture, a money-losing "charm school"? Well, she'd show him, she vowed as she recalled his cruel and biting words. He'd even had the nerve to say that if he had believed her—if!—he'd have given her the school.

Suddenly, in the midst of tying on her drawers, Lacie paused. He would have given her the school if he'd believed her? That made no sense at all, for wasn't it Sparrow Hill that he was fighting her for? And then he'd said it was only the tip of the iceberg.

For a moment she frowned, pondering his confusing words. Then, in a mind-boggling rush, the terrible truth became clear. She could do nothing but stand there, her mouth opened in a little circle, her eyes staring but not really seeing. He hadn't wanted Sparrow Hill at all. He probably *would* have given it to her, she realized with a mixture of horror and awe as the reality of the situation struck home. Frederick had supplemented the school's income from other sources—she knew that after going over the school's financial records. But only now did she see that it was those other sources that Dillon really wanted.

The tip of the iceberg. Once more his words reeled through her mind. Frederick must have been far richer than she'd known. Far, far richer, indeed.

Lacie finished dressing almost mechanically. Stockings, corset, chemise, petticoat, skirt, and matching bodice. Her mind was spinning with too many thoughts to even notice her clothes. Only when she glanced perfunctorily at herself in Frederick's triple tailor's mirror did she realize she'd forgotten to don mourning clothes. Still, what did that matter? she decided cynically. The truth was out—at least between her and Dillon. He knew she'd lied. And now she knew that he had lied too.

She lifted her chin a notch and stared boldly at her reflection. What she saw brought her both satisfaction and pain. She'd always loved this dress, for the striped tone-on-tone teal-blue cambric flattered her eyes well. And the snug-fitting pointed-basque waist gave her a decidedly shapely appearance. Yet despite that, Lacie was hardly pleased.

Anyone would surely be able to tell, simply by looking at her, that she was no longer intact. Why, it was obvious, she thought as she drew nearer the mirror. The color in her face was too high. Her lips were a deep rose color, full and tender looking. Even her eyes . . .

She let out a soft cry of despair and turned away from the heartless mirror. This was something that would never go away. She could never be an honest woman, or go to a husband unsullied.

But then, there was no man she wanted to marry. Except perhaps the very one who'd ruined her.

"No!" Her sharp denial restored her anger and buried her weak and self-pitying thoughts. She could not change what had happened, but she could make him very sorry he'd ever decided to play his hateful game with her. Vindictiveness was a sin, she knew. But she could not feel otherwise.

She took up her hairbrush and attacked her tangled hair with a vengeance. She would call his bluff, she thought spitefully. She would dare him to prove she wasn't Frederick's widow and taunt him with the fact that he could not prove either of his accusations, neither about Frederick nor about herself.

Impatient to confront him, she abandoned her unruly hair and only tied it back from her face with a black grosgrain ribbon. Then she found her shoes and hurried toward the door.

But once she opened it, Lacie was gripped with a crippling fear. She could not face him yet. She simply could not!

In anguish she closed the door, then leaned miserably against it. It was easy to be brave and angry and self-righteous when alone in her room. But could she face him? Could she face that mocking, knowing look and still maintain her control? Could she stare into his vivid green eyes and bury her pain—and any weakness she still felt for him—beneath a cool and composed facade?

She bit her lips in consternation trying to muster her courage. Then she saw his shirt lying in the corner— gray, ruined, forgotten in their passion last night. He'd risked his life in that shirt. He'd saved the horses and his friend.

But he'd turned around and destroyed her.

It was then that the tears came, cruel and hard, in hot burning sobs. She shook with pain and disappointment and a hollowness that seemed to consume her. He'd deceived her and led her on when all he had wanted was another weapon to use against her. It shouldn't matter, she tried to tell herself as her bowed head leaned against the closed door. It shouldn't matter because he meant nothing to her. Nothing at all.

But that was not true. No matter how much she might deny her feelings for him, her heart nonetheless ached cruelly. She was empty and drained inside, a hollow shell that once had hoped for fulfillment. Now it would never be.

Only half of the barn remained. The back wall and part of one side, plus most of the roof, had collapsed before the rains had extinguished the flames. Now it was a gray scorched wasteland, a pile of splintered timbers framed within the stark, roofless walls. Lacie gripped the gallery rail as she stared toward the barn. The fire had finally been defeated, but at what a cost! She was not sure it could even be repaired. It might be better simply to tear it down and rebuild it anew.

A bitter smile lifted her lips. Perhaps she should take her lesson from the barn, for she'd been burned herself last night. Even now she was still uncertain whether she should continue on with what she had, or let it all go and begin again. She could just leave. After all, she was a good teacher. She could always find another school to teach in. Perhaps she was being a fool, taking on responsibility for everyone else. Who was she to think she could manage a school by herself? And now she knew there was more than simply the school involved.

Lacie pressed her palms to her cheeks as she struggled against her doubts. She would be stealing much more than just the school from Dillon. Much more.

But he didn't deserve Frederick's inheritance either. At least she would use Frederick's wealth to keep his school going. Frederick would have approved. She was sure of it.

Still, no matter how she rationalized it, Lacie could not escape her terrible feelings of doubt. More than anything she dreaded facing Dillon again. But there was no way she could avoid it.

For a long while she stood on the gallery, watching the play of sunlight on the grounds as the clouds moved across the sky, but not really seeing anything. It wasn't until a carriage turned up the long drive that she roused. Then when she recognized the school's brett, she hurried down to greet it.

Dillon was already outside when she arrived, but she determinedly avoided his dark searching stare. It was cowardice, but she had no alternative. When Leland pulled up and Ada anxiously peered out at her, she knew an enormous relief.

"Oh, Lacie! Are you all right?" Ada cried after Dillon had handed her down.

"I'm quite well," Lacie murmured, hugging her friend a little too tightly. "Better than ever," she vowed as she managed a smile.

"I was so worried about you. But Leland said the horses couldn't take that muddy road again without a rest. We left as soon as we could this morning."

"How is your patient?" Lacie asked, watching cautiously as Dillon climbed into the brett.

"Oh, Neal will be fine, thank God. He insisted on returning with us despite what Dr. Cromwell said." Ada's face softened as she watched Neal alight with Dillon's help while Mrs. Gunter bustled about scolding her obstinate patient in German. Neal had one arm in a sling and a stark white bandage around his head. But despite his pallor and obvious weakness, he had a smile on his face.

"It's not my leg. I can walk, you know."

"*Ach!* Such a hard head! You think you know everything. Better than the doctor. Better than me!"

Unable to help herself, Ada quickly crossed to Neal's side. When Dillon stepped back she filled the void at once, holding Neal about the waist as he leaned on her, helping him up the steps. Mrs. Gunter flapped around them like a mother hen, leaving Lacie and Dillon to bring up the rear. On the surface, it was a very pleasant homecoming scene. Yet Lacie was acutely aware of Dillon's presence. Although she did not look at him, she sensed his nearness.

It was time, she told herself. Time to end this. Time to call his bluff. If she didn't do it now, she might never get up the nerve again.

On the gallery she cleared her throat. "I'd like to speak to you, Dillon." She did not look at him. "I'd like Neal to stay as well," she added, meeting Ada's curious glance.

Perhaps it was her odd tone, or maybe everyone could sense—as she'd feared—what had happened. Whatever it was, little surprise was expressed at her words. Ada gave her an anxious look and helped Neal to one of the painted white rockers, then stood a little nervously beside him. Dillon perched nonchalantly at the gallery rail, one leg hitched up, his arms folded across his chest expectantly. Mrs. Gunter looked from him to Lacie—hopefully at first, but then her expression fell. She turned and went into the house, muttering in distress about coffee and tea, biscuits and cookies.

In her absence, the quiet on the porch grew oppressive. Lacie stood at the top of the steps, her hands knotted and hidden in the folds of her skirt.

"I know this is perhaps a difficult time for this discussion," she began addressing Neal. "What with your injuries and all. However, what I have to say cannot wait any longer."

"It's all right. I'm happy to listen," he answered, glancing questioningly at Dillon.

"Are you sure you don't want to consider what you're doing, Lacie?"

At Dillon's quietly spoken words Lacie whirled to face him.

"I'm quite sure of what I'm doing," she snapped. "I may have played the fool up to now, but not anymore. I've figured you out."

Dillon did not respond, but his eyes became darker and his very calm seemed almost threatening. Yet she continued on with reckless abandon. "I know it's not just the school. Frederick was far wealthier than he let on, wasn't he? When I married him I stopped you from inheriting far more than just Sparrow Hill."

Neal could not prevent a quick look at Dillon. "So you finally told her." When he received no answer he looked back at Lacie.

"Oh, yes, he told me—in his own fashion." Lacie

fought back the ache in her heart and struggled to look the victor. "Of course, I don't know the entire extent of Frederick's holdings. No doubt you do, however. Since I believe there are laws against depriving a widow of her rights, surely I can expect the cooperation of a respectable lawyer like yourself, Mr. Camden."

At last Dillon reacted. "Widows, yes." He stood up slowly. "But you are hardly Frederick's widow."

Lacie faced his menacing stare with a heart that thundered and knees that shook. This was her moment of truth. She knew she risked her reputation and even Frederick's, but her hurt and anger were too strong to let her back down.

"I *am* his widow," she said in a soft, shaky voice. "I am, and you cannot prove otherwise."

He could *not* prove otherwise, she told herself as the silence stretched taut as a bowstring. He could not. Yet staring at his rigid expression, she was not so sure he wouldn't vent all his suspicions just for spite. She wasn't conscious of holding her breath, yet when his eyes finally turned from her to Neal she took an apprehensive breath. Still, there was an odd look on his face and his voice was too pleasant when he finally responded.

"We are not finished, Lacie. You may continue with your little farce, but in the end—" He gave her a sardonic smile. Then he made an abbreviated bow and unexpectedly quit the porch.

Lacie was stunned by her sudden and apparent victory, despite his parting threat. She could hardly believe her eyes as she watched him walk away. His back was no less straight; his head was no less erect and proud. His stride was even and relaxed, just as it had been that first day when he'd strolled into her life. He was as confident as ever—and as arrogant.

It was that arrogance that took the pleasure out of her triumph, she told herself as she watched him disappear. It was his arrogant threat of repercussions to come. Certainly she felt not the slightest regret to see him go. If she were lucky, she would never have to see him again.

If she were lucky, she thought morosely.

Neal propped himself against a thick-trunked pecan tree as he watched Dillon saddle his horse.

"What did you do to her?"

Dillon gave him a sharp, angry glance. "Nothing any man wouldn't do, given a chance. And when she gave me the chance, I took it." He turned back to the animal and tightened the girth strap.

"Dammit, Dillon! I thought you had more finesse than that. I've never known any woman to leave your bed angry."

"She's not like any other woman."

"Oh?"

At that interested reply Dillon let out a short oath. "She was a virgin," he muttered.

"Aha!" Neal gave his friend a searching look. "That means she was never a wife. May I say that was a very clever—if devious—way to prove your point. However, there's no way to use that proof to your advantage. You've destroyed the evidence."

"Hell's bells! You too?" Dillon whirled on his friend furiously. "I did not take her to bed to prove she wasn't married to Frederick! I already *knew* that. I took her to bed—" He stopped abruptly then ran his hand through his hair in frustration. "What in hell difference does it matter why I did it?"

"I think it would make a big difference to her."

"You don't know her. She doesn't trust me any farther than she can throw me. Especially now. Besides, as she sees it, she holds all the cards. As long as I can't prove she's a fake and she has the benefit of Frederick's estate, she's got no use for me."

"So you're leaving? Giving up, just like that?"

Dillon pulled the stirrup down, then adjusted his saddlebags. "You're the one who's been sending me urgent messages. I thought you wanted me to get back to Denver and back to business."

Neal pursed his lips in disapproval and rubbed his bandaged brow. "It appears you've got unfinished business here as well now." He studied Dillon's grim face. "What are you planning?"

Dillon glanced over at him. "I'm leaving you here to recuperate. Look over the school's situation if you want, but keep your eyes open and don't worry about hurrying back to Denver. I'll take care of things there."

"You're not giving up." It was a confident statement, not a question.

"Not on your life." Dillon took his hat from its perch on a branch and pulled it low over his eyes. Then he mounted his eager stallion. "There are a few leads I need to follow up on. In the meantime, I think I'll just let sweet Lacie stew awhile. But mark my words, she hasn't heard the last of me."

Lacie watched in agitation as Dillon cantered slowly from the orchard. The sun beat down blindingly, sending shimmers across the grass as the wet ground steamed in the June heat. As he rode across the lawn he looked as intimidating as ever. Like some black-garbed devil determined to torture her unceasingly.

Vowing to appear unmoved, Lacie concentrated on the chickens gathering around her. "C'mon, chick. Here you go, chick, chick, chick." She was acutely aware of Dillon when he stopped his horse at the gate to the chicken yard. Yet still she would not look up. She had wanted to hide inside all day. Only pride had forced her to assume her daily tasks. Yet not even pride could make her look up at him.

"I came to say good-bye, Lacie."

She threw the corn around her with a vengeance, trying desperately to ignore the ache in her heart caused by his quietly spoken words. "Good-bye," she muttered.

Just leave, she pleaded silently. Leave before she embarrassed herself by bursting into tears. She heard him shift in his saddle, heard the leather creak and his horse paw twice at the muddy ground. But she did not dare look up at him, for that would be her complete undoing.

"Neal is going to stay until he's well enough to travel. I trust you'll extend him every hospitality. I've left some money to cover his expenses."

At that insolent comment Lacie jerked around to glare at him. But his serious expression stopped her angry retort. Flustered, she immediately looked away.

"You've forgotten your crippled chicken. She's still waiting to be fed."

"I haven't forgotten," she muttered, even as her throat choked up with confusing emotions.

"Well." The leather saddle creaked once more. "I'd like you to let me know if there's a child."

Then, when she only stood there, staring unseeingly at the solitary hen across the soggy chicken yard, he turned his mount and without further comment rode away.

Lacie stood in the chicken yard a long time after the sound of his horse's hoofbeats had faded. The chickens dispersed one by one when it seemed their benefactress had no further corn for them. But she didn't move. She was too overwhelmed with emotion and too drained.

If there's a child. His parting words repeated over and over in her mind. *If there is a child.* It was the last thing she'd expected, a possibility she'd not considered at all. Yet he had.

Why not? He'd probably had lots of experience— perhaps a string of little bastards just like himself.

A tear fell, but she wiped it away. Then another came, and another. Still she stood there, the tears streaming down her face as she mourned her loss.

He was gone. It was what she wanted, she told herself. But that didn't change a thing. He was gone, and although she'd won all that she'd wanted, and more, it still felt as if she'd lost everything.

Everything.

14

Lacie was listening. At least she was trying to. But too much of what Neal was discussing brought unwelcome thoughts of Dillon to mind. Had he already arrived back in Denver? she wondered. He had been gone a week now, although it seemed more like a year. Then again, it seemed to have been only this morning that he had asked her to let him know if there was a child.

Her eyes were unfocused and staring, a clouded gray as she sat there. But her emotions were twisting painfully as once more she relived that last day with Dillon. He had planned it all. He'd plotted to seduce her in order to get the school—and everything else. But she had called his bluff.

Still, she simply could not fathom why he had backed down. If nothing else, he could have ruined her reputation—and therefore the school's—with just his accusations. Why hadn't he pressed on? She couldn't believe it was out of kindness, for she was certain he was incapable of such emotion. No, he must be planning something else. He'd even warned that she had not heard the last of him. . . .

"Do you see how the two are connected?" Neal interrupted her dark musings.

"What? Oh." Lacie tried to concentrate on the subject at hand. "We were speaking of Lockwood Lumber and—and the school?"

Neal gave her an exasperated look. "This is obviously beyond you."

"It is not!" Lacie declared heatedly. "Just because my mind was wandering doesn't mean I can't understand what you're talking about. Would you mind repeating what you said?"

He sighed and pushed a sheet of paper with three columns in front of her.

"This is a list of Frederick's investments. Here are Dillon's. This longer column in the middle is their joint holdings."

Lacie leaned forward and examined the paper. It appeared that Frederick had owned the school, investments in two holding companies, and stock in a mattress factory. Dillon owned Lockwood Mines, Lockwood Lumber, and a construction company. But it was the center list that caught her interest most. There were a wide variety of companies listed: Estes Carriage Works, L and K Transport, L and K Hardware, the Denver Palace Hotel, the Estes Livery, as well as several others. It seemed that Dillon and Frederick had been involved in almost every sort of business that a growing town might need.

Except a school, she thought smugly. The school was all hers.

"Where did Frederick get the money to keep the school going? What are these holding companies? Where is this mattress factory?"

"The mattress factory no longer exists except on the books. It was just east of New Orleans, but it burned down toward the end of the war. All you own is the name and four or five acres of land. The two holding companies are also defunct, good only on paper."

"What happened to them?"

"Financed with worthless Confederate scrip." He shrugged. "None of Frederick's business ventures were viable."

"Then how did he keep the school going?" Lacie asked in renewed concern.

"Dillon." Neal leaned back and scratched at the bandage that still bound his head.

"Dillon!" Lacie sat back in surprise, then quickly grew suspicious. "He wants nothing but to destroy this place! I saw Frederick's letter to him. No, I'll never believe Dillon willingly kept Sparrow Hill going."

"I didn't say willingly. You're right that he thought it a poor investment and wanted Frederick to sell it off. But it was Dillon's other investment choices—these in the center column—bought into jointly by the two of them that provided Frederick with the wherewithal to keep Sparrow Hill going. So you see, he's not quite as bad as you think."

Lacie purposefully ignored that comment. "Then I can continue on just as Frederick did," she said, her interest piqued.

"I suppose."

At his odd inflection Lacie peered over at him. "Is there any reason why I can't?"

Neal met her concerned gaze for a long moment, then pushed his chair back from the table they were sitting at and rose to his feet. She followed his restless pacing silently, waiting for a new bomb to fall.

"Damn," he began, then gave her an embarrassed glance. "Forgive me, but I find myself in a most difficult ethical position. You see, I sympathize completely with your situation, Lacie. Believe it or not, I do. And I like you and this school—".

"And Ada," Lacie supplied shrewdly.

"Ah . . . yes." Color crept into his face. "I like Ada very much. But you have to realize that I am still Dillon's friend."

"Yes. And his lawyer too."

"And his lawyer too," he conceded. "But that doesn't mean I am without professional ethics. As long as you remain legally Frederick's widow, I will deal with you as such."

"Good, because I plan to stay his widow for a long time to come. No matter what your boss may think," she added tartly.

"Yes, that may very well prove true."

"So I will continue, just as Frederick did, to use money from those other companies to finance the school."

It was easy, and it was logical. Neal gave her no reasons why she might not expect it to be so. Yet she felt a nagging doubt. If there was a way to prevent it, Dillon would find it.

But as one week led into another, they heard nothing from Dillon. If Lacie could have kept him out of her thoughts and out of her dreams, she would have described herself as very well content.

Then a wire arrived, and everything turned upside down.

Lacie knew even as she took the message from the young man that something was afoot. Deliveries were seldom made so far from town. Only Dillon had the pull to have it brought out to her.

As she held the envelope she could not prevent her hand from shaking. She looked over at Ada, who was anxiously wringing her hands, then at Neal, who had received a similar envelope. Neal's expression was at once both pained and curious. He knew what Dillon was up to, she realized, or at least he suspected. She wasn't so sure she wanted to know what it was. Still, there was nothing to do but open the envelope and face whatever was to come.

Instead of a message, what he'd sent her read like a shopping list. Company names and big numbers. It made no sense at all. Then at the bottom a short note was added:

"This budget breakdown will be presented to the Board of Directors at the annual meeting August 15. No monies are allotted to bolster those companies not financially solvent. Any budget deficits must be covered through internal means."

She didn't have to understand very much to know what he was doing. In a fury she raised her eyes to Neal. "He's cutting me off, isn't he?"

Neal nodded.

"Can he do that?"

"If the Board of Directors goes along with him." His voice grew more solemn. "They always do."

"I don't understand," Ada said in a worried voice. "Who are these directors? What do they have to do with anything?"

"They represent the stockholders. You see, one of the

reasons Dillon has done so well is that when he started each company he opened it to public investment. He sold stocks. He was already a well-known success in Denver starting with his gold strike in '59, followed by a killing he made in silver. Besides, he has a way of convincing people to go along with him."

He stopped abruptly, embarrassed by the unintended implication, but Lacie waved him on. "Keep going."

"Well, people saw his success and wanted a piece of it. So he sold as much stock as he could to raise capital. But he made sure he kept a controlling share."

"In other words, he owns more than half."

Neal paused and cleared his throat. "I suppose it would be more accurate to say that he and the stockholders friendly to him own more than half."

Lacie was silent a moment. She chewed her lip before turning her perceptive gaze on him.

"Was Frederick a friendly shareholder?"

"Ah, well, I would say so. Yes, he was."

"Well, I won't be!" she vowed, pounding her small fist on the table for emphasis. "If he thinks he can sink this school without any repercussions, he's a fool."

"I don't think you understand, Lacie." Neal scratched at his brow in agitation. "There's not much you can do to stop him. Frederick gave him power of attorney on business matters. Dillon votes Frederick's stocks as he wishes."

"But Frederick is dead. Those votes are mine now!"

"Not at the moment they aren't. Not legally."

Lacie stood up so fast her chair nearly toppled over. Her eyes were glittering with anger as she leveled Neal with a killing stare. "If Frederick gave him this power of attorney, there must be a way to get it back. How do I do it?"

"There's certain papers that have to be prepared."

"Fine. Will you do it? Or shall I hire some other lawyer?"

"I'll do it. I'll do it," he said placatingly. Then his eyes cleared and a slow smile lit his fair features. "There is another way, however. A way to insure that there's no mix-up since there's only four weeks until the Board of Director's meeting."

Lacie looked at him suspiciously. "Go ahead. Tell me."

"If you were to attend the board meeting, you could request power of attorney back again. It would be settled right then and there, in front of everyone. And you would be there to vote precisely as you wish."

It was, of course, the most obvious solution. Yet Lacie was aghast at the idea of having to face Dillon like that. Just considering it made her heart pound and her palms sweat. To have that dark knowing gaze upon her, to be in the same room and breathe the same air—

No, she could not do it.

But as she stared at Neal's expectant face, she wondered if she really had a choice. She needed money if Sparrow Hill was to survive. She hadn't gone through all this misery and guilt and humiliation to lose the school now. Fiddling with legal papers was too chancy. Besides, she had to keep in mind that she was dealing with a most devious person in Dillon Lockwood. If she wanted to keep the school going, she would simply have to go to Denver.

Slowly she sat down, filled now with terrible anxiety.

"The meeting is August fifteenth?" she asked quietly.

"Sometimes it lasts several days."

"And I would have to go to Denver."

"You could stay at the Denver Palace. You own it—at least partially. And for heaven's sake, don't look so frightened, Lacie. If you're going to challenge Dillon at the board meeting, you'd better go in there looking like you've already won, not like a scared little school-marm."

But that's what she was, Lacie was still thinking, not an hour later. She was a very scared—terrified—school-teacher. No matter what she did, she would never convince anyone otherwise. Oh, how had she gotten into this terrible predicament? It was like some medieval maze. For every step forward she took, two new threatening paths opened before her. Neither choice appealed to her. Both promised only further heartache. Yet she could not turn back for the path had already closed behind her.

She stared at her open armoire morosely, depressed anew by the pitiful array before her. Three simple day dresses she used for teaching. Her one good dress—dyed black, of course. Two plain skirts, several white blouses, and her teal dress. Certainly they would impress no one in Denver. Not one of the other board members would take her seriously at all!

"Lacie?" Ada entered when she spied her friend. "Neal told me. Are you really going to Denver?"

"Yes. I fear I must."

"Do you want me to accompany you?"

"I would love it, but I'm not sure we can afford train fare for both of us. Besides"—she sent Ada what she hoped was a reassuring smile—"someone must stay here to manage things. Neal says I might be gone almost three weeks. School will be resuming shortly after that."

"Three weeks?" Ada came to stand beside Lacie. "Then you'll need some new clothes."

"We really can't afford it."

"I don't think you have a choice. Neal told me you'll have to convince all those people to help the school. You'll have to gain their confidence and win them over. You can't do that if you look threadbare and forlorn. You have to appear capable."

"Oh, this is just hopeless!" Lacie wailed in despair.

"No, it's not." With a burst of energy Ada began to yank Lacie's clothes from the armoire, garment by garment. "You can travel in this. And this"—she indicated the black dress and the teal one—"this blouse will do. But not this one. And if you could find a basque waist to go with this skirt, it would do as well." She tossed the three plain dresses aside with a dismissive wave of her hand, then dragged Lacie to stand before Frederick's triple mirror. "You'll need an elegant suit. At least two more day dresses. And an evening dress. Perhaps a coat. Or, no—a cape!"

"We haven't the money." Lacie sighed.

"We can sew."

"We haven't the time," she explained patiently.

"We can try. Between the two of us and Mrs. Gunter —even the maids could help."

"The fabric alone will be dear," Lacie protested despite a little spark of enthusiasm.

"It will be worth it," Ada insisted. "Think of everything you stand to lose."

* * *

It will be worth it. It *will* be worth it, Lacie chanted as she stabbed her needle into the linen inset of the bodice she was working on. Her back ached, her eyes were swimming, and her fingers were beginning to cramp. The entire house had been in an upheaval since Ada had taken on the task of outfitting her for her trip.

Girding her for battle.

For the sake of time they had selected simple elegant styles devoid of excessive—and expensive—ornament, relying more on cunningly placed pleats, artful drapes of fabric, and discreet borders to give style.

Ada had taken on the hardest task. The suit she was making was of gray chambray with simple lines that befitted a young widow. However, the snug-fitting polonaise fell below the waist in deep, pointed scallops, trailing even longer in the back. She was edging the scallops as well as the cuffs with a band of midnight purple braid. All in all, it was turning out most beautifully. The dress Lacie was making, however, was less certain. It was of dark blue percale, the skirt box-pleated with a draped apron effect in the front. The bodice was close-fitting, and except for the overlapping inset she was working on now, it was not really a very difficult job. But stitching had never been her strong suit. She found it too boring. Still, she struggled on, reminding herself how much was at stake.

Mrs. Gunter was making her a gored basque with vest points to go with her dark red skirt. The basque was in a similar fabric but in a small red and black stripe. It promised to be a very handsome costume.

She'd bought two plain straw bonnets that they would dress with ribbons and remnants of fabric. But the worst was yet to come. Despite her opposition, Ada had insisted on getting a generous dress length of black figured sateen. It had been so dear that Lacie could not justify the expense. But Ada had refused to relent.

"You will be among wealthy, elegant people. You will no doubt be invited to dine and you must look your best."

"I doubt that rough-and-tumble town will have anyone of any breeding in it," Lacie retorted. "Besides, I can have dinner in the gray suit. Or in my teal dress."

"What if there's a reception? What would you do then?"

Lacie had no answer to that.

As the dress took shape, Lacie grew thankful for Ada's obstinance. The black sateen dress spoke of elegance and sophistication, of woman at the height of her feminine power. It was not a provocative dress with bare shoulders and bosom on display—that would have been most inappropriate for a widow. And yet as she stood for the fitting, staring at three different reflections of herself in the tailor's mirror, Lacie thought she'd never looked so womanly. Her waist appeared impossibly narrow, thanks to the multiple-gored bodice. Framed by the small set-back collar and open neckline, her skin looked as pale as ivory, delicate as eggshell. The sleeves were long and slim. The skirt was full, yet fell in softly moving folds. The figured black sateen was its own ornament, needing no more than simple ear bobs, her wedding ring, and an artfully arranged coiffure to be complete.

Here was her armor, she thought with a glimmer of hope. Dillon would not dismiss her in this dress. But perhaps—just perhaps—she would finally be able to dismiss him.

The day of her departure, she was not so sure. Every fear, every terrified imagining she'd had of meeting Dillon again filled her head, sweating her palms and knotting her stomach.

"I keep thinking of Daniel entering the lions' den," she confessed as she watched her small trunk being put aboard the train car. She gripped the carpetbag she had borrowed from Ada more tightly.

"Daniel was unharmed by the lions, as you may recall." But Lacie could tell that Ada was nearly as nervous as she was.

She hesitated at the cast-iron steps. The conductor stood patiently at the top of the rear deck, waiting for her to ascend. Neal stood beside her, his hand partly extended to help her up. For long seconds she stood there, caught halfway between going and staying, between anticipation and despair. She looked over at Ada and gave her a hopeful smile. Then she took Neal's hand and resolutely stepped up onto the railroad car.

There was no going back. She had picked her path, and now she must follow it to its end.

Ada and Neal watched from the wooden plank walkway as the train slowly picked up speed, then disappeared around a grove of birch trees.

"It's either peace or war now," Neal murmured. He patted the hand that Ada had slipped into the crook of his arm.

"I don't know if it was such a good idea to let her go all that way alone. Are you sure he won't do anything . . . ?" Ada trailed off, not sure what it was she feared Dillon might do to Lacie, but worried nonetheless.

"He wanted her to come. That means something."

"Is that what he said in the wire he sent you?"

Neal smiled down at Ada's worried face. "He didn't have to say it. He knew she would react to the threat in his wire as a bull reacts to a red flag. He dared her to come to Denver, and she promptly took up his dare."

"But you said it's either peace or war. Suppose it's war? What will happen to Lacie then?"

"It will only become a war if she doesn't give in to him easily."

"But Neal, that's precisely why she's going—to fight him. She wants to save the school, and she'll never give up."

His smile grew warmer then, and with one finger he touched the end of her nose. "Don't you worry about Lacie and Dillon. I've known him a long, long time. As far as I'm concerned, I've never seen two people better suited for each other. Except, of course, for us."

Then at her becoming blush he laughed out loud. "Come along, Miss Pierce. I'm going to buy you lunch and try very hard to make you forget about everything but me."

15

Despite her dread of reaching her destination, by the time the train finally pulled into Denver Lacie could not imagine a more welcome sight. She had left Kimbell only five days before, and yet she felt she had been traveling for years. From one railroad line to another, she'd switched. At Shreveport. In Dallas. In Red River City and again in Junction City. The names were all so similar that in her exhaustion they jumbled up so that she couldn't remember which was which. The New Orleans Mississippi and Texas Railroad—that was the one through Kimbell. But the others! The Texas Pacific Railroad. The Texas Central Railroad. The Missouri Kansas Texas Railroad, and now the Kansas Pacific.

One line was very like another, she thought as she peered bleary-eyed at the early morning landscape. The cars were all noisy and crowded. No matter how well upholstered the seats, after a few hours of sitting her posterior would be numb. And the spittoons! Such a disgusting feature in a public conveyance! Fortunately, with the hot weather the windows were kept open, and those who felt compelled to spit could do so discreetly.

The only commendable thing about her journey had been the spectacular views. From gently rolling hills, green with forests, to the vast open prairies, undulating so strangely in the wind, and now to the bluffs and foothills leading to the mountains of the Colorado Territory, it had all held her enthralled. She had seen huge herds of buffalo, the strange-looking long-horned cattle about which she'd often read, and myriads of odd little prairie dogs from her moving window, as well as hawks and foxes and coyotes.

Even the last night, the only one she had actually slept on the train, she had sat up in her Pullman booth and looked out over the moonlit plains, marveling at the strange beauty of it. It was stark compared with Louisiana but no less captivating. She had fallen asleep as the train had moved steadily through the wide empty plains. She had awakened to hills that rose slowly toward the distant mountains. Now, as they continued steadily west, winding their way past higher and higher hills and an occasional sharp bluff, she was dressed and packed, as ready as was possible for her upcoming confrontation.

When the train finally eased into the station in Denver, the sun shone brilliantly on snow-capped mountains and dusty streets; on leafy elms and the grassy plains that surrounded the town.

As she peered warily from the open window, Lacie saw a town quite unlike what she had expected. She had pictured a ramshackle collection of half-hearted buildings, perhaps the sod buildings she'd heard of or some otherwise equally inadequate structures. The streets would slant sharply; swift-flowing creeks would threaten on every side. After all, wasn't this the town that had been burned down and then washed away, peopled with the the most unreliable sorts?

What faced her, however, was a solid town of neat buildings. Although the mountains were clearly visible, Denver itself was situated in a fairly flat valley. And the river! The South Platte was little more than a wide sluggish stream. Its tributary, the Cherry, was a pale comparison to her own Brush Bayou. All in all, she found the town completely unlike any of her preconceptions.

Still, she knew its citizens were none too savory. Dillon Lockwood was proof of that. Determined to stay on her guard, she joined the other passengers in the push to disembark.

Once she stepped down from the train, Lacie straightened her back wearily. Sleeping on a train left much to be desired. She was tired, and she direly needed a bath. And she wished she never had to wear a corset again! When she got to the hotel she would take a long luxurious bath, wash her hair, and hang out her clothes to rid them of their wrinkles.

And take a nap.

She found a porter and with his help hired a hack to deliver her to the Denver Palace. She was fiddling with her bag and wondering about the fare when they pulled up before an imposing structure. It was only then that she began to get nervous.

The Denver Palace was not at all what she had expected. It was an ornate structure, three stories of blue beveled siding with cream-and-rust-colored gingerbread. The imposing Second Empire roof was faced with scallop-edged slates in a repeating diamond pattern. From its wide granite steps to the fanciful chimney pots, the Palace lived up to its name, and then some.

Somehow she'd envisioned a quickly thrown together building, perhaps with a saloon in its lower level and a few rooms above. Certainly she had not expected such a magnificent edifice as this.

But then, she'd not expected Denver to be so large either. The Colorado Territory was widely considered the realm of ruffians and deserters, populated by men who chased dreams of instant wealth in the gold and silver mines. Men like Dillon Lockwood.

Pensively she mounted the few steps, smiling a vague thanks as the uniformed doorman opened the door for her but thinking only of Dillon. Once she had thought he wanted Sparrow Hill because it was the symbol of the good life that had been denied him. Later she had learned it was not Sparrow Hill at all, but all the other properties that he wanted. But she had never thought of Dillon as being accustomed to the luxuries that she saw about her, to such quiet elegance in the best of taste.

She noted the grand Tall-case clock, the huge Chinese rug, and the facing set of mahogany upholstered sofas as she approached the hotel desk. Everything was perfect. She could not find a flaw in it. And it belonged —at least partially—to her!

"I believe you have a reservation for Mrs. Kimbell. Mrs. Frederick Kimb—"

"Mrs. Kimbell!" The clerk smiled at once and rang immediately for a porter. "Welcome to the Denver Palace, Mrs. Kimbell. We have your suite ready and waiting." He beamed at her as if she were a treasured customer, to her surprise. In an instant two young men

appeared—one for her trunk, one for her bag and key.
But the clerk would not relinquish the key.

"No, no. I shall escort you up myself."

"Why, thank you! Thank you," Lacie replied, somewhat bewildered by all the fuss.

Up one flight of stairs and down a beautifully appointed hall they went to a pair of tall double doors.

"I hope you find everything to your satisfaction," the
man was saying as he walked in. Lacie could only stare
at her surroundings mutely, astounded anew. The room
was furnished all in creams and mauves, with accents
here and there of pale olive green and royal purple.
The first chamber was a spacious sitting room, provided
with marble fireplace, bargello-upholstered parlor set,
and an intimate Queen Anne tea table arrangement for
two. It was even provided with a cunning kidney-
shaped desk set round about with glass-enclosed book-
cases.

All eyes, she followed the porters into the bedroom as
they deposited her luggage. There she found more of
the same, as well as the biggest canopy bed she had
ever laid eyes on. It was draped with yards and yards of
the most delicate Belgian lace looped in poufs and
swags and sumptuous gathers. Upon the high mattress
were a plethora of beautifully upholstered pillows and a
magnificently stitched comforter of shimmering cream
silk. It was all so rich, so exquisite, that she was sure
there must be a mistake. Her budget could never survive a stay in this suite.

"Are you quite certain this is the correct room?" she
asked in concern. "You see, I didn't expect . . . that
is—"

"Oh, I'm *quite* certain, Mrs. Kimbell. Although we

nèver had the opportunity to entertain your husband—
your late husband," he added with a quick bob of his
head. "You can be quite assured that you shall not lack
for the best."

"Yes, but . . . well, it's really not necessary."

"I'm afraid it is. Mr. Lockwood made it quite clear
that you should be very well settled. He said only the
best was good enough for you," the man beamed.

Lacie looked away in dismay. At the mention of Dillon's name her heart had begun to pound, and she
feared her emotions must be visible to all. She mum-
bled a vague thanks and tried to give the two young
men each a coin. But the clerk gave a sharp clap and
hurried them on their way. Then he gave her another
broad smile.

"It will not be necessary for you to tip anyone, ma-
dame."

"Mr. Lockwood?" she ventured to guess.

"Quite so. And now, may I get you anything else?
Perhaps a light repast?"

"No." Lacie turned away with a frown. "I couldn't
eat anything right now. But thank you." Then she
abruptly reconsidered. "Actually, I could do with a
bath. Where are the facilities?"

"Why, right through that door." He pointed toward a
three-panelled door with a cream pickled finish. "All
the rooms on this floor are equipped with private bathing chambers. With hot and cold running water," he
added proudly.

With hot and cold running water! Lacie marveled
after he was gone. She had only to turn each faucet. She
perched on the edge of the white enameled tub as she

watched the water stream out of the two spigots. *Very* hot and *very* cold, she amended. What a luxury!

She had been annoyed when she had learned that this grand suite was all Dillon's doing. It was just like him to begin managing her before she even saw him. Yet, hot and cold running water . . .

She flopped onto the bed and then rolled over to stare up at the canopy. The lace, backed with mauve silk, was gathered into an ornate knot at the center of the canopy. But she did not marvel at the mystifying workmanship of the bed dressings. She was marveling instead about the sort of man who could create a hotel such as this, who could build a fortune from the humblest of beginnings.

Whose very memory could make her quiver deep inside.

She moaned with dismay and threw one arm across her eyes. How would she ever survive the next few days?

It was late afternoon before she ventured downstairs. First she had bathed, washing her hair as she laid back in the oversized tub. Then she had filled the tub anew and rinsed off in the delectably warm water filled to a scandalous depth in the porcelain tub. A person could drown in such pleasure, she'd thought at the time. Brushing and drying her hair at the window had occupied another full hour. Besides that, she unpacked and hung out all her clothes. Finally, when there seemed no recourse but to dress and go out, she had resolved to take a nap instead. Determinedly she had lain there, certain sleep would never overcome her. But when she'd awakened to long shadows in the room, she knew it was time.

Now, meticulously outfitted in the dark blue dress she'd made, with her hair swept up as Ada had instructed her, and the glen straw hat trimmed with blue ribbons tied in love knots and dark rooster feathers, she had no excuse to linger any longer.

There was no reason to hide in her room, her logical side told her. Dillon no doubt knew she was here and she would eventually have to face him. After all, wasn't that the whole point of her journey?

But even so, the very idea had her on the edge of panic. It was clear he meant to intimidate her. Wasn't this suite he'd ordered just a way to show her how much power and authority he commanded? Everyone jumped when he said jump. The implication was that she should too.

But she was not going to.

Still, she could not quiet the nerves that tightened her stomach into knots as she finally left the suite.

Downstairs, the gaslights were being lit. In the lobby the golden light flickered warmly from ornate wall sconces. The huge chandelier in the dining room was being hoisted back aloft after its multitude of candles had been lit. Although it was a little early for dinner, she decided to have a relaxing meal, then retire to her room and get a good night's sleep. She needed to revive her energy after the long and tiresome trip. Her nap had helped, but rather than refreshing her, it had left her somewhat groggy and disoriented.

She was the first guest in the dining room. That accounted for all the fuss, she told herself. The maître d' hovered nearby as if he were worried the waiter might not be able to perform his duty. When the two of them finally faded away with her order for grilled trout, sautéed potatoes with parsley, and the soup du jour, she could feel the beginnings of a headache behind her eyes. She was fiddling with the crystal glass, filled with a clear red wine she hadn't really wanted, when a sudden tremor snaked up her spine.

She looked up quickly, but she knew even before she met his gaze that it was him. Dillon stood in the wide arched entrance to the dining room looking straight at her. He was dressed in a magnificently cut suit of charcoal black botany, relieved by a silver brocade waistcoat and a snowy linen shirt. He was hatless and his ebony hair was neatly combed.

It was longer, she noted obliquely as she drank in the sight of him. His hair was longer on his collar, and he was more handsome than she'd remembered. He didn't smile at her or acknowledge her in any other way. But his gaze seemed to devour her.

Lacie forgot her nervousness. She forgot the anger that had brought her here and the hurt that seemed always to haunt her. Her eyes and her mind—her entire being—filled with his presence so that nothing else mattered. How could she feel this way? she tried to reason with her traitorous heart.

She just did, the answer came. She just did.

For a moment she imagined that they might be able to find some peace between them. But then his attention was drawn by a woman who approached him from the foyer.

The woman was breathtakingly beautiful, with a cloud of silver-blond hair and skin so pale as to be almost ghostly. Her dress was a creamy peach, nipped in at an impossibly tiny waist and pulled snug across a well-displayed bosom. As Lacie watched with growing misgivings, the woman slid her hand most intimately into the crook of Dillon's arm. Although he pulled slightly away, she only leaned nearer him, crushing her generous bosom against his arm as she whispered something to him.

On the surface it appeared that Dillon had been alone and that the woman had come over to him of her own volition. But this stark reminder that her fascination with him was no less than what innumerable other women might also feel sent a shock through Lacie. She lowered her eyes in complete dismay.

Lacie had imagined her confrontation with Dillon many times on her long journey. Sometimes she had imagined it as cool yet cordial, sometimes as angry. In some versions she trounced him; in others, he won. Her favorite had been their reconciliation, although her rational self had always dismissed that foolish possibility.

But somehow she'd not considered this. Somehow she'd not thought that there might be other women in his life.

You're a fool, she berated herself as she reached shakily for the wineglass. She gulped the tart wine without tasting it, then only nodded as the hovering waiter refilled her glass.

He was so smooth, so greedy and devious and selfserving! How could she have overlooked this possibility? What he'd taken from her he'd obviously had from any number of women. She'd known all along she was nothing special to him. She was just that obstacle that he'd had to surmount.

And he had.

But that logic brought her no comfort. He was here, and it was obvious he could be with that blonde if he wanted to. Even if he hadn't done so intentionally, he'd hurt her in the most cruel fashion imaginable.

Tears burned her eyes, but she blinked them back. Her heart ached within her chest and she felt drained of every emotion she had ever felt. She was empty. Hollow. There was nothing left inside her to feel.

Yet still she hurt.

Lacie lifted the glass again and drank too quickly. Her empty stomach roiled at such abuse, but she was past caring about that. Dillon Lockwood would not see her defeated. He would not see her hurt, she vowed as she drained the glass. He was who he was, who he had always been: Frederick's grasping bastard brother.

She was the same too. She was Frederick's friend who was going to keep his school safe. Nothing had changed.

Yet when Dillon crossed alone to her table, she knew that was not true.

"Welcome to Denver, Lacie."

Each low, rumbling word seemed to pierce her heart. "Thank you for arranging for the lovely suite," she managed to say in a voice that hardly shook at all. She raised her eyes to him. "It's far more than I need."

She trailed off under his steady stare, so dark and unfathomable. So perceptive. Her fingers tightened around the stem of her glass as she fought an urge to hide from his astute gaze.

"What do you think of my—" He stopped and his eyes glinted like hard emerald chips. "Of *our* hotel?"

On the pretext of looking around, Lacie tore her gaze away from his mesmerizing one. Unfortunately it was the departing blonde that her eyes fastened on, and she swallowed convulsively. "I'm impressed. Is that what you want to hear?" She glared back at him. "Now, may I please enjoy my dinner in peace?"

"I thought perhaps we could have a quiet little talk."

"I believe your friend is more interested in speaking to you than I am."

He did not move his eyes from her at all. "That was just a chance meeting. Besides, she knows not to expect too much from me."

"Yes, and so do I." She stood up abruptly and flung her twisted napkin onto the table. Then before he could detect any pain behind her words, she swiftly exited the room.

He was the most hateful man alive! Cruel to her. Probably cruel to that other woman as well. Poor thing, Lacie seethed. She probably had no inkling what a cad he was.

Still, Lacie's consuming anger did not lessen the terrible pain she felt. She was nothing to him. She never had been, she mourned as she hurried up the broad carpeted stairs. Yet that realization could not relieve her grieving heart.

She was trembling like a leaf in a wind when she reached the entrance to her suite. She fumbled for the key in her drawstring purse, half blinded by unwelcome tears. Then she heard footsteps approaching, and her haste turned to panic.

"Lacie, we have to talk," Dillon said from right behind her.

"I don't want to talk to you," she muttered.

"Then why are you here?"

"To get my power of attorney back and have my say at the board meeting. Not to talk to you." She struggled to fit the key into the lock, but it slipped from her nerveless fingers.

"You won't be able to avoid me forever."

"I can try." She stooped down for the key, but just as she grasped it, so did he. At once she jumped, as if she had suddenly been burned. Only a few inches separated their faces, and for an electrifying moment their eyes met in silent combat. Then Lacie stood up and looked away.

"You can't avoid me forever," he reiterated as he unlocked her door.

"We can settle our business before the board," she insisted, but quietly now.

"Not all of it."

Alarmed at what he might be implying, Lacie took a step back. "Everything I have to say to you can be said in front of the board. Everything. Now, if you'll excuse me."

She tried to step past him but his arm shot out to block her way.

"Still playing the high-and-mighty Mrs. Kimbell, I see." He leaned a little nearer, forcing her back against the doorframe. "Perhaps I should warn you, Lacie. We're on my home ground now. We'll be playing by my rules." He traced the length of her jaw with one finger as he stared into her dark-lashed eyes. "You can't win, so why not compromise now?"

Lacie looked up into his handsome face as she struggled to contain her warring emotions. "Another of your infamous compromises?" she whispered. "Another of your disgusting plots?" She shook her head faintly and tried to catch her breath. "I'm not so stupid as to still trust you."

A shadow passed over his face, and he straightened up. "I may be guilty of many things. But what happened—I didn't expect it to turn out the way it did."

"No? Then you mean it was just your good fortune that I turned out to be a—" She blushed violently and looked away. There was an uncomfortable silence.

"My good luck. Your bad luck." He paused. "There's still the question of a child."

A knife could not have pierced her heart more cruelly than his words.

"There is no child!" she cried. "There is no child, and even if there were, I'd never want him to know what a horrible father he had!" Then in uncontrollable despair, she rushed past him and slammed the door behind her.

This time she could not hold back the tears. In a torrent they came, hot and salty, wetting the beautiful silk comforter and draining her completely. She was emotionally exhausted by the time they came to a painful sobbing end.

There was no child—thank God. But if there were, she would never let him know. Better to be raised not knowing your father than to be the bastard child of a heartless man.

After all, look how Dillon had turned out.

16

Dillon drummed his fingers on the wide mahogany table top. In the empty conference room it was a sharp, angry sound, frustrated and unrelieved.

Was she lying?

All night he'd lain awake debating that question. Was she lying about a child? His child? For some reason the thought bothered him very much.

He had always been careful in his dalliances, for a bastard was the last thing he wanted. No child of his would ever wonder about his father. No child of his would ever live with that hollow spot inside, that void of need that only a caring father could fill. No, he'd been very careful—except with her.

Dillon flung himself back in the chair and stared up at the dark coffered ceiling, shadowed now in the early morning light. What a fool he'd been where one Lacie Montgomery—Kimbell—was concerned. He should have just given her that infernal school and let her keep Frederick's name in exchange for the balance of his brother's properties. As one-sided a deal as it would have been, he realized now that she probably would have agreed. The school was all she had wanted, after all. She could have given management of the school her best effort. Then, when Sparrow Hill folded, as it inevitably would have, he could have bought it back from her for a reasonable sum, and they would have both been content.

But now it was unlikely that either of them would ever be satisfied. His only consolation was that he could easily determine if she was pregnant. Neal could keep him posted on that.

And if she were pregnant?

He ran his hand over his forehead, then closed his eyes and sighed. If she were pregnant it would make an already complicated situation even more unwieldy. There would be no reasoning with her whatsoever.

Yet even that knowledge could not stifle the strange quiver of emotion that stirred in him. He'd never thought about being a father before, at least not in other than preventive measures. But seeing Lacie last night had made the possibility seem much more alive. She had been so beautiful. So vulnerable.

So infuriating.

His jaw tightened in concern. It would be just like her to lie about it, when all the while that baby would be his heir!

Dillon's eyes widened as he considered the implications. If she kept it, she would have to claim it was Frederick's. No doubt she would love to torture him with that lie. But the child would still be his, heir to everything he'd built.

His resolve jelled at once. There was no way he would allow Lacie to fob off a child of his as Frederick's. He would claim it as his no matter what she said. A child of theirs would possess the rights to both properties—hers and his. Everything would come together quite naturally through a baby, just as it should.

At that unexpected realization he slowly straightened up. If they were to marry . . .

If they were to marry, it would solve everything. It wouldn't matter who owned what if there was a baby and they were married.

He frowned as he imagined the absolute delight she would take in turning down a marriage proposal from him. How she would love to taunt him with a refusal! But if she were pregnant—if!—she might feel a little differently.

And if he had to, he'd force her. No child of his would be born a bastard.

He smiled then and marveled at his immediate light-heartedness. The thought of Lacie growing big with his child held a perverse appeal that he could not begin to comprehend. The very thought made him want to hold her in his arms and press her close to him. He rose from the chair and stretched the stiff muscles of his back before leaving the dim boardroom. To his surprise, he actually hoped she had been lying when she had denied the existence of a child. Maybe it was too soon for her to even know. If she were pregnant he would be content, for to his amazement, he suddenly found that he wanted an heir. Very much.

Lacie was as ready as she ever would be, girded for battle behind the self-possessed facade of an elegant young widow. The gray suit was the perfect choice, for she looked tall and slender in it. Mature, she decided. Yet it still allowed her to be attractive. It was just the right touch. Still, no amount of chambray, linen, and ribbon could quite prepare her for the roomful of curious gazes that turned her way when she entered the imposing boardroom.

She should have known, she realized as she hesitated in the doorway, staring back at all the strange faces. After all, everyone in the Lockwood Office Building had cast her furtive looks as she'd passed: the doorman, the receptionist, the room of young clerks and secretaries. Even though they had all been quite polite, she had not had to identify herself to any of them. They already knew exactly who she was.

So, obviously, did the staring board members. She had to will herself to step farther into the room so that the young man at the door could close it behind her. But then what? How was she to act? What was she to do? Everyone else was milling around, chatting among themselves like old acquaintances. She was clearly the only outsider.

Then she saw Dillon, and the others were no longer important. He was leaning on a tall leather chair, his elbows propped on the high back, his hands loosely clasped. He appeared to be listening to an older gentleman's words, but his eyes were on her. Like sun shining through emeralds, his eyes glinted darkly as they swept over her. But he did not acknowledge her in any other way.

Why should he? she asked herself logically. Yet she could not ignore the pang in her heart. No matter how often she recounted his many sins against her, no matter how unyielding and cruel he continued to be, she nevertheless longed for nothing more than his smile and the sign of his approval. Oh, what was wrong with her that she could be so perverse?

Her heart was thumping painfully by the time she dragged her eyes away from him. She would sit down, she decided. There was no one she knew here, so she would simply take a seat at the long mahogany table and wait for the meeting to begin. She moved to a chair, but then she noticed the name cards: M. FERGU-SON. Next to it was R. ANDREWS.

Where had he decided to put her? Probably right next to him, the better to intimidate her. She read the next two: B. GRANT, S. CUNNINGHAM.

Had he left her name out?

At the end of the table she stopped and sent him a furious glare. But he only smiled and nodded ever so slightly. She yanked her skirts in annoyance as she rounded the table, preparing to check the cards on the other side. It was then that she found her name. L. KIMBELL was printed in sturdy letters, devoid of any swirls and curlicues. These were certainly not place cards for a luncheon, she noted obliquely. A nearby gentleman pulled her chair out for her and she thanked him as she settled herself. Then she looked up to see Dillon pulling out the chair on the opposite end of the table. As if on cue the other men drifted to their own chairs. There was much good-natured kidding as they jockeyed around one another and found their places. Once they were all settled, however, the situation could not have been clearer to everyone, she realized. Dillon anchored one end. She was squarely on the other. Between them at least a dozen and a half men sat, the rope in the coming tug-of-war.

Lacie already knew they would be pulling with Dillon against her. Still, she had not come this far only to cave in now. She took a deep breath and then raised her chin a notch. With her bitter smile she sent Dillon a message: *Let the battle begin.*

". . . Page seventeen summarizes the profit-and-loss statement for each of the companies we've reviewed so far."

Lacie stifled a yawn as she looked at still another page of small printed figures. Column upon column. Profits, losses, bottom lines. Estimated values at current market prices. Shares. Dividends. For six hours, with only a short break for a lunch that was brought in, they had been examining each company's financial position in endless detail. She was relieved that some of the others seemed just as bored as she. Whispered conversations were always going on even as the main discussion proceeded. But invariably, whenever another company was brought up for discussion, one group of whisperers would turn their attention toward Dillon while another group would lose interest. It wasn't hard to see that the board members held ownership in different companies. They felt compelled to listen only when their affairs were up for discussion.

But Frederick had owned large portions of each of the companies. Despite her boredom, Lacie felt compelled to follow every one of Dillon's explanations. He would have no reason to accuse her of negligence where her properties were concerned, she vowed. And he would not sneak anything by her either.

It was late in the afternoon when Dillon leaned back in his chair and closed the leather-bound book before him. "I think this is a very good point to adjourn today's discussion."

"Wait!"

At her unexpected outburst every eye turned toward Lacie. It was almost enough to unnerve her completely. But she doggedly held her ground.

"We've discussed every business venture imaginable but the one I am most interested in. I don't think we should adjourn until Sparrow Hill School for Young Ladies is discussed as well, for I have something to say on that matter."

"This is not the time." With that curt dismissal, Dillon rose from his seat.

Lacie stood up as well. "When *is* the time?"

For a tense moment they faced each other while the other men sat very still—waiting for the fireworks to start, she guessed. But Dillon was surprisingly pleasant.

"It is our usual practice to discuss the stock-owned companies the first day and the privately owned ones the second day. We follow that with general discussion, and on the third day go into the budgets." He smiled then, a warm, generous smile that caught her completely off guard. "I assure you, you'll have more than adequate opportunity to discuss the school."

In the ensuing melee of chairs being scraped back, papers being collected, and boisterous conversation as the room was vacated, Lacie continued to stand where she was. Why had he smiled at her like that? It hadn't been mocking or cruel. She'd not seen the sarcasm she would have expected under the circumstances. After all, he'd just put her in her place in front of everyone. Yet his smile . . .

Lacie sat down abruptly and began to straighten the

myriad papers before her. He must be up to something, she decided. He wanted to appear to be the good brother-in-law, in case the others felt any sympathy for her, the poor widow. She slapped the pile of papers down on the table, then reached angrily for her purse. It was just like him to affect one attitude when his real intentions were quite the opposite. Oh, he was truly devious.

She got up to leave, determined not to fall, even for an instant, under the charming spell he wove so well. She must remember not to trust him, she told herself. She must always remember not to trust him.

A few of the men still lingered in the antechamber as she left the room. Mr. Cunningham, who had been to her left, nodded as she passed. Two others whose names she'd already forgotten nodded as well. She was beginning to think she would escape without seeing Dillon again, when she rounded a corner and almost ran directly into him.

"Well, did you enjoy your first board meeting, Lacie?" His expression was relaxed, neither taunting nor condescending, but she refused to let down her guard.

"It was interesting," she answered, stepping back from his always-overwhelming presence.

"This was actually the most boring part. It should get more interesting as we go on."

"No doubt." She smiled stiffly, then looked beyond him. "If you'll excuse me?"

But his hand on her arm stopped her. She backed away immediately, alarmed that his casual touch could shake her so profoundly. They might not have been in a place of business, on opposite sides of a bitter struggle, so quickly did her blood heat and her pulse begin to race. She met his intense gaze with fearful eyes, then abruptly averted them. It was bad enough to feel as she did. Letting him suspect it was ever so much worse.

"We need to talk," he said quietly.

"No, we don't. Besides, I'm tired and would like to leave," she stated as firmly as she could, considering that her heart was pounding thunderously in her chest.

"Have dinner with me."

"What?" Lacie jerked her head up. He must be mad to think she would willingly do anything with him, even something as apparently harmless as eating a meal at the same table. She had already discovered, to her enormous dismay, that Dillon was never harmless. Never.

"Have dinner with me," he repeated, as a smile began to curve one side of his mouth.

"No." She purposefully pulled her skirts to one side and tried to pass him. She wanted nothing to do with him. But he was equally determined to have her assent.

"You will want to hear what I have to say," he informed her as he accompanied her down the hall. Then he took her arm and swung her around to face him. He pinned her to the wall with his warm green eyes. "Just tell me what time to come for you."

"No." Lacie shook her head for emphasis when her refusal came out so weakly.

His hands tightened slightly, although not painfully. Then his thumbs began to slide back and forth along her inner arms, and she felt herself beginning to melt.

"You're being foolish, Lacie, and overly emotional. Two traits that are deadly in business." Still his thumbs circled on her sensitive skin.

"If you want to talk business," she managed to gasp, "then you can save it for the board meeting."

"This is private business. Between you and me."

Lacie closed her eyes at his pointed words. Oh, dear God, help me, she prayed desperately. Give me the strength to resist him.

"It has to do with the school," he added.

At that her eyes flew open.

He was only inches away from her, holding her arms still as she leaned back against the wall for support. Yet he might have been pressed intimately against her, so clearly did she recall the precise feel of his body warm upon hers. Then they heard footsteps approaching, and he slowly released his grip on her. By the time two clerks clattered around the corner, Dillon was standing a respectable distance from her, but his eyes had not strayed from her face.

"I'll call for you at eight," he told her decisively.

"I won't be there," she whispered in a hoarse voice.

"Where else is there for you to be?" Then, as if he did not expect an answer, he took her arm, escorted her to the office door, and put her into a waiting carriage.

Infuriated by his high-handedness, Lacie promptly pulled the fringed curtain down. But on the lonely ride back to the Palace, she knew it had been a futile gesture. A woven shade faced with striped satin could hardly block Dillon Lockwood out of her life. Indeed, it seemed that nothing could.

17

Lacie decided to wear the black mourning dress. Then she squared her shoulders and swallowed hard as she contemplated what she was doing. It was just a dinner, she rationalized, a dinner with a business associate who wanted to discuss a matter of some importance to her.

But Dillon was not just *any* business associate, and Sparrow Hill was far more than a matter of *some* importance to her. It was home, yet it was also the source of all her problems, of her dilemma—the reason she and Dillon were embroiled in this winner-take-all confrontation. He had stopped at nothing to get Sparrow Hill—and the rest of Frederick's properties—from her. And so far she had stopped at nothing to oppose him. Now they were nearing the final showdown, and she was petrified with fear.

Yes, her dyed mourning costume seemed most appropriate indeed, for one of them was bound to win and the other to fold in this high-stakes gamble.

She was very careful as she dressed. Not to impress him, she assured herself, at least not as she would want to impress a handsome dinner partner under more normal circumstances. All she wanted was to force him to respect her as a person, as someone who could take on all the responsibilities for Frederick's properties and do a good job. Most of all, she wanted him to admit that she had bested him this time.

How many times had she been humiliated by him? she fumed as she fastened the endless row of jet-black buttons down the fitted front of her bodice. How many times had he manipulated and manhandled her? He'd lied to her from the beginning.

But she'd lied, too, her conscience reminded her.

She paused and stared at her pale face in the beveled mirror above the ornate vanity. Yes, she had lied, but she'd paid dearly for it. For a moment her resolve slipped, and wicked memories came rushing back, torturing her with their bittersweetness. Dillon had held her and kissed her. He'd seduced her and taught her what pleasure a man and woman might share together.

But it had all been calculated and insincere.

Her resolve stiffened as she recalled why he'd seduced her. But the so-called proof he'd found was just so many words. If he thought he could prove his claim, he would have done so by now, she reassured herself. The fact was, he had been bluffing all along. The only reason he hadn't won was that he had underestimated her dedication to the school. It was her home and her livelihood. Without it, she was no one and had nothing. She could never give that up.

Lacie straightened up and peered at herself critically. In the stiff bombazine outfit, she looked quite the widowed schoolteacher. She should loosen her feminine chignon and reknot her hair into a prim bun at the nape of her neck, she thought. That would complete her look perfectly.

But she couldn't bring herself to do it. Frowning at her own idiocy, she donned her small black bonnet. She was being vain and foolish and courting disaster, she fretted. But what difference would her hair truly make? The real danger was in meeting with him at all. He wouldn't care how she looked, as long as he was able to manipulate her again.

But he was going to fail this time. Nothing he could do or say would sway her in the least.

As she grabbed her small drawstring purse and turned to leave, she kept that thought uppermost in her mind. He would not sway her this time.

Unfortunately, the test of her resolve came far sooner than she would have liked. She had only begun to descend the hotel stairs when Dillon bounded up, taking the steps three at a time. When their eyes met they both stopped short. He was standing at the landing, one hand on the pineapple finial that capped the newel post, his eyes an unfathomable green. As impervious as emerald, she thought obliquely.

Yet he looked no less fine. Any other man in a black swallowtail evening suit, cut simply but elegantly, would have looked as good. Any other gentleman might have carried off the stark white shirt and simple satin band bow equally well. But no other man could duplicate that rare combination of carefully cultivated sophistication and raw animal magnetism. No man on earth would ever stir her so passionately.

Color stained her cheeks at such untoward thoughts, and she gripped the banister more tightly. She wanted to turn and flee, yet she knew she must not. Oh, why didn't he say something instead of just looking at her like that, as if he might devour her at any moment?

Then he smiled faintly and lifted a hand toward her. For long seconds she hesitated, unsure as all her resolve weakened into nothingness. Only when his smile broadened into a grin was she able to prod herself forward.

Step by step she descended, as stiff and resistant as if she were facing a firing squad. He merely stood waiting for her to come to him, clearly confident that he had only to beckon and she would.

At the landing she tried to ignore the proffered hand, but Dillon would not allow her even that small victory.

"Don't be a brat," he murmured almost jovially as he tucked her gloved hand into the crook of his arm, then kept his hand quite firmly over it.

"Don't tell me how to act," she hissed back as she unsuccessfully tried to pull her hand free. But there was nothing she could do as he guided her down the stairs and into the lobby. There were too many people about for her to create a scene, she fumed. And his very nearness was already robbing her of her resoluteness. It took only the feel of his arm beneath her palm, the brush of his sleeve against her, the warmth of his palm completely covering her hand. As if her emotions were at his command, she felt herself grow warm and weak. Even her heart was pounding a new too-rapid rhythm.

Why, why was she so perversely drawn to him?

Dillon did not wait for the maître d' to lead them to a table. Instead, he masterfully steered her to a partially curtained-off alcove. Before she could object, he seated her at a magnificently appointed table glittering with the finest china, crystal, and silver, festooned with a huge bouquet of red roses.

She glanced around nervously as he sat down across the small table from her. Candles shimmered in silver wall sconces, casting a warm glow over the cozy setting. The walls were exquisitely papered above an elaborately carved wainscot. Heavy velvet drapes with silk tassels were drawn open at the entrance to the alcove but she realized that it would take only one gentle tug of the pulls to close off the remainder of the restaurant. Within the alcove, they would then have complete privacy.

The faint smell of roses wafted sweetly around her as she contemplated that possibility. Privacy was the last thing she wanted where Dillon was concerned. Privacy was too threatening. It could lead nowhere but to total disaster.

"I don't want to eat in here." She stood up abruptly, sliding her chair back on the black-and-pink-silk Tabriz rug.

"The curtains will stay open, and I promise I won't bite you." He grinned and gestured toward her chair. "There's no reason to be so jumpy, Lacie. Just sit down and relax."

Sit down and relax? Lacie eyed him suspiciously. She would never be able to relax in his presence. Not now, not ever. Even the way he said her name . . .

"Sit down. There's something I need to talk to you about, and I don't think you want anyone to overhear us."

In sudden resignation she sat down, although she deliberately avoided the smug expression that surely covered his face. She wanted to know what he was up to but not for a moment would she relax her guard.

"Do you provide roses every time you have dinner with a member of the board?" she asked caustically, flicking her napkin open.

"No."

Lacie looked up at once, startled by his blatant honesty. But instead of smugness, she saw a disturbing frankness in his face. An unnerving perceptiveness. She looked away immediately, shaken more than she wanted to admit.

"I'd like to eat first," he said. "Perhaps I can answer any questions you have about today's meeting. Then we can go into the matter I mentioned earlier."

"Just what is this matter?" Lacie challenged, facing him fully.

His warm gaze slipped over her face and he smiled quite openly. "Let it lie for now. We'll get into it later."

"If you think you can lull me into complacency again, it won't work this time!" she blurted out. She was instantly chagrined by what her words revealed. But to her surprise Dillon's face grew more serious and he glanced down at his plate before replying.

"In business lunches and dinners, it is common practice for the meal to precede the business. Both parties are more relaxed then, and more receptive to the other's overtures—"

He stopped when she stiffened.

"Don't read more into it than I meant, Lacie."

But that only made her go scarlet. In desperation she glanced past the curtains to the main dining room and escape beyond. This dinner was a huge mistake, she told herself, a dreadful, dreadful mistake.

"I think it would be best if we dispensed with the meal and went directly to this business of yours," she choked out through gritted teeth. It was then, however, that the dapper waiter intruded.

"Ah, Toby," Dillon leaned back in his chair in obvious relief. "May I introduce Mrs. Lacie Kimbell." He turned to Lacie. "Toby has been at the Denver Palace since its origins before the big flood."

"It wasn't called the Denver Palace then," the graying little man told her with a sparkle in his eyes. "It was little more than a rowdy saloon with a few rooms. We've come up a bit in the world, don't you know."

"It is a wonderful hotel," Lacie offered as the man uncorked a bottle of wine, then filled their glasses. When he outlined the evening's choices on the menu, she felt compelled to make a selection despite herself. She just could not find it in herself to be anything less than gracious to as enthusiastic and efficient a fellow as Toby. Once he left, however, and she and Dillon were again alone, she turned her attention toward her cut-crystal wine goblet. She was jumpy and on edge, and certain that Dillon took profound pleasure in it.

"So how is Neal doing?"

Lacie looked up cautiously at his seemingly innocuous words.

"His head wound healed well. And his broken arm was doing much better when I left."

"I suppose he's getting the best of care if Ada and Mrs. Gunter have anything to do with it."

Lacie nodded a silent confirmation as she peered curiously at him. Making small talk was not what she expected of him. Chattiness was hardly his style. Up to now, she'd learned to be careful of everything he said.

Every word had seemed loaded with implications and innuendos. But this bland conversation . . .

"He seems quite enamored of your friend Ada."

"Really? I thought he was just following your orders," she replied cattily, pleased by the quick frown her words evinced.

"Always looking for a way to paint me black, aren't you?" he snapped. "I hope you haven't poisoned Ada against him with your unfair accusations."

"If I'm unfair in my assumptions about you and your cohorts, it's only because I've learned the hard way how disastrous it is to give you the benefit of the doubt." She brought the wineglass to her lips and took a rather unsteady sip as she waited for his response.

To her surprise, however, Dillon did not rise to her challenge. Instead, he also tasted his wine. But his clear-green eyes never left her face. The silence stretched out as they stared at each other. Between them the air was fraught with tension, yet the silence held steady, threatening to undo her completely.

When she could bear it no more, she took another drink, concentrating on the glass she held tightly in her hand.

"So, is Neal Camden sincere or not?" she asked, if only to break the dreadful stillness.

"Very sincere. In fact"—he paused and twirled the pale amber liquid around in his glass—"in fact, he tells me he plans to marry her."

"Marry her!" Lacie leaned forward in consternation at this unexpected news. "He's going to marry her? Take her away from Sparrow Hill?"

"I should think, as Ada's good friend, that you would

be pleased for her. She could hardly do better than Neal for a husband."

Lacie had no answer for that. She'd been around Neal enough to know that he was indeed a nice man and would probably make a good husband to Ada. In truth, it was only his association with Dillon that cast any shadow upon his character. His attention toward Ada had been unmistakable. But to marry her! That was an eventuality she had overlooked. Now her happiness for Ada was overshadowed by a sudden sense of doom for herself. It was hard enough to maintain her farce with Ada's support. She would never be able to do it alone.

"Ada and Neal," she murmured softly, her eyes focused somewhere in space. "Yes, I suppose he will be good for her." Then her gaze sharpened to take in Dillon's watchful expression. "But you've no doubt already determined that their union can only help you in your greedy little plan."

"I think it's a lot more accurate to say that it will hurt you in yours," he replied tersely.

She gave him a bitter smile, then shrugged in forced nonchalance. "Only time will tell. But I'm not really interested in this idle chitchat you're manufacturing. Why don't you just tell me what it is you want to say?"

So she could get away from the overwhelming pressure of his nearness, she added silently. So she could shake off the terrible confusion he created in her. It only made things worse to hear him speak of such things as love and marriage.

"Quite the businesswoman, aren't you?" He gave her a skeptical look. "And here I'd always thought that women loved nothing more than talk of weddings and true love. Of happily-ever-afters."

"I've learned the hard way not to believe in such foolishness," she muttered, then immediately regretted her words.

He was silent a moment. "I presume the implication is that I bear the blame for your cynicism, not Frederick."

Lacie could not reply. Her throat had suddenly tightened, as too many emotions competed for dominance. She had meant to be angry and resentful, but it was sorrow and longing that overcame her. His casual reference to true love and happily-ever-afters depressed her dreadfully. She wanted those things, too, but she knew her love would never be returned. Dillon would never love anything but power and money.

She blinked hard and looked down at the linen napkin now twisted in her hands. Love had nothing to do with how she felt, she admonished herself. But the thought would not be beaten back. She loved him, although for whatever perverse reason she did not know. But she did love him, and the realization made everything even worse than it already was. It was bad enough to be embroiled with him in this battle for Frederick's properties. It was worse to be drawn so unwisely to him, to be so desirous of his kiss and his touch. But love! To feel love for him was unthinkable! It was madness!

In a panic she looked around, desperate for an excuse to leave the table, to flee his presence, then to hide someplace where he would never find her, someplace where she could rid herself of this irrational compulsion. But her way was blocked by the beaming Toby, carrying a huge silver tray upon which myriad covered dishes were arranged.

As he unloaded the tray, spreading a veritable feast

upon the table, Lacie could do no more than sit there, watching the waiter with an unwarranted interest, and dreading his eventual departure.

After Toby left, to her surprise and enormous relief, Dillon did not resume the conversation where they had left off. For reasons known only to himself he seemed bent on keeping their meal pleasant, at least superficially, and he carefully skirted any issue that might lead to the real problems between them—either business or personal.

Dillon filled the uncomfortable silence with comments about the wonderful meal and the cook they'd lured away from a fancy San Francisco hotel, then proceeded on to the popular—and financial—success of the Denver Palace. Despite Lacie's complete disinterest in eating, she could not help paying attention to his astute comments about Denver's rapid growth. Without realizing it she slowly began to pick at the salad of fresh greens. The tender new potatoes in delicately flavored cream sauce were next, and she even tried the juicy filet mignon surrounded by local mountain mushrooms in a superb butter sauce.

". . . gold mine was marginally successful. But it was the mine tailings—the discarded ore left over after the gold was removed—that proved the most valuable. They were full of silver."

"And that's when Denver's boom times began?" she asked in spite of herself.

"Its second boom," he answered. "We're well on our way to being the most important city between St. Louis and San Francisco."

He reached over and filled her glass, all the while smiling warmly at her. It was enough to send her heart

racing, and Lacie averted her gaze in confusion. She
had no idea what he was up to, or why he was deliberately being so charming. But she was vitally aware that
it was working. He was giving her his undivided attention, without being overtly complimentary—he was far
too smooth for that, she told herself. Yet the way he
leaned toward her, the way he listened carefully to
whatever she said and kept his eyes constantly upon
her, and the way he smiled so sincerely at her seemed
to strike a responsive chord deep within her. She could
not ignore the tingle that had started in her stomach
and that now had every least portion of her humming
in tense anticipation.

She knew the color was high in her cheeks, but try as
she might, she could not counteract the effect he was
having on her. Her hand trembled as she reached for
her glass. Then she thought twice and decided that
more wine would only weaken her resolve further. She
pursed her lips as she leaned back in her chair, and with
an effort she raised her eyes to his handsome face.

"I'll admit that Denver is much larger—and more
civilized—than I had anticipated."

"It hasn't come overnight, but bit by bit we'll get
there. We need to build an opera house—"

"And more schools."

Dillon paused at her interjection. "We have a school,
down on Champion Street."

"A city this size should have more—especially if it's
growing as fast as you say. More people coming in
means more children. And they'll need more than just
the most rudimentary skills. Do you want people to
have to send their children off to San Francisco to get a
good education?" She shot him an arch look. "Of

course, we both know that you don't consider proper schools very important. They don't make very good investments, do they?"

She knew she'd touched a vulnerable spot then, for his eyes darkened and his smile faded somewhat. But he was clearly more determined to have a pleasant meal with her than she'd suspected.

"Perhaps you should consider opening a school here."

Lacie was taken aback by that unexpected suggestion. For a moment, she had no reply. Then she tossed her napkin down on the table. "With the full financial backing of you and the rest of your cronies?" she asked caustically.

In the long angry silence that followed, she told herself that she was three times a fool. Despite the charm he could turn on at will, he was as trustworthy as a rattlesnake. She was about to get up and leave, unable to take any more of his cat-and-mouse games, when he leaned forward, his elbows on the table.

"I can arrange for financial backing," he said quietly.

"What?" Lacie stared at him as if he were mad. "You must think I'm a complete fool if you believe I trust one word you say!"

A muscle in his cheek tensed as he stared seriously at her. "We can prepare legally binding papers, if that will make you happy."

That drew her up short, and for a moment she was speechless. He would help her start a school in Denver? But why? It made no sense whatsoever.

"I know you're thinking I must have had too much to drink, but I assure you, Lacie, this is a well-considered proposal. You see, despite what you think, I really have

no desire to fight you over Frederick's estate. We both
know the truth, and if it were to come out, you would
be completely disgraced—not to mention penniless."

"If this is another of your disgusting propositions, the
answer is no!" she muttered, alarmed by how fast her
pulse was racing. Although she wanted to attribute it to
pure anger, she knew that a part of it was because of his
implication that he still wanted her. No matter how she
fought such a sinful desire, that knowledge nonetheless
gave her an undeniable thrill.

"I think you may find what I have to say far from
disgusting. Unless, of course, you're opposed to marriage."

At first Lacie wasn't certain she had heard him correctly. But then he grinned a little crookedly at her, and
she knew she wasn't mistaken.

"Marriage?" she whispered, still stunned. "To—to
who?"

"To me."

Lacie's heart was in her throat, and she stared in
amazement at him. This could not be happening. It
couldn't. A marriage proposal from him was not a possibility she had considered. Certainly it had not been a
part of his plans up to now. And yet there he sat, smiling
broadly at her, clearly amused by her shock but no less
serious than before.

"If you'll think about it, you'll see that it's completely
logical," he continued. "We both win. I'd regain control
of my companies, and you'd get both the financial security you want and another school."

"But—" her thoughts were too scattered to be
quickly gathered. "But I already have a school."

"It's too far from here. Besides, as you already

pointed out, Denver could use another good school. And people here can afford to pay the price."

"But—but—" Lacie's head was spinning as she tried to grasp the ramifications of his unexpected proposal. "But I can't just abandon Sparrow Hill."

"You're not abandoning it," he said smoothly, leaning forward more eagerly now. "You would just be moving it here."

"Yes, but—" Lacie pressed her palms to her cheeks, trying to think clearly. Across the table Dillon watched her closely, awaiting her reply. He grinned at her, a blatantly sensual grin, beckoning and promising all sorts of rewards if she just answered him correctly. But Lacie closed her eyes to that overwhelming appeal of his. She couldn't let herself be swayed by the irrational pull he exerted over her. She had to be careful. She had to be smart.

She took a slow breath in an attempt to calm herself. Then she looked back at him with dark, troubled eyes.

"I want to be sure—to be sure I understand," she began haltingly. "If we marry, you will assume ownership of my portion of the companies. I would give up Sparrow Hill, and you would give me another school to occupy myself." She paused and a frown creased her forehead. "In other words, you would get everything you wanted and I would get—" The frown deepened. "I would get nothing."

"You would get another school."

"But you would close Sparrow Hill. That's what you've wanted from the very beginning."

"You make it sound like I have something against that school. Dammit, I don't. It's just that it's a losing proposition, Lacie. And it's stupid to waste any more money on it."

"It's not stupid!" she cried. "It may never be a great moneymaker like your gold and silver mines, but that doesn't mean it's worthless!" She started to rise, but his hand on her arm prevented her from leaving.

"I think you're overreacting. Can't we discuss this matter more calmly?"

But Lacie knew that was impossible. Already the warmth of his casual touch was raising her temperature to a fever pitch. If she let him go on, he would melt all her resolve and destroy her ability to reason. Worse, she was sure he knew it and wasn't above using such deplorable tactics.

With an effort she tore her arm from his grasp and pulled herself together.

"No doubt you can be calm about this," she began coldly. "After all, it's no more than a shrewd business merger you're planning. You call it a marriage proposal, but it's really just another underhanded attempt to get Frederick's properties. Since I haven't caved in to your other attempts, you've decided to marry me. Well"—she drew herself up as regally as she could—"I'm not interested."

His expression was calm in the face of her refusal, but Lacie saw his eyes flicker and turn a dark, stormy green. She tried to find some pleasure in having finally put him in his place. He had probably never considered that she might refuse him. It was very likely that no woman ever had up to now. But she found no solace in her triumph. If only he'd spoken of love, she thought morosely, or even of respect and affection. Perhaps then she might have been unable to deny him. Perhaps then she would have said yes.

But he'd made it sound more a practical business deal than a proposal. She was already embroiled in an uncomfortable business deal with him. She didn't need any more of the same.

It was a struggle to fight down the tears that rose in her eyes. All she wanted was to escape to her room and have a good cry. But Dillon was not ready to let her go.

"Don't turn me down without thinking over the repercussions," he said quietly.

"I think I already have," she muttered as she rose and turned to leave.

"If there is a child, it deserves to have a father."

Lacie whirled to face him then, her eyes filling with tears despite her best efforts to contain them. "I told you, there is no child!"

"You also said you wouldn't tell me if there were." He stood up and approached her, towering over her in the intimate dining alcove. "For all I know, you're lying to me. You've done it before."

Lacie could feel her heart pounding in her throat, beating so hard she was sure it would break. Dillon was so near, the heat of him, the subtle masculine scent of him seemed to envelop her, drawing her to him and weakening her resistance. She was trembling violently from the terrible emotions overwhelming her, unable to stop the two tears that spilled over her lashes.

"You've been no more honest than I have," she whispered hoarsely. "All you've ever wanted is Frederick's property, and I was only something in the way. Now you think you can marry me to get what you want and perhaps an heir to boot. Well, this is one time you're not going to have your way."

She faced him stiffly, trying hard not to show any weakness before him. He stood just a foot away, staring at her. Glaring, she thought, although for a moment she thought she saw a glimmer of contrition. But she quickly banished that silly notion. It was only that her vision was blurred by the tears building up in her eyes. Dillon didn't feel sorry for what he'd done or said. He didn't have it in him to see any way but his own.

She turned then to go but she was stopped by his one low, husky word.

"Lacie . . ."

It took everything she had to steel herself against the visceral pull of that simple entreaty. You can't trust him, she told herself harshly. Haven't you learned that after all that's happened? He only wants what's good for him, and he cares nothing at all for you.

She lifted her chin, although she kept her eyes trained on the fringed curtains and the public dining area beyond. "There is no child. And there will be no marriage." Then she pushed past the curtain and hurried toward the stairs, blinded by the tears that fell full force now.

She didn't see Dillon come out to watch her flight. She didn't see the desk clerk's concerned stare or notice any of the other hotel guests in the lobby. She had only one objective, and that was to get away from Dillon Lockwood before she fell completely to pieces.

18

Rain was beating a tattoo against the windows when Lacie awoke. In hundreds of angry drumbeats, it pounded futilely against the multi-paned glass. It seemed at once both mournfully sad and frustratingly angry, she thought.

Just as she felt.

With a weary sigh Lacie rolled to her side and stared at the beautifully curtained window. She was warm and comfortable in here. The Denver Palace provided every creature comfort imaginable, yet oh, how she longed to be back in her old familiar room at Sparrow Hill! She closed her eyes, picturing the huge old house with its wide inviting porches framed by towering white columns. Right now it was probably enveloped by a misty ground fog and looked for all the world like a strange white ship adrift in a murky sea, just waiting for the sun to bring it safely into the light.

The rooster would be crowing, calling the hens out to begin their daily routine. Lacie stretched her legs and flexed her feet beneath the covers, imagining the feel of wet grass and fine gravel beneath her bare feet along the path that led to the chicken yard.

Yet her warm memories were no real comfort to her. She thought of the chicken yard—and saw Dillon standing beside the gate. She pictured the porch—but imagined Dillon waiting there. The barn, the dining room, even the library in the second-floor hall—everything there was now associated with Dillon Lockwood! He had somehow left his stamp on it all. Or else on her.

Lacie compressed her lips tightly. He had most definitely left a permanent stamp on her. It might have been a brand imprinted on her heart, marking her forever as belonging to him, it was so deep. Yet it was not her heart that he wanted. Everything but.

With a morose sigh Lacie tossed back the cover, then slowly swung her legs around and sat up. She was still tired. Last night's confrontation with Dillon had been emotionally traumatizing, and once she had reached her room she had cried herself into exhaustion. Like a violent storm her emotions had battered her until, bruised and heartbroken, she had lain in the dark, drained and empty, unable to pretend she was strong enough to fight him anymore. All she wanted was to go home.

But there would be no comfort there either. As long as she maintained her deception, she would be connected to Dillon. And he would never give up until he got what he wanted.

Lacie rose from the bed and crossed to the window. The glass was cold against her brow as she leaned against it. Outside the world was gray and wet, and the clouds pressed down on the town as they let loose a steady stream of depressing rain. If only she could bury her woes beneath the covers and blot out the rain and this town. And Dillon Lockwood!

For a long while she stood at the window, staring blindly without, watching the erratic trickle of the drops running together down the glass. Like one of those little drops, she too was caught up in a torrent, unable to avoid being swept along on this path of no return. As much as she wished to flee, she could not. As desperate as she was to avoid Dillon and his heartless offer of marriage, she must nevertheless confront him again at the board meeting.

She turned away from the window at the thought of coming face to face with him once more. How would she be able to hold up during the long grueling hours of the meeting with him at the other end of the table staring at her, demanding things of her with his potent gaze? Her refusal was hardly likely to deter him from his single-minded goal. Indeed, knowing him as she did, she feared it would only encourage him. By turning him down, she had sent him a challenge he would not be able to ignore.

She shook her head in despair. What was she to do? Perhaps when he realized she wasn't lying about a baby he would relent, she thought hopefully.

Lacie pressed her hand to her flat tummy. For one weak moment, she wondered how it would feel to have Dillon's baby within her, to know something sweet and wonderful was growing deep inside her. She had never considered motherhood before, at least not seriously. Yet although she knew it was not the case, she couldn't help but imagine it now.

Maybe things would be different if she were pregnant. Maybe they would be better, for at least she and

Dillon would have some common ground. Unable to resist, she wondered what a child of theirs would look like. Green eyes or gray? Dark hair, of course. Dillon would prefer a boy, no doubt, but she had seen him with Nina, and it was obvious he could happily spoil a little girl of his own. She knew he would be a good father.

At that thought, she shook her head hard and jerked her hand away from her stomach. She was a fool to think such things. Dillon would be a terrible father and an even worse husband. He'd had a poor enough example in his own upbringing. As a result, he had grown up to be a cruel and calculating businessman. He wanted neither wife nor child and had only proposed to her because it was the easiest way to get what he wanted. Oh, but she was ten times a fool to be in love with him!

At least she could take solace that there had been no child resulting from that night. . . .

That night.

That night she could not put out of her head, no matter how hard she tried, no matter how many times she reminded herself of his ulterior motives for every tender gesture and every passionate caress. Even when he had shown kindness, it had only been a part of his selfish plot, she recalled with brutal clarity.

Lacie dressed with haste. It was easier to push Dillon Lockwood out of her mind when she was busy, and she wasted no time in preparing for her coming confrontation. Yesterday she had been cool and elegant, even demure in her gray suit. But today the board's polite hostility could very well erupt into open warfare. Today she would wear the new red and black basque that Mrs. Gunter had made to go with her slim-fitting skirt. Today she would not let Dillon Lockwood tear her emotions apart.

The lobby was quiet when she went downstairs. The desk clerk smiled respectfully as she hesitated at the bottom of the stairs. The only other person she saw was an early morning diner, smoking a cigar as he pored over a local newspaper.

Lacie was not hungry; her stomach was too tied up in knots to abide food. But the board meeting would not begin for at least another hour. Getting there early was absolutely out of the question, for she could not risk running into Dillon, especially if there was no one else around.

A trifle uncertain, she left the hotel, descended the steps to the rain-washed boardwalk, and looked up and down the street. Despite the early hour, people were already beginning to go about their business. A shopkeeper across the way had removed his wooden shutters and was unfurling a pair of awnings over his display windows. A skinny little boy pulled a two-wheeled cart laden with neatly stacked newspapers. Two well-dressed businessmen walked briskly toward a bank, while a white-haired gentleman settled himself on a bench in front of a barbershop.

The air smelled clean, washed by the early morning rain and sweetened now by bright sunlight chasing the clouds away. As Lacie looked around, she could almost feel the pulse of the city and sense the energy and growth of which Dillon had spoken so enthusiastically. It was a young, vital town, rushing into the future. And Dillon was a large part of that future.

Depressed by the thought, Lacie arbitrarily started to walk. She had no particular destination. She only

wanted to pass the time and, perhaps, to prepare herself for the coming ordeal. But before she had progressed to the end of the block, she was hailed by a low,
familiar voice.

"Let me show you Denver." Dillon gave her a speculative look as he strode up, as if he were not quite sure
of the response he would get.

For her part Lacie wanted nothing more than to send
him packing. How dare he assume she would want to
see Denver with him! After his unforgivable behavior
last night? How dare he even speak to her!

"I am not interested in seeing Denver," she snapped,
turning to continue on her way. Unfortunately, he just
matched his pace to hers and strolled nonchalantly at
her side. Even when she hurried to put him behind her,
he lengthened his own long stride to keep up with her.

"I told you before that we were on my turf now. As
long as we're both here, why not take advantage of the
situation?"

"You *told* me nothing," she hissed. "What you did—
what you always do—is *threaten* me."

He caught her arm and forced her to a halt. "Can't
we compromise? Let's just say that I *warned* you. That's
not a threat. And if you don't want me to show you
Denver, how about if I just accompany you on your
tour?"

Lacie was not fool enough to fall for this self-serving
line of reasoning. He was trying to talk her into letting
him do exactly as he pleased. But she was helpless
against the emotions that his touch stirred in her. His
hand on her arm was warm through the several layers
of fabric, and her reckless heart ignored the logical
warnings that circled in her head. For an endless mo-

ment their eyes clung. Dark serious gray met clear piercing green. When he tucked her hand beneath his arm she did not protest, though something deep inside her quivered.

"Denver is an unusual town," he began without preamble. He deftly guided her to the edge of the boardwalk and started across the street with her.

"I don't care to know anything about Denver," she responded at last. She tried to pull her hand from his possessive hold, but it was to no avail.

"You'll like Denver if you just give it a chance."

"I don't *want* to like Denver," she answered heatedly. "I didn't want to come here, and I hope never to come back again!"

"Dammit! Will you stop being so difficult, at least for a little while?" He turned her toward him and stared hard at her mutinous face. "You're here now, so accept it. And remember, Lacie, as long as you plan on pretending you're Frederick's widow, you'll have to keep coming back here at least once a year."

For some strange reason he seemed amused by his own words, but Lacie was dismayed by them. Indeed, during the long hours of the night she had fretted about that very possibility. If she wanted to keep Sparrow Hill going she would never be completely rid of Dillon Lockwood. He would always be there somewhere, lurking in the background, waiting to be dealt with. Even when he was not physically there, his memory would haunt her just the same, waiting in benign repose until, when she was least prepared, it would spring forward to reopen all the painful memories.

She could not handle the pain now. Was she likely to do any better in the future?

Lacie averted her eyes from his too perceptive stare. Unbidden, the thought occurred that she could always say yes to him. If she wanted to, she could simply agree to marry him. But she quickly forced such a foolish idea away. That was only wishful dreaming, she told herself stubbornly. It was a business deal he had proposed, not really a marriage. But as his hands slid slightly lower on her arms, she knew she would have to keep on reminding herself of that fact. That was the only way to prevent herself from succumbing to the heat that enveloped her whenever he touched her, whenever he was anywhere near her.

She took a deep breath and steadied herself as best she could. "All right, show me Denver." She raised her eyes briefly to his darkly handsome face, then looked away. "Since I plan to be here every year for the board meeting, I may as well learn my way around," she added tersely.

"How sensible of you," he chuckled. Then he tucked her hand back under his arm and guided her up onto the next boardwalk. Although it was no more than a gentlemanly gesture, Lacie was suddenly reminded of another time and another town they'd strolled arm in arm. She had been unwilling then too. But now her unwillingness had another more vulnerable face to it.

The stiffness in her gait eased, and the rigidity of her posture slowly relaxed as they walked along and he pointed out buildings, businesses, and people. All around them the town was slowly coming to life. Besides the bank and the dry goods, the saddlers and the several saloons and entertainment establishments, Dillon pointed out a milliner's shop, two doctors' offices, several buildings sporting lawyers' shingles, and a freshly whitewashed church.

"The newspaper office is recent too," he told her, pointing out a two-storied building where a pair of carts waited for more loads of the freshly printed newspapers. "The first building floated away in the flood of 'sixty-four." He laughed, a warm, infectious sound. "They kept right on printing, though. Never missed an issue."

"You were already in Denver then?" she asked, forgetting that she'd planned to remain reserved and aloof.

"I was near Denver, up in those foothills before you reach Lookout Mountain." He gestured toward a distant range of hills and mountains to the west. "But I came in to town pretty often."

"You were working in the mines?" she asked as he guided her around a corner onto a street where the boardwalk was now being extended. New houses were being built in the area, and one already sported window boxes with bunches of violets and ivy trailing from them.

"I worked in the mines. I worked on the transports. I worked at anything and everything I could." He looked down at her with no trace of mocking or teasing in his face. "I worked hard because I believed I could build a good life for myself here."

"You—you've done very well," she conceded, as their eyes held for a long disconcerting moment. Then she swallowed convulsively and looked away. "You seem to have gotten everything you wanted."

He didn't respond right away. When he did, she wasn't entirely certain of his meaning.

"I haven't gotten everything I want," he said enigmatically. "Not yet."

Her heart raced as she pondered his meaning. Did he mean her? Yet as soon as that thought occurred another took its place. No, he meant Frederick's properties. He didn't have them all yet because she stood in the way. He wanted the properties, therefore he wanted her. She was back to the same old coil.

They walked another half-block in silence, both wrapped up in their own thoughts. Then Dillon halted before a red-brick building of Gothic design.

"The Methodist School," he said, answering her curious look. "It's newly built, yet already full, enrolled with girls." He gave her an intent look. "I thought you might be interested in seeing it."

Lacie could not deny her curiosity, although Dillon's motives in bringing her here aggravated her no end. Still, she was unable to appear disinterested.

Although it was imposing in its own right, the Methodist School did not begin to compare with Sparrow Hill. Still, there was a reassuring familiarity about the place. The building was empty now, but she knew that once the summer harvests were over, it would be filled with the sounds of children's high-pitched voices. That sound must certainly be the same no matter what school a person was in, she thought with a faint smile.

Despite the unseemliness of it and the fact that Dillon was watching her, Lacie could not resist approaching the school and peering through one of the uncurtained windows. Although there were pronounced differences between this school and her own Sparrow Hill, as she squinted to see into the dim interior, Lacie was struck more by its similarities than its differences. The same rows of desks, the same shelves of books, and a globe on the teacher's table.

But the sameness was more than even that, and she smiled ruefully when she recognized it. This was a place where children learned and teachers taught. It was not as grand and steeped in tradition as Sparrow Hill, but it was a school with teachers and children, and that was always a step in the right direction.

She rubbed a spot clear on the window, leaning closer as she stared into the schoolroom. Despite herself, she found the place strangely appealing. But then she remembered Dillon's so-called proposal. He expected her to give up her beautiful school—and everything else Frederick had owned—for the dubious pleasure of becoming his wife and allowing him to give her a new school to occupy herself with. Wouldn't he just love to get all that property back in his clutches? she thought in returning annoyance. Then he would build her a little school—probably no match even for this one, and consider her well paid.

Lacie stepped back from the school and shook her head slowly. She'd be a fool to consider it, and he was quite mad to think she would. When she turned back to face him, her wavering emotions were buoyed by righteous anger. But she was brought up short by a middle-aged woman watching the two of them curiously.

"Have you children that require schooling?" the neatly dressed woman asked.

"What? Oh—um, no." Lacie glanced from Dillon to the woman, then back once more to Dillon. She was completely flustered by the woman's mistake, even as understandable as it was. "No, I . . . uh—we don't."

The woman smiled. "No doubt you one day will. And

when you do, my dear, you couldn't do better than this Methodist School. Even if you aren't Methodist," she added conspiratorially. "Of course, they're already filled to capacity, but if you talk to them well in advance, you can get yourself a place for your child. And it appears you've got plenty of time." She smiled at the two of them as she started on her way. "It's a good place. My Mary graduated from there this past May. First of her class."

"That's quite admirable," Dillon said with a winning smile at the beaming woman. "You must be very proud of her."

To his credit, Dillon did not press the point on their return walk. But there was no need, for Lacie was already too disconcerted by the woman's casual assumption that they were husband and wife. A part of her wondered why she was struggling so hard against what seemed the easiest and most logical solution to her dilemma. Just marry him, move the school, and be content.

But another part of her—her heart—knew that she would never be completely content with such an arrangement. She *would* marry him if he loved her, but he did not.

Lacie was buried in thought, quite morose indeed, when they reached the three-storied brick building that housed Dillon's offices. Lacie shook herself out of her gloomy mood and examined the building with more interest than she had the previous day. It was a magnificent new structure, among the finest in Denver from what she had seen, certainly in the best of taste. Dillon clearly had a knack for giving himself the trappings of respectability. From his clothes to his offices to the hotel he had created, he appeared every inch the cream of Denver society.

But that was only appearances, she reminded herself. Although he looked the part, inside he was all business and no feelings. Still, as she stared up at his prosperous-looking offices, she had to admit that his attitude was probably what accounted for his astounding success in business. He did what he had to do. He made the deals he had to make. No regrets, no apologies, as long as the profits increased.

She started up the steps only to be restrained by Dillon's hand on her arm. When she turned to face him, he stared at her with eyes too perceptive for her peace of mind. She could feel her pulse beginning to race.

"So, what do you think of Denver?" His gaze did not waver from her face.

"It's—well, it's bigger and more prosperous than I had expected. I thought there would be more miners and cowboys, fewer families and children," she admitted softly.

"Yes, I thought so." He took her arm and guided her up the granite steps. "How did you like the school?"

Lacie was so undone by the return of his hand to her arm that his words did not register at first. But once they paused at the doors, she looked up at him.

"The school was very nice. I'm sure it will do well." She paused, and her jaw tightened stubbornly. "Every town needs a good school." Then she pulled her arm free and reached for the doorknob.

Dillon was not so easily shaken off, however. He too reached for the knob, then kept his hand firmly over her smaller one, forcing them to open the door together.

"After you," he murmured quietly, but his voice had recaptured some of its more typical mocking tone.

"Thank you," she muttered reluctantly, suddenly too conscious of his warm palm encircling her hand. Then, before he could do any further damage to her shattered nerves, she gathered her skirts and hurried in, not stopping to see whether he followed or stayed, anxious only to put as much space between them as was possible.

But distance was not enough to prevent her from feeling the inexorable effects of Dillon's overwhelming presence. Even as she hurried down the hall toward the boardroom, she could feel his eyes upon her back. He might as well have been caressing her, so vivid was the effect on her devastated nerves. Why, oh, why had she consented to walk with him? she fretted as she paused before the boardroom, struggling to calm her breathing. It was hard enough to oppose him when he was being hateful and contrary. But when he played the gentleman, when he was pleasant and cordial, far too many foolish hopes started circling in her mind. How pleased he must be with himself! she thought miserably. How well-satisfied and content! Even now that smug grin was no doubt painted on his face as he contemplated everything he expected to gain when she finally gave in to him.

Unexpected tears stung her eyes as she once more recalled how businesslike his proposal had been last night. He didn't really want a wife, she reminded herself. He wanted a business partner, one he could control. And if the truth were known, he didn't really want that either. All he had ever really wanted from her was . . .

She stiffened and banished the tear before it could

fall. He wanted a mistress, and he wanted all of Frederick's property. His proposal to her would in effect get him both of those. He saw their marriage as no more than another business contract, and since he didn't love his business partners, why would he expect to love her?

It was just her poor misfortune to have fallen desperately in love with him.

The sound of voices approaching shook Lacie out of her self-pitying thoughts, and with a quick dab at her eyes she collected herself. She recognized Dillon's voice among the men coming toward her, but she refused to look over at him, fearing that he would see how emotionally overwrought she had become. Instead she grasped the door handle and entered the room, sending a few tight smiles to the men she had met the previous day, then hurrying to her now familiar place at the end of the long table.

She busied herself reviewing the papers before her as the last of the board members found their places. Even when Dillon called the meeting to order, she could not meet the sharp green gaze that she felt so clearly turned upon her. Her emotions were too raw, and she feared he would see how vulnerable she was. He no doubt already believed she was considering his unfeeling proposal, especially after the walk they'd shared this morning. What would he think if he saw tears glistening so near the surface of her eyes? She could not give him that advantage.

". . . my reason for discussing the financial status of the privately held companies before the entire board will soon be clear. I am proposing a three-year plan of aggressive expansion among the entire family of companies. The railroads are expanding. Denver is on the verge of experiencing an explosion of growth, and we are in the enviable position of being able to profit handsomely if we are willing to take some risks."

"I don't see how there are any risks under those circumstances," Mr. Cunningham remarked amiably. "Denver's growth means our growth."

"So it does. But I'm not talking about complacently benefiting from that growth. This is the right time to expand the carriage works to build railroad cars as well. This is the right time to build new hardware stores in all the neighboring towns. This is the right time to open a lumberyard and a construction outfit in every town where the railroad stops." He paused and looked over the crowd of now-interested members. Then his gaze rested on Lacie, and an ominous shiver of apprehension ran up her spine. He had been softening her up this morning, but she knew with an irrational certainty that he was about to launch his attack now. And she was far from ready.

"The risk I'm speaking of involves the personal financial commitment of every single one of you." Again he paused, but this time his eyes would not meet hers. "If you can all agree to forgo dividends for the next four quarters, each company will have the monetary resources to finance these projects."

There was a brief silence as everyone digested that proposal. Lacie frowned, trying to understand how that affected Sparrow Hill, but her thoughts were interrupted when someone asked a question.

"Didn't you say this would be a three-year proposal?"

"Yes, but I'm proposing that we evaluate our progress on a yearly basis."

"Makes it more palatable to those of us being socked, eh?" Mr. Cunningham chuckled.

Dillon grinned. "Hopefully." Then he became more serious. "I'm sure some of you count on your quarterly dividends to supplement the other business and personal expenses you incur. If you agree to my proposal, however, you will not be able to touch that money." His eyes paused briefly on Lacie, seeming to burn her with their intensity. Then they moved on.

"Any shortfalls in your income would have to be supplemented by other means."

In sudden comprehension Lacie sat bolt upright. Her eyes locked on Dillon as she realized with sickening clarity just what he was doing. Her hand went to her throat as he continued to speak, but she didn't hear the remainder of his words. She had already heard the crucial part, and she understood now exactly what he planned. He was blocking her only means of support for the school. With his track record of success and the promise of even greater financial rewards, he was enticing the other board members to go along with him.

She glanced around at the men who were listening so raptly to Dillon's well-calculated presentation. There wasn't one of them who did not appear sufficiently well off to weather a temporary absence of their usual dividends. From young to old, from lean and eager to fat and complacent, they might not have all been born gentlemen, but in the rough-and-tumble climate of the Colorado Territory they had all become quite rich. Although next to Dillon she held the most stock in the companies, she was very likely the poorest of them all, she suddenly realized.

Averting her gaze, Lacie stared unseeingly at her lap,

THIEF OF MY HEART

a hole in Dillon's logic. Surely there was a reason for the
board members not to go along with his plan. To her
dismay, however, they seemed to think it a well-considered idea. Her shoulders slumped as she tried to fight
off an awful feeling of defeat. Then her eyes focused on
the simple ring she had taken from Frederick's things,
the one she was passing off as her wedding band. At that
moment the plain little band felt very much like a wedding ring, a symbol of the trust that Frederick had
placed in her. Although he had not given it to her to
signify marriage, with his last dying words, he had
seemed to entrust to her the care of his beloved school.

Preserve my school, he had uttered before he had
fallen into that final coma. She knew with certainty that
he had wanted her to keep Sparrow Hill going. Although her methods in doing that might appear a little
suspect, her motives had nevertheless always been
pure.

Lacie twisted the ring about her finger, feeling the
lightly carved flowers and the warmth of the delicate
band. Strengthened and restored, she straightened her
shoulders and lifted her gaze to Dillon.

He had just finished his bid for their approval and was
smiling confidently at the group. When his eyes met
hers, however, his grin seemed to turn smug. She gritted her teeth as her resolve faltered. He seemed always
to affect her so, intimidating her both with his overwhelming magnetism and with his arrogant grasp of
every situation. But this was her last stand, her final
chance to keep the school solvent. Bravely, she met his
intense stare with her own.

"Before everyone blithely goes along with this proposal, I'd like to say a few things."

Every head turned toward her and all background whispering abruptly died. Lacie's mouth felt as dry as cotton as she faced the silent group. But after several long seconds it was not she but Dillon who spoke.

"I have no intention of calling for a vote on this matter today, Lacie. As the rest of the board members know, it is my custom to introduce a subject one day for discussion, and after everyone has had a night to mull it over, to call for a vote the following day."

Lacie felt the mild chastisement in his voice and her cheeks grew warm as she realized how silly she must appear to the other avidly watching men. Still, the damage was already done. Besides, she knew better than to trust Dillon, especially when he sounded so reasonable.

"Are you saying it's inappropriate to discuss the subject now?"

He studied her for a moment. "Not at all. I'm saying this *is* the time to discuss it. We'll discuss it as long as we need to today. And we'll discuss it even more tomorrow before we vote on it." He cocked his head as he regarded her. "No one is going to blithely go along with my proposal, as you put it."

There was a horrible silence after that, and Lacie could not have been more embarrassed. Everything he said was so logical and well thought out that he seemed moved by only the best of intentions. By contrast, she must seem like a suspicous, grasping shrew. She sat back a little as she peered dejectedly at him. Once more he had drawn her in, then allowed her to hang herself. If the wary faces of the other board members were any indication, they were hardly flattered to be depicted as sheep blindly following the shepherd's call. Now that she had inadvertently belittled them, she would have to work twice as hard to win them over.

She swallowed hard as she considered her response, for she knew every word she said from now on would count.

"I'm sorry if I misunderstood you, Dil—Mr. Lockwood," she amended hastily. "And I certainly did not mean to imply that the board members would not judge all sides of this proposal on their merit."

"Come now, Lacie, there's no reason to stand on ceremony here. You can call me Dillon at the board meetings, the same as you do in private."

She couldn't prevent the icy glare she sent him at that unsettling remark. He was deliberately trying to provoke her! It took all her willpower not to snap back at him. But that was what he wanted, she reminded herself. That was exactly what he wanted.

Still, she felt like a loser regardless of what she did, for as the meeting progressed it was clear that Dillon was enjoying her strenuous efforts to stay calm and polite almost as much as he would if she had pitched a fit in front of the board. That was obvious from the slight curve to his lips and the amused glint in his glass-green eyes as he watched her. Even when he spoke, she was conscious of a subtle goading in his tone, his impeccable manners and his unquestionably polite demeanor notwithstanding. He had never treated her so solicitously before, and that only proved it was all for show. Yet no one else knew what he was up to and that galled her to no end. She knew he was putting on an act. And he was aware that she knew his game. But he also knew there was nothing she could do about it, and that clearly was what amused him the most.

She struggled to compose herself as he responded to a question from another board member.

"Those numbers sound very good," she interjected with as much grace as she could muster. "But you are in effect asking this board to use money that is not its own to finance your elaborate plans."

"The money is all dividend money that is generated within the family of companies."

"Yes, but dividends are by their very nature the earnings of the stockholders," she interrupted with great heat. "You want to spend my earnings on your projects when you know very well—" She stopped herself before she said too much. "When you must know that others of us have definite plans for our dividend earnings—plans quite separate from the schemes you've been preparing."

"I never doubted that for a minute," he answered in an infuriatingly polite tone.

"Might I say, Mrs. Kimbell," Mr. Andrews put in, "that you've not had the benefit of observing Mr. Lockwood's successes in business as the rest of us have. If it will help to appease your concern, I am certain that the few years we do without our profits will reward us with far greater earnings in the many years to come." He smiled hopefully. "Perhaps you could put your other plans on hold for a year or two?"

And let Dillon win? Lacie thought in frustration. And let him close her school? Not a chance. Yet she knew better than to express any open hostility toward Dillon when it was clear that practically the entire board was in his camp. It took all her willpower to keep her expression pleasant as she responded to Mr. Andrews.

"Putting my plans on hold could mean the demise of a project near and dear to the heart of my late husband," she said very quietly, deciding it was time to pull out all the stops. If reason wouldn't sway them, perhaps appealing to their heartstrings would. "He cared more for the Sparrow Hill School for Young Ladies than he did for any of his other businesses. Indeed, I now see that for him, all these other investments were only the means to provide income for his school." She glanced around and tried to make herself look the needy widow. "His last words to me were of his school. I couldn't bear to let it go under. Yet, if I am denied my profits . . ." she trailed off, choking on emotions that were not affectation at all.

There was a brief silence and for a moment Lacie felt a glimmer of hope. She'd actually made them pause in their all-fired hurry to do whatever the wonderful Dillon Lockwood said. But Dillon was quick to answer her.

"Your plans to keep Frederick's school going are admirable, Lacie. Certainly I have no objection to that," he said easily. But the glint in his narrowed eyes said otherwise. "I think, however, that you would do well to make an effort to improve the school so that it could become financially solvent."

There was little Lacie could say to refute that argument, yet she refused to let Dillon have the final word. She gave him a smile, although her eyes shot daggers at him. "I assure you, that *is* my goal. However, it may take a while to do so. All I'm asking is not to be deprived of my rightful earnings in the meantime."

He stiffened at her use of the word *rightful*, and she

felt a small twinge of remorse. Oh, why must the two of them be at such an impasse? she fretted. Why couldn't they have met under better circumstances? Then perhaps he would have liked her more, maybe even fallen in love with her.

She tore her gaze away from him and folded her hands tightly. She was ten times a fool to think such maudlin thoughts, she told herself sternly. Under different circumstances he wouldn't have paid her the least attention. She was hardly the flashy sort that appealed to him. She wasn't at all like that blond woman she'd seen him with. No, he'd only paid this much flattering attention to her because she had opposed him and presented him with an obstacle to overcome. It behooved her to keep that in mind.

Restored by the memory of the hurt and humiliation she'd suffered at his hands, she quashed any weakness she felt for him. But it was nonetheless a long and exhausting meeting. By the afternoon she was no nearer winning a sufficient number of board members to her way of thinking than she'd been when she first walked in the door.

When one of the members called for an early adjournment, citing the coming evening's reception, Lacie was surprised by Dillon's agreeableness. She was more than relieved to escape the oppressive confines of the meeting, for she desperately needed to rethink her position. Tomorrow they would vote, she worried as she rose to leave. That meant she had to convince the other members to oppose Dillon's ambitious plans. And she had to find a reason for them to oppose it that affected all of them, not just her. That would be difficult, however, because even she could see the logic of his proposal. His plans for expanding the companies would make her a very rich woman if she went along, she realized. But such wealth would cost her the one thing she most wanted—Frederick's school. It was a depressing, seemingly impossible situation.

She was so caught up in her dismal thoughts that she did not notice the men milling around and slowly exiting in front of her. But when a hand caught her arm, preventing her from leaving, she knew at once whose warm grasp it was.

"I'll thank you never to touch me again," she hissed as she tried to free her arm.

"Careful, now," he taunted in a husky whisper. "You don't want to reveal to everyone what a devious little witch you are." He chuckled and pulled her back from the doorway and into the empty boardroom. "After all, you've been working so hard to perfect your image as the sweet little widow."

"No harder than you work to appear the well-mannered gentleman!"

"But I *am* a well-mannered gentleman."

"And I *am* a sweet little widow!"

It sounded ridiculous as soon as she said it. She'd meant it to sound scathingly sarcastic, since he knew the truth about her even if he couldn't prove it. But the words were no sooner out of her mouth when he let out a low chuckle. She herself had to fight back a smile that suddenly threatened to rise unbidden to her own lips.

"Ah, Lacie," he murmured, pulling her nearer now with a hand on each of her upper arms. "Such a sweet, sweet little widow." His face lowered toward hers, and her stomach lurched in instant awareness of him. "Such a sweet, sweet little liar."

Then his mouth found hers, and for an earth-shattering moment their lips clung together. It was a hot, searing kiss, made even more so by the complete unexpectedness of it. She had worked so hard to bury these wicked feelings she had for him, to hide the terrible desire that seethed within her. Yet with one kiss, with one tender touch, he had brought them rising to the surface, boiling over the edge until she was scalded with their intensity.

His lips moved sensually across hers. His teeth lightly tugged at her full lower lip, and then his tongue smoothed over it. Like the sleekest silk, the warmest velvet, he seemed to enfold her within his embrace, seducing her with that steadily heating kiss. Then his tongue slipped between her lips to meet with her own.

Lacie felt the shock of his kiss down to her toes. Everywhere she reacted: her heart pounded painfully in her chest, her blood roared like heated lava through her veins, and her stomach twisted and tightened, turning over deep inside her.

She leaned against his chest as the kiss deepened, wanting this security and warmth more than ever. Yet even as she accepted him, going more and more pliant against his hard masculine frame, she knew it could not be. Like an irritating voice, reality pricked her, reminding her—taunting her—with the knowledge that what he wanted and what she wanted were incompatible. What his kiss promised was physical pleasure. What her kiss sought was love. The two could go hand in hand, but only if both of them were willing. But love was not a part of Dillon's scheme, she knew.

With a small moan she turned her face away from his, but Dillon only moved his lips to her neck, moving in small torturous kisses from just below her jawline and down the soft sensitive skin to her collarbone. She gasped as his tongue made small circles at the base of her throat.

It would be heaven to just give in, the aberrant thought came into her mind. Just to give in and enjoy being with him. It would be wonderful, even more than it had been before, she conceded to herself as his hand moved to her waist and pressed her intimately against him.

But afterward it would be even worse.

Only that thought gave her the strength to disentangle herself from his adamant embrace. Even then, however, he did not let her go completely but only let his palms slide down her arms to grab hold of her hands.

They stood thus, a little apart, her face flushed and her breathing coming hard and fast. Dillon's eyes were bright upon her, vivid with a desire she recognized uncomfortably well. In dismay, she tried to tug her hands free, but he only tightened his hold and stepped nearer, pressing her palms against his chest.

"Ah, damn, but you are enough to tempt a saint." His eyes stared down into hers with an intensity that frightened her. She wanted so badly to see love there, yet she knew better than to read anything into his avid gaze. He wanted her, she told herself bleakly, but that was not the same as love. Still, the warmth in his eyes, the beguiling smile that curved his sensuous lips could almost be . . .

Lacie averted her eyes, terrified of where her thoughts were leading her. She must not be misled by wishful thinking, she had to remind herself. That would only lead to disaster.

"We already know you're no saint," she murmured in a quiet wavering voice.

"Nor, thank goodness, are you."

He went to put one hand around her again, but this time she prevented him, twisting away and freeing her hands from him. She took a step back and stared up at him with eyes wide and a dark, stormy gray.

"I may be no saint, but I know better than to court the devil." Then she had to bite her lower lip to still its trembling. She turned abruptly, blindly groping for the door as tears sprang unbidden to her eyes. She had to get away from him.

To her enormous relief, he did not try to stop her. It was only when she reached the door that he spoke at all.

"You may fight me. You may run from me. But one thing you cannot do, Lacie, is deny the pull we both feel so strongly. Call me the devil if you wish, but you are just as surely the devil's mistress."

As she ran from the room, his words seemed to echo all around her. In her head she tried to deny it, to shout down everything he had said. It wasn't true—it wasn't!

But her heart knew the truth. Her heart felt that pull even more strongly than her body, and it was her heart that could not deny him.

19

The engraved invitation read eight o'clock. Lacie, how-ever, did not plan to arrive before eight thirty, or per-haps even nine. After all, she reasoned, it was not a dinner where everyone must be present to sit down at a prescribed hour, so there was really no rush. She would go up to the Palace ballroom for the board members' reception only after it was safely filled with people. The last thing she wanted was to find herself alone with Dillon.

She paused while rolling up her good pair of silk stockings. Dillon once more consumed her every thought, indeed he had not been out of her mind since she had fled his presence after the board meeting. Over and over she had relived those passionate seconds when he'd kissed her and broken down her meager defenses. As if he were with her still, she could feel his arms around her and his body pressed hard against hers. She could taste his kiss on her lips, and she had only to close her eyes . . .

Lacie caught herself before she could imagine what else they might have done, where their fervent lovemaking might have taken them. To think about that was surely to court disaster!

And yet, trying to put him out of her mind was driving her quite mad.

With a frustrated sigh she pulled her garter over her foot, then slid it up and positioned it just above her knee. Then she stood up and shook out her slip. If she were planning to arrive late, why was she dressing so early? She had bathed and brushed out her hair as soon as she'd returned to her room. Then a maid had come to lace up her corset and arrange her coiffure.

The girl had done a truly remarkable job with her straight thick hair, Lacie thought as she examined herself in the vanity mirror. From a center part her hair was softly drawn back in two large waves, partially covering her ears but still allowing her ear bobs to show. A little above the nape of her neck, all her hair was caught up in a large knot, the shining mass woven through with velvet ribbons sewn with jet beading. Several large loops of hair hung down the back of her neck, twisted with the shining beads, and she held a small hand mirror up to catch the full effect. It was the most cunning of styles, at once both demure and striking. It was the perfect touch for the wonderful black dress she and Ada had made.

She put down the mirror and stared once more at her pale reflection. She had only to don her half-crinoline, tie on her shoes, and step into her dress to be ready. Yet it was not even eight o'clock. How was she to pass the time?

Certainly not by thinking about Dillon, she vowed earnestly. She picked up the crinoline and absently fastened it about her slip. She pulled the ribbons snug at her waist, then straightened it so that the wired portion was situated properly in the rear. She was fiddling with the lower ties when a firm knock sounded from the door.

At once Lacie's heart was in her throat. Who would call for her at this hour? Before she could gather her thoughts, the knock came once more—four sharp raps that sounded almost authoritative, so obvious was the command in them. Then she knew who it was, and her knees suddenly became so weak that she had to sit down on the bargello-upholstered settee.

Why, why, why? She shivered as she thought of Dillon standing just beyond that thin paneled door. He was so near, and she wanted him so badly.

The knock came a third time, louder than before. "Lacie, I know you're in there. Answer the door."

"Go away." She hardly wanted him to, but anything else would be quite insane. "Go away!" she insisted with more strength.

There was a brief silence from the door, but Lacie knew he was unlikely to leave so easily. When he spoke, his voice was lower and far more compelling.

"I've come to escort you to the reception, Lacie. I didn't want you to have to enter alone."

She wrapped her arms tightly about her waist. Her heart thundered in her chest, and her palms grew damp. Her voice was less than steady when she answered him.

"I don't mind arriving alone. And—and anyway, I'm not ready yet."

Again the unnerving silence as she strained to hear his reply.

"Perhaps I can help you dress." This time there was a

dark warmth to his voice that set all her senses clamoring. She leaped up from the settee in agitation and looked madly about for her wrapper. But then he was speaking again, and she stopped and whirled around to face the door.

"If you were considering coming late, I recommend you change your plans. As the two major stockholders in the family of companies, it's only natural that you and I act as host and hostess tonight." When she didn't answer right away, he rattled the doorknob. "Lacie? Answer me."

"N-no," she managed weakly. Then she crept nearer the door, holding her hands protectively around her tightly cinched waist. "I'm not ready. And I won't play the hostess for you!" she added with much heat.

He let out a low chuckle. "Do you think you could answer a question honestly?" He did not wait for her reply but continued on. "Just tell me: do you direct this obstinance at everyone you meet as much as at me? Or am I alone the one you vent your stubbornness on?"

"Only you!" she snapped in quick anger. "You're the only one who torments me. And you're the only one—" She trailed off in a mixture of confusion, anger, and humiliation.

"Well, I suppose I should feel flattered." The door creaked slightly as if he had leaned against it. "But no matter your obstinance, I have to insist that you finish dressing and come upstairs with me now. You would otherwise appear most impolite."

"To whom? You?"

"Not to me, Lacie. You should know by now that I like nothing better than to cross swords with you. Well, almost nothing," he added, causing her to stiffen. "It's all the other board members I'm referring to—the ones you desperately need to court if you're to best me in the vote tomorrow. They're the ones you risk offending tonight."

Lacie didn't know how to answer that. Did they all expect her to play the part of hostess? Was that one of those unwritten rules of business etiquette of which she knew nothing? She floundered between her suspicions of Dillon's motives and her fear of losing tomorrow's vote because of a social blunder. But Dillon gave her no time to make up her mind. Once more he rattled the doorknob.

"Let me in, Lacie. I'm tired of arguing through this door."

"Then go away. I'll—I'll be there in good time."

"No doubt you'll understand that I don't believe you. Fortunately, I have a key that opens every door in the hotel."

"No!" she shrieked as she dashed for the door. She grabbed the handle, holding on for dear life. "Don't you dare open this door," she warned, truly frightened now. Her only protection lay in surrounding herself with other people and never being alone with him. But if he should come into her room! In desperation she tightened her hold on the doorknob.

"Then promise me you'll get dressed right now." For emphasis he slid the key into the lock.

In the ensuing seconds Lacie struggled to contain her frustration. If she didn't agree he would most certainly push his way in. But it would be galling to once more bow to one of his unreasonable whims. Either way she would find herself alone with him. But one way she would be dressed; the other way she would be—

She had no time to relay her decision to him. With a distinctively metallic click, the key turned in the lock. Beneath her hand the doorknob twisted, and the door began to open.

"Stop! Wait!" she cried as she frantically leaned her weight against the door.

"I've waited long enough," he said, his voice much clearer now as the door steadily inched forward.

"Oh!" Lacie gave up with an alarmed cry and leaped clear of the door. As Dillon lurched suddenly into the room she had only to see his darkly handsome face and those perceptive jade eyes of his on her barely clad form to become completely unsettled.

She whirled away and dashed for the bedroom, slamming the door soundly behind her. Her hands shook as she turned the key, for she had no doubt he could breach this door just as easily. Without regard for the fine fabric or the careful ironing it had been given, she grabbed the black dress from the bed, stepped hurriedly into the skirt, and began madly to pull it on. She had no care for the meticulously sewn seams or the finely stitched details. The delicacy of the black figured sateen was completely lost to her as she frantically twisted the skirt around, trying to get the bodice properly aligned so that she could shove her arms into the sleeves.

She was struggling with the left sleeve and unsuccessfully trying to avoid stepping on the skirt when the bedroom door flew open. Framed in the doorway, Dillon came no farther into the room but simply stood staring at her. For a breathtaking moment their eyes remained locked. Lacie was caught with her left hand buried somewhere in the tight-fitting sleeve, but the

bodice was still twisted at her waist, and the voluminous skirts were caught under her foot and snagged on
the half-crinoline. Her shoulders and the upper swells
of her breasts were completely bared to his view, yet
for an endless moment she was unable to move to cover
herself. His steady gaze would not free her. Then she
felt his vivid green eyes slide down to take in her revealing disarray, and a rosy flush washed over her.

"Get out of here," she pleaded, whirling around to
hide her shameful dishabille. She shoved her hand farther into the sleeve, but to her absolute dismay she
became more tangled than ever in the beautiful yards
of sateen.

"I came to get you for the reception, and my motives
have not changed. Although I was fully prepared to
dress you if necessary, I hardly expected to be so fortunate." He paused and Lacie felt his gaze as clearly as a
bold and heated caress. "Can I give you a hand?"

"No!" She reached down with her right hand and
tried to free the fabric caught beneath her foot. But
when she moved her right foot, she lost her balance.
With her left hand still stuck in the sleeve, she could not
prevent toppling forward. Only Dillon's timely inter-
vention stopped her from landing painfully on the floor.
With one hand on each of her shoulders, he caught her
and turned her around to face him.

"Why didn't you send for a maid to help you?" he
murmured, keeping his hands quite possessively upon
her.

Lacie stared up at him, unnerved now by his overwhelming nearness. Where had her anger fled? she
wondered obliquely. Where was her resolve and her

righteous indignation? A proper lady would give him a proper set-down.

A proper lady would, but she just could not.

She averted her face, unwilling to stare up into his harshly beautiful face. He was so handsome in his formal clothes. Against the black doeskin jacket and vest and the pristine white of his shirt, his face glowed tan and healthy. His hair gleamed black as a raven's wing. Like a chameleon, he fitted as well into a society fête as he did into a small-town fair. He had been born a bastard in a little shack, then proved himself in the rough Colorado Territory. Now he was charming Denver—and he was charming her.

She pressed her lips together and took a shaky breath. "The maid was to return later," she whispered softly. "Then I would have gone up to the reception."

"You don't need her now. I'm here." So saying, he tugged lightly at her skirt to free it from beneath her foot. Then he moved his hands down to her waist and deftly twisted the fabric free of the stiff crinoline.

"Damned inconvenient, these undergarments you women wear." He grinned slightly and his hands settled firmly at her waist. "The only good thing I can say for them is that they do allow a man's imagination free rein. Especially when he already knows what all that wire and ribbon hide."

At her horrified gasp his grin turned decidedly wicked. Then he pulled her a little nearer and she began to panic.

"I don't need your help," she muttered as she jerked away from him. She started to turn away, for she was humiliated by how much of her bosom was exposed to his bold glance. But then she hesitated. To turn her

back on this untrustworthy man would be foolish indeed.

Yet to look at him, so tall and virile, so intensely male,
was not wise either, she realized. With her heart pounding in her throat and her breath coming quick and
shallow, she forced herself to look away from him and
slip her arms all the way into the sleeves.

She pulled up the bodice with hands that trembled,
then nervously lifted her eyes up to him. "If you'll just
summon a maid, I'll be ready—"

"I'll fasten your dress."

"No!" Lacie's cry was shrill, and she backed away at
once. But Dillon was not put off by her protest. With
the sure confidence of a predator, he moved steadily
toward her until she was backed into a corner and he
was only inches from her.

With eyes wide and wary Lacie faced him. She hated
him, she told herself. She truly did. Yet she could not
ignore the insidious warmth stealing up from her belly,
nor the rapid beating of her heart. She wanted to de-
nounce him, but no words came to mind. Instead she
kept thinking of the kiss they had shared earlier, and
like a mesmerized doll she could only stand there, painfully conscious of his scent, his warmth, and the pure
animal magnetism of him.

Dillon's eyes were as warm as molten lava as he
stared down at her, as sure and confident as ever. If he
kisses me, Lacie thought wildly, if he kisses me I am
lost.

He reached for her and drew her forward, but then
he turned her around and with clever fingers began to
button up her gown. Lacie was too stunned to react and
too appalled by the wave of disappointment that

washed over her. What in heaven's name was wrong with her that she could have such a perverse response to him? How could she have fallen so low?

It didn't make things any better that the smooth motion of his fingers was sending the most exquisite tremors up her spine.

"Is this so bad?" he said softly, his breath a warm tickle at her ear.

But Lacie was too unsure of her voice to answer.

When he reached the final top button he let his hands linger at her skin. Then he bent forward and placed a light kiss on the side of her neck. "May I help you to remove this dress later tonight?"

She swallowed hard at his seductive words, dismayed at her traitorous reaction to the very sound of his voice. Oh, how easy it would be to say yes!

But to say yes would only bring her more grief. It took all her willpower to slip away from his possessive touch.

"If you'll wait in the sitting room, I'll be ready in a moment," she managed to get out in a soft and breathless voice.

"I'd rather stay." He turned and followed her restless movement away from him.

"And what I want, naturally, matters not a whit," she shot back with returning heat.

"You're always too hasty to judge me, Lacie, too hasty to find fault with everything I do and say. The fact is, no matter how you deny it, you're just as eager for me as I am for you. Only that ridiculous facade of respectability that you maintain stops you."

Despite the truth of his words, Lacie refused to admit it to him. "You are so wicked and—and so crude that you think everyone is just like you!" She turned away before he could see the truth in her eyes, and picked up her gloves and evening purse. She was almost to the door, desperate to escape the intimate confines of the room, when she realized she had not yet donned her shoes. She halted and looked quickly around for them, but she found to her complete dismay that they now dangled in Dillon's raised hand, twisting back and forth from their black satin ribbons.

"Looking for these?"

"Give them to me," she muttered, tight-lipped.

"Come and get them."

Lacie stared at him, irritated by his smug taunt. Anger, frustration, longing—how many ways must he manipulate her emotions? Disheartened that he always managed to gain the upper hand, she abruptly turned and marched into the cream and mauve sitting room. There, with a great display of hauteur, she seated herself in a chair, fully intending to wait him out this time. After all, she wasn't thrilled about going to this reception. He was the one so anxious to get there.

When he followed her into the room she had a smug smile firmly in place. But Dillon quickly dissolved her hard-won posture.

"Allow me." He grinned as he stopped before her, then went down on one knee. With a quick lift of her skirts, he brought one of her feet up to rest on his thigh.

At once she tried to pull her foot free, but although his warm grasp slid a little along her silken hose, her foot remained nonetheless upon his leg.

"I can put my own shoes on!" she insisted as he pushed her skirt up almost to her knee. But he only grinned at her, then let his hand slip ever so slowly along her calf.

"But I'd rather do it." Then his hand gripped her foot and began to massage it very gently. Warm and knowing, his fingers squeezed the bottoms of her toes, then moved slowly up her foot along her arch and finally to her heel. Lacie caught her breath at his clever touch. It occurred to her that she was ticklish and that his light caress should have dissolved her into nervous laughter. But that was hardly the reaction he inspired in her. Oh, she was nervous all right, and her stomach had tightened into a knot. But she felt much more like moaning in pleasure than giggling in discomfort. She stared at him in sheer confusion as he raised her other foot to his knee as well.

What was there about this man that caused her to become so undone every time he touched her? This wasn't a kiss or a caress by any normal standards. And yet she recognized well enough the sizzling reaction that churned in her belly and radiated out through her body. How could he control her so?

Lacie sat as still as a mouse under Dillon's adept hands. She was unable to speak and, indeed, was afraid even to move, she was so overpowered by his simple act. But her eyes darkened with the intensity of her feelings, and she could not mistake the answering heat in Dillon's devouring gaze. Then both of his hands slid up the silken smoothness of her calves to stroke the tender flesh behind her knees, and her heart seemed actually to stop.

It was time to give in. Lacie could fathom no reason to hold back any longer, and she felt a strange, exhilarating relief to admit it.

She could not know that her expression softened, that her lips parted slightly, and that her lids lowered in mute acceptance of him. She only knew that he unexpectedly withdrew his hands from her legs and let out a short, muffled oath. When she looked back up at him, he was breathing hard and fumbling for her forgotten shoes, his eyes determinedly averted. To her complete dismay he quickly slipped her shoes onto her feet, wound the ties about her ankles, and tied them.

"Is that too tight?" he asked, finally raising his eyes back to her.

Lacie shook her head, too unsure of her voice to speak. Why was he torturing her so? She was too agitated to notice that he also seemed uncomfortable. She only knew that he seemed to take particular pleasure in manipulating her emotions until her longings for him were completely transparent. Then he could sit back and gloat over her helplessness.

As he stood up she looked down into her lap and the poor twisted mitts in her hands. Of all the men in the world, he was the most perverse, and of all the women, she was the most foolish. Yet no amount of self-recrimination could change the way she felt.

"Shall we go?" he asked, his voice low and subdued.

Lacie lifted her chin as bravely as she could, but she could not quite manage to meet his eyes. She stood up mutely, making a great display of pulling on her black lace evening mitts. She hesitated when he offered his arm to her, but to her surprise he did not press the issue when she refused. He only gave her a quick bow, then gestured for her to precede him. Still, as she passed by him, so near that her hem brushed against his shoes, the crackling attraction between them could not be mistaken.

In the hall he paused to lock her door. Lacie tried to put a little distance between them by hurrying on, but when she glanced back at him she knew it was a futile gesture. His eyes held hers captive as he moved down the hall to where she stood very still, seeming almost to wait for him. When he reached her side he paused, and in the soft golden light from the wall-mounted lamps he appeared the most magnificent of male creatures. He reached out as if to take her arm. But then he stopped and only touched her bottom lip so lightly she wasn't sure it happened at all.

"If you don't want to go . . ."

The remainder of his statement dangled in the air between them, unspoken yet understood. The temptation to accept his silent offer was so powerful she had to bite her lip to keep from answering him with a yes. But Dillon seemed to understand the cruel tug-of-war inside her, and his mouth turned up in rueful amusement. He took her hand and tucked it under his arm, pulling her so near that her arm was pressed warmly against his side.

"Perhaps later, then."

He said no more as he led her down the hall to the stairs, but those three words would not leave Lacie alone.

Perhaps later then . . . Perhaps later . . .

If he wanted her later, she would not be able to resist. If he wanted her she would melt into his arms and into his bed, no matter what the consequences were. Heart and brain—and body—were sadly at odds, and she knew now that logic would lose this time.

As they approached the entrance to the ballroom she was warm all over, filled with an exquisite awareness of herself—both her body and the needs that Dillon had aroused in her. If she gave in . . . She took a deep breath, conscious of her nipples pressing hard against her bodice.

If she gave in it would be madness. Yet she was already quite mad with longing for him.

Would it really change anything if she surrendered?

20

The ballroom at the Denver Palace was a magnificent space indeed. The ceilings soared the height of two floors, held up by twenty-four square Ionic columns. The ceiling was a series of rectangular coffers, the recesses painted a pale sky blue. On two walls huge windows stretched high, draped with sheers and swagged with elegant green damask. The third wall was faced with tall French doors that led out to a rooftop terrace.

Lush plants grew in pots all around the room, as if it were a huge solarium—well tended, comfortable, yet on this scale, quite grand as well. With the French doors thrown open and the cool evening breeze stirring the delicate curtains, the room felt more like a wonderful outdoor garden than a room in a fancy hotel.

Lacie paused at the entrance and looked around in awe. Once more Dillon Lockwood had surprised her, for she had expected a very formal room, designed to add to his prestige by intimidating those invited inside. But this room . . .

She let her eyes sweep the space once more, empty save for a group of musicians seated at the far end between two enormous palm trees. This room was designed to comfort and please. This room was for people to enjoy themselves in.

"Like it?"

Lacie looked up at Dillon's quiet inquiry. His hand moved to cover hers, but she quickly extricated her hand from his arm and took a step farther into the room.

"It's quite beautiful," she admitted despite the fierce pounding of her heart. It would be far easier to speak to him about this room than to discuss what was really on her mind.

"There's nothing else quite like it in Denver."

"Where did you get all the wonderful plants?" she asked as she moved slowly past a group of tall and fragrant flowers.

"Mexico. Japan. These are from Cuba. This is a Bird of Paradise. See the flower?" He moved a large leaf back to reveal a strangely shaped flower of orange and purple. "It came from South America."

Lacie sent Dillon a puzzled glance. Was there anything about this man that made sense? "Why a solarium?" she asked with genuine curiosity.

He stared down at her for a moment, then looked across the room. "My mother loved flowers."

Lacie was stunned once more. Yet she remembered the little cabin he had taken her to and the remnants of a garden that had lingered still in several sturdy plants. Even after all the years, several roses had grown wild along one side of the porch. Yet such sentimentality was not a trait she would have ascribed to Dillon.

"My mother grew flowers too."

Most mothers did, she thought as he took her arm

once more and identified several other rare species. Yet that one tiny fragment, that insignificant fact from their earlier lives, had formed a fragile connection between them. It was tenuous at best, and temporary, she told herself. If they were to stray onto any other topic they would most likely revert to accusations and criticisms, to insults and taunts. Still, for the moment at least, they walked on common ground. She glanced sidelong at him but lowered her lashes when he turned his perceptive gaze on her. If only it could go on like this forever!

Too quickly, however, the other guests began to arrive, and as conversation turned from flowers to business, the fragile connection broke. She tried to tell herself it was for the best. After all, this evening was her last chance to convince the other board members not to go along with Dillon's aggressive expansion plans. If it weren't for that she wouldn't even be here. Yet even as she circulated among the crowd, meeting the board members' wives and trying to strike the proper balance between social chatter and business talk, her eyes constantly searched out Dillon.

He was always easy to see due to his height. And he always seemed to be surrounded by people—ladies as well as gentlemen. Yet she knew she would be able to find him even in a room of giants, for the magnetism, the pull between them was impossible to resist. As the North Pole drew the compass arrow, so did he attract her in the most powerful and irresistible manner.

Sometimes when she chanced a look at him she would find his eyes already upon her, and she would quickly look elsewhere. One time she met his stare more boldly, unable to tear her eyes away. His expression was unexpected. He seemed almost surprised, or perhaps puzzled. But then he grinned ever so slightly at her, as if he knew her very thoughts, and she looked away, uncertain what his expression had meant.

"It'll be a hardship, perhaps," Mr. Ferguson was saying as she struggled to drive Dillon out of her thoughts and get back to business. "But in the long run we could all benefit enormously."

"Yes, but there's no certainty he'll meet with success," she countered, feeling the man slipping over to Dillon's side.

"If Dillon Lockwood is behind it, you can be certain. Why, that young fellow has so much energy—so many good ideas—that it's almost unfair to the competition. If you'll just tighten your belt a little, Miz Kimbell, when those dividends *do* start comin' in, I think you'll change your mind about your brother-in-law."

Another one lost, Lacie thought glumly as she watched the man polish off his whiskey. If she did no better than this, she wouldn't have a chance tomorrow. She turned to look for another likely candidate for her campaign against the expansion, but it was Dillon's smiling face she encountered instead.

She drew back at once, hardly ready to cross swords with him again.

"May I lead you out for the first dance?" He extended his hand expectantly, the very picture of correct manners and proper etiquette. But within his eyes a heated light glimmered. He was a wolf in sheep's clothing, she told herself, civilized and charming but a rogue nonetheless. Still, it was that dangerous quality about him that exerted the most powerful pull on her.

She shook her head, for it would be madness to put herself willingly within his arms. However, Dillon seemed to have read her mind. With a wicked smile he came nearer and, paying absolutely no mind to her rebuff, took her hand into his own.

He nodded to the musicians to begin a waltz, and then led her unresisting, into the middle of the dance floor. She did not pull away when he turned to face her, putting one hand on her waist. As the music began, filling the soft summer air with the sweet strains of "The Emperor's Waltz," she only followed his lead, moving easily with him as he led her in a slow elegant circle of the room.

It did not take long for the other guests to join in the dancing, but Lacie was hardly aware of them at all. Her mind was occupied solely with Dillon. Indeed, her every sense was flooded with awareness of him. He filled her vision and warmed her wherever they touched. He smelled of soap and skin and, faintly, of brandy. And though he said nothing, he spoke clearly to her nonetheless. Her stomach tightened in sweet torturous awareness of what he was silently saying to her.

As they whirled around the room, her skirts swinging wide as he expertly guided her in the dance, Lacie slowly began to relax in his arms. He was an excellent dancer and the perfect partner, although that did not really surprise her. After all, from the very first there had been a strong physical connection between them. They danced well together just as they made love well. . . .

Lacie quickly looked away, stumbling a bit as she did. But Dillon's embrace prevented her from falling, and as the closing notes of the song faded away, he gave her a quizzical look.

"Can I get you something to drink?"

A drink was not what she wanted, but Lacie was too undone by her own wanton thoughts to do other than nod her head. Dillon flagged down a circulating waiter and in a matter of seconds handed her a tall crystal glass of champagne. Without thinking, she finished the glass, then when the bubbles filled her nose, started coughing.

"Do you want another?" he asked, amusement in his voice.

"N-no." She shook her head hard. Why must she always be such a fool in his presence? She turned as if to depart, looking desperately for an excuse to leave his company. But just then the musicians began a new melody, and before she could protest, Dillon pulled her once more into his arms.

This time his embrace was not so polite. His arm circled her waist, drawing her nearer than was socially correct. Instead of looking around and meeting her eyes only occasionally, as any other gentleman would, he kept his head lowered and his dark eyes direct upon her. With each pass around the beautiful room, he seemed to pull her ever so slightly closer until, during one elegant whirl, her breasts brushed against his chest.

At once a new rush of heat suffused her entire body. It was so strong, so overpowering, that she knew he must be acutely aware of it, and when she looked up at him, his vivid green gaze confirmed it. He knew exactly how his nearness affected her, how her nipples tightened into hard, sensitive buds, and how something hot and restless curled tightly in her belly. Yet his gaze revealed even more than that, for as she stared up into his disturbing eyes she saw his desire as well, and although she had always known he wanted the physical pleasure of her in his bed, now she understood that he felt something more. He could torture her and make her long uncontrollably for him, but she could do the same to him. She desired him in the most shameless fashion, in a way she'd never dreamed possible. But he desired her too. It was more than just the physical attraction he might feel towards any pleasant-looking female. It had to do with her as the particular woman she was. He might desire other women at different times of his life. But right now, even though it wasn't love, he desired only her.

On the surface this was not an especially astonishing realization. But Lacie was quite overcome by her new knowledge of her place in Dillon's life. She did not doubt it had to do with her pose as Frederick's widow and her share of the companies that Dillon knew was his. Had she not presented him such a challenge, he would likely never have even noticed her. But she *had* become the challenge, and he *had* noticed her. It didn't really matter anymore why his attentions were focused on her. It was enough for her to know that they emphatically were.

Lacie could hardly think as Dillon swept her along in the dance. When another followed, she agreed mutely to his silent request, then put up only the flimsiest resistance when he clasped her even closer to him. Time and again her breasts grazed the buttons of his waistcoat. More than once his hand moved possessively around her waist, holding her much closer than he should, his fingers splaying wide to follow the contours of her waist and lower ribcage. When the dance ended she was breathless and flushed, buzzing with a building excitement that she could scarcely contain inside her.

When he offered her another glass of champagne, she took it with a soft murmur of thanks. She did not demur when he kept her arm in his as he spoke briefly to one of the other guests. She only sipped at the sparkling amber drink and surreptitiously watched Dillon.

He was the most handsome man in the world, she thought as she watched his alternately passive then animated face. He was quick to smile, yet his scowl could be most intimidating. Tall, dark, and handsome—the phrase came quickly to mind. Yet there was a harshness, an arrogance to his features that did not fit with ordinary expectations for the term *handsome*.

Did other women see him as she did? she wondered. Did he fill them with the same terrible longings that she felt every time he was near? Or perhaps it was only she that did, since she loved him.

That thought, however, brought a stab of pain to her chest. To love Dillon was to court disaster, to invite heartache and tragedy. Hadn't she already learned that the hard way?

But love was not an emotion a woman was able to control. If it were, she would not have allowed herself to love him. If she'd had a choice, she would have picked someone more reliable to love, someone steady and predictable.

Tears suddenly pricked her eyes at the absurdity of that idea. If she'd wanted a man like that she would not have discouraged Richard Beasley, or Walter Reynolds, or Angus Hawsley. No, it was plain that none of those men—nor any other—would ever do, now that Dillon had come into her life.

She looked down into her half-empty champagne glass and tried to banish the tears that fought so strenuously for release. Tears would accomplish nothing, she told herself sternly. She was in love with him, but he was not in love with her. Despite his businesslike proposal of marriage, he was not the best sort of man to marry. Yet how she wished his offer had been sincere! How she wished he wanted to marry her for nothing more than love!

"May I have this dance, Mrs. Kimbell?"

Mr. Andrews's polite request brought Lacie's morose thoughts up short. She felt the quick tensing in Dillon's arm as he looked over at Mr. Andrews.

"Why . . . ah, why, yes. How—how kind of you to ask," she managed to say. She felt quite odd as he escorted her onto the dance floor. But as he took her hand, then placed his fingertips politely at the side of her waist, Lacie knew it was only that there was no thrill from his touch. When she danced with him it was not an unconscious melding of her rhythm to his as it had been with Dillon. Dancing with the pale-faced Mr. Andrews was like dancing with her old dance instructor, or even with the other girls in her dance classes. It was not a warm floating fantasy, but merely ordinary mortal movement set to the cadence of a song.

Against her will, her eyes sought out Dillon, standing tall and handsome among the other, less vital men. Dancing would never be the same without him as her partner. No man could ever compare with him or be good enough for her. Not after Dillon.

Her decision came easily. It was not even a decision in the truest sense, but more an innate understanding. By the time Mr. Andrews returned her to Dillon's side, murmuring his blushing thanks, she already knew.

Mr. Andrews—Roger, as he'd insisted she call him—

was obviously enamored of her. With only a little encouragement, he would vote with her, yet that did not begin to be enough in a man. When Dillon again led her out to the dance floor, his hand possessively riding her waist, she knew that only *his* touch, only *his* caress would ever be enough for her. She would not marry him, not the way he wanted her. But she would have him in her arms at least one more time. She would have his love, or at least the physical expression of it one last time. Whether she won or lost tomorrow, whether she was able to keep the school going or not, Dillon was someone she would carry in her heart forever. After this, she would have to keep her distance from him. But tonight . . .

She determinedly ignored all the dire repercussions her rash decision might carry with it. They had nothing to do with her heart anyway. Without thinking she moved a little closer to Dillon. She became more pliable in his arms, more fluid in her movements.

Dillon looked down at her curiously, but she did not meet his astute gaze. She knew she was too transparent and that all her emotions were an open book to him. Although she was willing to surrender to his exquisite embrace and thrilling kisses, something in her feared to let him see how deeply she really felt about him. If he knew that she loved him, it would be too hard. It would be impossible.

They would be lovers, she decided. One more time they would be lovers. But she would never let him know that she loved him.

In the hours that followed Lacie felt like Cinderella at the ball. Dillon, a most convincing prince, was her constant escort, seeing to her needs most earnestly. He monopolized her on the dance floor, not hesitating to stop anyone who approached with his dark, quelling stare. Their conversation steered clear of business as if by mutual agreement. It occurred to her that he might be deliberately trying to prevent her from circulating among the other board members and garnering their support. But even if he were, she didn't care.

As the evening wore on, she knew that he sensed the change in her. It was in his eyes, intense now as he stared down into her upturned face.

"What are you thinking?" he asked as they swayed in slow, sensuous steps through the thinning crowd.

Lacie returned his steady gaze, searching still for an emotion she could never expect to find. "How unlike any other man you are," she replied without pausing to consider her words.

One of his dark brows arched at this unexpected honesty.

"And what should I read into that?"

"Whatever you like," she answered. Under differing circumstances, her reply would have been light and amusing, but here it was anything but. She felt his embrace tighten. With every breath, she felt the intimate pressure of his chest against her breasts. His voice lowered to a husky murmur.

"And you are quite unlike any other woman I've ever met, Lacie." She felt the warmth of his breath stirring her hair, teasing against her ear. "All fire and ice. Yesses and nos." He whirled her around until she was dizzy and faint. "My adversary. My partner."

"So you admit we are partners?" she asked breathlessly.

His answer was only a faint, heart-stopping smile. She

was hardly aware that he had danced her out onto the roof terrace, she was so undone by that smile. Then he pulled her firmly against him so that her every contour was fitted against his.

"I burn for you, Lacie. Here." His hand moved to her derriere, then pressed her against the hard warmth of his arousal. "And here." He lowered his head and took her lips in a deep, searing kiss.

Lacie had no thoughts of denial or resistance. This was their time. It would be their only time, and nothing on earth—or in heaven—would make her turn him away. Her mouth was pliant beneath his demanding kiss. Her lips opened to his searching, and her tongue crept readily forward to meet his.

There was no slow warming in their desperate embrace. It was more like an explosion, as if the entire evening had been a buildup and now they could release the powerful desires that gripped them both. They clung ferociously together, their bodies perfectly aligned, their two desires one.

The ground spun dizzily beneath Lacie's feet. Dillon was the center of the world, and everything—even the stars—circled them at his command. She was overwhelmed by the sheer power of it, the perfection, the inevitability. He was the center of the world, and she had been a fool to struggle against him for so long, when to give in was to find every pleasure she could want, every delight she could imagine, and more.

She was drowning in sweetness, engulfed in a fire that scorched her, both body and soul. Dillon's solid presence was the only constant, both the source and the relief of the torments that consumed her. When he raised his head, gasping raggedly for breath, she let out a low moan, then pressed her face against his chest. Her decision was right, she knew without doubt. He would be hers tonight, and she would be his.

"I won't let you go this time," he murmured hoarsely. "There's no turning back for you and me, Lacie. No turning back."

Tears caught in her throat, making her reply impossible. But her answer was clear in the way she clung to him so recklessly, in the way she stretched up to meet his kiss.

Soft yet demanding, her lips opened to him with an urgency that tortured them both. In that kiss their pact was sealed. In that moment her answer was clear, and she sensed the answering triumph in his tightened embrace. When he finally drew back from her, holding her at arm's length, he was breathing hard and for once he seemed almost as shaken as she. Still, that little distance did nothing to dim the fire that heated between them. Despite her voluminous skirts and his civilized attire, she could feel as distinctly as if they were clinging together the imprint of his virile masculine form upon her.

"I'll have you tonight—and forever," he said in a hoarse tone that seemed almost a warning. His eyes pierced her very soul with their intensity. When she nodded her mute acceptance, however, his hands tightened almost painfully on her upper arms. "I mean it, Lacie. I'll have everything from you tonight. Everything."

He would have more than he even knew, she thought. Tonight he would even have the love she could not admit to feeling. But tomorrow . . .

She refused to think about that. And as he pulled her

nearer for an achingly sweet kiss, thoughts of the future disappeared from her mind. Tonight was Dillon, and he was all there was. He was all there ever would be.

She was unsteady when he led her back to the ball-room. As they bade the other guests good-bye, her mind was focused only on Dillon. His voice as he spoke to the others warmed her with its deep resonance. His solid arm beneath her hand was her only reality. When his eyes met hers she was at once both faint with desire and energized by her powerful need for him. A part of her knew she was giving herself away to him, letting him see far too much of her feelings. But she had gone too far to turn back.

When the last couple departed, they watched the door close behind them. At the far end of the room she heard the musicians scraping back their chairs, packing their instruments for departure. Then silence descended, and they were alone.

Lacie was trembling. It started as a little quiver in her belly, then worked its way up until she was hot and shaking. Dillon pulled her into his embrace, wrapping his arms about her waist and pulling her back against his chest so that he could bury his face in her hair. It was an exquisite feeling to have him behind her yet hold her captive in his arms. Then one of his hands slid down and splayed open, flattening intimately against her belly and pressing her derriere against the rigid contours of his loins.

Like fire his touch burned her. Like a torch she ignited beneath his fiery caress. It flashed through her mind that she would love to give him a child, that carrying his baby inside her would be the most satisfying thing she could ever do. Then his hand slid a little lower, and she cried out at the exquisite torture of it.

"My sweet, sweet girl. Are you an angel—or a devil?" He pressed himself hard against her, then abruptly pulled away. With hard-won control he took her arm in a more civilized manner and led her without further word to the door. Yet even in their seemingly polite walk across the hall and down one flight of stairs, she was conscious of a barely restrained passion within him. To all eyes he might appear the sophisticated gentleman and she the proper lady. But beneath the surface lurked darker emotions, and when he let them into her room and then locked the door behind them, she was relieved to drop the facade.

Her heart was racing as he leaned back against the door. His eyes were so dark, so filled with fiery light, that she felt burned by their intimate caress. He shrugged out of his coat and flung it negligently aside. Then he stepped nearer, and she was sure he meant to take her in his arms. She was aching for him, ready to rip her clothes away, so desperate and impatient was she for his touch. But Dillon, like one transfixed, had decided already on a course of action, and she could only submit to his whim.

He loosened her hair first, letting the hairpins fall where they would, then filled his hands with her thick, dark tresses. The velvet ribbons were next, but he did not discard them. Instead, he left them lying across the back of her neck and looped the freed ends across his own shoulders. They made a black, glittering connection between the two of them, dark and shining, tenuous and fragile, yet unable to be ignored, like the unseen, powerful attraction that had pulled them unrelentingly toward one another since the day they had met.

He moved slowly around behind her, and she felt the ribbons slide slowly along her neck, as seductive as his own touch would be. Then he bent and lightly kissed the sensitive spot beneath her ear, teasing it with the tip of his tongue.

"Dillon . . ." Her word was a soft whisper, hardly more than a sigh.

His answer came in his touch. With hands less sure than they had been earlier when he had buttoned up her gown, he unfastened the long row of buttons. With each jet button he folded the fabric of her bodice back, revealing her pale trembling skin, planting more of those warm wet kisses as he went. By the time he had slid the gown over her hips and let it fall in a shimmering black heap at her feet, followed by her crinoline, she was shaking with longing, quite mad with desire.

Then he tugged lightly on the ribbon wound about her neck and drew her once more against him. With her derriere pressed intimately to him and her head fallen back against his shoulders, his hands were free to continue their task. Her corset ties were next, then her slip, until she was clad only in her chemise and pantalets.

His head lowered to her shoulder then, and his kisses grew more passionate as he licked and bit the soft skin near her throat.

When his hands moved up to cup her breasts, she gasped at the response that flooded her. Back and forth across her erect nipples he stroked, until the pleasure was so acute as to approach pain, and she struggled away from his masterful caress.

"Don't fight it," he whispered urgently.

"I—I can't help it," she groaned as he stepped up his sensual assault.

He moved one hand down to her belly and this time let his palm slide lower until he cupped her most intimately in his hand.

"I don't want you ever to fight me again," he ordered in a hoarse voice. He let one finger slip between her legs and slide langorously back and forth over the bud that marked the center of her sexual being. "Do you hear me, Lacie?"

She could do no more than nod weakly, for with his clever touch he had ignited a flame that already raced out of control. In fast mounting waves it raised her higher and higher, melting her, dissolving her until she was only what he wanted her to be. With each stroke he brought her closer until she was wet with desire, her whole body quivering on the brink of explosion.

But he knew what he was doing to her, and with a deliberateness that should have outraged her, he slowly pulled his hand away. To her soft cry of disappointment, she felt his answering shudder of self-imposed restraint, but when she turned to embrace him face to face, he held her a little away.

"You have tortured me without mercy, Lacie. Without mercy." His dark gaze raked over her barely clad form with an avidness that heightened all of her senses. Then his eyes leveled with hers. "You've tortured me night after night, and now I shall return the favor."

His sensuous threat sent a new thrill through her, for such a torture she would gladly endure from him. Slowly, as she watched his every move, he stripped his clothes away, waistcoat, neckcloth, collar, shirt, and studs. Then his boots and socks, followed by his trousers. When he finally stood before her clad only in his silkalines, she could hardly breathe for the emotions that choked her. He was so beautiful, so perfectly formed, with powerful shoulders and arms, and lean waist and belly. Where her own body was soft and pale, his was hard and brown. As her eyes drank in the sight, her skin tingled at the remembered feel of his naked form pressing down upon hers.

How long had she tried to bury that memory? And how vividly had it surfaced over and over again, tormenting her dreams and leaving her weak and aching for him? But now he was here and this time . . . this time . . .

He slid his last garment off, never letting his eyes veer from her face. She was unable not to stare at the mighty evidence of the desire he felt for her. Strong and proud, it proclaimed his intentions, and she felt herself grow weak at the very sight. When he approached, her eyes closed, for the intensity of it all was too much to bear. With one hand he slipped her chemise from her left shoulder, then from her right. The fabric caught on the prominent crests of her bosom, but with one finger at the shadow between her breasts he tugged at the flimsy garment, and like an excruciating caress the soft linen slid over her highly aroused nipples.

She heard his softly muttered words of appreciation and felt his hurried removal of her pantalets. But not until he pulled her into his arms, pressing their naked bodies together, did her eyes come open.

"Oh, Dillon," she murmured as fire leaped between them. It was a fever they both had, one that only burned hotter as they came together. Was ever a man born who could bring a woman to such heights as this? she wondered obliquely. But she knew the answer. Only his chest was meant to press against the soft fullness of her breasts. Only his iron-hewn thigh was meant to force her legs apart. And only his virile desire could ever inspire an answering desire in her.

His lips slanted across hers in a kiss that demanded everything of her, and she opened to meet it. He wanted to devour her. She sensed that in the hard possessiveness of his kiss. His tongue was a plunderer, taking without asking, forcing her to submit to his command. Yet even as she submitted, taking the deep thrust of his tongue within her mouth, then meeting it with her tongue until she was kissing him back, her very eagerness brought a new wonder to them both. To submit to him was to become victorious. To surrender to his demand was to win everything.

When he lowered his kisses to her throat and collarbone, she arched back in willing acceptance. When he found her out-thrust breasts, she cried out in wordless ecstasy. Each nipple was his to caress, to lick and suck and tug between his teeth until passion rose perilously close to pain. Like the most shameless hussy, she pressed herself hard against his thigh between her legs. Recklessly, she rubbed herself against the hairy roughness there, responding to a primitive need that had her in its grip.

Then without warning Dillon cupped her bottom in his hands and hoisted her off the floor. There was no need for them to speak, for they seemed to communicate in a manner far beyond words. She wrapped her legs instinctively around his waist. When she felt the

urgent pressure of his arousal against her damp entrance, she sank down without hesitation, accepting the
whole of him inside of her.

Lacie was at once overcome with intense and poi-
gnant love for Dillon—for this man who had captured
her heart and all her senses—and consumed with the
most incredibly wanton desire for him. He filled her
completely, her body and her heart, and she knew she
would never have enough of him. There would never
be a time when she would not need more and more of
him.

For a sweet suspended moment they stood thus, with
her intimately entwined about him. He was like a
Greek god, a marble statue capturing the essence of all
that was perfect in the male creature, and she was the
willing foil, soft and yielding yet empowered by his
strength and his very real need for her.

She was afraid to move, afraid that this moment was
too perfect to last. But Dillon felt no such hesitation.
With a groan, he buried his head in her wildly tossed
hair and tightened his hands against her bottom.

"Do you know how much I want you? How much I
need you?" he muttered hoarsely. "Do you know all the
things I want to do to you?"

Lacie gloried at his words and gripped him tighter.
"I'm here," she answered in a voice choked with emotion. "I'm here."

She did not know how they made it to the bed. One
moment she was in his arms, clinging to him in the most
wicked fashion, all propriety thrown to the winds. Then
she was beneath him on the cream-colored comforter.
The silk fabric was cool against her skin while Dillon,

above her, was an inferno, scorching her with the intensity of his passion.

He reared above her, taking in the full length of her pale trembling form. Her hair was a dark tangle against the mound of pillows, a sensuous fan of silken strands. Her eyes were luminous with desire; neither fear nor hesitation clouded their gray centers. He smiled then, the most beautiful possessive smile Lacie hoped ever to see, and she could have cried for joy.

"You're mine now. You belong to me, Lacie," he whispered. Then as if he did not want to hear her reply, he began to move within her.

At her gasp of breathless pleasure, he fitted her more snugly against his thighs and took her breasts into his hands. He cupped them and caressed them, circling the nipples with a maddening precision, even as he increased the ferocity of his heated thrusts. In and out he slid with long torturous strokes. In and out, sending her nerves skittering out of control.

Lacie thought she must die from the sheer pleasure of it. His hands excited her breasts beyond belief, while his thick presence within her raised her to heights beyond all imaginable passion.

She arched to meet every thrust, her eyes closed, her head tossing in mindless ecstasy. When his hands moved down to grip her waist, she felt as if she were being absorbed into him. Faster and deeper he thrust into her, filling her to overflowing, then pulling all the way out, only to plunge once more into her. She rose to his frantic rhythm, his deep, demanding possession of her. Then in a tidal wave of passion, she reached the crescendo.

Over and over she shuddered in endless all-consuming waves of release. He was in her; he was around her. He was everything to her.

Then her completion became his as he too tensed in a climax of passion. She clung to him as his warmth spilled into her, as he filled her with every powerful lunge.

Tears sprang to her eyes as the reality of their intimacy struck her. He gave her his finest gift when he made love to her this way, and she gave him hers. It needed only love to be the most perfect offering in the world, love from both of them. Although she knew the love was one-sided, she refused to torture herself with that knowledge. Tonight he was hers, and the rest she would leave for morning.

When he lowered himself over her, she felt as if she were melting into him, that she was becoming a part of him just as he was becoming part of her. The connection between them was too strong, too perfect to be otherwise. He completed her in every way and made her whole. Yet when he slowly rolled to his side, she knew she must cling to him, for their time would be short.

She was gratified when he pulled her close, nestling her next to his chest and wrapping his arms around her.

"Come here, sweetheart," he murmured in a low, sleepy voice.

With a satisfied sigh, she complied. It was her intention to stay like that, close and intertwined with him, listening to the steady beat of his heart beneath her ear. She would lie thus through the night, awake while he slept, memorizing everything about him so that she would never forget any of it. It was all she would ever have, and she didn't want to lose a single one of his caresses or even the least of his kisses.

But she had not counted on such warmth, such contentment. Lying within Dillon's comforting embrace, she slowly relaxed. Then, lulled by his easy breathing beside her, her eyes closed, and she succumbed to the intimacy of their shared slumber.

21

Lacie awoke to slivers of morning sunlight streaming through the heavily draped windows. All was quiet save for the steady breathing of the man beside her. For a moment she lay there, not ready to let the day begin, unwilling to give up the warmth and comfort of her bed, or of Dillon.

As much as she knew that this comfort was only illusion—he did not feel love for her, only physical desire— still, as long as she remained quiet in his arms she could pretend it was otherwise. Nevertheless she could not help but think that, as exquisite as it was to have Dillon hold her and make love to her, how much more wonderful would it be if he actually loved her?

A wayward tear slid down her cheek, and anguish flooded her heart. It was no use to pretend—that only brought her more pain. She needed to make a clean break from him, then never again let herself be alone with him. If it were possible, she would try to never even see him again. After all, she would be in Louisiana, and he would be in Denver. Still, she feared that avoiding him completely might prove impossible.

She rolled to her side and trembled at the warm slide of his arm against her skin as he shifted in his sleep. As she started to rise, his hand tightened at her waist. Then he pressed a kiss against her naked lower back, and her heart leaped in despair.

"Stay here," he murmured sleepily, moving the kiss up her spine as he tugged her back toward him. "Stay in bed with me, Lacie."

Her throat constricted with pain, so desperately did she wish to do as he said. If only it were possible, she would stay with him forever.

But that was not what he meant.

"I have to get up," she whispered in a voice close to cracking.

"You don't," he countered. As if to prove his point, his hand slipped down her side to caress her hip, then around to her belly to pull her more intimately against him. His chest now rested against her back. His thighs pressed against her own, tucking her derriere provocatively against his loins. She felt the heat of his arousal, and to her dismay, an answering fire flared deep within her belly.

This was madness, she told herself, pure madness! Yet a sudden flood of desire overwhelmed her, and its frightening power washed away all reason, all caution, until only her purest emotions were left. She loved him, and she wanted him. It was that simple, that incredible. She needed him as she would never need anyone again. To deny him—or herself—was beyond her ability.

When Dillon turned her to face him, she met him without a hint of hesitation. In a long sensuous embrace they clung, his body hard and unyielding against her softer, more pliable form. It was only in his kiss—sweet, beguiling, yet demanding—that she sensed the tender side of his passion. He wanted things from her, reckless wicked things. And he was willing to woo her to get them. He would see her writhing in ecstasy before he would seek his own pleasure.

Or was it that his pleasure was made sweeter by her enthusiastic response? She did not know, and she could not think further, for Dillon's kisses drove all logical thoughts from her mind.

He did not rush her. If anything, he was maddeningly slow in his thorough exploration of her mouth. In curious nibbles he tasted her, tormenting her lips apart as he slid his tongue along the full curve of her lower lip. It was sweet and tantalizing, and it provoked the most incredible reaction from her.

Shamelessly she pressed her willing body against him. Like a wanton she ran her hands down his back, reveling in the slick hardness of his well-formed muscles. He was like steel beneath her fingers, yet he was also warm, living silk.

With a sob Lacie clutched his head between her hands, deepening their kiss with a ferocity she could not contain. At once, Dillon rolled her beneath him. For a breathtaking moment he stared down at her, his eyes a vivid green, as clear as emeralds. It seemed to Lacie that he was seeing all the way into her, everything she was, everything she wanted, everything she needed. If she could have, she would have closed her eyes and turned away. But his intense gaze would not allow it.

For a moment she thought she saw confusion in his eyes, or sudden doubt. But it disappeared as quickly as it came, and she was not sure she had seen anything at all. Then he moved over her, and with a sureness that took her breath away, he came into her.

There was a rightness to their lovemaking, a perfection she recognized innately. With every long, purposeful stroke he proved that to her over and over again until they were moving together in a steadily increasing rhythm. She rose to meet his every thrust, wanting to take everything he had to give.

"Lacie . . ." She heard his gasping cry. "Lacie . . ." Then she felt a sudden quickening in her belly, and with a soft cry of her own she succumbed. Like a hot wet wave it came over her, drowning her in its perfect warmth until she was gasping for air and clinging to him for her very survival. A tempest tossed them, a storm of emotions that could never be controlled by mere rational thought. When they at last collapsed in final surrender, they were both fighting for breath, struggling to slow the frantic pace of their pounding hearts.

He was crushing her. His full weight pressed her down into the soft mattress, yet Lacie wanted him always to be just as he was. She wanted this moment never to change, never to end.

When he raised his head, he was still breathing hard. Their gasping breaths pressed his chest against her breasts in a manner that seemed almost as intimate as everything else they'd done. Face to face, he looked down at her, and not even the dimness of the curtained room could hide the warmth in his gaze. In abject pain she closed her eyes.

"Ah, my sweet Lacie," he murmured as he kissed each of her eyelids. "What a wonder you are!"

What a wonder she was? What a fool she was! she

thought miserably. What a completely willing fool she was where he was concerned. Tears stung her eyes, but she struggled to contain them. If only he would not be so tender afterward. If only he wouldn't hold her so near. Maybe then she would have the strength to leave him.

In frustration she pushed at his chest. When he obligingly moved to his side, she sat up at once and swung her legs over the side of the bed. If he would not leave the room, then she must.

"Where do you think you're going?" he murmured playfully as she rose from the bed. His hand slid out to catch her waist, but he came up only with a corner of the sheet she held protectively around her.

"I—I need to wash . . . to bathe," she faltered, desperate to find an excuse to escape.

"I'll join you." He tugged at the sheet, trying to free it from her grasp and thereby bare her to his laughing eyes. "The tub here, unlike Sparrow Hill's, is big enough to accommodate us both."

"No!" Lacie jumped in alarm, then backed away to the extent the length of the sheet would allow. "No . . . I want to bathe alone."

"I think we should bathe together, my little prude." His pull on the sheet became stronger.

For a split second Lacie hesitated. For a moment she considered giving in to him once more, just once more. But her emotions were too torn, too shattered for her to take such a terrible chance. Being rational was beyond her, and she wasn't certain she could even muster any anger. She was past being angry with Dillon, for she knew now that everything that had happened was her own fault. Devastated by that knowledge, she tried to fight down the anguished emotions that rose in her chest.

"I think—" She took a breath and forced a coolness to her voice. "I think it's time for you to leave."

It was awful to watch the warmth drain from his eyes as he looked up at her from his perch on the bed. He frowned slightly, as if he did not quite understand what she meant. But as she stood there, still and pale, she saw when he understood. For an excruciatingly long moment he stared at her, as if giving her a chance to change her mind. Then he rolled to a sitting position and put his hands on his knees.

"What if I don't want to leave?"

Lacie's heart pounded like thunder at his quietly said words. Although there was no inflection in his voice, no sign of emotion, she knew it was nonetheless there. She braced herself for what was to come, steeling herself to hide her feelings just as he always hid his. Remain aloof, she told herself. Just keep yourself remote. You can cry later, when he's gone.

"If you won't leave, then I will," she finally answered.

Again he only stared at her. Then his eyes narrowed and he stood up. In a sudden panic of what he might do, she began to speak. "You've had what you want from me—"

"Not quite," he interrupted curtly.

"Well, then, you've had all you're going to get." She raised her head and stared bitterly at him. "You've had me, and I've had you. We both got what we wanted, so let's not pretend. If you think last night changed my mind about today's vote, you're wrong."

There was disbelief on his face, disbelief and something that might have been pain. But if it was pain, it was only because he had lost this time, Lacie told herself. He'd thought her surrender to him last night was complete, not only physically, but emotionally as well. He'd thought she would be his now, willing to go along with anything he said. If he seemed hurt, it was only because he was not used to losing, she reasoned.

But she was not prepared for the cutting tone in his voice. " 'We both got what we wanted,' " he repeated her words sarcastically. His gaze slid over her with a thoroughness that caused her to clutch the sheet tighter. There was appreciation there. But there was a cold assessiveness too, even contempt. "I see that you did get what you wanted, Lacie. But I didn't, not quite." Then he moved toward her, unconcerned by his nakedness, as wary as a stalking predator.

"Stay away from me, Dillon! Do you hear me?" Lacie squeaked as her aloof facade began to crumble. "Stay away!"

"Why? You say you know what I wanted from you. And we both know you like it, so why the sudden squeamishness? That *is* all you wanted from me, isn't it? A hard male body between your legs?"

She cringed at his hateful words, yet she knew she must not deny them. When he grabbed her by the arms and pulled her cruelly against him, she stared up into his furious face. "That *is* all you wanted, isn't it, Lacie?"

"Yes," she whispered the lie. "That's all you wanted from me, and that's all—that's all I wanted from you."

His hands tightened like vises on her arms. For one heart-shattering moment, he stared down into her wide frightened eyes. Then he let go of her as if he'd been burned and took an abrupt step back from her.

Lacie was so weak, so completely drained by the

emotional trauma of the scene that she could hardly stand upright. For awful endless seconds they stood like that, near enough to touch, yet on opposite ends of the earth. Then without warning his hand snaked out and ripped the filmy sheet away from her.

She shrank away from him in horror, humiliated by his contemptuous expression as he raked his eyes boldly over her. But there was no place to hide from him, and nowhere to run. He flung the sheet aside and took a menacing step toward her, then another. As he stalked her she backed away, too numb to speak, too anguished even to think straight. She had finally bested him, perhaps even hurt him just a little. Yet she felt no joy in it at all. Not even fear was her foremost emotion. No, as he backed her against the vanity, it was not fear but sorrow that ripped through her. She had made him hate her. It was clear in his face and in his tense posture. She'd finally made him hate her, and she'd never been so miserable in her entire life.

Lacie was trembling uncontrollably when Dillon halted just inches from her. Her eyes were locked on his harsh face, drawn against all reason to the dark opaqueness of his eyes. What she saw there chilled her to the core, for although lust was clear in his hard jade stare, there was no warmth. He wanted her as he might want a fancy trollop. Then he spoke and confirmed what she already knew.

"It appears we've come full circle," he began in a voice that turned her to ice. "From the first I was sure you were a cold-hearted bitch, conniving to steal first from Frederick, and then from me. I was prepared to do anything to prove you were a liar." He reached out and stroked her cheek lightly with the back of his knuckles, then abruptly let his hand fall. "As time went by, I wasn't so sure anymore. You kept saying you only wanted to keep the school going for Frederick's sake, and I actually began to believe you. You weren't at all what I'd expected, and I—"

He stopped and shook his head slightly. "But that was just part of your act, wasn't it? You play the lady well, you know. So well that I foolishly offered to marry you—"

"You didn't want to marry me!" she burst out with a sob. "You didn't! All you wanted—"

"I wanted my property," he bit out. "And I wanted you."

"Well, you can't have either!" she cried. Blinded by a sudden burst of tears, Lacie tried to lunge past him, but Dillon refused to let her by. With hands of steel he whipped her around, then lowered his head until they were face to face.

"I already have both," he muttered hoarsely. "And tears won't help." Then he jerked her toward the bed and thrust her roughly onto the mattress. "I've had you. And I'll have you again," he stated as he caught her flailing arms and stilled her struggles by flinging himself down upon her. "And I have the properties," he muttered as he forced one of his knees between her thighs.

"Don't do this, Dillon," she cried as he thwarted her every move to get free.

"Why? Because you'll vote your shares against me?" He let out a short, harsh chuckle. "It's too late for that, Lacie. You should have agreed when I offered to buy you out way back in the beginning." He pulled her arms above her head, holding her immobile beneath him. "Or else accepted my proposal of marriage. But now it's too late."

"I wouldn't marry you if you were the last man on earth!" she sobbed, wishing more than anything that it were true.

"You won't get the chance," he growled. "Although Reverend Hainkel is going to be awfully disappointed."

Lacie stared up at him, startled by the name he taunted her with. Reverend Hainkel? What did he mean?

At her look of consternation a black laugh escaped him.

"Oh, yes. My agents found him only yesterday, living in St. Louis with his daughter. And can you believe it?" he mocked her cruelly. "He doesn't remember ever marrying you to my brother."

Lacie went very still at his words. At last it was out, she thought with a perverse sense of relief. At last it was over. She closed her eyes against the terrible triumph she saw on Dillon's face. Yet it was clear that for him, it was not quite over.

"Have you nothing to say? No feeble excuses for what you did?"

Lying beneath him, Lacie felt the angry tension in his body. He had found her out—every single lie—and he had a right to be angry. She could not deny that now. Anything she said in her defense would only sound weak and self-serving. In utter defeat she turned her face to the side and took a shaky breath. "Let me go."

When he did not move, she took another breath. "Please."

"Not yet."

At the odd inflection in his voice Lacie looked up in

sudden alarm. The look on his face confirmed her worst fear. "No!" she cried as he slid his hard body down, then back up along hers.

"Yes," he muttered. "I wanted to marry you, Lacie, but you refused. You thought you'd gain more by turning me away. Well, now you've got nothing." He slid down along her again, and despite her outrage, her skin leaped wherever his hair-roughened body rubbed against her.

"You would have made a troublesome wife," he taunted her in a hot whisper against her ear. "But you've proved quite well that you'll make a satisfactory mistress." He tightened his grasp on her wrists when she began to struggle. "You've got the mercenary heart of one," he murmured sarcastically. "And since you have no further options open to you—no job, no money—I suggest you set about earning your keep."

He could not have struck her a crueler blow, even if he'd actually hit her. She gasped at the pain, so brutally did it pierce her heart. He thought her no better than a whore. Tears stole from between her tightly clenched eyelids, but she was beyond caring. In vain she tried to twist her hands free, but he only strengthened his hold. Then she felt his free hand roam along her body, and she reacted as if she had been stung.

"No, no!" she pleaded as she tried to arch away from him. But it was no use. He was too strong and too determined, and as he pressed her down beneath him, Lacie knew her struggle was futile.

A part of her did not want to fight him. A part of her rose in willing anticipation as his rough caresses aroused her. He knew what to do, where to touch her and kiss her to bring her to the brink of trembling pleasure. But much more was involved than simply their mutual pleasure. This time he intended to use her in the cruelest, most callow manner. She would be no more than a physical release to him, only a way to vent his lust, and his anger. It was that which she could not accept.

When he sought her mouth, she turned her face desperately away. He held her captive beneath him. From her hands, which he held firmly above her head, to her bare legs and naked torso trapped helplessly beneath his powerful body, she was truly in his power. But she did not have to kiss him.

"Don't fight me," he ordered in a hoarse whisper. He began to kiss her cheek, then her ear, then slowly moved down her neck in damp nibbling kisses. Lacie struggled against his heated lips and his searching kisses. She tossed her head back and forth in frustration as his tongue slid in fiery circles along her collarbone.

She wanted him to stop, she told herself. What he was doing was no better than rape. Yet the gasp that caught in her throat when his prickly chin rubbed against one of her nipples was not a gasp of pain, nor even of anger. The emotion that clutched at her chest and tightened in her belly was passion, pure and simple. She wanted to deny it. She wanted to hate him and fight him and—and make him stop.

Yet when his lips moved to caress the aroused crest of her nipple, she could only moan in unwilling surrender. There was nothing right in what he was doing—in what she wanted him to do. But she had neither the strength nor the will to make him stop. When his hand cupped the fullness of her breast, she bit her lip at the intensity of her reaction. Like fire in her veins, heat burned

through her, melting her with its searing power. When
he moved his kisses back and forth from one breast to
the other, circling each aching nipple with his tongue,
then sucking at the hardened tips, she writhed in exquisite agony beneath him. She didn't notice when he
released his grasp on her hands. She only knew that his
kisses had moved lower to the soft flesh of her belly.
Then he slid farther down and parted her thighs with
his hands.

Lacie could not protest when he pressed his mouth
against the warm mound of her private place. She could
not speak or even catch her breath as his thumbs gently
parted her and his tongue found the sensitive core of all
her desires. Like a flame it burned her, yet in mindless
ecstasy she arched against him for more. It was like a
wonderful pain, something she feared yet could not get
enough of. Back and forth his tongue moved in long wet
strokes, evoking the most primitive response from her.
Then his lips took over until she was trembling helplessly beneath him. Higher and higher he pushed her,
and swifter and hotter she burned, until in a sudden
brilliant flash she arched in anguished completion.

Her hands pressed against his sweat-slicked shoulders
as she succumbed to the overpowering waves of passion
that consumed her. It was too painful and too perfect to
bear. Yet Dillon would not let go of her, and when she
collapsed weakly against the mattress, he pressed the
side of his face fiercely against her belly.

She did not mean to cry. She'd cried too many times
before him already, and anyway, her unhappiness
meant nothing to him. Yet despite everything, the tears
came. Down her cheeks, into her ears and her hair they

streaked, until Dillon could not help but notice. He rose onto his elbows, then hesitantly moved up over her.

"Lacie—" He halted and touched her cheek tentatively.

She could not bear it. She could not bear the tenderness in his voice because she knew it was only momentary, only a reaction to the physical desire that gripped him. Unwilling to be tortured that way, she did not hesitate. Her hands circled his neck, and she pulled him heedlessly down upon her.

"Love me," she whispered against the sob caught in her throat. "Love me," she demanded, pressing her belly shamelessly against his rigid arousal.

There was a moment of hesitation, a moment when she felt his searching gaze upon her face even though her eyes were tightly closed. Then he moved over her until his proud manhood touched the entrance to her.

"I want you to love me," she whispered once more, so softly it went almost unheard. Love me in every way there is for a man to love a woman, as I love you, she finished silently.

Then he came into her in one sure stroke, filling her and driving every thought from her but one. He was in her arms, for now he was hers, as much as he ever could be. If this was all she could have, then she must take all he would give.

She met him stroke for stroke. She rose up to his every powerful thrust and opened to him completely. There was a recklessness to their passion this time, a wildness she gladly embraced. Perhaps it was desperation, perhaps only the finality of it all. She did not know that tears still wet her face until he began to kiss her eyes and her cheeks. But not even that could halt the rushing momentum that carried both of them along. Like a wildfire, they burned out of control, scorching along a path that was bound to consume them both. Yet still they plunged madly on until in one violent explosion they reached that zenith of final fulfillment. In long shuddering thrusts he spent himself within her.

There were no words as they collapsed, utterly exhausted. They only lay as they were, Dillon above her, enveloping her with his big body as if to reinforce what she already knew in her heart: his imprint would forever be on her. Like a brand, he had marked her as his, both her heart and her flesh. No, there was no need for words, she thought in profound sorrow, for as complete as his victory was—he'd proven her a liar and a thief—he could surely not mistake his other triumph over her. She'd succumbed to his physical caress despite everything. She had even gone so far as to plead for his love. She'd pleaded for him to love her, knowing even as she had spoken the words that he never would. Love was not the emotion she inspired in him. She was a challenge to him, a woman he desired. But love was not a part of the question.

When Dillon rolled to his side, he slipped one arm beneath her, then pulled her securely against him. He was still breathing hard, still damp from his exertion, but he would not loosen his hold. Then he pushed a tangle of her hair back from her cheek and whispered in her ear.

"You don't have to fight me anymore, Lacie. It's over."

It was over. Yes, that was true, she thought forlornly. When she did not answer, he pressed a soft kiss against the back of her neck. "You'll stay with me now," he murmured against her hair. Then he sighed, and she felt his body relax against her.

For a long time she lay there, conscious of the pattern of his breathing, the rhythm of his heartbeat, the warm strength of him stretched out next to her in sleep. It was clear that he expected her to stay. After all, he knew better than anyone that she had nowhere else to go. She had no one and nothing, and since he thought her a liar and a thief—little better than a whore—he had no reason to believe she would not stay as his mistress. She would do it for the security, for the money, the clothes, and the other comforts he could afford for her.

But Lacie knew that was the one thing she could never do. For love she would stay with him. For his love she would be lover or wife to him, whichever he asked. Social convention would have no bearing on it.

But he did not love her, and that was the one thing she could not bear. To have him with her every day and yet not have his heart would destroy her.

She rolled over carefully, excruciatingly aware of his arm under her, of his hand resting heavily on her hip. But his warmth, his intimate, possessive touch, seemed only to stiffen her determination. She did not consciously plan her movements as she slipped from the bed on quiet careful feet. She did not think out exactly what she must do and where she must go. She only knew she must get away.

Far, far away.

22

Even the train reminded her of Dillon. Everything did.

He owned a lumber mill that provided millions of board feet for the construction of railroad lines. He owned the rights to build spur lines out of Denver, Leadville, and Castle Rock. His carriage works would probably expand soon to include construction of railroad cars as well. No matter where she looked or what she did, memories of him overwhelmed her. He had consumed her thoughts during the long trip she had made from Kimbell to Denver. It seemed only fitting that he consume them again on the return journey as she sat staring blankly at the flat, unchanging horizon.

It was over, he'd said so and it was true. But that knowledge did nothing to ease her pain. It was over, but she would never stop hurting. It was over, but his face would not stop haunting her. Through two long sleepless nights he'd tortured her. For three endless, arduous days he had tormented her. Her head ached, her stomach knotted queasily, and her shoulders were stiff from the strain. Yet still her thoughts turned constantly to him, and once more she ran everything over in her mind.

She had dressed hastily that morning, not caring what she wore, as long as she escaped before he awoke. Her hair had been uncombed, only hurriedly twisted into a knot with a hat pinned haphazardly upon it. Her mourning suit had been the easiest to don, and she had slipped into her stockings and shoes with desperate speed. She had started to shove her other clothes into her trunk until she realized she could not possibly get the trunk out of the room without waking Dillon. In a panic she had stuffed the gray suit and the teal dress into her traveling bag along with a few intimate items. The rest she left behind. Then with her bag in one hand and her small purse in the other, she had tiptoed to the door.

She had wanted to leave without looking back. She would not torture herself with regrets, for she knew she had no real choice. To stay with him as he wanted was to ensure a desperate unhappiness. She would always want more of him than he could give, and eventually he would tire of her and move on to a more challenging woman. What was it he'd said so long ago? Docile women did not particularly appeal to him.

Yet for all her resolve, she'd not been able to prevent herself from looking back, just one last time. He'd been sprawled on the bed, tangled within the top sheet, completely relaxed in slumber. Against the pale ivory of the delicate bed dressings, he'd appeared so dark and masculine, so powerful despite his repose. She'd had to fight the overwhelming urge to fling down her bags and return to his side.

But she had not run back to him, and now, as she sat

motionless on the thinly upholstered seat, she tried to reassure herself that she had been right. As the miles of prairie went by in a constant rhythmic clacking of steel wheels against steel rails, she told herself over and over again that she was right to leave. Sparrow Hill would hardly offer her a respite—indeed, Dillon must surely suspect that was where she was going. Still, she had no other choice. If only to lick her wounds and contemplate her future, she would go back to Sparrow Hill. Then she would leave and move on to another place and another life that would not include Dillon Lockwood.

Yet even as the landscape outside her window changed from the golden green of the late summer prairie to the lush green of east Texas and Louisiana, the life she had to look forward to was bleak indeed. Dillon's presence—or rather, his absence—would always be with her. He would be that empty part of her, the hole she felt so piercingly in her heart. It was a physical ache, as real as any wound could be. Only it went far deeper than merely the flesh—it went to her very soul.

Lacie sat small and stiff at the open window when the train slowed in anticipation of the stop at Kimbell. She watched as scrub willows and spindly pines gave way to fenced yards and hard-packed streets. As if she were seeing it for the first time, she stared at the small town, noticing the woodshake roofs above the neatly painted wood-siding walls. It was the town listed as her home. Any correspondence to her came via the Kimbell post office, although there was little enough mail for her. She had lived here for many years, yet Kimbell was hardly her home.

As she stepped off the train, accustoming herself again to solid ground, she felt even more alone than before. Sparrow Hill had kept her isolated from the town. Although she was well recognized and known to most people, she was still not a part of the townsfolk. She looked up and down the short station walk, then sighed in resignation. She would not really be missed in Kimbell—not for very long, anyway.

On that morose thought she sought out the stationmaster, who quickly found a farm boy to deliver her to the school. She was hardly aware of the late afternoon heat or the hard wooden seat of the buckboard that carried her. She was too busy staring around her, seeing anew all the sights she would soon be leaving. Off to her left, hidden by lush summer growth, Brush Bayou meandered. He'd ridden with her there. He'd been a terrible bully that day, ordering her around, scooping her up on his horse, then taking her on a long ride against her will. They had stopped at that little house, the tiny place he'd grown up in. That was the first time she had sensed any vulnerability in him, the first time she had felt a pang of sympathy and understanding.

But he had hidden that part of himself well since then. She frowned as the driver turned the farm wagon into the long drive up to the school. Off to the right, up a gentle hill, was the Allen-Kimbell graveyard. Oh, Frederick! she silently grieved. I failed you this time. I tried to keep your school going—as much for me as for you. But I failed.

"Here y'are, Miz Lacie," the wiry farm boy said with a shy grin. "Back home again."

"Thanks, Vincent. I appreciate you going out of your way for me."

"It wasn't really out of my way, Miz Lacie. It wasn't any trouble 'tall." Then he jumped down from the wagon and pulled his hat from his head. "I'd be happy to drive you again if you've a need," he added as his face turned a heated red.

He waved away the coins she offered after he deposited her bag on the porch, and Lacie was unable to mistake his painful interest in her. But instead of restoring her spirits, it only depressed her further. When he finally left, she was enormously relieved.

Once inside, she peered around the shadowed rooms. No one seemed to be home, although the doors and windows were all opened to catch the late afternoon breezes. She walked slowly through the big parlor and the dining room, removing her hat as she went. The huge house was still and solemn, as if it were waiting for something. For the girls to return, she thought sadly. Only they would not be coming this year. They would never come back again.

Whatever would become of this house now? What would Dillon do with it?

As she walked to the back gallery, Lacie saw Leland in the far pasture beyond the burned-out barn. A faint smell of bread baking told her that Mrs. Gunter was about. Then she heard a lighthearted laugh. There was a quiet murmur from a low male voice, then another giggle. At once Ada appeared around a huge gardenia bush. Her cheeks were flushed, and her face glowed with youthful happiness.

"Oh, Lacie!" She stopped abruptly, and almost at once Neal came up behind her.

"You're back," he said, almost as breathlessly as Ada.

"I'm back," she replied, trying to smile at the two of

them. Dillon had told her they planned to marry, and it was plain he'd spoken the truth. As Neal caught Ada by the waist and guided her up the steps to the gallery, Lacie was struck by the tenderness of his casual gesture.

Ada's face was creased in a worried frown as she approached her friend, but Lacie was determined that they not discuss her predicament. It was not Ada's problem, and Lacie wasn't going to let it ruin her happiness.

"I hear that you two are to wed," she began. "Is it a secret, or does everyone know?"

"We've announced it," Neal answered, beaming at his bride-to-be. "We wired everyone about our intentions, but she's keeping me up in the air over the date." He gave Ada a mock frown.

"Why, Ada!" Lacie laughed, happy for her best friend. "How long can you expect to keep poor Neal in limbo this way?"

Ada smiled softly at Neal, then turned her gaze on Lacie. Her face grew more serious. "I wanted to speak to you before we selected a date for the wedding."

"Me?" Lacie looked at her, puzzled at first. Then she realized that dear sweet Ada wanted to be sure her absence on a wedding trip would not disrupt the school.

"If you're worried about not being here—" she halted, hardly able to speak the words although she knew she must. In desperation she looked at Neal. "Hasn't Dillon wired you?"

His somber stare confirmed it, although the level of detail Dillon had conveyed was anybody's guess. She took a shaky breath and nervously turned her hat around and around in her hands.

"If he wired, then you must know I lost. I gambled on

the foolish hope that I could keep this school going."
She gave Neal a rueful smile, hoping he would understand her motives and that he would not judge her too
harshly. Despite their rocky first meeting, she had
grown to like him very much. "I gambled, and I lost. So
you see"—her smile grew more brittle, and she moved
her eyes to gaze blindly at the shell of the burned-out
barn—"there's no need to put off your wedding. The
school won't be opening this year—or ever again."

It was out in all its dreadful truth, and the admission
brought unanticipated tears to her eyes. She had
thought she was resigned to it, but she could not prevent the terrible stinging behind her eyelids. As she
blinked the tears back, she was unprepared for what
Ada had to say next.

"Sparrow Hill may not have to close."

Lacie glanced over at her friend and shook her head.
"I'm afraid you don't know Dillon very well, Ada. He'll
close it, all right. He won't waste either his time or his
money on a business that doesn't turn a big profit. He's
going to close this school and probably sell the property."

"Then *we'll* buy it."

Neal's confident statement took Lacie completely
aback. She stared at him dumbfounded, and it was a
few moments before she could assimilate her thoughts
enough to respond. "What—what do you mean?"

"Neal wants to buy it," Ada answered in a voice filled
with excitement. "He wants to buy it and keep the
school open!"

"But—but how? And why?" Lacie asked, unable to
believe what she was hearing.

"Here, let's sit down while he explains everything,"

Ada said. "Oh, Lacie, you won't believe how well Neal has figured everything out!"

Indeed, as Neal began to outline his plan, it did seem well thought out.

"You've room for many more students. Ada told me that in its heyday, Sparrow Hill had nearly a hundred girls. If we could get that sort of enrollment again, we'd be back on a sound financial footing."

"But this area has been depressed since the war. People haven't the money to pay for private schools for their sons, let alone their daughters."

"Maybe around here they don't, but other parts of the country are booming. You saw Denver, Lacie. Tell me there aren't people there able to afford school tuition."

"But that's Denver," she argued. "Things aren't the same here."

"You're right about that, but you're forgetting one thing. There's a special mystique about sending your children away to school. Think about your own circumstances. Weren't there any schools in Natchez your father could have sent you to? Why did he send you to Sparrow Hill for Young Ladies?"

Lacie thought about it a moment, but she still wasn't sure. "I suppose you have a point. But—"

"It's just a matter of letting people know what a special place Sparrow Hill is. The right people," he emphasized.

"Neal has all sorts of ideas," Ada broke in excitedly. She leaned forward and clutched Lacie's arm. "He's going to run advertisements in the newspapers in all the big cities—Denver, St. Louis, Kansas City, Topeka."

Lacie felt a glimmer of hope as she stared first at

Ada's shining face, then at Neal's determined one. "But why?" she asked the question wonderingly. "Why should any of this matter to you?"

Neal's warm gaze turned to Ada, and in that brief moment Lacie had her answer. Neal loved Ada and would do everything in his power to make her happy— even if it meant spending his valuable time on an ailing girls' school. As she stared at them, she was suddenly struck by the enormous gulf between Neal's unselfish feelings for Ada, and Dillon's wholly self-centered response to herself. Neal would give Ada anything she wanted. Dillon took from her more than she had been willing to give.

That was not exactly true, she told herself. She couldn't blame him entirely for her inability to resist him. She must take part of the blame for herself. But the difference between the two men depressed her anew. Here was Neal, giving her what she really wanted, and still thoughts of Dillon circled in her mind, dragging her down.

". . . and so we could live here still. You could manage the school and hire more teachers."

Lacie came out of her reverie and refocused on Neal. "But if you stay here, what about your job? With Dillon?" she added, his name rolling hesitantly from her mouth.

"Dillon has enough investments to keep me traveling back and forth to St. Louis and Kansas City pretty regularly. There's no reason why I can't be based here instead of Denver."

A small warning sounded in Lacie's head. "Then— then there'd always be a chance he might come here."

In the awkward silence, Ada and Neal glanced at

each other, then back at Lacie. "You wouldn't have to see him if you didn't want to," Neal said quietly.

Lacie stood up from the wicker rocker and crossed nervously to the porch railing. "You know him better than that." Then she laughed, a harsh mirthless sound. "Of course, there's no reason to believe he'd want to see me either." She took a slow, shaky breath, then another. "But I don't know if I could face either possibility."

She turned back and met both of their sympathetic faces. "Your idea is wonderful, Neal. I really believe you can pull it off. And with Ada as headmistress—"

"You *have* to stay," Ada interrupted. She jumped up and approached Lacie, her fair brow creased earnestly. "I couldn't begin to manage Sparrow Hill, especially with more students and more teachers. Why, I wouldn't know what to do at all!" She clasped Lacie's hands in her own. "You're the only one who can do it."

"At least think about it, Lacie," Neal joined in. "At least consider the possibility."

Lacie looked from Ada to Neal, then down the wide shady gallery. "I'll consider it," she murmured softly. She would consider it, for preserving Sparrow Hill was the one thing she had wanted from the beginning. It was what had driven her to pursue her mad pretense in the first place. Oh yes, she desperately wanted to stay, for just as before, she truly had no place else to go.

But deep in her heart, she knew it was impossible. As much as she wanted Sparrow Hill to survive, as much as Neal's idea fired her enthusiasm, she knew she could never stay anyplace where she might run into Dillon. She'd wanted Sparrow Hill to survive, and now it seemed as if it might—only she would not be a part of it.

23

Lacie wiped a trickle of perspiration from her brow with the back of her hand. Despite the wide straw hat that shaded her face and the rolled-up sleeves of her loose cotton blouse, she was unbearably hot. Beneath her single petticoat and her skirt, her legs felt as if they were in an oven. In the blazing August heat, the entire world seemed to be wilting, waiting for day to end and evening to fall with its modicum of relief. No one was about, for everyone had sought a shady spot: Leland on the old hammock he'd slung between two magnolias, and Mrs. Gunter to her bed. Ada and Neal had gone to town very early, before the heat had risen so miserably. Even the horses across the field sought the shade of a pecan tree, standing head to tail as they lazily switched away flies with their long tails.

Only she was foolish enough to venture out in this unforgiving heat.

With a grimace, Lacie pushed away a damp tendril that clung to her neck, but she did not turn back. Doggedly she made her way across the road, then carefully clambered over the wood-plank fence. She held her long skirt up as she picked her way across the uncut field, clutching a split-oak basket in her free hand. It was only a little farther until she reached the shade of the trees, she told herself. Then she would stop and catch her breath.

At the treeline she stopped, put down the basket, and turned back to look across the field toward the big white house in the distance. How beautiful it was! she thought, caressing the scene with her eyes. The wide green fields, the two ancient oak trees. It was at once both grand and homey, impressive and familiar. How hard it would be to leave!

But no matter how hard it might be, the time had come. It was time to leave, and the sooner the better. Ada would object, of course, as would Neal. Mrs. Gunter would fuss and dab at her eyes. But it couldn't be helped. She had deluded herself for the past three days, but she could do so no longer. For today her trunk had arrived quite unexpectedly from Denver, and like a harbinger of trouble to come, it had given her a warning.

The trunk had been delivered earlier in the morning, after Ada and Neal had left. As she had stared at it, sitting so square and solid in the wide hall, she'd been acutely aware of Dillon's part in its arrival. He had sent it on behind her, and it was as if he were telling her to pack and begone. As much as she hated to accede to even one more of his arrogant demands, as much as she resented his continued interference in her life, she knew she could not oppose him on this. He didn't want to see her, and she most certainly did not want to see him.

She had decided to leave the next morning, but there

were still a few things she needed to do before she
went. Now, as she contemplated the task she had set for
herself, she could not help but wonder at the vagaries of
her own emotions. That little cabin was nothing to her
—it truly wasn't. But it mattered to Dillon, and somehow that changed things. Out of all the elegant and
expensive things his money could buy—the hotel she
had stayed in, his office building—it was that humble
little cottage that affected him the most. He had been
vulnerable when he'd taken her there. It had only been
for a moment, and he'd hidden it behind a sarcastic
comment. But she'd seen it, and it had touched her.

Was that when she had started to fall in love with
him? Lacie shook her head and picked up the basket. It
was hard to tell now when it had begun, for she could
hardly recall her life before Dillon. It seemed she had
loved him forever, and as for the years before he strode
so imperiously into her life, well, during those years
she'd just been waiting to love him.

She moved deeper into the woods, following an overgrown trail that led toward the bayou. When Ada and
Neal came home, she would announce her decision.
Leland could take her to the station in the morning,
and by evening she would be in Natchez. She would
send a message to her mother's second cousin's daughter. Perhaps she could visit with her for a while as she
searched for a teaching position. Or if that wasn't possible, she could go on to New Orleans, or perhaps At-
lanta.

She stepped over a fallen log and continued on, lost in
thought. With a little persuasion Ada would write her a
letter of recommendation, signing it as Headmistress of
Sparrow Hill School for Young Ladies. After all, that's

who Ada soon would be. Surely that letter would stand her in good stead. It might take her a little time, but eventually she would find a position in a school and she could go on with her life.

If only she could find some enthusiasm for the idea.

When the path broadened to an open grassy bank, Lacie halted. Before her, Brush Bayou lay still, barely moving in the thick afternoon heat. The sun struck yellow sparks across its golden green surface, sending shimmering waves of heat dancing before her eyes. Across the water, in a shaded pool, three white herons stood, awkward and elegant on their long stick legs. They stalked the shallow water searching for food, dipping low to feed, then raising their heads up to peer around for more.

She moved quietly to a shady hummock, then put the basket down, and the three birds all looked over at her. When she pulled her old shoes off and flung her hat down, they crooked their necks, following her every movement curiously. It was only when she tucked the hem of her skirt and petticoat into her waistband, then moved barefoot toward the beckoning water, however, that they evidenced any alarm. For a moment they tensed, crouching down a little, prepared to spring skyward at the least sign of threat. Then, as Lacie moved ankle deep into the cool water and bent down to refresh herself by trickling water onto her arms, the birds relaxed. She moved slowly along one bank, feeling the sand and gravel give way to soft, squishy clay beneath her toes while the birds resumed their peaceful search for prey.

When had she first done this? Lacie wondered as she meandered through the shallows of the lazy bayou.

That first spring at Sparrow Hill, when she had been so lonely, so lost? Or later, after the war had ended, and there wasn't so much fear of encountering Yankees in the woods? She wasn't sure, and anyway, it didn't really matter. She had done it for years, whenever she could —only this would be the last time.

With a heavy sigh she moved into deeper water, relieved as the cool liquid lapped up to her knees. She hiked her skirt a little higher with one hand, while with the other she loosened the pin that held her hair in a wilting coil at the nape of her neck. Down came the thick gleaming mass of hair. Up came the skirt a little higher. The sun beat furiously upon her and reflected up from the amber surface of the deeper water. It was so hot. So hot, she thought.

When she made the decision to take a swim she turned abruptly for shore. The three herons paused again as she unbuttoned her skirt and removed her slip. They stared as she shed her blouse, then turned back toward the water. But as she stepped into the bayou, clad only in chemisette and pantalets, and propelled herself forward in a shallow dive, they decided it was all too much. As if of one mind, they all rose in unison, flapping for a moment in alarm as they lifted high above the water. Then they glided across the clearing and disappeared into the trees like three society matrons, aghast at her unseemly behavior.

Lacie watched them flee her presence as she floated on her back. She let her head slip beneath the water, then turned and kicked forward, swimming through the murky bayou until her lungs ached for want of air and she had to surface with a sudden splash.

Although the water felt heavenly on her heated skin,

Lacie was hardly comforted by her swim. In the past she had enjoyed her solitude in this place. Today, however, it only made her feel more alone.

Would it always be like this? she brooded. Would she always feel so completely empty, so horribly desolate?

She struggled against the sorrow that seemed to overwhelm her. She would simply have to keep busy, she told herself sternly, and find new things to occupy her days.

But what about her nights? a wayward thought rose in her mind.

Frowning, Lacie swam back to the shore. Finding her footing, she climbed up the shallow bank. She would not think like this, she decided angrily. If she went on this way, daydreaming about him, burying all the hurtful things he'd done and remembering only those few good times—those wonderful times—she would drive herself mad.

With a vengeance she pulled her slip and skirt up over her sopping wet pantalets, then buttoned her blouse over her clinging-wet chemisette. She snatched up her hat and shoes in one hand and grabbed the basket with the other. With new and inexplicable haste, she hurried down the overgrown trail that paralleled Brush Bayou.

Lacie wasn't sure precisely where the little cabin was. She only knew it was beyond the area where she normally wandered. But as she proceeded along through the thick woods at a brisk walk, she became more and more confident of her destination. Up this rise, circling the bayou, then down and across a sandy shaded branch that was little more than a trickle.

When she finally reached the tangled, overgrown

clearing, she found it even more neglected than she had remembered. Blackberry vines scrambled across the path, catching at her skirt as she passed. Morning glories, with their blue trumpet flowers already beginning to close in the afternoon, climbed up the porch in profusion and dangled from the rotting eaves. For a moment she was taken aback, dismayed by the task she'd set herself and daunted by the absolute futility of it. What did it really matter? she asked herself. Who would know or even care about a few pitiful rose bushes struggling in a long-forgotten and abandoned garden?

No one would, she acknowledged. No one would know or care—but then, that did not matter. She had come to tend the rose bushes because she wanted to. There was no other reason.

With a sense of purpose she approached the house and set the basket down. She frowned at the tangle of rose bushes, thickly grown and coiled about themselves at the edge of the porch. With the help of one of the school's library books, she had identified the plants as Apothecary Roses. The famous Rose of Lancaster, she thought with a faint smile. But she grew more serious as she contemplated her task. The suckers must go first, she decided, and the faded blooms and hips. Then she would tie them up so they wouldn't shade themselves and perhaps learn to grow along the porch rail, as they had so many years ago. After that, she would work the bag of rotted stable sweepings she'd brought into the soil, then mulch the roots with leaves.

She swept a thick strand of still-wet hair behind her shoulders and removed a pair of garden clippers from the basket. Considering that the old-fashioned roses were doing so well with absolutely no attention or care, she could only imagine how magnificently they must have bloomed when Dillon's mother had tended them. Once again, she hitched her skirt into her waistband as she stepped up to her task. She would not be there to see the results of her efforts, but she knew they would be spectacular.

As Lacie worked, birds twittered and sang in the trees around her. Squirrels paused in their busy work to stare down at her curiously, then went back to their own private concerns. Without hesitation, she clipped off every one of the long budless suckers, intent as she worked, hardly conscious of the musical forest sounds all around her. As she focused on the roses, their intensely sweet fragrance surrounded her, and she breathed deeply of the intriguing scent. They reminded her of a favorite perfume and a sachet she kept tucked in her drawer among her undergarments. Oh, yes—and of the restaurant in the Denver Palace.

She stopped in midmotion, not wanting to remember, yet unable to forget. In that cozy dining alcove the scent of roses had been distinct, making everything seem sweeter than it was.

Only Dillon had not been sweet. The table had been beautifully laid, the room had been exquisite, but his proposal had been so calculated, so selfish. He had wooed her with flowers, then crushed her with his self-serving logic.

Lacie took a shaky breath as that memory pressed down on her. He had offered her a business deal and called it a marriage proposal! Still, she could not help but wonder for a moment how things might have turned out if she had accepted. Then she laughed out loud at her own idiocy. Even if she had accepted his twisted proposal that night, he would not have married her. The next day was when he had found out about Reverend Hainkel. With his proof at last in hand, he would have ended their engagement just as abruptly as he had begun it. There would no longer have been any need for him to wed her.

No, she thought with a desolate sigh, it would have turned out the same. She had lied to him from the beginning, and now she had to accept the consequences. Dillon had been heartless, but she could not place the blame entirely on him.

Depressed by her thoughts, Lacie clipped the stem in her hand, then grimaced in dismay. She had just cut off the most perfect rose on the vine—an unfurling bloom still caught between bud and full flower. Annoyed by her carelessness, she brought the scarlet flower to her nose and sniffed appreciatively of its mysterious scent.

"You're so beautiful," she murmured to the velvety red petals that were just opening to reveal their bright yellow center. "So beautiful, and yet so fleeting."

"I might say the same of you."

Lacie froze at the unexpected voice. For a fraction of a second she refused to recognize it. For the merest fragment of time she denied that he could be here, that it could be Dillon. But her heart was already racing painfully, and her breathing came fast and shallow. When she could bear the suspense no longer, she turned and stared into his dark, unsmiling face.

He stood at the corner of the house watching her, not twenty feet away. How had he snuck up on her so easily? she wondered vaguely. Yet that question was not what really dominated her thoughts. In those first seconds as they faced each other in the sun-dappled clearing, all she saw—all she thought—was how truly splendid he looked. He was dressed for riding. His white shirt was open at the throat; the sleeves were carelessly rolled up to the middle of his forearms. His tall black boots were dusty, and his snug-fitting broadcloth trousers clung noticeably to his muscular thighs.

He was almost too beautiful to behold and Lacie struggled between absolute joy and complete horror as she stared helplessly at him. She had hoped never to see him again, yet—yet seeing him now was like the answer to her prayers.

He frowned at her continued silence and impatiently slapped his slouch hat against his thigh. At once Lacie's joy fled, leaving in its wake only a miserable sinking feeling. He had come to this cabin—for whatever reason that drove him—expecting solitude. Instead, he had found her—the cause of all his recent troubles—digging in his mother's garden as if she had any right to be here. As the full force of how unfeeling she must look occurred to her, her eyes veered guiltily away from his unyielding gaze.

"I—um, I was just . . ." She stumbled to a humiliating halt, unable to explain her presence there at all. How could she? Was she to explain that caring for his mother's roses somehow brought her closer to him? That it was her only way—albeit a feeble one—to apologize for what she had done? Could she say that she had long passed being angry with him and knew now that she had to accept at least half the blame for bringing all this down on herself? Perhaps all the blame?

Even if she could say it, it was highly unlikely that he would want to hear it. If anything, he would only want to gloat at his complete victory over her.

Miserable beyond description, Lacie rose awkwardly from her knees, conscious of the dirt and leaves that clung to her feet and lower legs and of the soil wedged beneath her fingernails. Her wet blouse clung to her almost indecently, and her hiked-up skirt revealed her knees and calves to his keen gaze. Her hair was an unkempt mess, still damp as it fell in a heavy tangle to her waist. Contrasted to his neat if casual attire, she looked like a poor country bumpkin, dirty and pitiful, hardly worth an iota of his concern.

Without looking up at him she fumbled to release the hem of her wet skirt from where it was tucked into her waistband. But when Dillon took a step forward, she looked up in alarm, forgetting her skirt in her dismay.

"Don't," he said as he took another step nearer. The odd tone in that one husky word only added to Lacie's misery and confusion. "Leave your skirt as it is," he ordered, continuing his steady approach.

"I—I can explain," she stammered, feeling like a frightened rabbit stalked by a hungry wolf.

"About what?" He stopped an arm's length from her.

"About—about the roses." She held up the solitary bloom she clutched in her hand.

"Give it to me."

Lacie cringed as he held out his hand to receive the deep scarlet bloom.

"Can you also explain why you ran back to Sparrow Hill?" His fingers closed lightly around the flower.

Lacie's eyes were huge as she stared at him, their serene gray now a dark troubled color. Her heart hammered painfully in her chest as she struggled to gather her thoughts and compose a reply. She pulled her hand back, then knotted her fingers tightly together at her waist.

"I'm—I'm leaving. Tomorrow. I only came here be-cause—because . . ."

"Why did you leave Denver?"

Lacie's fumbling answer was abruptly halted by this new question. Yet if the previous question had been hard to answer, this one was impossible.

Because I love you! she wanted to scream. Because everything I am is suddenly—despite my every wish— connected to you. But mostly because you don't love me. She blinked and lowered her gaze from his brilliant emerald eyes.

"It was over," she whispered, wishing desperately that anger would overwhelm this awful pain in her heart. Must he humiliate her completely in order to be satisfied?

"It was over." He repeated her words quietly. Then in a sudden harsh movement he crushed the rose in his hand and flung the mangled petals onto the ground between them. His eyes ran scathingly over her, not missing a single aspect of her disheveled appearance— the damp blouse clinging too revealingly to her breasts, the bared ankles and legs so immodestly displayed. She looked like a wild forest urchin, she realized shame-fully, whereas he appeared a magnificent forest god, one mightily displeased by what he saw before him.

"If it's over, then why are you digging in these roses? *My* roses?" he asked furiously. His hand whipped out to drag her hand forward. "What are you doing here?" he thundered as he forced her grimy palm open between them.

"They needed attention!" she burst out defensively. She was caught between guilt at his rightful accusation and anger at his unreasonableness. Or was it anger that he was here at all? She'd thought to escape the possibility of ever seeing him again. In one more day she would have succeeded. Yet here he was, once more confronting her, accusing her of things that weren't precisely true.

As the moment stretched out unbearably, as her wrist remained a captive of his blazing grasp, her heart began to race and her anger ebbed away. She tugged to no avail to free her hand, then turned a pleading expression on him.

"I only wanted to take care of them," she began in a trembling voice. "They—they were so overgrown and tangled and wild. The suckers . . ."

She trailed off as his hard gaze remained locked on her face. He was so angry and so—so— She couldn't describe the other emotions that colored his face and darkened his eyes. In abject defeat she finished in a whisper. "These roses were loved once. I thought—I thought I would give them a little love again."

She stared up at him, trying hard to control her tears. Crying before him would do no good—it never did. If anything, it would only confirm what he surely must know. She had no more resources where he was concerned. He was the undeniable victor in this battle between them. This war. In every way, from the school, to her physical desire for him, to her unwilling love, he had won.

But it was Dillon's turn to drop his gaze from hers. His eyes moved to her small hand, dirty from the garden soil. He moved his thumb lightly across her open palm, then back and forth once more.

"Why couldn't you be willing to do the same for me?"

His words were so soft that at first Lacie could hardly credit him with them. Surely it was her imagination. Yet when his eyes came up to meet her bewildered stare and she saw his painful expression, she doubted her own reasoning. As if those few words had been cruelly wrenched from him, his face seemed etched with pain. Then his expression grew fierce, and his eyes burned into hers with an intensity that took her breath away. His hand tightened on her wrist. He pulled her closer, and she took a hesitant step toward him.

"Give me your answer, Lacie," he muttered hoarsely. "I have to know why you continue to run away from me even when you have no place to go."

Lacie felt an aberrant flicker of hope at his words, wrung so harshly from him, a wild unreasonable longing for what she was so sure would never be.

"You—you hate me," she managed in little more than a whisper.

"No." He shook his head and frowned. "Hardly that."

Lacie looked away, searching for a source of strength to prevent her from falling to pieces. "I know you—I know you *want* me. That's not what I mean."

His other hand came up to caress her cheek. But for Lacie the tender gesture was far more painful than a blow from his mighty fist would have been. She recoiled from him as if she had been burned. He was breaking her heart, and she was certain she could never survive without him.

"I want you," he admitted. "I want you in ways you

cannot even begin to imagine." At her painful blush at his blunt admission he reached for her, but Lacie drew back a step. She was too weak where he was concerned to risk letting him touch her again.

"You say that now," she whispered. "But—but what about everything that has happened? What about Frederick?"

"I don't care about that anymore, Lacie. God, but I don't. Frederick's property—" He stopped, and this time he took her by the arms and pulled her against his chest. He rested his chin on her head. "You're the only thing I want. I know that now."

With every fiber of her being Lacie wished to say yes, to just give in to him. It would be so easy, and at least for a while, she would have him all to herself. But there had been so much animosity between them, so much suspicion.

"I never wanted to steal from you, Dillon. When I lied about Frederick—about marrying him—"

"I know," he said in the low, husky voice that always made her want to melt. "It was only the school you wanted. I realized that before I left Sparrow Hill for Denver. I also knew I wanted to keep you in my life, but by then you seemed determined to keep me at arm's length."

But I failed, she thought as she responded to the warmth of his embrace. He planted a kiss on the top of her head, then another against her temple.

"Thank God you came to Denver," he murmured into her wet tangled hair.

She looked up at him then, suddenly understanding that he'd manipulated her on that score as well. "The telegram. You knew I'd come."

He had the good grace to look embarrassed. "Like a bull chasing a red cape."

For a long moment they stared at one another, and his face slowly became more serious.

"I want you to come back to Denver with me, Lacie." He hesitated as she stood stock-still in his arms. "I need you there."

She heard his words. They were simple and to the point, yet they raised endlessly complex emotions in her.

Just go, one voice urged her. Go with him and stay as long as he wants you to. Maybe you can make him love you.

Yet everything else told her no. To go would be pure madness. If it was awful to lose him now, it would be unbearable later.

Tears blurred her vision, and in humiliation she pressed her face against his chest. She shook her head no, yet she could not tear herself away from him.

"I'll make you go back. No one can stop me," he said, increasing the strength of his hold on her. "You can't."

A sob escaped her despite all her efforts to hide her tears. In utter misery she buried her face against his shirt, unable to hold back the torrent any longer. As she stood sobbing in his arms, she felt his muscles tense. His hold tightened around her until she felt he must crush her into him. But still her tears would not stop.

"Don't, sweetheart. Please, Lacie, don't cry like this."

She felt his kisses in her hair, desperate searching kisses seeking her face in an effort to stem her tears. But she would not turn her face up to him. She couldn't. In a moment he would convince her. If he kissed her, she would be lost.

"Listen to me, sweetheart. Listen," he whispered huskily against the wet tangles of her hair. "I love you. You can't leave me now. You can't!"

At those startling words—longed for, yet never truly expected—Lacie went very still. Only a few lingering sobs shook her as she clung to him. Only his heart pounding beneath her ear grounded her in reality.

"I love you." The words came again, soft and low, and she tremulously raised her head to peer up at him. Through her watery gaze she saw his earnest face, his serious expression.

"I love you," he stated almost ferociously. "I didn't know it before—oh, God! Maybe I did know, but I just couldn't, or wouldn't, admit it." His eyes burned into hers with such intensity, he seemed to see into her soul. And for once, she was able to see into his. "I was a fool when I asked you before. I guess I knew you would turn me down, but I had to ask anyway. Now I'm asking again. I love you, Lacie. Marry me, and I promise you— I promise you, sweetheart, that you'll never be sorry."

Marry him. He wanted her to marry him!

Lacie shook her head, unable to believe what she heard. "But—can you really forgive me for all I've done? For lying? For trying to steal from you?"

"There's nothing to forgive. I know you did it for Frederick, to keep his school going." His hands slid up her back. "Marry me, and the school will be my wedding gift to you. Whatever you want, Lacie. I'll do anything. Just say you'll marry me."

She was so stunned, so undone by his rush of words— by everything—that for a moment she could not respond at all. Then her heart began to swell, and it was as if everything in the world had turned from wrong to right, as if she would burst from the incredible happiness that filled her.

"I love you," she whispered, although emotions choked her words.

It was his turn to stare at her in amazement. "Does that mean you will? Will you be my wife?"

Her answer was a kiss, swift and sure and passionate. Words were quite beyond her. As she wrapped her arms recklessly around his neck, molding herself to his tall masculine form, she felt both his stunned surprise and his eager response.

"Yes," she whispered, kissing his lips, his cheek, his rough chin. "Yes," she promised, finding his mouth once more as he lifted her clear of the ground and spun her around in an exuberant embrace. "Yes!"

If she had stopped to think, she might have reassured herself that this proposal was sincere. After all, she had nothing he wanted anymore. Not the school, nor any of the other properties he and Frederick had owned together. Likewise, she might have comforted herself with the knowledge that Sparrow Hill would go on as Frederick had wanted it to after all, better than ever under Ada and Neal's capable control. If she had paused to think about any of that, she would have felt secure in her decision to marry him. Everything was turning out better than she could possibly have dreamed.

But Lacie did not need logic to guide her any longer. Dillon's arms around her felt so right, so perfect. She needed only to feel his possessive embrace and return his demanding kiss to know that this time she was not making a mistake with him. For once, she was absolutely certain where Dillon Lockwood was concerned.

"Was that a yes?" he murmured in delicious nibbles against her upturned lips.

"Oh, yes."

Epilogue

Lacie stepped out onto the gallery, then moved silently on bare feet to the wide wooden rail. Beyond her, bathed in the silver-gold of moonlight, the grounds of Sparrow Hill looked at once familiar and mysterious. From her vantage point she could see the fields and the woods, the long drive and the meandering paths.

She was right to have come back to Sparrow Hill to have the baby, she thought as contentment wrapped around her like a warm blanket. It was all so dear to her that she wondered if she would be able to leave it after this long, pleasant visit with Ada and Neal. Still, there would be other visits. And one day her own little girl would come back here to go to school. She smiled to think of her sweet little Elizabeth going to classes in this very school.

Then a strong pair of arms slipped around her, circling her waist, and she leaned gratefully against the comforting bulk of her husband.

"She's asleep," Dillon whispered. Then he continued

in a huskier, more suggestive tone. "She's asleep and I finally have you all to myself."

Lacie smiled at that and let her head fall back against his shoulder. "Surely you're not jealous of such a helpless little innocent as your own daughter?"

"No, not jealous." He turned her around so that they faced each other. "Not really." Then he smiled down at her, that familiar, heart-stopping smile that never failed to send a warm thrill through her. "It's just that these long weeks of waiting have driven me slightly mad." He pulled her closer with a soft groan. "I love you so much. I need you so badly."

Lacie smiled in complete satisfaction as she pressed her cheek against the warm skin of his bare chest. Dressed as she was in only a thin cotton nightgown, she could easily feel every muscle, every contour of his chest and waist, and farther down, his hard muscular thighs and the thickening evidence of his desire. She moved her hips slightly, sliding her belly against his loins. At his swift intake of breath, she moved even more seductively against him, pleased beyond measure at how quickly he responded to her shamelessly wicked actions.

For a moment his grasp tightened, as if he would absorb her, body and soul, into him. Then with a groan of agony he pushed himself away, holding her at arm's length as he took a ragged breath.

"Witch," he muttered as he stared at her with eyes glazed with desire. "Cruel, heartless witch."

"If I'm heartless, it's only because you stole it away from me long ago," she murmured silkily as she slid her hands along his rigid forearms.

"Lacie, don't," he choked out in a voice thick with

longing. "There's only so much I can take. It's been hard enough keeping my distance from you these weeks since Elizabeth was born—"

"And I intend to reward you for it," she answered, sliding her hands back up to grip both of his strong wrists. She smiled at him beckoningly. "Right now," she added breathlessly.

For a moment Dillon only stared at his wife, hardly able to think for the intensity of his desire for her, the impossible power of his love for her. From the moment he had first laid eyes on her, she had driven him crazy, frustrating him at every turn, torturing him first with her primness and later with her passion. There had been times . . .

He shook his head slowly, holding her beautiful moonlit features within his loving gaze. Then he gathered her into his arms, holding her fast within his embrace, molding her soft womanly form against his. She felt so good, so right. He'd been a fool to pit himself against such a one as she, when there was such happiness to be found in this joining of forces. Such unbelievable happiness and love.

It had begun in this place, this school she so loved. How fitting it had been for them to return for the birth of their first child. They would return here often, no doubt, although Denver was now their home. But then, he knew that he would be at home wherever he was, as long as Lacie was at his side.

He felt her move in his arms and looked down into her upturned face. Then he planted a sweet lingering kiss on her waiting lips.

"Shall we"—she colored a little as she stared up at

him with shining eyes—"shall we go inside now? To our bedroom?"

"Yes," he answered. He lifted her off her feet and held her high in the snug warmth of his arms. "Oh, yes."